Robert Dodsley

The King and the Miller of Mansfield

Robert Dodsley

The King and the Miller of Mansfield

ISBN/EAN: 9783743389625

Manufactured in Europe, USA, Canada, Australia, Japa

Cover: Foto ©Andreas Hilbeck / pixelio.de

Manufactured and distributed by brebook publishing software (www.brebook.com)

Robert Dodsley

The King and the Miller of Mansfield

THE
KING
AND THE
MILLER of MANSFIELD.

A
DRAMATIC TALE.

As it is Acted at the

THEATRE-ROYAL in DRURY-LANE.

By R. DODSLEY.

LONDON:

Printed for and sold by W. OXLADE, at Shakespeare's
Head, in George-Street, Old-Bailey.
M DCC LXXV.

Dramatis Personæ.

M E N.

The KING.

The MILLER.

RICHARD, the *Miller*'s Son.

Lord LUREWELL.

Courtiers and Keepers of the Forest.

W O M E N.

PEGGY.

MARGERY.

KATE.

SCENE, *Sherwood Forest.*

THE

KING

AND THE

MILLER of MANSFIELD.

SCENE, *Sherwood Forest.*

Enter several COURTIERS *as lost.*

FIRST COURTIER.

'TIS horrid dark! and this wood, I believe, has neither end nor side.

Fourth Courtier. You mean to get out at, for
we have found one in, you see.

Second Courtier. I wish our good King *Harry*
had kept near home to hunt; in my mind, the
pretty, tame deer in *London* make much better
sport than the wild ones in *Sherwood* forest.

Third Courtier. I can't tell which way his Majesty went, nor whether any body is with him
or not; but let us keep together, pray.

Fourth Courtier. Ay, ay, like true courtiers,
take care of ourselves, whatever becomes of
master.

Second Courtier. Well, it's a terrible thing to
be lost in the dark.

Fourth Courtier. It is. And yet it's so common a case, that one would not think it should

be

be at all fo. Why, we are all of us loft in the dark every day of our lives. Knaves keep us in the dark by their cunning, and fools by their ignorance. Divines lofe us in dark myfteries; lawyers in dark cafes, and ftatefmen in dark intrigues: nay, the light of reafon, which we fo much boaft of, what is it but a dark-lanthorn, which juft ferves to prevent us from running our nofe againft a poft, perhaps; but is no more able to lead us out of the dark mifts of error and ignorance, in which we are loft, than an *ignis fatuus* would be to conduct us out of this wood.

Firft Courtier. But, my lord, this is no time for preaching, methinks. And, for all your morals, day-light would be much preferable to this darknefs, I believe.

Third Courtier. Indeed wou'd it. But come, let us go on; we fhall find fome houfe or other by and by.

Fourth Courtier. Come along. [*Exeunt.*

Enter the King *alone.*

No, no, this can be no public road, that's certain: I am loft, quite loft indeed. Of what advantage is it now to be a King? Night fhews me no refpect: I cannot fee better, nor walk fo well as another man. What is a King? Is he not wifer than another man? Not without his counfellors, I plainly find. Is he not more powerful? I oft have been told fo, indeed; but what now can my power command? Is he not greater and more magnificent? When feated on his throne, and furrounded with nobles and flatterers, perhaps he may think fo; but when loft in a wood, alas! what is he but a common man? His wifdom knows not which is north and which is fouth; his power a beggar's dog would bark at; and his greatnefs the beggar would not bow to. And yet how oft are we puffed up with thefe

thefe falfe attributes ? Well, in lofing the monarch, I have found the man.

[*The report of a gun is heard.*

Hark! fome villain fure is near! What were it beft to do ? Will my Majefty protect me ? No. Throw Majefty afide then, and let manhood do it.

Enter the Miller.

Miller. I believe I hear the rogue! Who's there ?

King. No rogue, I affure you.

Miller. Little better, friend, I believe. Who fir'd that gun ?

King. Not I, indeed.

Miller. You lie, I believe.

King. Lie! lie! how ftrange it feems to me to be talked to in this ftile. [*Afide.*] Upon my word I don't.

Miller. Come, come, firrah, confefs ; you have fhot one of the King's deer, have you not ?

King. No, indeed ; I owe the King more refpect. I heard a gun go off, indeed, and was afraid fome robbers might have been near.

Miller. I'm not bound to believe this, friend: Pray who are you ? what's your name !

King. Name !

Miller. Name ! yes name. Why you have a name, have not you ? Where do you come from? What is your bufinefs here ?

King. Thefe are queftions I have not been us'd to, honeft man.

Miller: May be fo ; but they are queftions no honeft man would be afraid to anfwer, I think. So if you can give no better account of yourfelf, I fhall make bold to take you along with me, if you pleafe.

King. With you ! what authority have you to——

Miller. The King's authority, if I muft give

A 3   you

you an account, Sir. I am *John Cockle*, the Miller of *Mansfield*, one of his Majesty's keepers in this foreft of *Sherwood*; and I will let no fuf-pected fellow pafs this way that cannot give a better account of himfelf than you have done, I promife you.

King. I muft fubmit to my own authority. [*Aſide.*] Very well, Sir, I am glad to hear the King has fo good an officer; and fince I find you have his authority, I will give you a bet-ter account of myfelf, if you will do me the fa-vour to hear it.

Miller. It's more than you deferve, I believe; but let's hear what you can fay for yourfelf.

King. I have the honour to belong to the King as well as you, and, perhaps, fhould be as un-willing to fee any wrong done him. I came down with him to hunt in this foreft, and the chace leading us to-day a great way from home, I am benighted in this wood, and have loft my way.

Miller. This does not found well; if you have been a hunting, pray where is your horfe?

King. I have tired my horfe, fo that he lay down under me, and I was obliged to leave him.

Miller. If I thought I might believe this now.

King. I am not ufed to lie, honeft man.

Miller. What! do you live at court, and not lie! that's a likely ftory indeed.

King. Be that as it will, I fpeak truth now, I affure you; and to convince you of it, if you will attend me to *Nottingham*, if I am near it, or give me a night's lodging in your own houfe, here is fomething to pay you for your trouble, and if that is not fufficient, I will fatisfy you in the morning to your utmoft defire.

Miller. Ay, now I am convinced you are a courtier; here is a little bribe for to-day, and

a large

a large promife for to-morow, both in a breath: here, take it again, and take this along with it——*John Cockle* is no courtier; he can do what he ought——without a bribe.

King. Thou art a very extraordinary man I muft own, and I fhould be glad, methinks, to be farther acquainted with thee.

Miller. Thee! and thou! pr'ythee don't thee and thou me: I believe I am as good a man as yourfelf at leaft.

King. Sir, I beg your pardon.

Miller. Nay, I am not angry, friend; only I don't love to be too familiar with any body, before I know whether they deferve it or not.

King. You are in the right.   But what am I to do?

Miller. You may do what you pleafe.   You are twelve miles from *Nottingham*, and all the way thro' this thick wood; but if you are refolved upon going thither to night, I will put you in the road, and direct you the beft I can; or if you will accept of fuch poor entertainment as a miller can give, you fhall be welcome to ftay all night, and in the morning I will go with you myfelf.

King. And cannot you go with me to-night?

Miller. I would not go with you to-night if you were the King.

King. Then I muft go with you, I think.

[*Exeunt.*

Scene changes to the town of Mansfield.

DICK *alone.*

Well, dear *Mansfield*, I am glad to fee thy face again.   But my heart aches, methinks, for fear this fhould be only a trick of theirs to get me into their power.   Yet the letter feems to be wrote with an air of fincerity, I confefs; and the girl was never us'd to lie till fhe kept a

.lord

lord company. Let me fee, I'll read it once more.

Dear Richard,

I am at laft (tho' much too late for me) convinc'd of the injury done to us both by that bafe man, who made me think you falfe; he contriv'd thefe letters which I fend you, to make me think you juft upon the point of being married to another, a thought I could not bear with patience; fo, aiming at revenge on you, confented to my own undoing. But, for your own fake, I beg you to return hither, for I have fome hopes of being able to do you juftice, which is the only comfort of your moft diftrefs'd, but ever affectionate, PEGGY.

There can be no cheat in this, fure! The letters fhe has fent are, I think, a proof of her fincerity. Well, I will go to her however : I cannot think fhe will again betray me : If fhe has as much tendernefs left for me, as, in fpite of her ill ufage, I ftill feel for her, I'm fure fhe won't. Let me fee, I am not far from the houfe, I believe. [*Exit.*

Scene changes to a room.

PEGGY *and* PHOEBE.

Phœbe. Pray, madam, make yourfelf eafy.

Peggy. Ah! *Phœbe,* fhe that has loft her virtue, has with it loft her eafe, and all her happinefs. Believing, cheated fool! to think him falfe.

Phoebe. Be patient, madam, I hope you will fhortly be reveng'd on that deceitful lord.

Peggy. I hope I fhall, for that were juft revenge. But will revenge make me happy? Will it excufe my falfehood? Will it reftore me to the heart of my much-injur'd love? Ah! no. That blooming innocence he us'd to praife, and call the greateft beauty of our fex, is gone.

, I have

I have no charm left that might renew that flame I took such pains to quench.

[*Knocking at the door.*

See who's there. O heavens, 'tis he! Alas! that ever I shou'd be asham'd to see the man I love!

Enter Richard, *who stands looking on her at a distance, she weeping.*

Dick. Well, *Peggy*, (but I suppose you're madam now in that fine dress) you see you have brought me back; is it to triumph in your falsehood? or am I to receive the slighted leavings of your fine lord?

Peggy. O *Richard!* after the injury I have done you, I cannot look on you without confusion: But do not think so hardly of me; I stay'd not to be slighted by him, for the moment I discover'd his vile plot on you, I fled his sight, nor could he ever prevail to see me since.

Dick. Ah, *Peggy!* you were too hasty in believing; and much I fear, the vengeance aim'd at me, had other charms to recommend it to you: such bravery as that [*pointing to her cloaths*] I had not to bestow; but if a tender honest heart could please, you had it all; and if I wish'd for more, 'twas for your sake.

Peggy. O *Richard!* when you consider the wicked stratagem he contriv'd to make me think you base and deceitful, I hope you will, at least, pity my folly, and, in some measure, excuse my falshood; that you will forgive me, I dare not hope.

Dick. To be forc'd to fly from my friends and country, for a crime that I was innocent of, is an injury that I cannot easily forgive, to be sure: but if you are less guilty of it than I thought, I shall be very glad; and if your design be really as you say, to clear me, and to expose the baseness of him that betray'd and ruin'd you,

I will

I will join with you with all my heart. But how do you propose to do this?

Peggy. The King is now in this forest a hunting, and our young lord is every day with him: Now, I think, if we could take some opportunity of throwing ourselves at his Majesty's feet, and complaining of the injustice of one of his courtiers, it might, perhaps, have some effect upon him.

Dick. If we were suffer'd to make him sensible of it, perhaps it might; but the complaints of such little folks as we, seldom reach the ears of Majesty.

Peggy. We can but try.

Dick. Well, if you will but go with me to my father's, and stay there till such an opportunity happens, I shall believe you in earnest, and will join with you in your design.

Peggy. I will do any thing to convince you of my sincerity, and to make satisfaction for the injuries which have been done you.

Dick. Will you go now?

Peggy. I'll be with you in less than an hour.

[*Exeunt.*

Scene changes to the mill.

MARGERY *and* KATE *knitting.*

Kate. O dear, I would not see a spirit for all the world; but I love dearly to hear stories of them. Well, and what then?

Margery. And so at last, in a dismal, hollow tone it cry'd———

[*A knocking at the door frights them both, they scream out, and throw down their knitting.*]

Margery and *Kate.* Lord bless us! What's that?

Kate. O dear mother, it's some judgment upon

on us, I'm afraid. They fay, talk of the devil, and he'll appear.

Margery. Kate, go and fee who's at the door.

Kate. I durft not go, mother; do you go.

Margery. Come, let's both go.

Kate. Now don't fpeak as if you was afraid.

Margery. No, I won't if I can help it. Who's there?

Dick. [*Without*] What! won't you let me in?

Kate. O gemini! it's like our *Dick*, I think: He's certainly dead, and it's his fpirit.

Margery. Heav'n forbid! I think in my heart it's he himfelf. Open the door, *Kate*.

Kate. Nay, do you.

Margery. Come, we'll both open it.

[*They open the door.*

Enter Dick.

Dick. Dear mother, how do you do? I thought you would not have let me in.

Margery. Dear child, I'm overjoy'd to fee thee; but I was fo frighted, I did not know what to do.

Kate. Dear brother, I am glad to fee you; how have you done this long while?

Dick. Very well, *Kate.* But where's my father?

Margery. He heard a gun go off juft now, and he's gone to fee who 'tis.

Dick. What they love venifon at *Mansfield* as well as ever, I fuppofe?

Kate. Ay, and they will have it too.

Miller. [*Without.*] Hoa! *Madge!* *Kate!* bring a light here.

Margery. Yonder he is.

Kate. Has he catch'd the rogue, I wonder?

Enter the King *and the* Miller.

Margery. Who have you got?

Miller.

Miller. I have brought thee a stranger, *Madge* ; thou must give him a supper, and a lodging if thou can'st.

Margery. You have got a better stranger of your own, I can tell you : *Dick*'s come.

Miller. Dick ! Where is he ? Why *Dick !* How it's, my lad ?

Dick. Very well, I thank you, father.

King. A little more, and you had push'd me down.

Miller. Faith, Sir, you must excuse me ; I was overjoy'd to see my boy. He has been at *London,* and I have not seen him these four years.

King. Well, I shall once in my life have the happiness of being treated as a common man ; and of seeing human nature without disguise.

[*Aside.*

Miller. What has brought thee home so unexpected ?

Dick. You will know that presently.

Miller. Of that by-and-by then. We have got the King down in the forest a hunting this season, and this honest gentleman, who came down with his Majesty from *London,* has been with 'em to-day, it seems, and has lost his way. Come, *Madge,* see what thou can'st get for supper. Kill a couple of the best fowls ; and go you, *Kate,* and draw a pitcher of ale. We are famous, Sir, at *Mansfield,* for good ale, and for honest fellows that know how to drink it.

King. Good ale will be acceptable, at present, for I am very dry. But pray, how came your son to leave you, and go to *London ?*

Miller. Why, that's a story which *Dick,* perhaps, won't like to have told.

King. Then I don't desire to hear it.

Enter Kate, *with an earthen pitcher of ale and a horn.*

Miller. So, now do you go help your mother. —Sir, my hearty service to you.

King.

King. Thank ye, Sir. This plain fincerity and freedom, is a happinefs unknown to kings.

[*Afide.*

Miller. Come, Sir.

King. Richard, my fervice to you.

Dick. Thank you, Sir.

Miller. Well, *Dick,* and how doft thou like *London?* Come, teli us what thou haft feen

Dick. Seen! I have feen the land of promife.

Miller. The land of promife! What doft thou mean?

Dick. The court, father.

Miller. Thou wilt never leave joking,

Dick. To be ferious then, I have feen the dif-appointment of my hopes and expectations; and that's more than one would wifh to fee.

Miller. What! would the great man, thou waft recommended to, do nothing at all for thee at laft?

Dick. Why, yes; he would promife me to the laft?

Miller. Zoons! do the courtiers think their dependents can eat promifes?

Dick. No, no; they never trouble their heads to think, whether we eat at all or not. I have now dangled after his lordfhip feveral years, tan-taliz'd with hopes and expectations; this year promifed one place, the next another, and the third, in fure and certain hope of——a difap-pointment. One falls, and it was promifed be-fore; another, and I am juft half an hour too late; a third, and it ftops the mouth of a cre-ditor; a fourth, and it pays the hire of a flat-terer; a fifth, and it bribes a vote; and, the fixth, I am promifed ftill. But having thus flept away fome years, I awoke from my dream: My lord, I found, was fo far from having it in his power to get a place for me, that he had been all this while feeking after one for himfelf.

Miller.

Miller. Poor *Dick!* And is plain honesty then a recommendation to no place at court?

Dick. It may recommend you to be a footman, perhaps, but nothing further, nothing further, indeed. If you look higher, you must furnish yourself with other qualifications: You must learn to say Ay, or No; to run, or stand; to fetch, or carry, or leap over a stick at the word of command. You must be master of the arts of flattery, insinuation, dissimulation, application, and [*pointing to his palm.*] right application too, if you hope to succeed.

King. You don't consider I am a courtier, methinks.

Dick. Not I, indeed; 'tis no concern of mine what you are. If, in general, my character of the court is true, 'tis not my fault if it's disagreeable to your worship. There are particular exceptions I own, and I hope you may be one.

King. Nay, I don't want to be flatter'd, so let that pass. Here's better success to you the next time you come to *London.*

Dick. I thank ye; but I don't design to see it again in haste.

Miller. No, no, *Dick;* instead of depending upon lords promises, depend upon the labour of thine own hands; expect nothing but what thou can'st earn, and then thou wilt not be disappointed. But come, I want a description of *London;* thou hast told us nothing thou hast seen yet.

Dick. O! 'tis a fine place! I have seen large houses with small hospitality; great men do little actions; and fine ladies do nothing at all. I have seen the honest lawyers of *Westminster-hall,* and the virtuous inhabitants of *'Change-Alley;* the politic madmen of coffee-houses, and the wise statesmen of *Bedlam.* I have seen merry trage-
dies,

dies, and fad comedies; devotion at an opera, and mirth at a fermon; I have feen fine cloaths at St. *James's*, and long bills at *Ludgate-Hill*. I have feen poor grandeur, and rich poverty; high honours, and low flattery; great pride, and no merit. In fhort, I have feen a fool with a title, a knave with a penfion, and an honeft man with a thread-bare coat. Pray how do you like *London?*

Miller. And is this the beft defcription thou can'ft give of it?

Dick. Yes.

King. Why, *Richard*, you are a fatirift, I find.

Dick. I love to fpeak truth, Sir; if that happens to be fatire, I can't help it.

Miller. Well! if this is *London*, give me my country cottage; which, tho' it is not a great houfe, nor a fine houfe, is my own houfe, and I can fhew a receipt for the building on't. But come, Sir, our fupper, I believe, is ready for us, by this time; and to fuch as I have, you're welcome as a prince.

King. I thank you.   [*Exeunt.*

Scene changes to the wood.

Enter feveral K E E P E R S.

Firft Keeper. The report of a gun was fome-where this way, I'm fure.

Second Keeper. Yes; but I can never believe that any body would come a deer-ftealing fo dark a night as this.

Third Keeper. Where did the deer harbour to-day?

Fourth Keeper. There was a herd lay upon *Hamilton-Hill*, another juft by *Robin Hood*'s chair, and a third here in *Mansfield* wood.

Firft Keeper. Ay; thofe they have been amongft.

Second Keeper. But we fhall never be able to find 'em to-night, 'tis fo dark.

Third Keeper. No, no; let's go back again.

Firft Keeper. Zoons! you're afraid of a broken head, I fuppofe, if we fhould find 'em; and fo had rather flink back again. Hark! ftand clofe. I hear 'em coming this way.

Enter *the* Courtiers.

Firft Courtier. Did not you hear fomebody juft now? Faith, I begin to be afraid we fhall meet with fome misfortune to-night.

Second Courtier. Why if any body fhould take what we have got, we have made a fine bufinefs of it.

Third Courtier. Let them take it if they will; I am fo tir'd I fhall make but fmall refiftance.

[*The Keepers rufh upon them.*

Second Keeper. Ay, rogues, rafcals, and villains; you have got it, have you?

Second Courtier. Indeed we have got but very little, but what we have, you are welcome to, if you will but ufe us civilly.

Firft Keeper. O, yes! very civilly; you deferve to be us'd civilly, to be fure.

Fourth Courtier. Why, what have we done that we may not be civilly us'd?

Firft Keeper. Come, come, don't trifle, furrender.

Firft Courtier. I have but three half-crowns about me.

Second Courtier. Here's three and fix-pence for you, gentlemen.

Third Courtier. Here's my watch; I have no money at all.

Fourth Courtier. Indeed I have nothing in my pocket but a fnuff-box.

Fourth Keeper. What! the dogs want to bribe us, do they? No, rafcals; you fhall

go

go before the juftice to-morrow, depend
on't.

Fourth Courtier. Before the juftice! What, for
being robb'd?

Firft Keeper. For being robb'd! What do you
mean? Who has robb'd you?

Fourth Courtier. Why, did not you juft now
demand our money, gentlemen?

Second Keeper. O, the rafcals! they will fwear
a robbery againft us, I warrant.

Fourth Courtier. A robbery! Ay, to be fure.

Firft Keeper. No, no; we did not demand
your money, we demanded the deer you have
kill'd.

Fourth Courtier. The devil take the deer, I
fay; he led us a chace of fix hours, and got
away from us at laft.

Firft Keeper. Zoons! ye dogs, do ye think to
banter us? I tell ye you have this night fhot one
of the King's deer; did not we hear the gun go
off? Did not we hear you fay, you was afraid
it fhould be taken from you?

Second Courtier. We were afraid our money
fhould be taken from us.

Firft Keeper. Come, come, no more fhuffling:
I tell ye, you're all rogues, and we'll have you
hang'd, you may depend on't. Come, let's
take them to old Cockle's; we're not far off;
we'll keep 'em there all night, and to-morrow
morning we'll away with 'em before the juftice.

Fourth Courtier. A very pretty adventure!
                                    [*Exeunt.*

Scene

Scene changes to the Mill.

King, Millery, Margery, *and* Dick, *at Supper.*

Miller. Come, Sir, you muſt mend a bad
ſupper with a glaſs of good ale ; here's King
Harry's health.

King. With all my heart. Come, Richard
here's King Harry's health; I hope you are
courtier enough to pledge me, are not you ?

Dick. Yes, yes, Sir, I'll drink the King's
health with all my heart.

Margery. Come, Sir, my humble ſervice to
you, and much good may do ye with your poor
ſupper ; I wiſh it had been better.

King. You need make no apologies.

Margery. We are obliged to your goodneſs
in excuſing our rudeneſs.

Miller. Prithee, Margery, don't. trouble the
gentleman with compliments.

Margery. Lord, huſband, if one had no more
manners than you, the gentleman would take
us all for hogs.

Miller. Now I think the more compliments
the leſs manners.

King. I think ſo too. Compliments in diſ-
courſe, I believe, are like ceremonies in religion ;
the one has deſtroy'd all true piety, and the
other all ſincerity and plain dealing.

Miller. Then a fig for all ceremony and
compliments too : give us thy hand ; and let
us drink and be merry.

King. Right, honeſt Miller, let us drink and
be merry. Come, have you got e'er a good
ſong ?

Miller. Ah ! my ſinging days are over, but
my

my man Joe has got an excellent one; and if
you have a mind to hear it, I'll call him in.

King. With all my heart.

Miller. Joe.

Enter Joe.

Miller. Come, *Joe,* drink boy; I have promis'd this gentleman that you shall sing him
your last new song.

Joe. Well, master, if you have promis'd it
him, he shall have it.

SONG.

I.

How happy a State does the Miller possess?
Who wou'd be no greater, nor fears to be less;
On his Mill and himself he depends for Support,
Which is better than servilely cringing at Court.

II.

What tho' he all dusty and whiten'd does go,
The more he's be-powder'd, the more like a Beau;
A Clown in this Dress may be honester far
Than a Courtier who struts in his Garter and Star.

III.

Tho' his Hands are so dawb'd they're not fit to be seen,
The Hands of his Betters are not very clean;
A Palm more polite may as dirtily deal;
Gold, in handling, will stick to the Fingers like
  Meal.

IV.

IV.

What if, when a Pudding for Dinner he lacks,
He cribs, without Scruple, from other Men's Sacks;
In this of right noble Examples he brags,
Who borrow as freely from other Men's Bags.

V.

Or should he endeavour to heap an Estate,
In this he wou'd mimick the Tools of the State;
Whose Aim is alone their own Coffers to fill,
As all his Concern's to bring Grist to his Mill.

VI.

He eats when he's hungry, he drinks when
      he's dry,
And down when he's weary contented does lie;
Then rises up chearful to work and to sing:
If so happy a Miller, then who'd be a King?

Miller. There's a Song for you.
King. He should go sing this at Court, I
think.
Dick. I believe, if he's wise, he will chuse
to stay at home tho'.

Enter Peggy.

Miller. What wind blew you hither, pray!
you have a good share of impudence, or you
wou'd be asham'd to set your foot within my
house, methinks.
Peggy. Asham'd I am, indeed, but do not
call me impudent.   [*Weeps.*
Dick. Dear father, suspend your anger for
                                        the

the prefent; that fhe is here now is by my direction, and to do me juftice.

Peggy. To do that is all that is now in my power; for as to myfelf, I am ruin'd paft redemption; my character, my virtue, my peace, are gone: I am abandoned by my friends, defpis'd by the world, and expos'd to mifery and want.

King. Pray let me know the ftory of your misfortunes; perhaps it may be in my power to do fomething towards redreffing them.

Peggy. That you may learn from him whom I have wrong'd; but as for me, fhame will not let me fpeak, or hear it told. [*Exit.*

King. She's very pretty.

Dick O, Sir, I once thought her an angel; I lov'd her dearer than my life, and did believe her paffion was the fame for me: but a young nobleman of this neighbourhood happening to fee her, her youth and blooming beauty prefently ftruck his fancy; a thoufand artifices were immediately employ'd to debauch and ruin her. But all his arts were vain; not even the promife of making her his wife, could prevail upon her: in a little time he found out her love to me, and, imagining this to be the caufe of her refufal, he, by forg'd letters, and feign'd Stories, contriv'd to make her believe I was upon the point of marriage with another woman. Poffefs'd with this opinion, fhe, in a rage, writes me word, never to fee her more; and, in revenge, confented to her own undoing. Not contented with this, nor eafy while I was fo near her, he brib'd one of his caft off miftreffes to fwear a child to me, which fhe did: this was the occafion of my leaving my friends, and flying to London.

King. And how does fhe propofe to do you juftice?

Dick.

Dick. Why, the king being now in this foreſt a hunting, we deſign to take ſome opportunity of throwing ourſelves at his majeſty's feet, and complaining of the injuſtice done us by this noble villain.

Miller. Ah! *Dick!* I expect but little redreſs from ſuch an application. Things of this nature are ſo common amongſt the great, that I am afraid it will only be made a jeſt of.

King. Thoſe that can make a jeſt of what ought to be ſhocking to humanity, ſurely deſerve not the name of great or noble men.

Dick. What do you think of it, Sir? if you belong to the court, you, perhaps, may know ſomething of the king's temper.

King. Why, if I can judge of his temper at all, I think he would not ſuffer the greateſt nobleman in his court, to do an injuſtice to the meaneſt ſubject in his kingdom. But pray, who is the nobleman that is capable of ſuch actions as theſe?

Dick. Do you know my lord Lurewell?

King. Yes.

Dick. That's the man.

King. Well, I would have you put your deſign in execution. 'Tis my opinion the king would not only hear your complaint, but redreſs your injuries.

Miller. I wiſh it may prove ſo.

Enter the Keepers *leading in the* Courtiers.

Firſt Keeper. Hola! Cockle! where are ye? why, man, we have nabb'd a pack of rogues here juſt in the fact.

King. Ha, ha, ha! what, turn'd highway-men, my lords? or deer-ſtealers?

Firſt Courtier. I am very glad to find your majeſty in health and ſafety.

Second

Second Courtier. We have run thro' a great many perils and dangers to-night : but the joy of finding your majefty fo unexpectedly, will make us forget all we have fuffer'd.

Miller and Dick. What! is this the king ?

King. I am very glad to fee you, my lords, I confefs ; and particularly you, my lord Lurewell.

Lurewell. Your majefty does me honour.

King. Yes, my lord, and I will do you juftice too ; your honour has been highly wrong'd by this young man.

Lurewell. Wrong'd, my liege !

King. I hope fo, my lord ; for I would fain believe you can't be guilty of bafenefs and treachery.

Lurewell. I hope your majefty will never find me fo. What dares this villain fay ?

Dick. I am not to be frighted, my lord. I dare fpeak truth at any time.

Lurewell. Whatever ftains my honour muft be falfe.

King. I know it muft, my lord : yet has this man, not knowing who I was, prefum'd to charge your lordfhip, not only with great injuftice to himfelf, but alfo with ruining an innocent virgin whom he lov'd, and who was to have been his wife ; which, if true, were bafe and treacherous ; but I know 'tis falfe, and therefore leave it to your lordfhip to fay what punifhment I fhall inflict upon him, for the injury done to your honour.

Lurewell. I thank your majefty, I will not be fevere ; he fhall only afk my pardon, and to-morrow morning be oblig'd to marry the creature he has traduc'd me with.

King. This is mild. Well, you hear your fentence.

Dick.

Dick. May I not have leave to fpeak before your majefty?

King. What canft thou fay?

Dick. If I had your majefty's permiffion, I believe I have certain witneffes which will undeniably prove the truth of all I have accus'd his lordfhip of.

King. Produce them.

Dick. Peggy!

Enter Peggy.

King. Do you know this woman, my lord?

Lurewell. I know her, pleafe your majefty, by fight; fhe is a tenant's daughter.

Peggy. [*Afide.*] Majefty! What, is this the king?

Dick. Yes.

King. Have you no particular acquaintance with her?

Lurewell. Hum—I have not feen her thefe feveral months.

Dick. True, my lord; and that is part of your accufation; for, I believe, I have fome letters which will prove your lordfhip once had a more particular acquaintance with her. Here is one of the firft his lordfhip wrote to her, full of the tendereft and moft folemn proteftations of love and conftancy; here is another which will inform your majefty of the pains he took to ruin her; there is an abfolute promife of marriage before he could accomplifh it.

King. What fay you, my lord, are thefe your hand?

Lurewell. I believe, pleafe your majefty, I might have a little affair of gallantry with the girl fome time ago.

King. It was a little affair, my lord; a mean affair;

affair; and what you call gallantry, I call infamy. Do you think, my lord, that greatnefs gives a fanction to wickednefs? Or that it is the prerogative of lords to be unjuft and inhumane? You remember the fentence which yourfelf pronounc'd upon this innocent man; you cannot think it hard that it fhould pafs on you who are guilty.

Lurewell. I hope your majefty will confider my rank, and not oblige me to marry her.

King. Your rank? my lord. Greatnefs that ftoops to actions bafe and low, deferts its rank, and pulls its honours down. What makes your lordfhip great! is it your gilded equipage and drefs? then put it on your meaneft flave, and he's as great as you. Is it your riches or eftate? the villain that fhould plunder you of all, would then be as great as you. No, my lord, he that acts greatly, is the true great man. I therefore think you ought, in juftice, to marry her you thus have wrong'd.

Peggy. Let my tears thank your majefty. But alas! I am afraid to marry this young lord: that would only give him power to ufe me worfe, and ftill encreafe my mifery: I therefore beg your majefty will not command him to do it.

King. Rife then, and hear me. My lord, you fee how low the greateft nobleman may be reduced by ungenerous actions. Here is, under your own hand, an abfolute promife of marriage to this young woman, which, from a thorough knowledge of your unworthinefs, fhe has prudently declin'd to make you fulfil. I fhall therefore not infift upon it; but I command you, upon pain of my difpleafure, immediately to fettle on her three hundred pounds a year.

Peggy. May heaven reward your majefty's goodnefs. 'Tis too much for me; but if your

C majefty

majefty thinks fit, let it be fettled upon this much-injur'd man, to make fome fatisfaction for the wrongs which have been done him. As to myfelf, I only fought to clear the innocence of him I lov'd and wrong'd, then hide me from the world, and die forgiven.

Dick. This act of gen'rous virtue cancels all paſt failings ; come to my arms, and be as dear as ever.

Peggy. You cannot fure forgive me !

Dick. I can, I do, and ſtill will make you mine.

Peggy. O ! why did I ever wrong fuch gene-rous love ?

Dick. Talk no more of it. Here let us kneel, and thank the goodnefs which has made us bleſt.

King. May you be happy.

Miller. [*Kneels.*] After I have feen fo much of your majefty's goodnefs, I cannot defpair of pardon, even for the rough ufage your majefty received from me.

[*The king draws his fword, the miller is frighted,
    and rifes up, thinking he was going to kill him.*
What have I done that I fhould lofe my life ?

King. Kneel without fear. No, my good hoſt, fo far are you from having any thing to pardon, that I am much your debtor. I can-not think but fo good and honeſt a man will make a worthy and honourable knight ; fo rife up, Sir John Cockle : and to fupport your ſtate, and in fome fort requite the pleafure you have done us, a thoufand marks a year ſhall be your revenue.

Miller. Your majefty's bounty I receive with thankfulnefs ; I have been guilty of no mean-nefs to obtain it, and hope I ſhall not be obliged to keep it upon bafe conditions ; for tho' I am

willing

willing to be a faithful fubject, I am refolved to be a free, and an honeft man.

King. I rely upon your being fo : and, to gain the friendfhip of fuch a one, I fhall always think an addition to my happinefs, tho' a king.

> *Worth, in whatever ftate, is fure a prize,*
> *Which kings, of all men, ought not to defpife;*
> *By felfifh fycophants fo clofe befieg'd,*
> *'Tis by mere chance a worthy man's oblig'd:*
> *But hence, to every courtier be it known,*
> *Virtue fhall find protection from the throne.*

T H E   E N D.

EPISTLES

AND

POEMS

ON

SEVERAL OCCASIONS.

By R. DODSLEY.

An EPISTLE *to Mr.* POPE, *occasion'd by his*
ESSAY ON MAN.

GREAT bard! in whom united we admire,
   The sage's wisdom, and the poet's fire:
And whom at once the great and good commend,
A safe companion, and a useful friend:——
'Twas thus the Muse her eager flight began,
Ardent to sing the poet and the man:
But truth in verse is clad too like a lie,
And you, at least, would think it flattery;
Hating the thought, I check my froward strain,
I change my style, and thus begin again.

                      As

As when fome ftudent firft with curious eye,
Thro' nature's wond'rous frame attempts to pry:
His doubtful reafon feeming faults furprife,
He asks, if this be juft? if that be wife?
Storms, tempefts, earthquakes, virtue in diftrefs,
And vice unpunifh'd, with ftrange thoughts op-
    prefs:
Till thinking on, unclouded by degrees,
His mind is open'd, fair is all he fees;
Storms, tempefts, earthquakes, virtue's ragged
    plight,
And vice's triumph, all are juft and right:
Beauty is found, and order, and defign,
And the whole fcheme acknowledg'd all divine.

So when at firft I view'd thy wond'rous plan,
Leading thro' all the winding maze of man;
Bewilder'd, weak, unable to purfue,
My pride would fain have laid the fault on YOU.
This falfe, that ill-expreft, this thought not good,
And all was wrong which I mifunderftood.
But reading more attentive, foon I found
The diction nervous, and the doctrine found.
Saw man, a part of that ftupendous whole,
" Whofe body nature is, and God the foul."
Saw in the fcale of things his middle ftate,
And all his powers adapted juft to that.
Saw reafon, paffion, weaknefs, how of ufe,
How all to good, to happinefs conduce.
Saw my own weaknefs, thy fuperior power,
And ftill the more I read, admire thee more.

*This fimile drawn out, I now began
To think of forming fome defign or plan,
To aid my mufe, and guide her wond'ring lay,
When fudden to my mind came honeft GAY.
For form or method I no more contend,
But ftrive to copy that ingenious friend:**

    * In his firft epiftle.

Like him to catch my thoughts juſt as they roſe——
And thus I caught them, laughing at thy fees.

Where are ye now——ye criticks, ſhall I ſay ?
Or owls, who ſicken at this god of day ?
What ! mighty ſcriblers, will you let him go
Uncenſur'd, unabus'd, unhonour'd ſo ?
Step forth ſome great diſtinguiſh'd daring dunce,
Write but one page, you ſilence him at once :
Write without fear ; you will, you muſt ſuc-
            ceed :
He cannot anſwer——for he will not read.

Here pauſ'd the muſe—— alas, the jade is bit,
She fain would copy GAY, *but wants his wit.*
She pauſ'd, indeed——broke off as he had done,
Wrote four unmeaning lines, and then went on.

Ye Wits, and Fools ; ye Libertines, and Saints,
Come pour upon the foe your joint complaints.
Firſt, you who oft, with wiſdom too refin'd,
Can cenſure and direct th' *Eternal Mind,*
Ingenious Wits, who modeſtly pretend
This bungling frame, the univerſe, to mend ;
How can you bear, in your great reaſon's
            ſpight,
To hear him prove, " *Whatever is, is right ?*"
Alas ! how eaſy to confute the ſong !
If all is right, how came your heads ſo wrong ?

And come, ye ſolemn Fools, a numerous band,
Who read, and read, but never underſtand,
Pronounce it nonſenſe—Can't you prove it too ?
Good faith, my friends, it may be ſo—to You.

Come too, ye Libertines, who luſt for power,
Or wealth, or fame, or greatneſs, or a whore ;
All who true ſenſual happineſs adhere to,
And laugh him out of this old-faſhion'd virtue :
                                    Virtue,

Virtue, where he has whimſically plac'd
Your only bliſs——How odd is ſome men's taſte?

And come, ye rigid Saints, with looks de-
    mure,
Who boaſt yourſelves right holy, juſt, and pure;
Come, and with pious zeal the lines decry,
Which gave your proud hypocriſy the lie:
Which own the beſt have failings, not a few;
And prove the worſt, ſometimes, as good as You.

What? ſhall he taint ſuch perfect ſouls with ill?
Shall ſots not place their bliſs in what they will?
Nor fools be fools? nor wits ſublime deſcend
In charity to heaven its works to mend?
Laughs he at theſe?--'Tis monſtrous. To be plain,
I'd have you write—he can but laugh again.

*Here l ſting up my head, ſurpriz'd, I ſee
Cloſe at my elbow, flattering Vanity.
From her ſoft whiſpers ſoon I found it came,
That I ſuppos'd myſelf not one of them.
Alas! how eaſily ourſelves we ſooth!
I fear, in juſtice, he muſt laugh at both.*

*For, Vanity abaſh'd, up to my ear
Steps honeſt Truth, and theſe harſh words I hear;
" Forbear, vain bard, like them forbear thy lays;
" Alike to* POPE *ſuch cenſure and ſuch praiſe.
" Nor that can ſink, nor this exalt his name,
" Who owes to virtue, and himſelf, his fame."*

MODERN REASONING.

An EPISTLE *to Mr.* L———.

WHENCE comes it, L——, that ev'ry
   fool,
In reafon's fpite, in fpite of ridicule,
Fondly his own wild whims for truth maintains,
And all the blind deluded world difdains ;
Himfelf the only perfon bleft with fight,
And his opinion the great rule of right ?

 'Tis ftrange, from folly this conceit fhould rife,
That want of fenfe fhould make us think we're
   wife ;
Yet fo it is. The moft egregious elf
Thinks none fo wife or witty as himfelf.
Who nothing knows, will all things comprehend;
And who can leaft confute, will moft contend.

 I love the man, I love him from my foul,
Whom neither weaknefs blinds, nor whims
   controul ;
With learning bleft, with folid reafon fraught,
Who flowly thinks, and ponders every thought;
Yet, confcious to himfelf how apt to err,
Suggefts his notions with a modeft fear ;
Hears every reafon, every paffion hides,
Debates with calmnefs, and with care decides ;
More pleas'd to learn, than eager to confute,
Not victory, but truth his fole purfuit.

 But thefe are very rare. How happy he
Who taftes fuch converfe, L——, with thee !
Each focial hour is fpent in joys fublime,
Whilft hand in hand o'er learning's Alps you
   climb ;.
        Thro'

Thro' reafon's paths, in fearch of truth,
  proceed,
And clear the flow'ry way from every weed;
'Till, from her ancient cavern, rais'd to light,
The beauteous ftranger ftands reveal'd to fight.

How far from this the furious noify crew,
Who, what they once affert, with zeal purfue?
Their greater right infer from louder tongues;
And ftrength of argument from ftrength of
  lungs.
Inftead of fenfe, who ftun your ears with found,
And think they conquer, when they but con-
  found
Taurus, a bellowing champion, ftorms and
  fwears,
And drives his argument thro' both your ears;
And whether truth or falfhood, right or wrong,
'Tis ftill maintain'd, and prov'd by dint of—
  tongue;
In all difputes he bravely wins the day,
No wonder——for he hears not what you fay.

But tho' to tire the ear's fufficient curfe,
To tire one's patience is a plague ftill worfe.
Prato, a formal fage, debates with care,
A ftrong opponent, take him up who dare.
His words are grave, deliberate, and cool,
He looks fo wife———'tis pity he's a fool.
If he afferts, tho' what no man can doubt,
He'll bring ten thoufand proofs to make it out.
This, this, and this——is fo, and fo, and fo;
And therefore, therefore——that, and that, you
  know.
Circles no angles have; a fquare has four;
A fquare's no circle therefore——to be fure.
The fum of Prato's wond'rous wifdom is,
This is not that, and therefore, that not this.

Oppos'd

Oppos'd to him, but much the greater dunce,
Is he who throws all knowledge off at once.
The firſt for every trifle will contend ;
But this has no opinions to defend.
In fire no heat, no ſweetneſs in the roſe,
The man impos'd on by his very noſe :
Nor light nor colour charms his doubting eye,
The world's a dream, and all his ſenſes lie.
He thinks, yet doubts if he's poſſeſs'd of
  thought ;
Nay, even doubts his very power to doubt.
Aſk him if he's a man, or beaſt, or bird;
He cannot tell, upon his honeſt word.
'Tis ſtrange, ſo plain a point's ſo hard to prove;
I'll tell you what you are—a fool, by Jove.

Another claſs of diſputants there are,
More num'rous than the doubting tribe by far ;
Theſe are your wanderers, who from the point
Run wild in looſe harangues, all out of joint.
Vagarius, and confute him if you can,
Will hold debate with any mortal man.
He roves from Geneſis to Revelations,
And quite confounds you with divine quotations.
Should you affirm that Adam knew his wife,
And by that knowledge loſt the Tree of Life ;
He contradicts you, and in half an hour
Moſt plainly proves——Pope Joan the ſcarlet
  whore.
Nor head nor tail his argument affords,
A jumbling, incoherent. maſs of words ;
Moſt of them true, but ſo together toſt
Without connection, that their ſenſe is loſt.

But leaving theſe to rove, and thoſe to doubt,
Another clan alarms us ; face about :
See, arm'd with grave authority, they come,
And with great names and numbers ſtrike us
  dumb.

With

With thefe an error ven'rable appears,
For having been believ'd three thoufand years.
Reafon, nay common fenfe, to names muft fall,
And ftrength of argument's no ftrength at all.
But on, my mufe, tho' multitudes oppofe us,
Alas! Truth is not prov'd by counting nofes ;
Nor fear, tho' antient fages are fubjoin'd ;
A lie's a lie, tho' told by all mankind.
'Tis true, I love the ancients——but what then?
Plato and Ariftotle were but men.
I grant 'em wife——the wifeft difagree,
And therefore no fufficient guides for me.
An error, tho' by half the world efpous'd,
Is ftill an error, and may be oppos'd ;
And truth, tho' much from mortal eyes con-
      ceal'd, .
Is ftill the truth, and may be more reveal'd.
How foolifh then will look your mighty wife,
Should half their *ipfe dixits* prove plain lies !

    But on, my mufe, another tribe demands
Thy cenfure yet; nor fhould they 'fcape thy
      hands.
Thefe are the paffionate ; who, in difpute,
Demand fubmiffion, monarchs abfolute.
Sole judges, in their own conceit, of wit,
They damn all thofe for fools that won't fubmit.
Sir Tefty (thwart Sir Tefty if you dare)
Swears there's inhabitants in every ftar.
If you prefume to fay this may'nt be true,
You lie, Sir, you're a fool and blockhead too.
What he afferts, if any difbelieve,
How folks can be fo dull he can't conceive.
He knows he's right; he knows his judgment's
      clear ;
But men are fo perverfe they will not hear.
With him, Swift treads a dull trite beaten way ;
In Young no wit, no humour fmiles in Gay ;
                     Nor

Nor truth, nor virtue, Pope, adorns thy page;
And Thompſon's *Liberty* corrupts the age.
This to deny, if any dare preſume,
Fool, coxcomb, ſot, and puppy fill the room.
Hillario, who full well this humour knows,
Reſolv'd one day his folly to expoſe,
Kindly invites him with ſome friends to dine,
And entertains 'em with a roaſt Sir Loin :
Of this he knew Sir Teſty could not eat,
And purpoſely prepar'd it for his treat.
The reſt begin——Sir Teſty, pray fall to——
You love roaſt beef, Sir, come—I know you do.
" Excuſe me, Sir, 'tis what I never eat."
How, Sir ! not love roaſt beef ! the king of
      meat !
" 'Tis true indeed." Indeed it is not true ;
I love it, Sir, and you muſt love it too.
" I can't upon my word." Then you're a fool,
And don't know what's good eating, by my ſoul.
Not love roaſt beef !——Come, come, Sirs fill
      his plate,
I'll make him love it—Sir, G—d——you, eat.
Sir Teſty finding what it was they meant,
Roſe in a paſſion, and away he went.

The Wonder.

Published May 10, 1775.

THE
WONDER!

A

WOMAN KEEPS A SECRET.

A

COMEDY.

As it is ACTED at the

THEATRES-ROYAL

IN

DRURY-LANE

AND

COVENT-GARDEN.

Written by Mrs. CENTLIVRE.

LONDON:
Printed for and fold by W. OXLADE, at SHAKESPEARE'S
HEAD, in GEORGE-STREET, OLD-BAILEY.
M DCC LXXV.

PROLOGUE.

OUR Author fears the criticks of the stage,
Who, like Barbarians, spare nor sex, nor age;
She trembles at those censors in the pit,
Who think good-nature shews a want of wit:
Such malice, O! what muse can undergo it?
To save themselves, they always damn the poet.
Our author flies from such a partial jury,
As wary lovers from the nymphs of Drury:
To the few candid judges for a smile
She humbly sues to recompence her toil.
To the bright circle of the fair, she next
Commits her cause, with anxious doubts perplext.
Where can she with such hopes of favour kneel,
As to those judges, who her frailties feel?
A few mistakes, her sex may well excuse,
And such a plea, no Woman *shu'd refuse:*
If she succeeds, a Woman *gains applause;*
What Female *but must favour such a cause?*
Her faults — whate'er they are—e'en pass 'em by,
And only on her beauties fix your eye.
In plays, like vessels floating on the sea,
There's none so wise to know their destiny:
In this, howe'er, the pilot's skill appears,
While by the stars his constant course he steers;
Rightly our Author *does her judgment shew,*
That for her safety she relies on you.
Your approbation, fair-ones, can't but move
Those stubborn hearts, which first you taught to love:
The men must all applaud this play of ours,
For who dare see with other eyes than yours?

EPILOGUE.

Written by Mr. PHILLIPS.

CUſtom, with all our modern laws combin'd,
  Has given ſuch power deſpotic to mankind,
That we have only ſo much virtue now,
As they are pleas'd in favour to allow.
Thus like mechanic work we're us'd with ſcorn,
And wound up only for a preſent turn;
Some are for having our whole ſex enſlav'd,
Affirming we've no Souls *, and can't be ſav'd.
But were the women all of my opinion,
We'd ſoon ſhake off this falſe uſurp'd dominion.
We'd make the tyrants own, that we cou'd prove
As fit for other buſineſs as for love.
Lord! what prerogative might we obtain,
Could we from yielding a few months refrain!
How fondly wou'd our dangling lovers doat?
What homage wou'd be paid to petticoat?
'Twou'd be a jeſt to ſee the change of fate,
How might we all of politicks debate;
Promiſe and ſwear what we ne'er meant to do,
And what's ſtill harder, Keep our Secrets too.
Ay, marry! Keep a Secret, ſays a beau,
And ſneers at ſome ill-natur'd wit below;
But faith, if we ſhou'd tell but half we know,
There's many a ſpruce young fellow in this place,
Wou'd never more preſume to ſhow his face;
Women are not ſo weak, whate'er Men prate:
How many tip-top beaus have had the fate,
T' enjoy from Mamma's Secrets their eſtate.
Who, if her early folly had made known,
Had rid behind the coach that's now their own.
But here the Wond'rous Secret you diſcover;
A Lady ventures for a Friend, ———— A Lover.
Prodigious! for my part I frankly own,
I'ad ſpoil'd the Wonder, and the Woman ſhown.

---

* Alluding to an ironical Pamphlet tending to prove that
  Women had no Souls.

Dramatis Personæ.

At DRURY-LANE.

MEN.

Don Lopez,	a Grandee of *Portugal,*	Mr. *Baddeley.*
Don Felix,	{ his Son, in Love with *Violante,* }	Mr. *Garrick.*
Frederick,	A Merchant, - - -	Mr. *Packer.*
Don Pedro,	Father to *Violante,*	Mr. *Burton.*
Col. *Britton,*	A Scotchman, - -	Mr. *Jefferson.*
Gibby,	His Footman, - - -	Mr. *Johnston.*
Liſſardo,	Servant to *Felix,* - -	Mr. *King.*

WOMEN.

Donna Violante,	{ Deſign'd for a Nun by her Father, in Love with *Felix,* }	Mrs. *Barry.*
Donna Iſabella,	Siſter to *Felix,* - - -	Mrs. *W. Barry*
Flora,	Her Maid, - - -	Miſs *Pope.*
Inis,	Maid to *Violante,*	Mrs. *Bradſhaw*

At COVENT-GARDEN.

MEN.

Don Lopez,	a Grandee of *Portugal,*	Mr. *Dunſtal.*
Don Felix,	{ his Son, in Love with *Violante,* }	Mr. *Benſey.*
Frederick,	A Merchant, - -	Mr. *Gardiner.*
Don Pedro,	Father to *Violante,*	Mr. *Morris.*
Col. *Britton,*	A Scotchman, - -	Mr. *Wroughton.*
Gibby,	His Footman, --	Mr. *Shuter.*
Liſſardo,	Servant to *Felix,*	Mr. *Woodward.*

WOMEN.

Donna Violante,	{ Deſign'd for a Nun by her Father, in Love with *Felix,* }	Miſs *Macklin.*
Donna Iſabella,	Siſter to *Felix,* -	Mrs. *Mattocks.*
Flora,	Her Maid, - -	Mrs. *Pitt.*
Inis,	Maid to *Violante,*	Mrs. *Green.*

SCENE, *LISBON.*

THE
WONDER!

ACT I. SCENE I.

Enter Don Lopez *meeting* Frederick.

Fred. MY lord, Don Lopez.

Don Lopez. How d'ye, Frederick?

Fred. At your lordship's service; I am glad to see you look so well, my lord; I hope Antonio's out of danger.

Don Lop. Quite contrary; his fever increases, they tell me; and the surgeons are of opinion his wound is mortal.

Fred. Your son Don Felix is safe, I hope.

D. Lop. I hope so too, but they offer large rewards to apprehend him.

Fred. When heard your lordship from him?

D. Lop. Not since he went; I forbad him writing till the publick news gave him an account of Antonio's health. Letters might be intercepted, and the place of his abode discovered.

Fred. Your caution was good, my lord; tho' I am impatient to hear from Felix, yet his safety is my chief concern. Fortune has maliciously struck a bar between us in the affairs of life, but she has done me the honour to unite our souls.

D. Lop. I am not ignorant of the friendship between my son and you. I have heard him commend your morals, and lament your want of noble birth.

Fred. That's nature's fault, my lord; 'tis some comfort not to own one's misfortune to one's self, yet 'tis impossible not to regret the want of noble birth.

D. Lop. 'Tis a pity indeed such excellent parts as you are master of, should be eclipsed by mean extraction.

Fred. Such commendation would make me vain, my lord, did you not cast in the allay of my extraction.

D. Lop. There's no condition of life without its cares, and it is the perfection of a man to wear 'em as easy as he can; this unfortunate duel of my son's does not pass without impression. But since it's past prevention, all my concern is

now,

now, how he may escape the punishment; if Antonio dies, Felix shall for England.   You have been there; what sort of people are the English?

Fred. My lord, the English are by nature, what the ancient Romans were by discipline, courageous, bold, hardy, and in love with liberty.   Liberty is the idol of the English, under whose banner all the nation lists; give but the word for liberty, and straight more armed legions would appear, than France and Philip keep in constant pay.

D. Lop. I like their principles; who does not wish for freedom in all degrees of life? Tho' common prudence sometimes makes us act against it, as I am now obliged to do, for I intend to marry my daughter to Don Guzman, whom I expect from Holland every day, whither he went to take possession of a large estate left him by his uncle.

Fred. You will not surely sacrifice the lovely Isabella, to age, avarice, and a fool; pardon the expression, my lord; but my concern for your beauteous daughter transports me beyond that good manners which I ought to pay your lordship's presence.

D. Lop. I can't deny the justness of the character, Frederick; but you are not insensible what I have suffered by these wars; and he has two things which render him very agreeable to me for a son-in-law, he is rich and well-born; as for his being a fool, I don't conceive how that can be any blot in a husband, who is already possessed of a good estate.—A poor fool indeed is a very scandalous thing, and so are your poor wits, in my opinion, who have nothing to be vain of, but the inside of their skulls: now for Don Guzman, I know I can rule him, as I think fit; this is acting the politic part, Frederick, without which it is impossible to keep up the port of this life.

Fred. But have you no consideration for your daughter's welfare, my lord?

D. Lop. Is a husband of twenty thousand crowns a year no consideration? Now I think it a very good consideration.

Fred. One way, my lord. But what will the world say of such a match?

D. Lop. Sir, I value not the world a button.

Fred. I cannot think your daughter can have any inclination for such a husband.

D. Lop. There I believe you are pretty much in the right, tho' it is a secret which I never had the curiosity to inquire into, nor I believe ever shall.—Inclination quotha! parents would have a fine time on't if they consulted their children's inclination! I'll venture you a wager, that in all the garrison towns in Spain and Portugal, during the late war, there was not three women who have not had

ah

an inclination to every officer in the whole army; does it
therefore follow, that their fathers ought to pimp for them?
No, no, Sir, it is not a father's bufinefs to follow his children's inclinations till he makes himfelf a beggar.

Fred. But this is of another nature, my lord.

D. Lop. Look ye, Sir, I refolve fhe fhall marry Don
Guzman the moment he arrives; tho' I could not govern
my fon, I will my daughter, I affure you.

Fred. This match, my lord, is more prepofterous than
that which you propofed to your fon, from whence arofe
this fatal quarrel.—Don Antonio's fifter, Elvira, wanted
beauty only, but Guzman every thing, but——

D. Lop. Money—and that will purchafe every thing, and
fo adieu.   [*Exit.*

Fred. Monftrous! thefe are the refolutions which deftroy
the comforts of matrimony — he is rich, and well born,
powerful arguments indeed! could I but add them to the
friendfhip of Don Felix, what might I not hope? but a
merchant, and a grandee of Spain, are inconfiftent names—
Liffardo! from whence came you?

Enter Liffardo in a riding habit.

Liff. That letter will inform you, Sir.

Fred. I hope your mafter's fafe.

Liff. I left him fo; I have another to deliver which requires hafte—your moft humble fervant, Sir.   [*bowing.*

Fred. To Violante, I fuppofe.

Liff. The fame.   [*Exit.*

Fred. (*Reads.*) Dear Frederick, the two chief bleffings of
this life, are a friend, and a miftrefs; to be debarred the fight
of thofe is not to live. I hear nothing of Antonio's death,
and therefore refolve to venture to thy houfe this evening,
impatient to fee Violante, and embrace my friend.

Yours,   *Felix.*

Pray heaven he comes undifcover'd——Ha! Colonel Britton.

Enter Colonel Britton in a riding habit.

Col. Frederick, I rejoice to fee thee.

Fred. What brought you to Lifbon, Colonel.

Col. La fortune de la Guerre, as the French fay; I have
commanded thefe three laft years in Spain, but my country
has thought fit to ftrike up a peace, and give us, good
Proteftants, leave to hope for Chriftian burial; fo I refolved
to take Lifbon in my way home.

Fred. If you are not provided of a lodging, Colonel, pray
command my houfe, while you ftay.

Col. If I were fure I fhould not be troublefome, I wou'd
accept your offer, Frederick.

Fred. So far from trouble, Colonel, I fhall take it as a
particular favour; what have we here?

Col.

Col. My footman ; this is our country dress, you must
know, which, for the honour of Scotland, I make all my
servants wear.

Enter Gibby *in a* Highland *dress.*

Gib. What mun I de with the horses, and like yer
honour, they will tack cold gin they stand in the cause
way.

Fred. Oh! I'll take care of them, what hoa Vasquez.·
 [*Enter* Vasquez
Put those horses which that honest fellow will shew you,
into my stable, do ye hear, and feed them well.

Vas. Yes, Sir.——Sir, by my master's orders,· I am, Sir,
your most obsequious humble servant. Be pleas'd to lead
the way.

Gib. 'Sbleed gang yer gat, Sir,· and I sall follow yee : If
tee hungry to feed on compliments.   [*Exit*

Fred. Ha, ha, a comical fellow—Well, how do you like
our country, Colonel ?

Col. Why faith, Frederick, a man might pass his time
agreeable enough with-inside of a nunnery ; but to behold
such troops of soft, plump, tender, melting, wishing, nay
willing girls too, thro' a damn'd grate, give us Britons
strong temptations to plunder. Ah, Frederick, your priests
are wicked rogues. They immure beauty for their own
proper use, and shew it only to the laity to create desires
and inflame accompts, that they may purchase pardons at a
dearer rate.

Fred. I own wenching is something more difficult here than
in England, where women's liberties are subservient to their
inclinations, and husbands seem of no effect, but to take care
of the children which their wives provide.

Col. And does restraint get the better of inclination with
your women here ? No, I'll be sworn not, even in fourscore
Don't I know the constitution of the Spanish ladies ?

Fred. And of all ladies where you come, Colonel ; you
were ever a man of gallantry.

Col. Ah, Frederick, the kirk half starves us Scotchmen
We are kept so sharp at home, that we feed like cannibal
abroad. Hark ye, hast thou never a pretty acquaintance now
that thou would'st consign over to a friend for half an
hour, ha ?

Fred. Faith, Colonel, I am the worst pimp in Christen
dom ; you had better trust to your own luck ; the women wil
soon find you out, I warrant you.

Col. Ay, but it is dangerous foraging in an enemy's coun
try, and since I have some hopes of seeing my own again,
had rather purchase my pleasure, than run the hazard of
stilletto in my guts. 'Egad I think I must e'en marry, and

facrifice my body for the good of my foul; wilt thou recommend me to a wife then, one that is willing to exchange her moidores for English liberty; ha friend?

Fred. She muft be very handfome, I fuppofe.

Col. The handfomer the better——but be fure fhe has a nofe.

Fred. Ay, ay, and fome gold.

Col. Oh, very much gold; I fhall never be able to fwallow the matrimonial pill, if it be not well gilded.

Fred. Puh, beauty will make it flide down nimbly.

Col. At firft perhaps it may, but the fecond or third dofe will choak me——I confefs, Frederick, women are the prettieft play-things in nature; but gold, fubftantial gold, gives 'em the air, the mien, the fhape, the grace, and beauty of a goddefs.

Fred. And has not gold the fame divinity in their eyes, Colonel?

Col. Too often——Money is the very god of marriage: the poets drefs him in a faffron robe, by which they figure out the golden deity, and his lighted torch blazons thofe mighty charms, which encourage us to lift under his banner.

> *None marry now for love, no, that's a jeft:*
> *The felf-fame bargain ferves for wife and beaft.*

Fred. You are always gay, Colonel; come, fhall we take a refrefhing glafs at my houfe, and confider what has been faid?

Col. I have two or three compliments to difcharge for fome friends, and then I fhall wait on you with pleafure: where do you live?

Fred. At yon corner houfe with the green rails.

Col. In the clofe of the evening I will endeavour to kifs your hand. Adieu.   [*Exit.*

Fred. I fhall expect you with impatience.   [*Exit.*

Enter Ifabella *and* Inis *her Maid.*

Inis. For goodnefs fake, madam, where are you going in this pet!

Ifab. Any where to avoid matrimony; the thoughts of a hufband is as terrible to me as the fight of a hobgoblin.

Inis. Ay, of an old hufband; but if you may chufe for yourfelf, I fancy matrimony would be no fuch frightful thing to you.

Ifab. You are pretty much in the right, Inis; but to be forc'd into the arms of an ideot, a fneaking, fniveling, driveling, avaricious fool, who has neither perfon to pleafe the eye, fenfe to charm the ear, nor generofity to fupply thofe defects. Ah, Inis! what pleafant lives women lead in England, where duty wears no fetter but inclination: The cuftom of our country

inflaves

inflaves us from our very cradles, firft to our parents, next to
our hufbands; and when heaven is fo kind to rid us of both
thefe, our brothers ftill ufurp authority, and expect a blind
obedience from us; fo that maids, wives, or widows, we are
little better than flaves to the tyrant man; therefore, to
avoid their power, I refolve to caft myfelf into a monaftery.

Inis. That is, you'll cut your own throat to avoid another's
doing it for you. Ah, madam, thofe eyes tell me you
have no nun's flefh about you: a monaftery, quotha! where
you'll wifh yourfelf into the green-ficknefs in a month.

Ifab. What care I, there will be no man to plague me.

Inis. No, nor what's much worfe, to pleafe you neither
—Odflife, madam, you are the firft woman that e'er defpair'd in a Chriftian country—were I in your place—

Ifab. Why what would your wifdom do if you were?

Inis. I'd embark with the firft fair wind with all my jewels,
and feek my fortune on t'other fide the water; no fhore
can treat you worfe than your own; there's ne'er a father
in Chriftendom fhould make me marry any man againft
my will.

Ifab. I am too great a coward to follow your advice; I
muft contrive fome way to avoid Don Guzman, and yet
ftay in my own country.

Enter Don Lopez.

Lop. Muft you fo, miftrefs? but I fhall take care to
prevent you. (*Afide.*) Ifabella, whither are you going,
my child?

Ifab. Ha! my father! to church, Sir.

Inis. The old rogue has certainly over-heard her. [*Afide.*

Lop. Your devotion muft needs be very ftrong, or your memory very weak, my dear; why, vefpers are over for this
night; come, come, you fhall have a better errand to church
than to fay your prayers there. Don Guzman is arrived in
the river, and I expect him afhore to-morrow.

Ifab. Ha, to-morrow!

Lop. He writes me word, that his eftate in Holland is
worth 12000 crowns a year, which, together with what he had
before, will make thee the happieft wife in Lifbon.

Ifab. And the moft unhappy woman in the world. Oh,
Sir! if I have any power in your heart, if the tendernefs
of a father be not quite extinct, hear me with patience.

Lop. No objection againft the marriage, and I will hear
whatfoever thou haft to fay.

Ifab. That's torturing me on the rack, and forbidding
me to groan; upon my knees I claim the privilege of flefh
and blood.   ˎ [*Kneels.*

Lop. I grant it, thou fhalt have an arm full of flefh
and blood to-morrow; flefh and blood, quotha: heaven
                                                      forbid

forbid I fhould deny thee flefh and blood, my girl.

Inis. Here's an old dog for you. [*Afide.*

Ifab. Do not miftake, Sir; the fatal ftroke which fepa-
rates foul and body, is not more terrible to the thoughts of
finners, than the name of Guzman to my ear.

Lop. Puh, puh; you lye, you lye.

Ifab. My frighted heart beats hard againft my breaft, as
if it fought a paffage to your feet, to beg you'd change
your purpofe.

Lop. A very pretty fpeech this; if it were turn'd into
blank verfe, it would ferve for a Tragedy; why, thou haft
more wit than I thought thou hadft, child.—I fancy this
was all *extempore*, I don't believe thou did'ft ever think one
word on't before.

Inis. Yes, but fhe has, my lord, for I have heard her
fay the fame things a thoufand times.

Lop. How, how? what, do you top your fecond-hand
jefts upon your father, huffy, who knows better what's good
for you than you do yourfelf? remember 'tis your duty
to obey.

Ifab. (*Rifing*) I never difobey'd before, and wifh I had
not reafon now; but nature has got the better of my duty,
and makes me loath the harfh commands you lay.

Lop. Ha, ha, very fine! ha, ha.

Ifab. Death itfelf would be more welcome.

Lop. Are you fure of that?

Ifab. I am your daughter, my lord, and can boaft as
ftrong a refolution as yourfelf; I'll die before I'll marry
Guzman.

Lop. Say you fo? I'll try that prefently. [*Draws.*
Here, let me fee with what dexterity you can breathe a vein
now (*offers her his fword.*) The point is pretty fharp. 'Twill
do your bufinefs, I warrant you.

Inis. Blefs me, Sir, what do you mean to put a fword
into the hands of a defperate woman?

Lop. Defperate, ha, ha, ha, you fee how defperate fhe is;
what, art thou frighted, little Bell? ha!

Ifab. I confefs, I am ftartled at your morals, Sir.

Lop. Ay, ay, child, thou hadft better take the man, he'll
hurt thee the leaft of the two.

Ifab. I fhall take neither, Sir; death has many doors, and
when I can live no longer with pleafure, I fhall find one to let
him in at without your aid.

Lop. Say'ft thou fo, my dear Bell? Ods, I'm afraid thou
art a little lunatick, Bell. I muft take care of thee, child.
(*takes hold of her, and pulls out of his pocket a key.*) I fhall

B   make

make bold to fecure thee, my dear : I'll fee if locks and bars
can keep thee till Guzman come ; go, get into your
chamber.

There I'll your boafted refolution try,
And fee who'll get the better, you or I.

        [*pufhes her in, and locks the door.*

ACT II.

SCENE, *a Room in* Don Pedro's *Houfe.*
Enter Donna Violante *reading a letter, and* Flora *following.*
Flora. WHAT, muft that letter be read again ?
        Vio, Yes, and again, and again, and again, a
thoufand times again ; a letter from a faithful lover can ne'er
be read too often ; it fpeaks fuch kind, fuch foft, fuch tender
things——   [*Kiffes it.*

Flo. But always the fame language.

Vio. It does not charm the lefs for that.

Flo. In my opinion nothing charms that does not change ;
and my compofition of the four and twenty letters, after the
firft effay, from the fame hand, muft be dull, except a bank
note, or a bill of exchange.

Vio. Thy tafte is my averfion.—(*Reads.*) My all that's
charming, fince life's not life exil'd from thee, this night fhall
bring me to thy arms. Frederick and thee are all I truft ;
thefe fix weeks abfence has been in love's accompt fix hundred
years ; when it is dark, expect the wonted fignal at thy window, till when, adieu, thine more than his own.   *Felix.*

Flo. Who would not have faid as much to a lady of her
beauty, and twenty thoufand pounds ?——Were I a man,
methinks, I could have faid a hundred finer things ; I would
have compar'd your eyes to the ftars, your teeth to ivory, your
lips to coral, your neck to alabafter, your fhape to——

Vio. No more of your bombaft, truth is the beft eloquence
in a lover—What proof remains ungiven of his love ? When
his father threaten'd to difinherit him, for refufing Don Antonio's fifter, from whence fprung this unhappy quarrel, did
it fhake his love for me ? And now, tho' ftrict enquiry runs
thro' every place, with large rewards to apprehend him, does
he not venture all for me ?

Flo. But you know, madam, your father Don Pedro de-
figns you for a nun, and fays your grandfather left you your
fortune upon that condition.

Vio. Not without my approbation, girl, when I come to
                                        one

one and twenty, as I am informed. But however, I shall run the risk of that; go, call in Liffardo.

Flo. Yes, madam; now for a thousand verbal questions.

[*Exit, and re-enter with* Liffardo.

Vio. Well, and how do you do, Liffardo?

Liff. Ah, very weary, madam—Faith, thou look'st wondrous pretty, Flora. [*Aside to* Flora.

Vio. How came you?

Liff. En Chevalier, madam, upon a hackney jade, which they told me formerly belong'd to an English colonel. But I should have rather thought she had been bred a good Roman Catholick all her life-time; for she down on her knees to every stock and stone we came along by.——My chops water for a kiss, they do, Flora. [*Aside to* Flora.

Flo. You'd make one believe you are wondrous fond now.

Vio. Where did you leave your master?

Liff. Od, if I had you alone, house-wife, I'd show you how fond I cou'd be —— [*Aside to* Flora.] At a little farm-house, madam, about five miles off; he'll be at Don Frederick's in the evening——Od, I will so revenge myself of those lips of thine. [*To* Flora.

Vio. Is he in health?

Flo. Oh, you counterfeit wondrous well. [*To* Liffardo.

Liff. No, every body knows I counterfeit very ill. [*To* Flora.

Vio. How say you? Is Felix ill? What's his distemper? Ha!

Liff. A pies on't, I hate to be interrupted —— love, madam, love——in short, madam, I believe he has thought of nothing but your ladyship ever since he left Lisbon. I am sure he cou'd not, if I may judge of his heart by my own. [*Looking lovingly upon* Flora.

Vio. How came you so well acquainted with your master's thoughts, Liffardo?

Liff. By an infallible rule, madam; words are the pictures of the mind, you know; now to prove he thinks of nothing but you, he talks of nothing but you —— for example, madam, coming from shooting t'other day, with a brace of partridges, Liffardo, said he, go bid the cook roast me these Violantes——I flew into the kitchen, full of thoughts of thee, cry'd, Here, cook, roast me these Florellas. [*To* Flora.

Flo. Ha, ha, excellent——you mimick your master then it seems.

Liff. I can do every thing as well as my master, you little rogue:——another time, madam, the priest came to make him a visit, he call'd out hastily, Liffardo, said he, bring a Violante for my father to sit down on;——then he often mistook my name, madam, and call'd me Violante;

B 2 in

in fhort, I heard it fo often, that it became as familiar to me as my prayers.

Vio. You live very merrily then it feems.

Liff. Oh, exceeding merry, madam. [*Kiffes* Flora's *Hand.*

Vio. Ha! exceeding merry; had you treats and balls?

Liff. Oh! yes, yes, madam, feveral.

Flo. You are mad, Liffardo, you don't mind what my ady fays to you.   [*Afide to* Liffardo.

Vio. Ha! balls——is he fo merry in my abfence? and did your mafter dance, Liffardo?

Liff. Dance, madam! where, madam?

Vio. Why, at thofe balls you fpeak of.

Liff. Balls! what balls, madam?

Vio. Why, fure you are in love, Liffardo; did not you fay, but now, you had balls where you have been?

Liff. Balls, madam! Odflife, I afk your pardon, madam! I, I, I, had miflaid fome wafh-balls of my mafter's t'other day; and becaufe I could not think where I had laid them, juft when he afk'd for them, he very fairly broke my head, madam, and now it feems I can think of nothing elfe. Alas! he dance, madam! no, no, poor gentleman, he is as melancholy as an unbraced drum.

Vio. Poor Felix! there, wear that ring for your mafter's fake, and let him know I fhall be ready to receive him.

[*Exit* Vio.

Liff. I fhall, madam—(*puts on the ring*) methinks a diamond ring is a vaft addition to the little finger of a gentleman.   [*admiring his hand.*

Flo. That ring muft be mine——Well, Liffardo! what hafte you make to pay off arrears now? look how the fellow ftands!

Liff. Egad, methinks I have a very pretty hand ——and very white,—— and the fhape! —— faith I never minded it fo much before!———in my opinion it is a very fine fhaped hand——and becomes a diamond ring, as well as the firft grandee's in Portugal.

Flo. The man's tranfported! Is this your love! This your impatience!

Liff. (*Takes fnuff.*) Now in my mind——I take fnuff with a very *jantee* air——Well, I am perfuaded I want nothing but a coach and a title, to make me a very fine gentleman.

[*Struts about.*

Flo. Sweet Mr. Liffardo, (*curtefying*) if I may prefume to fpeak to you, without affronting your little finger—

Liff. Odfo, Madam, I afk your pardon—Is it to me, or to the ring—you direct your difcourfe, madam?

Flo. Madam! Good lack! How much a diamond ring improves one!

Liff.

Liff. Why, tho' I say it—I can carry myself as well as any body—But what wert thou going to say, child?

Flo. Why I was going to say, that I fancy you had best let me keep that ring; it will be a very pretty wedding-ring, Liffardo, would it not?

Liff. Humph! Ah! But——but——but——I believe I shan't marry yet awhile.

Flo. You shan't, you say.——Very well! I suppose you design that ring for Inis.

Liff. No, no, I never bribe an old acquaintance——Perhaps I might let it sparkle in the eyes of a stranger a little, till we come to a right understanding——But then, like all other mortal things, it would return from whence it came.

Flo. Insolent——Is that your manner of dealing?

Liff. With all but thee——Kiss me, you little rogue you.
[*Hugging her*

Flo. Little rogue! prithee, fellow, don't be so familiar, (*pushing him away*), if I mayn't keep your ring, I can keep my kisses.

Liff. You can you say! Spoke with the air of a chamber-maid.

Flo. Reply'd with the spirit of a serving man.

Liff. Prithee, Flora, don't let you and I fall out, I am in a merry humour, and shall certainly fall in somewhere.

Flo. What care I, where you fall in.

Enter Violante.

Vio. Why do you keep Liffardo so long, Flora? when you don't know how soon my father may awake, his afternoon naps are never long.

Flo. Had Don Felix been with her, she would not have thought the time long; these ladies consider no body's wants but their own. [*Aside.*

Vio. Go, go, let him out, and bring a candle.

Flo. Yes, madam.

Liff. I fly, madam. [*Exeunt Liff. and Flora*

Vio. The day draws in, and night,—the lover's friend, advances—Night more welcome than the sun to me, because it brings my love.

Flo. (*Shrieks within.*) Ah thieves, thieves! murder, murder!

Vio. (*Shrieks.*) Ah! defend me heaven! What do I hear? Felix is certainly pursu'd, and will be taken.

. Enter Flora running.

Vio. How now! why dost stare so? Answer me quickly! What's the matter?

Flo. Oh, madam! as I was letting out Liffardo, a gentleman rushed between him and I, struck down my candle, and is bringing a dead person in his arms into our house.

B 3 *Vio.*

Vio. Ha! a dead perfon! Heav'n grant it does not prove my Felix.

Flo. Here they are, madam.

Enter Colonel *with* Ifabella *in his arms.*

Vio. I'll retire till you difcover the meaning of the accident.
[*Exit.*

Col. (*Sets* Ifabella *down in a chair, and* addreffes *himfelf to* Flora.)

Madam, The neceffity this lady was under, of being conveyed into fome houfe with fpeed and fecrefy, will, I hope, excufe any indecency I might be guilty of, in preffing fo rudely into this——I am an entire ftranger to her name and circumftances; would I were fo to her beauty too. [*Afide.*] I commit her, madam, to your care, and fly to make her retreat fecure, if the ftreet be clear; permit me to return, and learn from her own mouth, if I can be farther ferviceable : pray, madam, how is the lady of this houfe called ?

Flo. Violante, fignior——He is a handfome Cavalier, and promifes well. [*Afide.*

Col. Are you fhe, madam ?

Flo. Only her woman, fignior.

Col. Your humble fervant, miftrefs. Pray be careful of the lady——(*Gives her two moidores.*) [*Exit Col.*

Flo. Two moidores ! Well, he is a generous fellow. This is the only way to make one careful ; I find all countries underftand the conftitution of a chamber-maid.

Enter Violante.

Vio. Was you diftracted, Flora ? to tell my name to a man you never faw ! Unthinking wench ! who knows what this may turn to—What, is the lady dead ? Ah ! defend me heaven, 'tis Ifabella, fifter to my Felix, what has befallen her ? Pray heaven he's fafe.——Run and fetch fome cold water. [*Exit* Flora, *and enters with water.*] Ifabella, friend, fpeak to me ; Oh ! fpeak to me, or I fhall die with apprehenfion.

Flo. See, fhe revives.

Ifab. O ! hold, my deareft father, do not force me, indeed I cannot love him.

Vio. How wild fhe talks.——

Ifab. Ha ! where am I ?

Vio. With one as fenfible of thy pain as thou thyfelf can'ft be.

Ifab. Violante ! What kind ftar preferved, and lodg'd me here ?

Flo. It was a terreftrial ftar, call'd a man, madam ; pray Jupiter he proves a lucky one.

Ifab. Oh ! I remember now ; forgive me, dear Violante ; my thoughts ran fo much upon the danger I efcap'd, I forgot.   *Vio.*

Vio. May I not know your ſtory?

Iſab. Thou art no ſtranger to one part of it; I have often told thee that my father deſign'd to ſacrifice me to the arms of Don Guzman, who it ſeems is juſt return'd from Holland, and expected aſhore to-morrow, the day that he has ſet to celebrate our nuptials. Upon my refuſing to obey him, he lock'd me into my chamber, vowing to keep me there till he arriv'd, and force me to conſent. I know my father to be poſitive, never to be won from his deſign; and having no hope left me, to eſcape the marriage, I leap'd from the window, into the ſtreet.

Vio. You have not hurt yourſelf, I hope.

Iſab. No, a gentleman paſſing by, by accident, caught me in his arms; at firſt my fright made me apprehend it was my father, till he aſſured me to the contrary.

Flo. He is a very fine gentleman, I promiſe you, madam, and a well-bred man, I warrant him. I think I never ſaw a grandee put his hand into his pocket with a better air in my whole life-time; then he open'd his purſe with ſuch a grace, that nothing but his manner of preſenting me with the gold cou'd equal.

Vio. There is but one common road to the heart of a ſervant, and 'tis impoſſible for a generous perſon to miſtake it.— But how came you hither, Iſabella?

Iſab. I know not; I deſired the ſtranger to convey me to the next Monaſtery, but ere I reach'd the door, I ſaw, or fancy'd that I ſaw, Liſſardo, my brother's man, and the thought that his maſter might not be far off, flung me into a ſwoon, which is all that I remember: Ha! What's here [*takes up a letter*] For Colonel Britton, *to be left at the Poſt-Houſe in* Liſbon; this muſt be brought by the ſtranger which brought me hither.

Vio. Thou art fallen into the hands of a ſoldier; take care he does not lay thee under contribution, girl.

Iſab. I find he is a gentleman; and if he is but unmarried, I could be content to follow him all the world over.—But I ſhall never ſee him more I fear.   [*Sighs and pauſes.*

Vio. What makes you ſigh, Iſabella?

Iſab. The fear of falling into my father's clutches again.

Vio. Can I be ſerviceable to you?

Iſab. Yes, if you conceal me two or three days.

Vio. You command my houſe and ſecreſy.

Iſab. I thank you, Violante.——I wiſh you would oblige me with Mrs. Flora awhile.

Vio. I'll ſend for her to you—I muſt watch if Dad be ſtill aſleep, or here will be no room for Felix.   [*Exit.*

Iſab. Well, I don't know what ails me, methinks I wiſh I could find this ſtranger out.

Enter

Enter Flora.

Flo. Does your ladyſhip want me, madam?

Iſab. Ay, Mrs. Flora, I reſolve to make you my confident.

Flo. I ſhall endeavour to diſcharge my duty, madam.

Iſab. I doubt it not, and deſire you to accept this as a token of gratitude.

Flo. O dear ſigniora, I ſhould have been your humble ſervant without a fee.

Iſab. I believe it——But to the purpoſe——Do you think if you ſaw the gentleman which brought me hither, you ſhou'd know him again.

Flo. From a thouſand, madam; I have an excellent memory where an handſome man is concerned; when he went away he ſaid he would return again immediately. I admire he comes not.

Iſab. Here, did you ſay? You rejoice me——Tho' I'll not ſee him if he comes: cou'd not you contrive to give him a letter?

Flo. With the air of a duenna——

Iſab. Not in this houſe——you muſt veil and follow him ——He muſt not know it comes from me.

Flo. What, do you take me for a novice in love affairs? Tho' I have not practiſ'd the art ſince I have been in Donna Violante's ſervice, yet I have not loſt the theory of a chamber-maid——Do you write the letter, and leave the reſt to me ——Here, here, here's pen, ink, and paper.

Iſab. I'll do it in a minute.   [*Sits down to write.*

Flo. So I this is a buſineſs after my own heart; love always takes care to reward his labourers, and Great-Britain ſeems to be his favourite country.—Oh, I long to ſee the other two moidores with a Britiſh air——Methinks there's a grace peculiar to that nation in making a preſent.

Iſab. So I have done; now if he does but find this houſe again!

Flo. If he ſhould not——I warrant I'll find him if he's in Liſbon.   [*Puts the letter into her boſom.*

Enter Violante.

Vio. Flora, watch my papa, he's faſt aſleep in his ſtudy —if you find him ſtir give me notice.—Hark, I hear Felix at the window; admit him inſtantly, and then to your poſt.
          [*Exit* Flora.

Iſab. What ſay you, Violante? is my brother come?

Vio. It is his ſignal at the window.

Iſab. (*Kneels*) Oh! Violante, I conjure thee by all the love thou bear'ſt to Felix——by thy own generous nature— nay more by that unſpotted virtue thou art miſtreſs of, do not diſcover to my brother I am here.

Vio.

Vio. Contrary to thy defire, be affur'd I never fhall. But where's the danger?

Ifab. Art thou born in Lifbon, and afk that queftion? he'll think his honour blemifh'd by my difobedience, and would reftore me to my father, or kill me; therefore, dear, dear girl——

Vio. Depend upon my friendfhip, nothing fhall draw the fecret from thefe lips, not even Felix, tho' at the hazard of his love; I hear him coming; retire into that clofet.

Ifab. Remember, Violante, upon thy promife my very life depends. [*Exit.*

Vio. When I betray thee, may I fhare thy fate.

Enter Flora *and* Felix.

Vio. My Felix, my everlafting love. (*runs into his arms*

Fel. My life, my foul! my Violante!

Vio. What hazards doft thou run for me? oh, how fhall I requite thee?

Fel. If, during this tedious painful exile, thy thoughts have never wander'd from thy Felix, thou haft made me more than fatisfaction.

Vio. Can there be room within this heart for any but thy-felf? No, if the god of love were loft to all the reft of human kind, thy image wou'd fecure him in my breaft; I am all truth, all love, all faith, and know no jealous fears.

Fel. My heart's the proper fphere where Love refides; could he quit that, he wou'd be no where found; and yet, Violante, I'm in doubt.

Vio. Did I ever give thee caufe to doubt, my Felix?

Fel. True love has many fears, and fear as many eyes as fame; yet fure I think they fee no fault in thee——what's that?.. (*the Colonel pats at the window without.*

Vio. What? I heard nothing. (*He pats again.*

Fel. Ha! What means this fignal at your window?

Vio. Somebody, perhaps, in paffing by, might accidentally hit it; it can be nothing elfe.

Col. (*Within*) Hift, hift, Donna Violante, Donna Violante.

Fel. They ufe your name by accident too, do they, madam? [*Enter* Flora.

Flo. There is a gentleman at the window, madam, which I fancy to be him who brought Ifabella hither; fhall I ad-mit him? [*Afide to* Flora.

Vio. Admit diftraction rather; thou art the caufe of this, unthinking wretch!

Fel. What, has Mrs. Scout brought you frefh intelligence? death, I'll know the bottom of this immediately! [*Offers to go.*

Flo. Scout! I fcorn your words, fignior.   *Vio.*

Vio. Nay, nay, nay, you muſt not leave me.
[*Runs and catches hold of him.*

Fel. Oh! 'Tis not fair, not to anſwer the gentleman, madam. It is none of his fault, that his viſit proves unſea-
ſonable; pray let me go, my preſence is but a reſtraint upon
you. [*Struggles to get from her.*
[*The Colonel pats again.*

Vio. Was ever accident ſo miſchievous! [*Aſide.*

Flo. It muſt be the Colonel; now to deliver my letter to
him. [*Exit.*

Fel. Hark! he grows impatient at your delay—Why do
you hold the man, whoſe abſence wou'd oblige you? Pray let
me go, madam; conſider, the gentleman wants you at the
window, Confuſion! [*Struggles ſtill.*

Vio. It is not me he wants.

Fel. Death, not you? Is there another of your name in
the houſe? But, come on, convince me of the truth of what
you ſay: open the window; if his buſineſs does not lie with
you, your converſation may be heard.——This, and only
this, can take off my ſuſpicion——What, do you pauſe?
Oh, guilt! guilt! Have I caught you? Nay, then I'll leap
the balcony. If I remember, this way leads to it.
[*Breaks from her, and goes to the door where* Iſabella *is.*

Vio. Oh, heaven! What ſhall I do now, hold, hold, hold,
hold, not for the world——You enter there——Which
way ſhall I preſerve his ſiſter from his knowledge? [*Aſide.*

Fel. What, have I touch'd you? do you fear your lover's
life?

Vio. I fear for none but you——for goodneſs ſake, do
not ſpeak ſo loud, my Felix. If my father hear you, I am
loſt for ever; that door opens into his apartment. What
ſhall I do if he enters? there he finds his ſiſter——if he
goes out, he'll quarrel with the ſtranger——nay do not
ſtruggle to be gone, my Felix—if I open the window, he
may diſcover the whole intrigue, and yet of all evils we
ought to chuſe the leaſt. Your curioſity ſhall be ſatisfied.
Whoe'er you are that with ſuch inſolence dare uſe my name,
and give the neighbourhood pretence to reflect upon my conduct, I charge you inſtantly to be gone, or expect the
treatment you deſerve.
[*Goes to the window, and throws up the ſaſh.*

Col. I aſk pardon, madam, and will obey; but when I
left this houſe to night——

Fel. Good.

Vio. It is moſt certainly the ſtranger: what will be the
event of this heaven knows. [*Aſide.*] You are miſtaken in
the houſe, I ſuppoſe, Sir.

Fel. No, no, he's not miſtaken——Pray, madam, let the
gentleman go on. *Vio.*

Vio. Wretched misfortune! pray be gone, Sir, I know of no bufinefs you have here.

Col. I wish I did not know it neither——But this houfe contains my foul, then can you blame my body for hovering about it.

Fel. Excellent!

Vio. Diftraction! He will infallibly difcover Ifabella. I tell you again you are miftaken; however, for your own fatisfaction, call to-morrow.

Fel. Matchlefs impudence! An affignation before my face—No, he fhall not live to meet your wifhes.

[*Takes out a piftol, and goes towards the window; fhe catches hold of him.*

Vio. Ah! [*Shrieks*] Hold I conjure you.

Col. To-morrow's an age, madam! May I not be admitted to-night?

Vio. If you be a gentleman, I command your abfence. Unfortunate! What will my ftars do with me? [*Afide.*

Col. I have done——Only this——Be careful of my life, for it is in your keeping. (*Exit from the window.*

Fel. Pray obferve the gentleman's requeft, madam.
(*Walking off from her.*

Vio. I am all confufion. (*Afide*

Fel. You are all truth, all love, all faith: Oh thou all woman!——How have I been deceived? S'death, cou'd you not have impos'd upon me for this one night? cou'd neither my faithful love, nor the hazard I have run to fee you, make me worthy to be cheated on.

Vio. Can I bear this from you? [*Weeps.*

Fel. [*Repeats*] When I left this houfe to-night——To-night! the devil! return fo foon!

Vio. Oh Ifabella! What haft thou involv'd me in! [*Afide*

Fel. [*Repeats*] This houfe contains my foul.

Vio. Yet I refolve to keep the fecret. [*Afide.*

Fel. [*Repeats*] Be careful of my life, for 'tis in your keeping,——Damnation!——How ugly fhe appears!
[*Looking at her.*

Vio. Do not look fo fternly on me, but believe me, Felix, I have not injur'd you, nor am I falfe.

Fel. Not falfe, not injur'd me! Oh Violante, loft and abandoned to thy vice! Not falfe, oh monftrous!

Vio. Indeed I am not—— There is a caufe which I muft not reveal———Oh think how far honour can oblige your fex———Then allow a woman may be bound by the fame rule to keep a fecret.

Fel. Honour, what haft thou to do with honour, thou that canft admit plurality of lovers? A fecret? Ha, ha, ha, his affairs are wondrous fafe, who trufts his fecret to a woman's keeping;

keeping; but you need give yourself no trouble about clearing this point, madam, for you are become so indifferent to me, that your truth and falsihood are the same!

Vio. My love!   [*Offers to take his hand.*

Fel. My torment!   [*Turns from her.*

Enter Flora.

Flo. So I have deliver'd my letter to the Colonel, and receiv'd my fee. [*Afide.*] Madam, your father bade me see what noise that was—for goodness sake, Sir, why do you speak so loud?

Fel. I understand my cue, mistress; my absence is necessary, I'll oblige you.   [*Going.*

Vio. Oh let me undeceive you first!   [*takes hold of him.*

Fel. Impossible!

Vio. 'Tis very possible if I durst.

Fel. Durst? ha, ha, ha, durst, quotha?

Vio. But another time I'll tell thee all.

Fel. Nay, now or never————

Vio. Now it cannot be.

Fel. Then it shall never be—thou most ungrateful of thy sex, farewell.   [*Breaks from her and Exit.*

Vio. Oh exquisite trial of my friendship! Yet not even this, shall draw the secret from me.

> *That I'll preserve, let fortune frown or smile,*
> *And trust to love, my love to reconcile.*   [*Exit.*

ACT III.

Enter Don Lopez.

Lop. WAS ever man thus plagu'd? Odsheart, I cou'd swallow my dagger for madness: I know not what to think; sure Frederick had no hand in her escape— She must get out of the window; and she could not do that without a ladder: and who cou'd bring it her, but him? Ay, it must be so. The dislike he shew'd to Don Guzman in our discourse to-day, confirms my suspicion, and I will charge him home with it; sure children were given me for a curse! Why, what innumerable misfortunes attend us parents, when we have employed our whole care to educate, and bring our children up to years of maturity? Just when we expect to reap the fruits of our labour, a man shall, in the tinkling of a bell, see one hang'd, t'other whor'd—This graceless baggage—But I'll to Frederick immediately, I'll take the Alguazil with me and search his house; and if I find her, I'll use her——by St. Anthony, I don't know how I'll use her.

[*Exit.*

The

The Scene changes to the Street.
Enter Colonel *with* Isabella's *letter in his hand, and* Gibby *following.*

Col. Well, tho' I cou'd not see my fair *incognita*, fortune, to make me amends, has flung another intrigue in my way. Oh! How I love these pretty, kind, coming females, that wont give a man the trouble of racking his invention to deceive them.—Oh Portugal! Thou dear garden of pleasure—where love drops down his mellow fruit, and every bough bends to our hands, and seems to cry, Come, pull and eat; how deliciously a man lives here without fear of the stool of repentance. —— This letter I received from a lady in a veil——Some Duenna! Some necessary implement of Cupid! I suppose the stile is frank and easy, I hope like her that writ it. *(Reads.)* " Sir, I have seen your person, and like it"—— *Very concise* —— " And if you'll meet at five " o'clock in the morning upon the *Terriero de passa*, half an " hour's conversation will let me into your mind."—*Ha, ha, ha, a philosophical wench: this is the first time I ever knew a woman had any business with the mind of a man*—— " If your intellects answer your outward appearance, the " adventure may not displease you. I expect you'll not at- " tempt to see my face, nor offer any thing unbecoming the " gentleman I take you for:"————Humph, the gentleman she takes me for; I hope she takes me to be flesh and blood, and then, I am sure I shall do nothing unbecoming a gentleman. Well, if I must not see her face, it shall go hard if I don't know where she lives.——Gibby.

Gib. Here, an lik yer honour.

Col. Follow me at a good distance, do you hear, Gibby?

Gib. In troth dee I, weel eneugh, Sir.

Col. I am to meet a lady upon the *Terriero de passa*.

Gib. The deel an mine eyn gin I kenn her, Sir.

Col. But you will when you come there, sirrah.

Gib. Like eneugh, Sir; I have as sharp an eyn tul a bony lass, as ere a lad in aw Scotland; and what mun I dee wi her, Sir?

Col. Why, if she and I part, you must watch her home, and bring me word where she lives.

Gib. In troth sal I, Sir, gin the deel tak her not.

Col. Come along then, 'tis pretty near the time—I like a woman that rises early to pursue her inclination.

Thus we improve the pleasures of the day,
Whilst tasteless mortals sleep their time away. [*Exit.*

Scene changes to Frederick's *House.*
Enter Inis *and* Lissardo.

Liss. Your lady run away, and you know not whither! say you?

C · · · *Inis.*

Inis. She never greatly car'd for me after finding you and I together ; but you are very grave, methinks, Liffardo.

Liff. [*Looking on the ring.*] Not at all—I have some thoughts indeed of altering my course of living ; there is a critical minute in every man's life, which if he can but lay hold of, he may make his fortune.

Inis. Ha ! What do I see, a diamond ring ! Where the de ce had he that ring ? You have got a very pretty ring there, Liffardo.

Liff. Aye, the trifle is pretty enough—But the lady which gave it to me is a *bona roba* in beauty, I assure you.
[*Cocks his hat and struts.*

Inis. I can't bear this—The lady !—What lady, pray ?

Liff. O fye ! There's a question to ask a gentleman.

Inis. A gentleman ! Why the fellow's spoil'd ! Is this your love for me ? Ungrateful man, you'll break my heart, so you will.   [*Bursts into tears.*

Liff. Poor tender-hearted fool.——

Inis. If I knew who gave you that ring, I'd tear her eyes out, so I wou'd.   [*Sobs.*

Liff. So, now the jade wants a little coaxing : Why what dost thou weep for now, my dear ? Ha !

Inis. I suppose Flora gave you that ring ; but I'll—

Liff. No, the devil take me if she did ; you make me swear now—so, they are all for the ring, but I shall bob 'em : I did but joke, the ring is none of mine, it is my master's ; I am to give it to be new set, that's all ; therefore prithee dry thy eyes, and kiss me, come.   [*Enter* Flora.

Inis. And do you really speak truth now ?

Liff. Why, do you doubt it ?

Flo. So so, very well ! I thought there was an intrigue between him and Inis, for all he has forsworn it so often.
[*Aside.*

Inis. Nor han't you seen Flora since you came to town ?

Flo. Ha ! How dares she name my name ?   [*Aside.*

Liff. No, by this kiss I han't.   [*Kisses her.*

Flo. Here's a dissembling varlet.   [*Aside.*

Inis. Nor don't you love her at all ?

Liff. Love the devil ; why, did not I always tell thee she was my aversion ?

Flo. Did you so, villain ?   [*Strikes him a box on the ear.*

Liff. Zounds, she here ! I have made a fine spot of work on't.   [*Aside.*

Inis. What's that for ? Ha !   [*Brushes up to her.*

Flo. I shall tell you by and by, Mrs. Frippery, if you don't get about your business.

Inis. Who do you call Frippery, Mrs. Trolup ? Pray get about your business : If you go to that, I hope you pretend to no right and title here.

Lif. What the devil do they take me for an acre of land, that they quarrel about right and title to me ? [*Afide.*

Flo. Pray what right have you, miſtreſs, to aſk that queſtion ?

Inis. No matter for that, I can ſhew a better title to him than you, I believe.

Flo. What, has he given thee nine months earneſt for a living title ? Ha, ha.

Inis. Don't fling your flaunting jeſts at me, Mrs. Bold-face, for I won't take 'em, I aſſure you.

Lif. So ! now I am as great as the fam'd Alexander. But my dear Statira and Roxana, don't exert yourſelves ſo much about me : now I fancy, if you wou'd agree lovingly together, I might, in a modeſt way, ſatisfy both your demands upon me.

Flo. You ſatisfy ! No, ſirrah, I am not to be ſatisfy'd ſo ſoon as you think, perhaps.

Inis. No, nor I neither.—What, do you make no differ-ence between us ?

Flo. You pitiful fellow you ; what, you fancy, I warrant, that I gave myſelf the trouble of dogging you, out of love to your filthy perſon ; but you are miſtaken, ſirrah—It was to detect your treachery.——How often have you ſworn to me that you hated Inis, and only carried fair for the good chear ſhe gave you ; but that you could never like a woman with crooked legs, you ſaid.

Inis. How, how, ſirrah, crooked legs ! Ods ! I cou'd find in my heart— [*Snatching up her petticoat a little.*

Lif. Here's a lying young jade now ! Prithee, my dear, moderate thy paſſion. [*Coaxingly.*

Inis. I'd have you to know, ſirrah, my legs were never— your maſter, I hope, underſtands legs better than you do, ſirrah. [*paſſionately.*

Lif. My maſter ! ſo, ſo. [*Shaking his head and winking.*

Flo. I am glad I have done ſome miſchief, however. [*Afide.*

Lif. [*To Inis*] Art thou really ſo fooliſh to mind what an enrag'd woman ſays ? Don't you ſee ſhe does it on purpoſe to part you and I ? [*Runs to* Flora] Cou'd not you find the joke without putting yourſelf in a paſſion ! You ſilly girl you ; why, I ſaw you follow us plain enough, mun, and ſaid all this, that you might not go back with only your labour for your pains——But you are a revengeful young ſlut tho', I tell you that ; but come kiſs, and be friends.

Flo. Don't think to coax me ; hang your kiſſes.

Fel. [*Within.*] Liſſardo.

Lif. Odſheart, here's my maſter ; the devil take both theſe jades for me, what ſhall I do with them ?

Inis. Ha ! 'Tis Don Felix's voice ; I wou'd not have him find me here, with his footman, for the world. [*afide.*

Fel.

Fel. [*Within.*] Why, Liffardo, Liffardo!

Liff. Coming, Sir. What a pox will you do?

Flo. Bless me, which way shall I get out?

Liff. Nay, nay, you must e'en set your quarrel aside, and be content to be mewed up in this clothes-press together, or stay where you are, and face it out——there is no help for it.

Flo. Put me any where, rather than that; come, come, let me in.   [*He opens the press, and she goes in.*

Inis. I'll see her hang'd, before I'll go into the place where she is.—I'll trust fortune with my deliverance : here us'd to be a pair of back-stairs, I'll try to find them out.   [*Exit.*

Enter Felix and Frederick.

Fel. Was you asleep, sirrah, that you did not hear me call?

Liff. I did hear you, and answer'd you, I was coming, Sir.

Fel. Go, get the horses ready ; I'll leave Lisbon to-night, never to see it more.

Liff. Hey day ! what's the matter now?   [*Exit.*

Fred. Pray tell me, Don Felix ! what has ruffled your temper thus?

Fel. A woman—O friend, who can name woman, and forget inconstancy !

Fred. This from a person of mean education were excusable; such low suspicions have their source from vulgar conversation; men of your politer taste never rashly censure—Come, this is some groundless jealousy—Love raises many fears.

Fel. No; my ears conveyed the truth into my heart, and reason justifies my anger : Violante's false, and I have nothing left but thee, in Lisbon, which can make me wish ever to see it more, except revenge upon my rival, of whom I am ignorant. Oh, that some miracle wou'd reveal him to me, that I might thro' his heart punish thy infidelity !

Enter Liffardo.

Liff. Oh ! Sir, here's your father Don Lopez coming up.

Fel. Does he know that I am here?

Liff. I can't tell, Sir, he ask'd for Don Frederick.

Fred. Did he see you?

Liff. I believe not, Sir; for, as soon as I saw him, I ran back to give my master notice.

Fel. Keep out of his sight then——and, dear Frederick, permit me to retire into the next room, for I know the old gentleman will be very much displeased at my return without his leave.   [*Exit.*

Fred. Quick, quick, begone, he is here.

Enter Don Lopez, *speaking as he enters.*

Lop. Mr. Alguazil, wait you without till I call for you. Frederick, an affair brings me here—which—requires pri-

vacy

vacy—fo that if you have any body within ear-fhot, pray order them to retire.

Fred. We are private, my lord, fpeak freely.

Lop. Why then, Sir, I muft tell you, that you had better have pitch'd upon any man in Portugal to have injur'd, than myfelf.

Fel. (Peeping) What means my father?

Fred. I underftand you not, my lord.

Lop. Tho' I am old, I have a fon——alas! why name I him? he knows not the difhonour of my houfe.

Fel. I am confounded! The difhonour of his houfe!

Fred. Explain yourfelf, my lord! I am not confcious of any difhonourable action to any man, much lefs to your lordfhip.

Lop. 'Tis falfe! you have debauch'd my daughter.

Fel. Debauch'd my fifter! Impoffible! He could not, durft not be that villain.

Fred. My lord, I fcorn fo foul a charge.

Lop. You have debauch'd her duty at leaft, therefore inftantly reftore her to me, or by St. Anthony I'll make you.

Fred. Reftore her, my lord! where fhall I find her?

Lop. I have thofe that will fwear fhe is here in your houfe.

Fel. Ha! in this houfe!

Fred. You are mifinformed, my lord; upon my reputation I have not feen Donna Ifabella, fince the abfence of Don Felix.

Lop. Then pray, Sir——if I am not too inquifitive, what motive had you for thofe objections you made againft her marriage with Don Guzman yefterday?

Fred. The difagreeablenefs of fuch a match, I fear'd, wou'd give your daughter caufe to curfe her duty, if fhe comply'd with your demands; that was all, my lord!

Lop. And fo you help'd her thro' the window to make her difobey.

Fel. Ha, my fifter gone! Oh fcandal to our blood!

Fred. This is infulting me, my lord, when I affure you I have neither feen, nor know any thing of your daughter ——if fhe is gone, the contrivance was her own, and you may thank your rigour for it.

Lop. Very well, Sir; however, my rigour fhall make bold to fearch your houfe: here, call in the Alguazil——

Flo. (Peeping) The Alguazil! What, in the name of wonder, will become of me?

Fred. The Alguazil! My lord, you'll repent this.

     Enter Alguazil and attendants.

Lop. No, Sir 'tis you that will repent it: I charge you,

in

in the king's name, to affift me in finding my daughter ————be fure you leave no part of the houfe unfearch'd ;— come, follow me.   [*Gets towards the door where* Felix *is ;*

[Frederick *draws, and plants himfelf before the door.*

Fred. Sir, I muft firft know by what authority you pretend to fearch my houfe, before you enter here.

Alg. How ! Sir, dare you prefume to draw your fword upon the reprefentative of majefty ? I am, Sir, I am his majefty's Alguazil, and the very quinteffence of authority ————therefore put up your fword, or I fhall order you to be knock'd down————for, know, Sir, the breath of an Alguazil is as dangerous as the breath of a demi Culverin.

Lop. She is certainly in that room, by his guarding the door————if he difputes your authority, knock him down, I fay.

Fred. I fhall fhew you fome fport firft. The woman you look for is not here, but there is fomething in this room, which I'll preferve from your fight at the hazard of my life.

Lop. Enter, I fay ; nothing but my daughter can be there—force his fword from him.

[Felix *comes out and joins* Frederick.

Fel. Villains, ftand off ! affaffinate a man in his own houfe !

Lop. Oh, oh, oh, *mifericordia* ! What do I fee, my fon !

Alg. Ha, his fon ! Here's five hundred pounds good, my brethren, if Antonio dies, and that's in the furgeon's power, and he's in love with my daughter, you know—Don Felix ! I command you to furrender yourfelf into the hands of juftice, in order to raife me and my pofterity ; and in confideration you lofe your head to gain me five hundred pounds, I'll have your generofity recorded on your tomb-ftone————at my own proper coft and charge—I hate to be ungrateful.

Fred. Here's a generous dog now————

Lop. Oh that ever I was born—Hold, hold, hold.

Fred. Did I not tell you, you wou'd repent, my lord ? What oh ! Within there [*Enter fervants*] arm yourfelves, and let not a man in nor out but Felix————Look ye, Alguazil, when you would betray my friend for filthy lucre, I fhall no more regard you as an officer of juftice, but as a thief and robber thus refift you.

Fel. Generous Frederick ! Come on, Sir, we'll fhew you play for the five hundred pounds.

Alg. Fall on, feize the money, right or wrong, ye rogues.

[*They fight.*

Lop. Hold, hold, Alguazil ; I'll give you the five hundred pounds ; that is, my bond to pay upon Antonio's death, and twenty piftoles however things go, for you and thefe honeft fellows to drink my health.   *Alg.*

Alg. Say you fo, my lord! Why look ye, my lord, I bear the young gentleman no ill-will, my lord; if I get but the five hundred pounds, my lord——why, look ye, my lord—— 'Tis the fame thing to me whether your fon be hang'd or not, my lord.

Fel. Scoundrels.————

Lop. Ay, well thou art a good-natur'd fellow, that is the truth on't——Come then we'll to the tavern, and fign and feal this minute. O Felix, be careful of thyfelf, or thou wilt break my heart. [*Exit* Lopez, Alguazil *and Attendants.*

Fel. Now, Frederick, though I ought to thank you for your care of me, yet till I am fatisfied as to my father's accufation, I can't return the acknowledgments I owe you: know you aught relating to my fifter?

Fred. I hope my faith and truth are known to you——And here by both I fwear, I am ignorant of every thing relating to your father's charge.

Fel. Enough, I do believe thee. Oh fortune! where will thy malice end?

Enter Servant.

Ser. Sir, I bring you joyful news, I am told that Don Antonio is out of danger, and now in the palace.

Fel. I wifh it be true, then I'm at liberty to watch my rival, and purfue my fifter. Prithee, Frederick, inform thyfelf of the truth of this report.

Fred. I will this minute—do you hear, let nobody in to Don Felix till my return. [*Exit.*

Ser. I'll obferve, Sir. [*Exit.*

Flo. (*Peeping.*) They have almoft frighted me out of my wits——I'm fure——now Felix is alone, I have a good mind to pretend I came with a meffage from my lady; but then how fhall I fay I came into the cupboard? [*Afide.*

Enter a Servant, feeming to oppofe the Entrance of fomebody.

Ser. I tell you, madam, Don Felix is not here.

Vio. (*Within.*) I tell you, Sir, he is here, and I will fee him. (*breaks in*) You are as difficult of accefs, Sir, as a firft minifter of ftate.

Flo. My ftars! My lady here! [*Shuts the prefs clofe.*

Fel. If your vifit was defign'd to Frederick, madam, he is abroad.

Vio. No, Sir, the vifit is to you.

Fel. You are very punctual in your ceremonies, madam.

Vio. Tho' I did not come to return your vifit, but to take that which your civility ought to have brought me.

Fel. If my ears, my eyes, and my underftanding ly'd, then I am in your debt; elfe not, madam.

Vio. I will not charge them with a term fo grofs, to fay they ly'd, but call it a miftake, nay call it any thing to excufe

cufe my Felix—Cou'd I, think ye, cou'd I put off my pride
fo far, poorly to diffemble a paffion which I did not feel? Or
feek a reconciliation, with what I did not love? Do but confider, if I had entertained another, fhou'd not I rather embrace
this quarrel, pleas'd with the occafion that rid me of your
vifits, and gave me freedom to enjoy the choice which you
think I have made; have I any intereft in thee but my love?
Or am I bound by aught but inclination to fubmit and follow
thee—No law whilft fingle binds us to obey; but you, by nature and education, are oblig'd to pay a deference to all wo-
man-kind.

Fel. Thefe are fruitlefs arguments: 'tis moft certain thou
wert dearer to thefe eyes than all that heaven e'er gave to
charm the fenfe of man; but I wou'd rather tear them out,
than fuffer them to delude my reafon, and enflave my
peace.

Vio. Can you love without efteem? and where is the
efteem for her you ftill fufpeƈt? Oh, Felix! There is a deli-
cacy—in love, which equals even a religious faith! True love
ne'er doubts the objeƈt it adores, and fceptics there will difbelieve their fight.

Enter Servant.

Fel. Your notions are too refin'd for mine, madam. How
now, what do you want?

Ser. Only my mafter's cloak out of this prefs, Sir, that's
all——Oh! the devil, the devil.

[*Opens the prefs, fees Flora, and roars out.*

Vio. Ha, a woman conceal'd! Very well, Felix!

Flo. Difcover'd! Nay then legs befriend me.   [*Runs out.*

Fel. A woman in the prefs!   [*Enter Liffardo.*
How the devil came a woman there, firrah?

Liff. What fhall I fay now?

Vio. Now, Liffardo, fhew your wit to bring your mafter off.

Liff. Off, madam! Nay, nay, nay, there, there needs no
great wit to, to, to bring him off, madam, for fhe did, and fhe
did not come as, as, as, a, a, a man may fay direƈtly to, to, to,
to fpeak with my mafter, madam.

Vio. I fee by your ftammering, Liffardo, that your invention is at a very low ebb.

Fel. 'Sdeath, rafcal! Speak without hefitation, and the
truth too, or I fhall ftick my ftilletto in your guts.

Vio. No, no, your mafter miftakes, he wou'd not have you
fpeak the truth.

Fel. Madam, my fincerity wants no excufe.

Liff. I am fo confounded between one and the other, that I
can't think of a lye.   [*Afide.*

Fel. Sirrah, fetch me this woman back inftantly; I'll know
what bufinefs fhe had here.

Vio.

Vio. Not a step; your master shall not be put to the blush.
—Come, a truce, Felix! Do you ask me no more questions
about the window, and I'll forgive this.

Fel. I scorn forgiveness where I own no crime; but your
soul, conscious of its guilt, wou'd fain lay hold of this occasion
to blend your treason with my innocence.

Vio. Insolent! Nay, if instead of owning your fault, you
endeavour to insult my patience, I must tell you, Sir, you
don't behave yourself like that man of honour you wou'd be
taken for; you ground your quarrel with me upon your own
inconstancy; 'tis plain you are false yourself, and wou'd make
me the aggressor——It was not for nothing the fellow oppos'd
my entrance——This last usage has given me back my liberty, and now my father's will shall be obeyed without the
least reluctance [*Exit.*

Fel. Oh, stubborn, stubborn heart, what wilt thou do? Her
father's will shall be obeyed: Ha! That carries her to a cloi-
ster, and cuts off all my hopes at once——By heaven she shall
not, must not leave me! No, she is not false, at least my love
now represents her true, because I fear to lose her: Ha!
villain, art thou here [*turns upon* Liffardo] tell me this moment who this woman was, and for what intent she was here
conceal'd. Or——

Liff. Ay, good Sir, forgive me, and I'll tell you the whole
truth. (*falls on his knees.*

Fel. Out with it then——

Liff. It, it, it, was Mrs. Flora, Sir, Donna Violante's woman——you must know, Sir, we have had a sneaking kind-
ness for one another a great while——She was not willing you
should know it; so when she heard your voice she ran into the
clothes-press; I wou'd have told you this at first, but I was
afraid of her lady's knowing it: this is the truth as I hope for
a whole skin, Sir.

Fel. If it be not, I'll not leave you a whole bone in it, sirrah
——fly, and observe if Violante goes directly home.

Liff. Yes, Sir, yes. [*Exit.*

Fel. I must convince her of my faith: oh! how irreso-
lute is a lover's heart! My resentments cool'd when her's
grew high—nor can I struggle longer with my fate; I cannot quit her, no I cannot, so absolute a conquest has she
gain'd—woman's the greatest sovereign power on earth.

> *In vain men strive their tyranny to quit,*
> *Their eyes command and force us to submit.*
> *So have I seen a mettled courser fly,*
> *Tear up the ground, and toss his rider high,*
> *Till some experienc'd master found the way,*
> *With spur and rein to make his pride obey.*

SCENE

SCENE the *Terriero de Passa*.

Enter Colonel *and* Isabella *veil'd.* Gibby *at a distance.*

Col. Then you say, it is impossible for me to wait of you home, madam.

Isab. I say it is inconsistent with my circumstances, Colonel, and that way impossible for me to admit of it.

Col. Consent to go with me then—I lodge at one Don Frederick's, a merchant just by here, he is a very honest fellow, and I dare confide in his secrecy.

Isab. Ha, does he lodge there? pray heaven I am not discover'd. [*Aside.*

Col. What say you, my charmer? shall we breakfast together? I have some of the best bohea in the universe.

Isab. Puh! Bohea! is that the best treat you can give a lady at your lodgings——Colonel!

Col. Well hinted——No, no, no, I have other things at thy service, child.

Isab. What are those things pray?

Col. My heart, soul, and body into the bargain.

Isab. Has the last no incumbrance upon it; can you make a clear title, Colonel?

Col. All freehold, child, and I'll afford thee a very good bargain. [*embraces her.*

Gib. Au my sol, they mak muckle wards about it. Ise seer weary with standing, Ise e'en tak a sleep. [*Lies down.*

Isab. If I take a lease, it must be for life, Colonel.

Col. Thou shalt have me as long, or as little time as thou wilt; my dear, come, let's to my lodging, and we'll sign and seal this minute.

Isab. Oh, not so fast, Colonel, there are many things to be adjusted before the lawyer and parson comes.

Col. The lawyer and parson! No, no, ye little rogue, we can finish our affairs without the help of the law ——or the gospel.

Isab. Indeed but we can't, Colonel.

Col. Indeed! Why, hast thou then trepann'd me out of my warm bed this morning for nothing! Why, this is shewing a man half famish'd a well-furnish'd larder, then clapping a padlock on the door, till you starve him quite.

Isab. If you can find in your heart to say grace, Colonel, you shall keep the key.

Col. I love to see my meat before I give thanks, madam; therefore uncover thy face, child, and I'll tell thee more of my mind——if I like you.——

Isab. I dare not risk my reputation upon your If's, Colonel; and so adieu. [*Going.*

Col. Nay, nay, nay, we must not part.

Isab. As you ever hope to see me more, suspend your curiosity

riofity now; one ſtep farther loſes me for ever.———Shew-
yourſelf a man of honour, and you ſhall find me a woman
of honour. [*Exit.*

Col. Well, for once I'll truſt to a blind bargain, madam
———(*Kiſſes her hand and parts.*) But I ſhall be too cunning for your ladyſhip if *Gibby* obſerves my orders: methinks theſe intrigues, which relate to the mind, are very
inſipid—The converſation of bodies is much more diverting
———Ha! What do I ſee, my raſcal aſleep? Sirrah, did not I
charge you to watch the lady? And is it thus you obſerve my
orders, ye dog?
[*kicks him all this while, and he ſhrugs and rubs his eyes and yawns*

Gib. That's treu, an lik yer honour; but I thought that
when ence ye had her in yer awn honds, yee mit a ordered
her yer ſal weel eneugh without me, en ye ken, and lik yer
honour.

Col. Sirrah, hold your impertinent tongue, and make haſte
after her: if you don't bring me ſome account of her, never
dare to ſee my face again. [*Exit.*

Gib. Ay! This is bony wark indeed, to run three hundred
mile to this wicked town, and before I can weel fill my weem,
to be ſent a whore-hunting after this black ſhee devil—What
gat ſal I gang to ſpeer for this wutch now? Ah, for a ruling
elder—or the kirk's treaſurer—or his mon—I'd gat my mai-
ter mak twa of this———But I am ſeer there's na ſike honeſt
people here, or there wou'd na be ſo muckle ſculdurie.*

(*Enter an* Engliſh *ſoldier paſſing along.*)

Gib. Geud mon, did ye ſee a woman, a lady, ony gate here
away enow?

Eng. Man. Yes, a great many. What kind of a woman
is it you enquire after?

Gib. Geud troth, ſhe's ne kenſpekle, ſhe's aw in a cloud.—

Eng. Man. What! 'Tis ſome high-land monſter which
you brought over with you, I ſuppoſe; I ſee no ſuch, no I,
kenſpekle, quotha!

Gib. Huly, huly, mon, the deel pike out yer eyn, and
then you'll ſee the bater, ye Engliſh bag pudin tike.

Eng. Man. What ſays the fellow? [*Turning to* Gibby.

Gib. Say! I ſay I am a better fellow than e'er ſtude upon
yer ſhanks————an gin I heer meer a yer din, deel a
my ſaul, Sir, but Iſe crack yer crown.

Eng. Man. Get you gone, you Scotch raſcal, and thank
your heathen dialect, which I don't underſtand, that you
han't your bones broke.

Gib. Ay! an ye de no underſtond a Scots man's tongue
—Iſe ſee gin ye can underſtond a Scots man's gripe: wha's
the better mon now, Sir? [*Lays hold of him, ſtrikes up his*
[*heels, and gets aſtride over him.*

* Fornication. *Here*

Here Violante *croffes the ftage;* Gibby *jumps up from the man, and brufhes up to* Violante.

Gib. I vow, madam, but I am glad that yee and I are foregather'd.

Vio. What wou'd the fellow have?

Gib. Nothing, away, madam, wo worthy yer heart, what a muckle deel of mifchief had you like to bring upon poor Gibby?

Vio. The man's drunk——

Gib. In truth am I not——An gin I had not fond ye, madam, the laird knows when I fhould; for my mafter bat me nere gang heam, without tydings of yee, madam.

Vio. Sirrah, get about your bufinefs, or I'll have your bones drubb'd.

Gib. Geuh faith, my mafter has e'en dun that te yer honds, madam.

Vio. Who is your mafter, friend?

Gib. Money e'en fpiers the gat they ken right weel——It is no fo lang fen ye parted wi him, I wifh he ken yee hafe as weel as he ken him.

Vio. Pugh, the creature's mad, or miftakes me for fome body elfe; and I fhou'd be as mad as he, to talk to him any longer.

Enter Liffardo *at the upper end of the ftage.*

Lif. So, fhe's gone home, I fee. What did that Scotch fellow want with her? I'll try to find it out; perhaps I may difcover fomething that may make my mafter friends with me again.

Gib. Are you gaune, madam, a deel fcope in yer company; for I'm as weefe as I was? but I'll bide and fee whafe houfe it is, gin I can meet with ony civil body to fpier at.——Weel of aw men in the warld, I think our Scots men the greateft feuls, to leave their weel favoured honeft women at heam, to rin walloping after a pack of gycarlings hero, that fhame to fhew their faces, and peer men, like me, are forc'd to be their pimps! a pim! Godfwarbit, Gibby's ne'er be a pimp——An yet in troth it is a threving trade; I remember a countryman aw mi aen, that by ganging a fikle like errants as I am now, came to gat preferment: My lad, wot yee wha lives here? [*Turns and fees* Liffardo.

Lif. Don Pedro de Mendofa.

Gib. And did you fee a lady gang in but how?

Lif. Yes, I did.

Gib. And dee ken her tee?

Lif. It was Donna-Violante, his daughter; what the devil makes him fo inquifitive? Here is fomething in it, that's certain. 'Tis a cold morning, brother; what think you of a dram?

Gib.

Gib. In troth, very weel, Sir.

Lif. You feem an honeft fellow ; prithee let's drink to our better acquaintance.

Gib. Wi aw my heart, Sir, gang your gat to the next houfe, and Ife follow ye.

Lif. Come along then. [*Exit.*

Gib. Don Pedro de Mendofa ——— Donna Violante, his daughter ; that's as right as my leg now——Ife need na meer, I'll tak a drink, an then to my mafter.——

Ife bring him news will mak his heart full blee ;
Gin he rewards it not, deel pimp for me. [Exit..

A C T   IV.

S C E N E Violante's *Lodgings.*

Enter Ifabella *in a gay Temper, and* Violante *out of humour.*

Ifab. **M**Y dear, I have been feeking you this half hour to tell you the moft lucky adventure.

Vio. And you have pitched upon the moft unlucky hour for it, that you could poffibly have found in the whole four and twenty.

Ifab. Hang unlucky hours, I won't think of them ; I hope all my misfortunes are paft.

Vio. And mine all to come.

Ifab. I have feen the man I like.

Vio. And I have feen the man that I could wifh to hate.

Ifab. And you muft affift me in difcovering whether he can like me or not.

Vio. You have affifted me in fuch a difcovery already, I thank ye.

Ifab. What fay you, my dear ?

Vio. I fay I am very unlucky at difcoveries, Ifabella ; I have too lately made one pernicious to my eafe ; your brother is falfe.

Ifab. Impoffible !

Vio. Moft true.

Ifab. Some villain has traduc'd him to you,

Vio. No, Ifabella, I love too well to truft the eyes of others ; I never credit the ill-judging world, or form fufpicions upon vulgar cenfures ; no, I had ocular proof of his ingratitude.

Ifab. Then am I moft unhappy ; my brother was the only pledge of faith betwixt us ; if he has forfeited your favour, I have no title to your friendfhip.

Vio. You wrong my friendſhip, Iſabella ; your own merit entitles you to every thing within my power.

Iſab. Generous maid——But may I not know what grounds you have to think my brother falſe ?

Vio. Another time——But tell me, Iſabella, how can I ſerve you ?

Iſab. Thus then——The gentleman that brought me hither, I have ſeen and talk'd with upon the *Terriero de Paſſa* this morning, and I find him a man of ſenſe, generoſity and good-humour ; in ſhort, he is every thing that I could like for a huſband, and have diſpatched Mrs. Flora to bring him hither ; I hope you'll forgive the liberty I have taken.

Vio. Hither, to what purpoſe ?

Iſab. To the great univerſal purpoſe, matrimony.

Vio. Matrimony ! Why, do you deſign to aſk him ?

Iſab. No, Violante, you muſt do that for me.

Vio. I thank you for the favour you deſign me, but deſire to be excus'd : I manage my own affairs too ill, to be truſted with thoſe of other people ; beſides, if my father ſhould find a ſtranger here, it might make him hurry me into a monaſtery immediately ; I can't for my life admire your conduct, to encourage a perſon altogether unknown to you.——'Twas very imprudent to met him this morning, but much more to ſend for him hither, knowing what inconveniency you have already drawn upon me.

Iſab. I am not inſenſible, how far my misfortunes have embarraſſed you ; and, if you pleaſe, ſacrifice my quiet to your own.

Vio. Unkindly urg'd——Have not I preferr'd your happineſs to every thing that's dear to me ?

Iſab. I know thou haſt—Then do not deny me this laſt requeſt, when a few hours, perhaps, may render my condition able to clear thy fame, and bring my brother to thy feet for pardon.

Vio. I wiſh you don't repent of this intrigue. I ſuppoſe he knows you are the ſame woman that he brought in here laſt night.

Iſab. Not a ſyllable of that ; I met him veil'd, and to prevent his knowing the houſe, I order'd Mrs. Flora to bring him by the back-door into the garden.

Vio. The very way which Felix comes ; if they ſhould meet, there would be fine work—Indeed, my dear, I can't approve your deſign.

Enter Flora.

Flo. Madam, the Colonel waits your pleaſure.

Vio. How durſt you go upon ſuch a meſſage, miſtreſs, without acquainting me ?

Iſab. 'Tis too late to diſpute that now, dear Violante, I acknowledge the raſhneſs of the action —— But conſider the neceſſity of my deliverance.

Vio. That indeed is a weighty confideration ; well, what am I to do?

Ifab. In the next room I'll give you inftruftions ! in the mean time, Mrs. Flora, fhow the Colonel into this.

[*Exit* Flora *one way, and* Ifabella *and* Violante *another*.

Re-enter Flora *with the* Colonel.

Flo. The lady will wait on you prefently, Sir.   [*Exit.*

Col. Very well — This is a very fruitful foil. I have not been here quite four and twenty hours, and I have three intrigues upon my hands already, but I hate the chace, without partaking of the game. [*Enter* Violante *veil'd.*] Ha, a fine fiz'd woman—Pray heaven fhe proves handfome — I am come to obey your ladyfhip's commands.

Vio. Are you fure of that, Colonel?

Col. If you be not very unreafonable indeed, madam ; a man is but a man.   [*Takes her hand and kiffes it.*

Vlo. Nay, we have no time for complements, Colonel.

Col. I underftand you, madam—*Montre moi votre chambre.*
    [*Takes her in his arm.*

Vio. Nay, nay, hold Colonel, my bed-chamber is not to be enter'd without a certain purchafe.

Col. Purchafe ! Humph, this is fome kept miftrefs, I fuppofe, who induftrioufly lets out her leifure hours. [*Afide.*] Look ye, madam, you muft confider we foldiers are not overftock'd with money—But we make ample fatisfaftion in love ; we have a world of courage upon our hands now, you know —Then prithee ufe a confcience, and I'll try if my pocket can come up to your price.   [*Puts his hand into his pocket.*

Vio. Nay, don't give yourfelf the trouble of drawing your purfe, Colonel, my defign is levell'd at your perfon, if that be at your own difpofal.

Col. Ah, that it is faith, madam, and I'll fettle it as firmly upon thee——

Vio. As law can do it.

Col. Hang law in love-affairs ; thou fhalt have right and title to it out of pure inclination. —— A matrimonial hint again ! Gad, I fancy the women have a project on foot to tranfplant the union into Portugal.

Vio. Then you have an averfion to matrimony, Colonel ; did you never fee a woman, in all your travels, that you cou'd like for a wife?

Col. A very odd queftion——Do you really expeft that I fhould fpeak truth now?

Vio. I do, if you expeft to be dealt with, Colonel.

Col. Why then —— Yes.

Vio. Is fhe in your country, or this?

Col. This is a very pretty kind of a catechifm : but I don't

conceive

conceive which way it turns to edification : in this town, I believe, madam.

Vio. Her name is ———

Col. Ay, how is she call'd, madam ?

Vio. Nay, I ask you that, Sir.

Col. Oh, oh, why she is call'd—Pray, madam, how is it you spell your name ?

Vio. Oh, Colonel, I am not the happy woman, nor do I wish it.

Col. No, I'm sorry for that.——What the devil does she mean by all these questions ?   [*Aside.*

Vio. Come, Colonel, for once be sincere.——Perhaps you may not repent it.

Col. Faith, madam, I have an inclination to sincerity, but I'm afraid you'll call my manners in question. This is like to be but a silly adventure, here's so much sincerity required.   [*Aside.*

Vio. Not at all: I prefer truth before compliment, in this affair

Col. Why then, to be plain with you, madam, a lady left night wounded my heart by a fall from a window, whose person I cou'd be content to take, as my father took my mother, till death do us part.——But whom she is, or how distinguish-ed, whether maid, wife, or widow, I can't inform you ; per-haps you are she.

Vio. Not to keep you in suspence, I am not she, but I can give you an account of her : that lady is a maid of condi-tion, has ten thousand pounds ; and if you are a single man, her person and fortune are at your service.

Col. I accept the offer, with the highest transports; but say, my charming angel, art thou not she ? *(offers to embrace her)* This is a lucky adventure.   [*Aside.*

Vio. Once again, Colonel, I tell you I am not she—but at six this evening you shall find her on the *Terriero de passa*, with a white handkerchief in her hand ; get a priest ready, and you know the rest.

Col. I shall infalliby observe your directions, madam.

Enter Flora *hastily, and whispers* Violante, *who starts and seems surprised.*

Vio. Ha, Felix crossing the garden, say you, what shall I do now ?

Col. You seem surpriz'd, madam.

Vio. Oh, Colonel, my father is coming hither, and if he finds you here, I am ruin'd !

Col. Odslife, madam, thrust me any where; can't I go out this way ?

Vio. No, no, no, he comes that way : how shall I pre-vent their meeting ? Here, here, step into my bed-chamber, and be still, as you value her you love ; don't stir till you've notice, as ever you hope to have her in your arms.

Col. On that condition, I'll not breathe.   [*Exit.*

Enter Felix.

Fel. I wonder where this dog of a fervant is all this while——but she is at home I find——how coldly she regards me.——You look, Violante, as if the fight of me were troublesome to you.

Vio. Can I do otherwise, when you have the assurance to approach me, after what I saw to-day!

Fel. Assurance, rather call it good-nature, after what I heard last night; but such regard to honour, have I in my love to you, I cannot bear to be suspected, nor suffer you to entertain false notions of my truth, without endeavouring to convince you of my innocence; so much good-nature have I more than you, Violante——Pray give me leave to ask your woman one question; my man assures me she was the person you saw at my lodgings.

Flo. I confess it, madam, and ask your pardon.

Vio. Impudent baggage, not to undeceive me sooner; what business cou'd you have there?

Fel. Lissardo and she, it seems, imitate you and I.

Flo. I love to follow the example of my betters, madam.

Fel. I hope I am justified——

Vio. Since we are to part, Felix, there needs no justification.

Fel. Methinks you talk of parting as a thing indifferent to you; can you forget how I have lov'd?

Vio. I wish I could forget my own passion; I shou'd with less concern remember yours——but for mistress Flora——

Fel. You must forgive her;——must, did I say? I fear I have no power to impose, tho' the injury was done to me.

Vio. 'Tis harder to pardon an injury done to what we love than to ourselves: but at your request, Felix, I do forgive her: go watch my father, Flora, lest he should awake and surprize us.

Flo. Yes, madam.   [*Exit Flora.*

Fel. Dost thou then love me, Violante?

Vio. What need of repetition from my tongue, when every look confesses what you ask?

Fel. Oh! let no man judge of love but those who feel it; what wonderous magic lies in one kind look!——One tender word destroys a lover's rage, and melts his fiercest passion into soft complaint: Oh the window, Violante, would'st thou but clear that one suspicion!

Vio. Prithee, no more of that my Felix, a little time shall bring thee perfect satisfaction.

Fel. Well, Violante, on that condition you think no more of a monastery——I'll wait with patience for this mighty secret.

Vio. Ah, Felix, Love generally gets the better of religion

in

in us women : refolutions made in the heat of paffion, ever diffolve upon reconciliation.

Enter Flora *haftily.*

Flo. Oh, madam, madam, madam! my lord your father has been in the garden, and lock'd the back-door, and comes muttering to himfelf this way.

Vio. Then we are caught : now, Felix, we are undone.

Fel. Heavens forbid, this is moft unlucky! let me ftep into your bed-chamber, he won't look under the bed ; there I may conceal myfelf. [*runs to the door, and pufhes it open a little.*

Vio. My ftars! if he goes in there he'll find the Colonel—— No, no, Felix, that's no fafe place, my father often goes thither ; and fhould you cough, or fneeze, we are loft.

Fel. Either my eye deceiv'd me, or I faw a man within ; I'll watch him clofe —— She fhall deal with the devil, if fhe conveys him out without my knowledge. [*Afide.*] What fhall I do then ?

Vio. Blefs me, how I tremble!

Flo. Oh, invention, invention! —— I have it, madam ; here, here, here, Sir, off with your fword, and I'll fetch you a difguife.   (*Runs in and fetches out a riding hood.*

Fel. Ay, ay, any thing to avoid Don Pedro.

Vio. Oh! quick, quick, quick, I fhall die with apprehenfion.   (*Flora puts the riding-hood on* Felix.

Flo. Be fure you don't fpeak a word!

Fel. Not for the Indies.——But I fhall obferve you clofer than you imagine.   [*Afide.*

Pedro. (*Within.*) Violante, where are you, child ? [*Enter* Don Pedro] Why, how came the garden-door open ? Ha! How now, who have we here ?

Vio. Humph ; he'll certainly difcover him.   [*Afide.*

Flo. 'Tis my mother, and pleafe you, Sir.

        [*She and* Felix *both courtfy.*

Pedro. Your mother! By St. Andrew, fhe's a ftrapper ; why, you are a dwarf to her —— How many children have you, good woman ?

Vio. Oh! if he fpeaks we are loft.   [*Afide.*

Flo. Oh! dear fignior, fhe cannot hear you, fhe has been deaf thefe twenty years.

Pedro. Alas, poor woman—Why, you muffle her up as if fhe were blind too.

Fel. Would I were fairly off.   [*Afide.*

Pedro. Turn up her hood.

Vio. Undone for ever.—— St. Anthony forbid : Oh, Sir, fhe has the dreadfulleft unlucky eyes——Pray don't look upon them ; I made her keep her hood fhut on purpofe —— Oh, oh, oh, oh!

Pedro, Eyes! Why, what's the matter with her eyes ?

        Flo.

Flo. My poor mother, Sir, is much afflicted with the cho-lick; and about two months ago she had it grievously in her stomach, and was over-persuaded to take a dram of filthy English geneva—which immediately flew up into her head, and caused such a defluxion in her eyes, that she could never since bear the day-light.

Pedro. Say you so?—Poor woman!—Well, make her sit down, Violante, and give her a glass of wine.

Vio. Let her daughter give her a glass below, Sir; for my part, she has frighted me so, I shan't be myself these two hours. I am sure her eyes are evil eyes.

Fel. Well hinted.

Pedro. Well, well, do so: evil eyes, there is no evil eyes, child. *[Exeunt Felix and Flora.*

Vio. I'm glad he's gone.

Pedro. Hast thou heard the news, Violante?

Vio. What news, Sir?

Pedro. Why, Vasquez tells me, that Don Lopez's daugh-ter Isabella is run away from her father; that lord has very ill fortune with his children——Well, I'm glad my daughter has no inclination to mankind, that my house is plagu'd with no suitors. *[Aside.*

Vio. This is the first word I ever heard of it; I pity her frailty.——

Pedro. Well said, Violante.——Next week I intend thy happiness shall begin. *[Enter Flora.*

Vio. I don't intend to stay so long, thank you, papa. *[Aside*

Pedro. My lady Abbess writes word she longs to see thee, and has provided every thing in order for thy reception.—Thou wilt lead a happy life, my girl——fifty times before that of matrimony, where an extravagant coxcomb might make a beg-gar of thee, or an ill-natur'd surly dog break thy heart.

Flo. Break thy heart! She had as good have her bones broke as to be a nun; I am sure I had, rather of the two. —You are wonderous kind, Sir; but if I had such a father, I know what I would do.

Pedro. Why, what wou'd you do, minx, ha?

Flo. I would tell him I had as good a right and title to the law of nature, and the end of the creation, as he had——

Pedro. You wou'd, mistress; who the devil doubts it? A good assurance is a chamber-maid's coat of arms! and lying, and contriving the supporters. — Your inclinations are on tip-toe, it seems—if I were your father, housewife, I'd have a penance enjoin'd you, so strict, that you should not be able to turn you in your bed for a month——you are enough to spoil your lady, housewife, if she had not abundance of devotion.

Vio.

Vio. Fye, Flora, are you not afhamed to talk thus to my father ? you faid yefterday you wou'd be glad to go with me into the monaftery.

Pedro. She go with thee! No, no, fhe's enough to de-bauch the whole convent. —— Well, child, remember what I faid to thee : next week————

Vio. Ay, and what I am to do this too ?— 　　*(Afide.)* I am all obedient, Sir; I care not how foon I change my condition.

Flo. But little does he think what change fhe means.
　　　　　　　　　　　　　　　　　　　　[Afide.

Pedro. Well faid, Violante. —— I am glad to find her fo willing to leave the world, but it is wholly owing to my pru-dent management, did fhe know that fhe might command her fortune when fhe came at age, or upon day of marriage, perhaps fhe'd change her note.——But I have always told her that her grandfather left it with this provifo, that fhe turn'd nun : now a fmall part of this twenty thoufand pounds provides for her in the nunnery, and the reft is my own ; there is nothing to be got in this life without policy. *(Afide.)* Well, child, I am going into the country for two or three days, to fettle fome affairs with thy uncle.——And then— Come, help me on with my cloak, child.

Vio. Yes, Sir.　　　　　*[Exeunt* Pedro *and* Violante.

Flo. So, now for the Colonel.　*[Goes to the chamber door.]* Hift, hift, Colonel.　　　　　　　*[Colonel peeping.*

Col. Is the coaft clear ?

Flo. Yes, if you can climb; for you muft get over the wafh-houfe, and jump from the garden-wall into the ftreet.

Col. Nay, nay, I don't value my neck if my incognita anfwers but thy lady's promife. *[Exeunt* Colonel *and* Flora.

Re-enter Pedro *and* Violante.

Ped. Good-bye, Violante, take care of thyfelf, child.

Vio. I wifh you a good journey, Sir. Now to fet my pri-foner at liberty.　　　　　*[Enter* Felix *behind* Violante.

Fel. I have lain perdue under the ftairs, till I watch'd the old man out.

Vio. Sir, Sir, you may appear.　　　*[Goes to the door.*

Fel. May he fo, madam ?—I had caufe for my fufpicion, I find, treacherous woman.

Vio. Ha, Felix here! Nay, then, all's difcover'd.

Fel. *[Draws.]* Villain, who e'er thou art, come out I charge thee, and take the reward of thy adulterous errand.

Vio. What fhall I fay ?——Nothing but the fecret which I have fworn to keep can reconcile this quarrel.　　*[Afide.*

Fel. A coward ! Nay, then I'll fetch you out ; think not to hide thyfelf ; no, by St. Anthony, an altar fhould not pro-
　　　　　　　　　　　　　　　　　　　　　tect-

yect thee, even there I'd reach thy heart, tho' all the faints were arm'd in thy defence. [*Exit.*

Vio. Defend me, heaven! What fhall I do? I muft difcover Ifabella, or here will be murder.——

Enter Flora.

Fl. I have help'd the Colonel off clear, madam.

Vio. Say'ft thou fo, my girl? then I am arm'd.

Re-enter Felix.

Fel. Where has the devil in compliance to your fex convey'd him from my refentment?

Vio. Him, who do you mean, my dear inquifitive fpark? Ha, ha, ha, ha, you will never leave thefe jealous whims?

Fel. Will you never ceafe to impofe upon me?

Vio. You impofe upon yourfelf, my dear; do you think I did not fee you? Yes, I did, and refolved to put this trick upon you; I knew you'd take the hint, and foon relapfe into your wonted error: How eafily your jealoufy is fired? I fhall have a bleffed life with you.

Fel. Was there nothing in it then, but only to try me?

Vio. Won't you believe your eyes?

Fel. No, becaufe I find they have deceived me; well, I am convinc'd that faith is as neceffary in love as in religion; for the moment a man lets a woman know her conqueft, he refigns his fenfes, and fees nothing but what fhe'd have him.

Vio. And as foon as that man finds his love return'd, fhe becomes as errant a flave, as if fhe had already faid after the prieft.

Fel. The prieft, Violante, would diffipate thofe fears which caufe their quarrels; when wilt thou make me happy?

Vio. To-morrow, I will tell thee; my father is gone for two or three days to my uncle's, we have time enough to finifh our affairs.——But prythee leave me now, for I expect fome ladies to vifit me.

Fel. If you command it.——Fly fwift, ye hours, and bring to-morrow on.——You defire I wou'd leave you, Violante.

Vio. I do at prefent.

Fel. *So much you reign the fovereign of my foul,*
That I obey without the leaft controul. [*Exit.*

Enter Ifabella.

Ifab. I am glad my brother and you are reconcil'd, my dear, and the Colonel efcap'd without his knowledge; I was frighted out of my wits when I heard him return.——I know not how to exprefs my thanks, woman—for what you fuffer'd for my fake, my grateful acknowledgement fhall ever wait you; and to the world proclaim the faith, truth, and honour of a woman.——

Vio. Prithee don't compliment thy friend, Ifabella.——You heard the Colonel, I fuppofe.

Ifab.

Isab. Every syllable, and am pleas'd to find I do not love
in vain.

Vio. Thou haft caught his heart, it feems; and an hour
hence may fecure his perfon.——Thou haft made hafty work
on't girl.

Isab. From thence I draw my happinefs, we fhall have no
accounts to make up after confummation.

> *She who, for years, protects her lover's pain,*
> *And makes him wifh, and wait, and figh in vain,*
> *To be his wife, when late fhe gives confent,*
> *Finds half his paffion was in courtfhip fpent;*
> *Whilft they who boldly all delays remove,*
> *Find every hour a frefh fupply of love.*

ACT V.

SCENE, Frederick's Houfe.

Enter Felix and Frederick.

Fel. THIS hour has been propitious, I am reconcil'd to
Violante, and you affure me Antonio is out of
danger.

Fred. Your fatisfaction is doubly mine.

Enter Liffardo.

Fel. What hafte you made, firrah, to bring me word if
Violante went home?

Liff. I can give you very good reafons for my ftay, Sir——
Yes, Sir, fhe went home.

Fred. O! Your mafter knows that; for he has been there
himfelf, Liffardo.

Liff. Sir, may I beg the favour of your ear?

Fel. What have you to fay?

[*Whifpers, and Felix feems uneafy.*

Fred. Ha, Felix changes colour at Liffardo's news. What
can it be?

Fel. A Scots footman, that belongs to Colonel Britton, an
acquaintance of Frederick's, fay you? the devil! if fhe be
falfe, by heaven I'll trace her. Prithee, Frederick, do you
know one Colonel Britton, a Scotchman?

Fred. Yes; why do you afk me?

Fel. Nay, no great matter; but my man tells me that he
has had fome little differences with a fervant of his, that's all.

Fred. He is a good harmlefs innocent fellow, I am forry
for it; the Colonel lodges in my houfe; I knew him formerly
in England, and met him here by accident laft night, and
gave him an invitation home; he is a gentleman of a good
eftate,

estate, besides his commission; of excellent principles, and strict honour, I assure you.

Fel. Is he a man of intrigue?

Fred. Like other men, I suppose; here he comes.——

[*Enter* Colonel.

Colonel, I began to think I had lost you.

Col. And not without some reason, if you knew all.

Fel. There's no danger of a fine gentleman's being lost in this town, Sir.

Col. That complement don't belong to me, Sir. But I assure you I have been very near being run away with.

Fred. Who attempted it?

Col. Faith, I know her not——only that she is a charming woman, I mean as much as I saw of her.

Fel. My heart swells with apprehension.——Some accidental rencounter.——

Fred. A tavern, I suppose, adjusted the matter.—

Col. A tavern! No, no, Sir, she is above that rank, I assure you; this nymph sleeps in a velvet bed, and lodgings every way agreeable.

Fel. Ha, a velvet bed?—I thought you said but now Sir, you knew her not.

Col. No more I don't, Sir.

Fel. How came you then so well acquainted with her bed?

Fred. Aye, aye, come, come, unfold.

Col. Why then you must know, gentlemen, that I was conveyed to her lodgings, by one of Cupid's emissaries, call'd a chambermaid, in a chair thro' fifty blind alleys, who by the help of a key let me into a garden.

Fel. 'Sdeath, a garden, this must be Violante's garden.

[*Aside.*

Col. From thence conducted me into a spacious room, then dropt me a courtesy, told me her lady would wait on me presently; so without unveiling, modestly withdrew.

Fel. Damn her modesty; this was Flora.   [*Aside.*

Fred. Well, how then, Colonel?

Col. Then, Sir, immediately from another door issued forth a lady, arm'd at both eyes, from whence such showers of darts fell round me, that had I not been cover'd with the shield of another beauty, I had infallibly fall'n a martyr to her charms: for you must know, I just saw her eyes: eyes did I say? No, no, hold, I saw but one eye, though I suppose it had a fellow equally as killing.

Fel. But how came you to see her bed, Sir? 'Sdeath, this expectation gives a thousand racks.   [*Aside.*

Col. Why, upon her maid's giving notice her father was coming, she thrust me into the bed-chamber.

Fel.

Fel. Upon her father's coming?

Col. Ay, so she said; but putting my ear to the key-hole of the door, I found it was another lover.

Fel. Confound the jilt! 'Twas she without dispute. [*Aside.*

Fred. Ah poor Colonel! Ha, ha, ha.

Col. I discover'd they had had a quarrel, but whether they were reconcil'd or not, I can't tell; for the second alarm brought the father in good earnest, and had like to have made the gentleman and I acquainted, but she found some other stratagem to convey him out.

Fel. Contagion seize her, and make her body ugly as her soul! There is nothing left to doubt of now.——'Tis plain 'twas she.——Sure he knows me, and takes this method to insult me: 'Sdeath, I cannot bear it. [*Aside.*

Fred. So when she had dispatch'd her old lover, she paid you a visit in her bed-chamber; ha, Colonel?

Col. No, pox take the impertinent puppy, he spoil'd my diversion, I saw her no more.

Fel. Very fine! Give me patience, heaven, or I shall burst with rage. [*Aside.*

Fred. That was hard.

Col. Nay, what was worse, the nymph that introduced me conveyed me out again over the top of a high wall, where I ran the danger of having my neck broke; for the father, it seems, had locked the door by which I enter'd.

Fel. That way I miss'd him:——damn her invention. (*Aside.*) Pray, Colonel, was this the same lady you met upon the *Terriero de passa* this morning?

Col. Faith, I can't tell, Sir; I had a design to know who that lady was, but my dog of a footman, whom I had ordered to watch her home, fell fast asleep——I gave him a good beating for his neglect, and I have never seen the rascal since.

Fred. Here he comes.

Enter Gibby.

Col. Where have you been, Sirrah?

Gib. Troth ise been seeking yee an' lik yer honour these twa hoors an meer. I bring ye glad teedings, Sir.

Col. What, have you found the lady?

Gib. Geud faite, ha I Sir——and she's call'd Donna Violante, and her parent Don Pedro de Mendosa, en gin yee will gan wa mi, an't lik yer honour, ife make yee ken the huse right weel.

Fel. O torture! torture! [*Aside.*

Col. Ha! Violante! That's the lady's name of the house where my incognita is, sure it could not be her, at least it was not the same house, I'm confident. [*Aside.*

Fred. Violante? 'Tis false; I would not have you credit him, Colonel. *Gib.*

Gib. The deel burſt my bladder, Sir, gin I lee.

Fel. Sirrah, I ſay you do lye, and I'll make you eat it, you dog, *(kicks him)* and if your maſter will juſtify you.——

Col. Not I, faith, Sir.——I anſwer for no body's lyes but my own; if you pleaſe, kick him again.

Gib. But gin he dus, iſe ne tak it, Sir, gin he was a thouſand Spaniards.   [*walks about in a paſſion.*

Col. I ow'd you a beating, Sirrah, and I'm oblig'd to this gentleman for taking the trouble off my hands; therefore ſay no more, d'ye hear, Sir?   [*Aſide to* Gibby.

Gib. Troth de I, Sir, and feel tee.

Fred. This muſt be a miſtake, Colonel, for I know Violante perfectly well, and I am certain ſhe would not meet you upon the *Terriero-de Paſſa.*

Col. Don't be too poſitive, Frederick, now I have ſome reaſons to believe it was that very lady.

Fel. You'd very much oblige me, Sir, if you'd let me know theſe reaſons.

Col. Sir?

Fel. Sir, I ſay I have a right to enquire into theſe reaſons you ſpeak of.

Col. Ha, ha, really, Sir? I cannot conceive how you or any man can have a right to enquire into my thoughts.

Fel. Sir, I have a right to every thing that relates to Violante.——And he that traduces her fame, and refuſes to give his reaſons for't, is a villain.   [*Draws.*

Col. What the devil have I been doing! now bliſters on my tongue, by dozens.   [*Aſide.*

Fred. Prythee, Felix, don't quarrel, till you know for what: this is all a miſtake I'm poſitive.

Col. Look ye, Sir, that I dare draw my ſword; I think will admit of no diſpute——but tho' fighting's my trade, I'm not in love with it, and think it more honourable to decline this buſineſs, than purſue it. This may be a miſtake; however I'll give you my honour never to have any affair directly or indirectly with Violante, provided ſhe is your Violante; but if there ſhould happen to be another of her name, I hope you would not engroſs all the Violantes in the kingdom.

Fel. Your vanity has given me ſufficient reaſon to believe I'm not miſtaken; I'll not be impos'd upon, Sir.

Col. Nor I bully'd, Sir.

Fel. Bully'd! 'Sdeath, ſuch another word, and I'll nail thee to the wall.

Col. Are you ſure of that, Spaniard?   [*Draws.*

Gib. (*Draws.*) Say ne meer, mon, aw my ſol here's twa to-twa, dona fear, Sir, Gibby ſtonds by ye for the honour of Scotland.   [*Vapours about.*

E   *Fred.*

Fred. By St. Anthony, you shan't fight *(Interpofes)* on bare fufpicion; be certain of the injury, and then——

Fel. That I will this moment, and then, Sir——I hope you are to be found——

Col. Whenever you pleafe, Sir. [*Exit* Felix.

Gib. 'Sbleed, Sir, there neer was a Scotfman yet that fham'd to fhow his face. [*Strutting about.*

Fred. So, quarrels fpring up like mufhrooms, in a minute: Violante and he were but juft reconcil'd, and you have furnifh'd him with frefh matter for falling out again; and I am certain, Colonel, Gibby is in the wrong.

Gib. Gin I be, Sir, the man that tald me lced, and gin he dud, the deel be my landlord, hell my winter-quarters, and a rope my winding-fheet, gin I dee not lik him as lang as I can hold a ftick in my hond, now fee yee.

Col. I am forry for what I have faid, for the lady's fake; but who could divine that fhe was his miftrefs? prythee, who is this warm fpark?

Fred. He is the fon of one of our grandees, nam'd Don Lopez de Pimentell, a very honeft gentleman, but fomething paffionate in what relates to his love.——He is an only fon, which may perhaps be one reafon for indulging his paffion.

Col. When parents have but one child, they either make a madman or a fool of him.

Fred. He is not the only child, he has a fifter; but I think, thro' the feverity of his father, who would have married her againft her inclination, fhe has made her efcape, and notwithftanding he has offered five hundred pounds, he can get no tidings of her.

Col. Ha! how long has fhe been miffing?

Fred. Nay, but fince laft night, it feems.

Col. Laft night! The very time! How went fhe?

Fred. No body can tell; they conjecture thro' the window.

Col. I'm tranfported! This muft be the lady I caught. What fort of a woman is fhe?

Fred. Middle-fiz'd, a lovely brown, a fine pouting lip, eyes that roll and languifh, and feem to fpeak the exquifite pleafure her arms could give!

Col. Oh! I'm fir'd with this defcription——'Tis the very fhe—what's her name?

Fred. Ifabella——you are tranfported, Colonel.

Col. I have a natural tendency in me to the flefh, thou know'ft, and who can hear of charms fo exquifite and yet remain unmov'd? Oh, how I long for the appointed hour! I'll to the *Terriero de Paffa*, and wait my happinefs; if fhe fails to meet me, I'll once more attempt to find her at Violante's in fpite of her brother's jealoufy. *(Afide.)*

Dear.

Dear Frederick, I beg your pardon, but I had forgot, I was
to meet a gentleman upon bufinefs at five; I'll endeavour to
difpatch him, and wait on you again as foon as poffible.——

Fred. Your humble fervant, Colonel. 　　　　*[Exit.*

Col. Gibby, I have no bufinefs with you at prefent.
　　　　　　　　　　　　　　　　[Exit Colonel.

Gib. That's weel——naw will I gang and feek this loon,
and gar him gang with me to Don Pedro's hufe.——Gin he'll
no gang of himfel, ife gar him gang by the lug, Sir; godfwarbit, Gibby hates a lear. 　　　　　　　*[Exit.*

Scene changes to Violante's *Lodging.*

Enter Violante *and* Ifabella.

Ifab. The hour draws on, Violante, and now my heart
begins to fail me, but I refolve to venture for all that.

Vio. What, does your courage fink, Ifabella?

Ifab. Only the force of refolution a little retreated, but
I'll rally it again for all that.

Enter Flora.

Flo. Don Felix is coming up, madam.

Ifab. My brother! which way fhall I get out——difpatch
him as foon as you can, dear Violante.
　　　　　　　　　　　[Exit into the clofet.

Vio. I will. *(Enter* Felix *in a furly pofture.)* Felix,
what brings you home fo foon, did I not fay to-morrow?

Fel. My paffion choaks me, I cannot fpeak; oh! I fhall
burft! *(Afide.)* 　　　*[Throws himfelf into a chair.]*

Vio. Blefs me, are you not well, my Felix?

Fel. Yes,—no,—I don't know what I am.

Vio. Hey day! What's the matter now? another jealous
whim!

Fel. With what an air fhe carries it!——I fweat at her
impudence. 　　　　　　　　　　　　　*[Afide.*

Vio. If I were in your place, Felix, I'd chufe to ftay at
home when thefe fits of fpleen are upon me, and not trouble
fuch perfons as are not obliged to bear with them.
　　　　　　　　　(Here he affects to be carelefs of her.

Fel. I am very fenfible, madam, of what you mean: I
difturb you, no doubt; but were I in a better humour I
fhould not incommode you lefs. I am but too well convinc'd
you could eafily difpenfe with my vifit.

Vio. When you behave yourfelf as you ought to do, no
company fo welcome—but when you referve me for your
ill-nature, I wave your merit, and confider what's due to
myfelf—and I muft be fo free to tell you, Felix, that thefe
humours of your's will abate, if not abfolutely deftroy, the
very principles of love.

Fel. (Rifing.) And I muft be fo free to tell you, madam, that fince you have made fuch ill returns to the refpect

　　　　　　　E 2 　　　　　　　　　　　　that

that I have paid you, all you do shall be indifferent to me
for the future, and you shall find me abandon your empire
with so little difficulty, that I'll convince the world your
chains are not so hard to break as your vanity would tempt
you to believe —— I cannot brook the provocation you give.

Vio. This is not to be borne — insolent! You abandon!
You! Whom I have so often forbad ever to see me more!
Have you not fall'n at my feet? Implor'd my favour and
forgiveness?—did not you trembling wait, and with, and
sigh, and swear yourself into my heart? ungrateful man! If
my chains are so easily broke, as you pretend, then you are
the silliest coxcomb living you did not break 'em long ago;
and I must think him capable of brooking any thing on whom
such usage could make no impression.

. *Isab. (Peeping)* A deuce take your quarrels; she'll never
think on me.

Fel. I always believed, madam, my weakness was the
greatest addition to your power; you would be less imperious,
had my inclination been less forward to oblige you.——You
have indeed forbad me your sight; but your vanity even then
assured you I would return, and I was fool enough to feed
your pride—your eyes, with all their boasted charms, have
acquired the greatest glory in conquering me. — And the
brightest passage of your life is, wounding this heart with
such arms as pierce but few persons of my rank.

[Walks about in a great pet.

Vio. Matchless arrogance! True, Sir, I should have kept
measures better with you, if the conquest had been worth
preserving; but we easily hazard what gives us no pain to
lose.——As for my eyes, you are mistaken if you think
they have vanquished none but you; there are men above
your boasted rank who have confess'd their power, when
their misfortune in pleasing you made them obtain such a
disgraceful victory.

Fel. Yes, madam, I am no stranger to your victories.

Vio. And what you call the brightest passage of my life,
is not the least glorious part of your's.

Fel. Ha, ha, don't put yourself into a passion, madam,
for I assure you after this day I shall give you no trouble.--
You may meet your sparks on the *Terryero de Passa* at four
in the morning, without the least regard to mine—for when
I quit your chamber, the world shan't bring me back.

Vio. I am so well pleas'd with your resolution, I don't
care how soon you take your leave.—But what you mean
by the *Terriero de Passa* at four in the morning, I can't guess.

Fel. No, no, no, not you—— You was not upon the
Terriero de Passa at four this morning?

Vio. No, I was not; but if I was, I hope I may walk
                                                    where

where I pleafe, and at what hour I pleafe, without afking your leave.

Fel. Oh, doubtlefs, madam! And you might meet Colonel Britton there, and afterwards fend your emiffary to fetch him to your houfe.————And upon your father's coming in, thruft him into your bed-chamber—without afking my leave. 'Tis no bufinefs of mine if you are expofed among all the footmen in town. — Nay, if they ballad you, and cry you about at a half-penny a piece——they may without my leave.

Vio. Audacious! Don't provoke me——don't; my reputation is not to be fported with, *(going up to him)* at this rate.——No, Sir, it is not, *(burfts into tears)* inhuman Felix!——Oh, Ifabella, what a train of ills haft thou brought on me.! [*Afide.*

Fel. Ha! I cannot bear to fee her weep.—A woman's tears are far more fatal than our fwords. [*Afide.*] Oh, Violante——'Sdeath! what a dog am I? now have I no power to ftir:——doft not thou know fuch a perfon as Colonel Britton? prythee tell me, didft not thou meet him at four this morning upon the *Terriero de Paffa?*

Vio. Were it not to clear my fame, I would not anfwer thee, thou black ingrate!——But I cannot bear to be reproached with what I even blufh to think of, much lefs to act; by heaven, I have not feen the *Terriero de Paffa* this day.

Fel. Did not a Scots footman attack you in the ftreet neither, Violante?

Vio. Yes, but he miftook me for another, or he was drunk, I know not which.

Fel. And do not you know this Scots Colonel?

Vio. Pray afk me no more queftions, this night fhall clear my reputation, and leave you without excufe for your bafe fufpicions; more than this I fhall not fatisfy you, therefore pray leave me.

Fel. Didft thou ever love me, Violante?

Vio. I'll anfwer nothing.——You was in hafte to be gone juft now, I fhould be very well pleas'd to be alone, Sir.
[*She fits down and turns afide.*

Fel. I fhall not long interrupt your contemplation.—Stubborn to the laft. [*Afide.*

Vio. Did ever woman involve herfelf as I have done?

Fel. Now would I give one of my eyes to be friends with her; for fomething whifpers to my foul fhe is not guilty.
——(*He paufes, then pulls a chair, and fits by her at a little diftance, looking at her fome time without fpeaking.—Then draws a little nearer to her.*) Give me your hand at parting

however,

however, Violante, won't you, *(Here he lays his open upon her knee several times.)* won't you——won't you——won't you ?

Vio. *(Half regarding him)* Won't I do what ?

Fel. You know what I would have, Violante. Oh, my heart !

Vio. *(Smiling.)* I thought my chains were easily broke. *(Lays her hand into his.)*

Fel. *(Draws his chair close to her, and kisses her hand in a rapture.)* Too well thou knowest thy strength——oh my charming angel, my heart is all thy own. Forgive my hasty passion, 'tis the transport of a love sincere !

Don Pedro *within.*

Ped. Bid Sancho get a new wheel to my chariot presently.

Vio. Bless me ! my father return'd ! what shall we do now, Felix ! we are ruin'd, past redemption.

Fel. No, no, no, my love ; I can leap from thy closet window.   *(Runs to the door where* Isabella *is, who claps to (the door, and bolts it within side.*

Isab. *(Peeping.)* Say you so ? but I shall prevent you.

Fel. Confusion ! Some body bolts the door within side ; I'll see who you have conceal'd here, if I die for't ; oh Violante ! hast thou again sacrific'd me to my rival. *(Draws.*

Vio. By heaven thou hast no rival in my heart, let that suffice—nay, sure, you will not let my father find you here ——distraction !

Fel. Indeed but I shall—except you command this door to be open'd, and that way conceal me from his sight.

[He struggles with her to come at the door.

Vio. Hear me, Felix——Though I were sure the refusing what you ask would separate us for ever, by all that's powerful you shall not enter here : either you do love me, or you do not ; convince me by your obedience.

Fel. That's not the matter in debate—I will know who is in this closet, let the consequence be what it will. Nay, nay, nay, you strive in vain ; I will go in.

Vio. You shall not go in——

Enter Don Pedro.

Ped. Hey day ! What's here to do ! I will go in, and, you shan't go in——and I will go in——why, who are you, Sir ?

Fel. 'Sdeath ! What shall I say now ?   *[Aside.*

Ped. Don Felix, pray what's your business in my house ? ha, Sir.

Vio. Oh Sir, what miracle return'd you home so soon ? some angel 'twas that brought my father back to succour the distress'd——this ruffian he, I cannot call him gentle-

man

man——has committed such an uncommon rudeness, as the
moſt profligate wretch would be aſham'd to own.

Fel. Ha, what the devil does ſhe mean! *(Aſide.*

Vio. As I was at my devotion in my cloſet, I heard a
loud knocking at my door, mix'd with a woman's voice,
which ſeem'd to imply ſhe was in danger——

Fel. I am confounded! *[Aſide.*

Vio. I flew to the door with the utmoſt ſpeed, where a
lady veil'd, ruſh'd in upon me; who falling on her knees
begged my protection, from a gentleman, who, ſhe ſaid,
purſued her: I took compaſſion on her tears, and lock'd her
into this cloſet; but in the ſurpriſe, having left open the
door, this very perſon whom you ſee, with his ſword drawn,
ran in proteſting, if I refus'd to give her up to his revenge,
he'd force the door.

Fel. What in the name of goodneſs does ſhe mean to do!
Hang me! *[Aſide.*

Vio. I ſtrove with him till I was out of breath, and had
you not come as you did, he muſt have enter'd——But he's in
drink, I ſuppoſe, or he could not have been guilty of ſuch an
indecorum. *[Leering at Felix.*

Ped. I'm amaz'd!

Fel. The devil never fail'd a woman at a pinch: what a
tale has ſhe form'd in a minute——In drink, quotha; a good
hint; I'll lay hold on't to bring myſelf off. *(Aſide.*

Ped. Fie, Don Felix! No ſooner rid of one broil, but you
are commencing another—to aſſault a lady with a naked
ſword, derogates much from the character of a gentleman,
I aſſure you.

Fel. (Counterfeits drunkenneſs) Who, I aſſault a lady——
upon honour the lady aſſaulted me, Sir; and would have
ſeiz'd this body politick upon the King's highway—let her
come out, and deny it if ſhe can—pray, Sir, command the door
to be open'd, and let her prove me a liar if ſhe knows how—
I have been drinking right French claret, Sir, but I love my
own country for all that.

Ped. Ay, ay, who doubts it, Sir?—Open the door, Violante, and let the lady come out—Come, I warrant thee he
ſhan't hurt her.

Fel. Ay, now which way will ſhe come off.

Vio. (Unlocks the door) Come forth, madam, none ſhall
dare to touch your veil——I'll convey you out with ſafety,
or loſe my life—I hope ſhe underſtands me. *(Aſide.*

Enter Iſabella *veil'd and croſſes the Stage.*

Ped. Excellent girl! *(Exit.*

Fel. The devil! a woman! I'll ſee if ſhe be really ſo.
(Offers to follow her.

Ped.

Ped. (Draws) Not a ftep, Sir, till the lady be paft your recovery.—I never fuffer the laws of hofpitality to be violated in my houfe, Sir.——I'll keep Don Felix here till you fee her fafe out, Violante.

Vio. Get clear of my father, and follow me to the *Ter-riero de paffa*, where all miftakes fhall be rectified. *(Afide to* Felix.   [*Exit* Violante.

Ped. Come, Sir, you and I will take a pipe and a bottle together.

Fel. Damn your pipe, Sir, I won't fmoak—I hate tobacco —Nor I, I, I, I won't drink, Sir——No, nor I won't ftay neither, and how will you help yourfelf ?

Ped. As to fmoaking or drinking, you have your liberty, but you fhall ftay, Sir.   *(Gets between him and the door, Felix ftrikes up his heels and Exit.*

Fel. Shall I fo, Sir ?——But I tell you, old gentleman, I am in hafte to be married——And fo God be with you.

Ped. Go to the devil—In hafte to be married, quotha, thou art in a fine condition to be married truly !

Enter a Servant.

Ser. Here's Don Lopez de Pimentell to wait on you, fignior.

Ped. What the devil does he want ? Bring him up, he's in purfuit of his fon, I fuppofe.

Enter Don Lopez.

Lop. I am glad to find you at home, Don Pedro; I was told that you was feen upon the road to —— this afternoon.

Ped. That might be, my Lord ; but I had the misfortune to break the wheel of my chariot, which obliged me to re-turn—What is your pleafure with me, my Lord ?

Lop. I am inform'd that my daughter's in your houfe, Don Pedro.

Ped. That's more than I know, my lord ; but here was your fon juft now as drunk as an emperor.

Lop. My fon drunk ! I never faw him in drink in my life; where is he, pray, Sir ?

Ped. Gone to be married.

Lop. Married ! To whom ? I don't know that he courted any body.

Ped. Nay, I know nothing of that——Within there !
[*Enter fervant.*] Bid my daughter come hither, fhe'll tell you another ftory, my lord.

Ser. She's gone out in a chair, Sir.

Ped. Out in a chair ! What do you mean, Sir ?

Ser. As I fay, Sir ; and Donna Ifabella went in another juft before her, and Don Felix followed in another ; I over-heard them all bid the chair go to the *Terriero de paffa.*

Ped.

Ped. Ha! What bufinefs has my daughter there? I am confounded, and know not what to think.————Within there.   [*Exit.*

Lop. My heart mifgives me plaguily————Call me an Alguazil, I'll purfue them ftrait.

SCENE *changes to the Street before* Don Pedro's *Houfe.*

Enter Liffardo.

Lif. I wifh I cou'd fee Flora————Methinks I have an hankering kindnefs after the flut————We muft be reconcil'd.

Enter Gibby.

Gib. Aw my fol, Sir, but Ife blithe to find yee here now.

Lif. Ha! brother! Give me thy hand, boy.

Gib. No fe fait, fe yee me—Brether, me ne brethers, I fcorn a lyar as muckle as a thiefe, fe ye now, and yee muft gang intul this houfe with me, and juftifie to Donna Violante's face, that fhe was the lady that gang'd in here this morn, fe yee me, or the deel ha my ful, Sir, but ye and I fhall be twa folks.

Lif. Juftify it to Donna Violante's face, quotha, for what? Sure you don't know what you fay.

Gib. Troth de I, Sir, as weel as yee de; therefore come along, and make no meer words about it.

[*Knocks haftily at the door.*

Lif. Why, what the devil do you mean? Don't you confider you are in Portugal? Is the fellow mad?

Gib. Fallow! Ife none of yer fallow, Sir; and gin this place were hell, id gar yee de me juftice. [*Liffardo going.*] Nay the deel a feet yee gang.   [*Lays hold of him, and knocks again.*

Enter Don Pedro.

Ped. How now! What makes you knock fo loud?

Gib. Gin this be Don Pedro's houfe, Sir, I wou'd fpeak with Donna Violante, his doughter.

Lif. Ha! Don Pedro himfelf, I wifh I were fairly off.
                                                       [*Afide.*

Ped. Ha! What is it you want with my daughter, pray?

Gib. An fhe be your doughter, and lik your honour, command her to come out, and anfwer for herfel now, and either juftify or difprove what this fhield told me this morn.

Lif. So, here will be a fine piece of work.   [*Afide.*

Ped. Why, what did he tell you, ha?

Gib. By my fol, Sir, Ife tell yee aw the truth; my mafter got a pratty lady upon the how de call't————

Paffa

Paſſa——here at five this morn, and he gar me watch her heam——And in troth I lodg'd her here ; and meeting this ill-favour'd thiefe, ſe yee me, I ſpiered wha ſhe was—— And he told me her name was Donna Violante, Don Pedro de Mendoſa's doughter.

Ped. Ha! My daughter with a man abroad at five in the morning : death, hell, and furies, by St. Anthony I'm un-done.

Gib. Wounds, Sir, ye put yer ſaint intul bony com-pany.

Ped. Who is your maſter, you dog yon ? Adſheart I ſhall be trick'd of my daughter, and my money too, that's worſt of all.

Gib. You dog you ! 'Sblead, Sir, don't call names —— I won't tell yee who my maſter is, ſe yee me now.

Ped. And who are you, raſcal, that knows my daughter ſo well ? Ha!   [*Holds up his cane.*

Liſſ. What ſhall I ſay to make him give this Scots dog a good beating ? *(Aſide.)* I know your daughter, ſignior ?. not I, I never ſaw your daughter in all my life.

Gib. (Knocks him down with his fiſt.) Deel ha my ſol, ſar, gin ye get no your carich for that lye now.

Ped. What, hoa! Where are all my ſervants ? *Enter ſer-vants on one ſide,* Colonel, Felix, Iſabella, *and* Violante *on the other ſide.)* Raiſe the houſe in purſuit of my daughter.

Serv. Here ſhe comes, ſignior.

Col. Hey day ! What's here to do ?

Gib. This is the loon like tik, an lik your honour, that ſent me heam with a lye this morn.

Col. Come, come, 'tis all well, Gibby ; let him riſe.

Ped. I am thunder-ſtruck—and have no power to ſpeak one word.

Fel. This is a day of Jubilee, Liſſardo ; no quarrelling with him this day.

Liſſ. A pox take his fiſts :—egad theſe Britons are but a word and a blow.

Enter Don Lopez.

Lop. So, have I found you, daughter ? Then you have not hang'd yourſelf yet, I ſee.

Col. But ſhe is married, my lord.

Lop. Married ! Zounds, to whom ?

Col. Even to your humble ſervant, my lord. If you pleaſe to give us your bleſſing.   *(Kneels.*

Lop. Why, hark ye, miſtreſs, are you really married ?

Iſab. Really ſo, my lord.

Lop. And who are you, Sir ?

Col. An honeſt North Briton by birth, and a Colonel by commiſſion, my lord.   *Lop.*

Lop. An heretic! The devil! 			[*Holding up his hands.*

Ped. She has play'd you a flippery trick indeed, my lord.—
Well, my girl, thou haft been to fee thy friend married.—
Next week thou fhalt have a better hufband, my dear.
						[*To* Violante.]

Fel. Next week is a little too foon, Sir; I hope to live
longer than that.

Ped. What do you mean, Sir? you have not made a rib of
my daughter too, have you?

Vio. Indeed but he has, Sir; I know not how, but he took
me in an unguarded minute,—when my thoughts were not
over-ftrong for a nunnery, father.

Lop. Your daughter has play'd you a flippery trick too,
fignior.

Ped. But your fon fhall never be the better for't, my lord;
her twenty thoufand pounds was left on certain conditions, and
I'll not part with a fhilling.

Lop. But we have a certain thing call'd law, fhall make
you do juftice, Sir.

Ped. Well, we'll try that,—my lord, much good may it
do you with your daughter-in-law. 			[*Exit.*

Lop. I wifh you much joy of your rib. 			[*Exit.*

Enter Frederick.

Fel. Frederick, welcome!———I fent for thee to be
witnefs of my good fortune, and make one in a country
dance.

Fred. Your meffenger has told me all, and I fincerely fhare
in all your happinefs.

Col. To the right about, Frederick; wifh thy friend
joy.

Fred. I do with all my foul;———and, madam, I congratulate your deliverance.———Your fufpicions are clear'd now, I
hope, Felix.

Fel. They are; and I heartily afk the Colonel pardon, and
wifh him happy with my fifter; for love has taught me to
know, that every man's happinefs confifts in chufing for
himfelf.

Liff. After that rule I fix here. 			[*To* Flora.

Flo. That's your miftake; I prefer my lady's fervice,
and turn you over to her that pleaded right and title to you
to-day.

Liff. Chufe, proud fool, I fhan't afk you twice.

Gib. What fay ye now, lafs; will ye ge yer maidenhead
to poor Gibby?———What fay you, will ye dance the reel of
Bogie with me?

Inis. That I may not leave my lady———I take you at
your word,———And, tho' our wooing has been fhort, I'll by
her example love you dearly. 			[*Mufick plays.*
						Fel.

Fel. Hark! I hear the mufick; fomebody has done us the favour to fend them, call them in.

A Country Dance.

Gib. Wounds, this is bony mufick — how caw ye that thing that ye pinch by the craig, and tickle the weam, ond make it cry, Grum, Grum?

Fred. Oh! that's a guitar, Gibby.

Fel. Now, my Violante, I fhall proclaim thy virtues to the world.

> *No more let us thy fex's conduct blame,*
> *Since thou'rt a proof to their eternal fame,*
> *That Man has no advantage but the name.* }

F I N I S.

The Provok'd Husband.

Publish'd by W. Oxlade George Street July 1 1776.

THE
Provok'd Huſband;
OR, A
Journey to London.
A COMEDY.

As it is Acted at the

THEATRES-ROYAL
IN
DRURY-LANE
AND
COVENT-GARDEN.

Written by the late
Sir JOHN VANBRUGH and Mr. CIBBER.

—— *Vivit tanquam Vicina Mariti.* Juv. Sat. VI.

LONDON:
Printed for and ſold by W. OXLADE, at SHAKESPEARE'S
HEAD, in GEORGE-STREET, OLD-BAILEY.
MDCCLXXV.

PROLOGUE,

Spoken by Mr. WILKS.

*T*HIS Play took Birth from Principles of Truth,
   To make amends for Errors paſt of Youth.
A Bard, that's now no more, in riper Days,
Conſcious review'd the Licence of his Plays:
And though Applauſe his wanton Muſe had fir'd,
Himſelf condemn'd what ſenſual Minds admir'd.
At length he own'd, that Plays ſhould let you ſee
Not only, what you are, but ought to be;
Though Vice was natural, 'twas never meant
The Stage ſhould ſhew it, but for Puniſhment!
Warm with that Thought, his Muſe once more took Flame,
Reſolv'd to bring licentious Life to Shame.
Such was the Piece his lateſt Pen deſign'd,
But left no Traces of his Plan behind.
Luxuriant Scenes, unprun'd, or half contriv'd;
Yet, through the Maſs, his native Fire ſurviv'd:
Rough, as rich Ore, in Mines the Treaſure lay,
Yet ſtill 'twas rich, and forms at length a Play.
In which the bold Compiler boaſts no Merit,
But that his Pains have ſav'd you Scenes of Spirit.
Not Scenes, that would a noiſy Joy impart,
But ſuch as huſh the Mind and warm the Heart.
From Praiſe of Hands no ſure Account he draws,
But fix'd Attention is ſincere Applauſe:
  If then (for hard you'll own the Taſk) his Art
Can to thoſe Embryon-ſcenes new Life impart,
The Living proudly would exclude his Lays,
And to the buried Bard reſigns the Praiſe.

E P

EPILOGUE,

Spoken by Mrs. OLDFIELD.

METHINKS I hear some powder'd Critics say,
  "Damn it! this Wife reform'd has spoil'd the Play!
" The Coxcomb should have drawn her more in Fashion,
" Have gratify'd her softer Inclination,
" Have tipt her a Gallant, and clinch'd the Provocation."
  But there our Bard stopt short: For 'twere uncivil
T'have made a modern Belle, all o'er a Devil!
He hop'd, in Honour of the Sex, the Age
Would bear one mended Woman———on the Stage.
  From whence, you see, by Common Sense's Rules,
Wives might be govern'd, were not Husbands Fools.
Whate'er by Nature Dames are prone to do,
They seldom stray but when they govern you.
When the wild Wife perceives her Deary tame,
No wonder then she plays him all the Game.
But Men of Sense meet rarely that Disaster;
Women take Pride, where Merit is their Master:
Nay, she that with a weak Man wisely lives,
Will seem t'obey the due Commands he gives!
Happy Obedience is no more a Wonder,
When Men are Men, and keep them kindly under.
But modern Consorts are such high-bred Creatures,
They think a Husband's Power degrades their Features;
That nothing more proclaims a reigning Beauty,
Than that she never was reproach'd with Duty:
And that the greatest Blessing Heav'n e'er sent,
Is in a Spouse, incurious and content.
To give such Dames a diff'rent Cast of Thought,
By calling home the Mind, these Scenes were wrought.
If with a Hand too rude the Task is done,
We hope the Scheme by Lady Grace laid down,
Will all such Freedom with the Sex attone,
That Virtue there, unsoil'd by modish Art,
Throws out Attractions for a Manly's Heart.
  You, You, then, Ladies, whose unquestion'd Lives
Give you the foremost Fame of happy Wives,
Protect, for its Attempt, this helpless Play;
Nor leave it to the vulgar Taste a Prey;
Appear the frequent Champions of its Cause,
Direct the Crowd, and give yourselves Applause.

Dra-

Dramatis Personæ.

MEN.

Lord *Townly*, of a Regular Life.
Mr *Manly*, an Admirer of Lady *Grace*.
Sir *Francis Wronghead*, a Country Gentleman.
Squire *Richard*, his Son, a mere Whelp.
Count *Basset*, a Gamester.
John Moody, Servant to Sir *Francis*, an honest Clown.

WOMEN.

Lady *Townly*, immoderate in her Pursuit of pleasures.
Lady *Grace*, Sister to Lord *Townly*, of exemplary
    Virtue.
Lady *Wronghead*, Wife to Sir *Francis*, inclined to
    be a fine Lady.
Miss *Jenny*, her Daughter, pert and forward.
Mrs. *Motherly*, one that lets Lodgings.
Myrtilla, her Niece, seduced by the Count.
Mrs. *Trusty*, Lady *Townly*'s Woman.

×××××××××××××××××××××××××××××××××××××

THE

Provok'd Huſband;

OR, A

Journey to London.

×××××××××××××××××××××××××××××××××××××

ACT I. SCENE I.

SCENE, *Lord* Townly's *Apartment.*

Lord Townly *ſolus.*

WHY did I marry!——Was it not evident, my plain, rational ſcheme of life was impracticable, with a woman of ſo different a way of thinking?——Is there one article of it, that ſhe has not broke in upon?——Yes,——let me do her juſtice ——her reputation——that——I have no reaſon to believe is in queſtion——but then how long her profligate courſe of pleaſures may make her able to keep it—is a ſhocking queſtion! and her preſumption while ſhe keeps it—inſupportable!ʼ for on the pride of that ſingle virtue ſhe ſeems to lay it down, as a funda‐ mental point, that the free indulgence of every other vice, this fertile town affords, is the birth-right prerogative of a woman of quality——amazing! that a creature ſo warm in the purſuit of her pleaſures, ſhould never caſt one thought towards her hap‐ pineſs——thus, while ſhe admits no lover, ſhe thinks it a greater merit ſtill, in her chaſtity, not to care for her huſband; and while ſhe herſelf is ſolacing in one continual round of cards and good company, he, poor wretch! is left at large, to take care of his own contentment——ʼtis time, indeed, ſome care were taken, and ſpeedily there ſhall be——yet let me not

be‐

be rash——perhaps this disappointment of my heart may make
me too impatient; and some tempers, when reproach'd, grow
more untractable.—Here she comes——let me be calm a while.

Enter Lady Townly.

Going out so soon after dinner, madam?

Lady *Town.* Lard, my lord! what can I possibly do at home?

Lord *Town.* What does my sister, lady Grace, do at home?

Lady *Town.* Why, that is to me amazing! have you ever
any pleasure at home?

Lord *Town.* It might be in your power, madam, I confess,
to make it a little more comfortable to me.

Lady *Town.* Comfortable! and so, my good lord, you would
really have a woman of my rank and spirit, stay at home to
comfort her husband! lord! what notions of life some men have!

Lord *Town.* Don't you think, madam, some ladies notions
are full as extravagant?

Lady *Town.* Yes, my lord, when the tame doves live
coop'd within the penn of your precepts, I do think 'em prodigious indeed!

Lord *Town.* And when they fly wild about this town, madam, pray what must the world think of 'em, then?

Lady *Town.* Oh! this world is not so ill bred as to quarrel
with any woman for liking it.

Lord *Town.* Nor am I, madam, a husband so well-bred, as
to bear my wife's being so fond of it; in short, the life you
lead, madam——

Lady *Town.* Is, to me, the pleasantest life in the world.

Lord *Town.* I should not dispute your taste, madam, if a
woman had a right to please no body but herself.

Lady *Town.* Why, whom would you have her please?

Lord *Town.* Sometimes her husband.

Lady *Town.* And don't you think a husband under the same
obligation?

Lord *Town.* Certainly.

Lady *Town.* Why then we are agreed, my lord——for
if I never go abroad, 'till I am weary of being at home——
which you know is the case——is it not equally reasonable, not
to come home 'till one's weary of being abroad!

Lord *Town.* If this be your rule of life, madam, 'tis time
to ask you one serious question.

Lady *Town.* Don't let it be long a coming then——for I
am in haste.

Lord *Town.* Madam, when I am serious, I expect a serious
answer.

Lady *Town.* Before I know the question?

Lord *Town.* Pshah——have I power, madam, to make
you serious by intreaty?

Lady *Town.* You have.

Lord *Town.* And you promise to answer me sincerely?

Lady *Town.* Sincerely.

Lord

Lord *Town.* Now then recollect your thoughts, and tell me seriously, why you married me?

Lady *Town.* You insist upon truth, you say?

Lord *Town.* I think I have a right to it.

Lady *Town.* Why then, my lord, to give you, at once, a proof of my obedience and sincerity——I think——I married ——to take off that restraint, that lay upon my pleasures, while I was a single woman.

Lord *Town.* How, madam! is any woman under less restraint after marriage, than before it?

Lady *Town.* O my lord! my lord! they are quite different creatures! wives have infinite liberties in life, that would be terrible in an unmarried woman to take.

Lord *Town.* Name one.

Lady *Town.* Fifty, if you please!——to begin then, in the morning——A married woman may have men at her toilet; invite them to dinner; appoint them a party in a stage box at the play; ingross the conversation; there call 'em by their christian names; talk louder than the players;——from thence jaunt into the city——take a frolicksome supper at an India house——perhaps, in her Gaieté de Cœur, toast a pretty fellow ——then clatter again to this end of the town; break, with the morning, into an assembly; crowd to the hazard-table; throw a familiar Levant upon some sharp lurching man of quality, and if he demands his money, turn it off with a loud laugh, and cry——you'll owe it him, to vex him! ha! ha!

Lord *Town.* Prodigious! [*Aside.*

Lady *Town.* These now, my lord, are some few of the many modish amusements, that distinguish the privilege of a wife, from that of a single woman.

Lord *Town.* Death! madam! what law has made these liberties less scandalous in a wife, than in an unmarried woman?

Lady *Town.* Why, the strongest law in the world, custom ——custom time out of mind, my lord.

Lord *Town.* Custom, madam, is the law of fools: but it shall never govern me.

Lady *Town.* Nay then, my lord, 'tis time for me to observe the laws of prudence.

Lord *Town.* I wish I could see an instance of it.

Lady *Town.* You shall have one this moment, my lord: for I think, when a man begins to lose his temper at home; if a woman has any prudence, why——she'll go abroad 'till he comes to himself again. [*Going.*

Lord *Town.* Hold, madam——I am amaz'd you are not more uneasy at the life you lead! you don't want sense! and yet seem void of all humanity: for, with a blush I say it, I think I have not wanted love.

Lady *Town.* Oh! don't say that, my lord, if you suppose I have my senses.

Lord *Town.* What is it I have done to you? what can you complain of?

Lady

Lady *Town.* Oh! nothing in the leaſt : 'tis true, you have heard me ſay, I have owed my lord Lurcher an hundred pounds theſe three weeks——but what then——a huſband is not liable to his wife's debts of honour, you know——and if a ſilly woman will be uneaſy about money, ſhe can't be ſu'd for, what's that to him ? as long as he loves her, to be ſure, ſhe can have nothing to complain of.

Lord *Town.* By heav'n, if my whole fortune thrown into your lap, could make you delight in the chearful duties of a wife, I ſhould think myſelf a gainer by the purchaſe.

Lady *Town.* That is, my lord, I might receive your whole eſtate, provided you were ſure I would not ſpend a ſhilling of it.

Lord *Town.* No, madam ; were I maſter of your heart, your pleaſures would be mine ; but different, as they are, I'll feed even your follies, to deſerve it——perhaps you may have ſome other trifling debts of honour abroad, that keep you out of humour at home——at leaſt it ſhall not be my fault, if I have not more of your company——there, there's a bill of five hundred——and now, madam——

Lady *Town.* And now, my lord, down to the ground I thank you——now am I convinced, were I weak enough to love this man, I ſhould never get a ſingle guinea from him.   [*Aſide.*

Lord *Town.* If it be no offence, madam——

Lady *Town.* Say what you pleaſe, my lord; I am in that harmony of ſpirits, it is impoſſible to put me out of humour.

Lord *Town.* How long, in reaſon then, do you think that ſum ought to laſt you ?

Lady *Town.* Oh, my dear, dear lord! now you have ſpoil'd all again ; how is it poſſible I ſhould anſwer for an event, that ſo utterly depends upon fortune ? but to ſhew you, that I am more inclin'd to get money, than to throw it away——I have a ſtrong poſſeſſion, that with this five hundred, I ſhall win five thouſand.

Lord *Town.* Madam, if you were to win ten thouſand, it would be no ſatisfaction to me.

Lady *Town.* O! the churl! ten thouſand! what! not ſo much as wiſh I might win ten thouſand !——ten thouſand! O! the charming ſum ! what infinite pretty things might a woman of ſpirit do, with ten thouſand guineas! O' my conſcience, if ſhe were a woman of true ſpirit——ſhe—ſhe might loſe 'em all again.

Lord *Town.* And I had rather it ſhould be ſo, madam ; provided I could be ſure, that were the laſt you would loſe.

Lady *Town.* Well, my lord, to let you ſee I deſign to play all the good houſe-wife I can; I am now going to a party at Quadrille, only to piddle with a little of it, at poor two guineas a fiſh, with the ducheſs of Quiteright.   [*Exit Lady* Townly.

Lord *Town.* Inſenſible creature ! neither reproaches or indulgence, kindneſs, or ſeverity, can wake her to the leaſt reflexion : continual licence has lull'd her into ſuch a lethargy of

care, that she speaks of her excesses with the same easy confidence,
as if they were so many virtues. What a turn has her head
taken!——but how to cure it——I am afraid the physic must
be strong, that reaches her — lenitives, I see, are to no purpose——take my friend's opinion——Manly will speak freely
——my sister with tenderness to both sides. They know my
case——I'll talk with 'em.

Enter a Servant.

Serv. Mr. Manly, my lord, has sent to know, if your lordship was at home.

Lord Town. They did not deny me?

Serv. No, my lord.

Lord Town. Very well; step up to my sister, and say, I desire to speak with her.

Serv. Lady Grace is here, my lord.   [*Exit Serv.*

Enter Lady Grace.

Lord Town. So, lady fair; what pretty weapon have you
been killing your time with?

Lady Grace. A huge folio, that has almost kill'd me—I
think I have half read my eyes out.

Lord Town. O! you should not pore so much just after dinner, child.

Lady Grace. That's true; but any body's thoughts are better
than always one's own, you know.

Lord Town. Who's there?

Enter a Servant.

Leave word at the door, I am at home to nobody but Mr. Manly.

Lady Grace. And why is he excepted, pray, my lord?

Lord Town. I hope, madam, you have no objection to his
company?

Lady Grace. Your particular orders, upon my being here,
look, indeed, as if you thought I had not.

Lord Town. And your ladyship's enquiry into the reason of
those orders, shews at least, it was not a matter indifferent to
you!

Lady Grace. Lord! you make the oddest constructions,
brother!

Lord Town. Look you, my grave lady Grace——in one serious word——I wish you had him.

Lady Grace. I can't help that.

Lord Town. Ha! you can't help it, ha! ha! the flat sim-
plicity of that reply was admirable!

Lady Grace. Pooh! you teize one, brother!

Lord Town. Come, I beg pardon, child——this is not a
point, I grant you, to trifle upon; therefore I hope you'll give
me leave to be serious.

Lady Grace. If you desire it, brother! though upon my
word, as to Mr. Manly's having any serious thoughts of me—
I know nothing of it.

Lord

Lord *Town.* Well——there's nothing wrong, in your mak‑
ing a doubt of it——but in short, I find, by his conversation of
late, that he has been looking round the world for a wife; and if
you were to look round the world for a husband, he's the first
man I would give to you.

Lady *Grace.* Then, whenever he makes me any offer, bro‑
ther, I will certainly tell you of it.

Lord *Town.* O! that's the last thing he'll do: he'll never
make you an offer, 'till he's pretty sure it won't be refus'd.

Lady *Grace.* Now you make me curious. Pray! did he ever
make any offer of that kind to you?

Lord *Town.* Not directly; but that imports nothing; he is
a man too well acquainted with the female world to be brought
into a high opinion of any one woman, without some well‑
examined proof of her merit; yet I have reason to believe, that
your good sense, your turn of mind, and your way of life, have
brought him to so favourable a one of you, that a few days will
reduce him to talk plainly to me : which as yet (notwithstanding
our friendship) I have neither declin'd, nor encourag'd him to.

Lady *Grace.* I am mighty glad we are so near, in our way
of thinking; for to tell you the truth, he is much upon the same
terms with me : You know he has a satirical turn; but never
lashes any folly, without giving due encomiums to its opposite
virtue : and upon such occasions, he is sometimes particular, in
turning his compliments upon me, which I don't receive with
any reserve, left he should imagine I take them to myself.

Lord *Town.* You are right, child : when a man of merit
makes his addresses, good sense may give him an answer, with‑
out scorn, or coquetry.

Lady *Grace.* Hush! he's here——

Enter Mr. Manly.

Man. My lord! your most obedient.

Lord *Town.* Dear Manly, yours——I was thinking to send
to you.

Man. Then, I am glad I am here, my lord——Lady Grace,
I kiss your hands!——What only you two! how many
visits may a man make, before he falls into such unfashionable
company! A brother and sister soberly sitting at home, when
the whole town is a gadding! I question if there is so particular
a Tête à Tête, again, in the whole Parish of St. James's.

Lady *Grace.* Fy! fy! Mr. Manly; how censorious you are!

Man. I had not made the reflection, madam, but that I saw
you an exception to it—where's my lady?

Lord *Town.* That I believe is impossible to guess.

Man. Then I won't try, my lord——

Lord *Town.* But, 'tis probable I may hear of her, by that
time I have been four or five hours in bed.

Man. Now, if that were my case——I believe I——but I
beg pardon, my lord.

Lord

Lord Town. Indeed, Sir, you shall not : you will oblige me, if you speak out ; for it was upon this head I wanted to see you.

Man. Why then, my lord, since you oblige me to proceed —— If that were my case——I believe I should certainly sleep in another house.

Lady *Grace.* How do you mean ?

Man. Only a compliment, madam.

Lady *Grace.* A compliment!

Man. Yes, madam, in rather turning myself out of doors than her.

Lady *Grace.* Don't you think, that would be going too far ?

Man. I don't know but it might, madam ; for, in strict justice, I think she ought rather to go than I.

Lady *Grace.* This is new doctrine, Mr. Manly.

Man. As old, madam, as Love, Honour, and Obey! when a woman will stop at nothing that's wrong, why should a man balance any thing that's right ?

Lady *Grace.* Bless me, but this is fomenting things——

Man. Fomentations, madam, are sometimes necessary to dispel tumours ; tho' I don't directly advise my lord to do this ——this is only what, upon the same provocation, I would do myself.

Lady *Grace.* Ay! ay! you would do! batchelors wives indeed are finely govern'd.

Man. If the married men's were as well——I am apt to think we should not see so many mutual plagues taking the air, in separate coaches.

Lady *Grace.* Well! but suppose it your own case ; would you part with a wife, because she now and then stays out, in the best company ?

Lord Town. Well said, Lady Grace 1 come, stand up for the privilege of your sex ! This is like to be a warm debate ! I shall edify.

Man. Madam, I think a wife, after midnight, has no occasion to be in better company than her husband's ; and that frequent unreasonable hours make the best company——the worst company she can fall into.

Lady *Grace.* But if people of condition are to keep company with one another ; how is it possible to be done unless one conforms to their hours ?

Man. I can't find, that any woman's good breeding obliges her to conform to other people's vices.

Lord Town. I doubt, child, here we are got a little on the wrong side of the question.

Lady *Grace.* Why so, my Lord ? I can't think the case so bad, as Mr. Manly states it——————people of quality are not ty'd down to the rules of those, who have their fortunes to make.

Man. No people, Madam, are above being ty'd down to some rules, that have fortunes to lose.

Lady

Lady *Grace.* Pooh! I'm fure, if you were to take my fide of the argument, you would be able to fay fomething more for it.

Lord *Town.* Well, what fay you to that, Manly?

Man. Why, 'troth, my Lord, I have fomething to fay.

Lady *Grace.* Ay! that I fhould be glad to hear now!

Lord *Town.* Out with it!

Man. Then in one word, this, my Lord, I have often thought that the mif-conduct of my Lady has, in a great meafure, been owing to your lordfhip's treatment of her.

Lady *Grace.* Blefs me!

Lord *Town.* My treatment!

Man. Ay, my Lord, you fo idoliz'd her before marriage, that you even indulg'd her, like a miftrefs, after it: In fhort, you continu'd the lover, when you fhould have taken up the hufband.

Lady *Grace.* O frightful! this is worfe than t'other! can a hufband love a wife too well!

Man. As eafy, Madam, as a wife may love her hufband too little.

Lord *Town.* So! you two are never like to agree, I find.

Lady *Grace.* Don't be pofitive, brother!—I am afraid we are both of a mind already. [*Afide.*] And do you, at this rate, ever hope to be married, Mr. Manly?

Man. Never, Madam; 'till I can meet with a woman that likes my doctrine.

Lady *Grace.* 'Tis pity but your miftrefs fhould hear it.

Man. Pity me, Madam, when I marry the woman that won't hear it.

Lady *Grace.* I think, at leaft, he can't fay, that's me.

[*Afide.*

Man. And fo, my Lord, by giving her more power than was needful, fhe has none where fhe wants it; having fuch intire poffeffion of you, fhe is not miftrefs of herfelf! and, mercy on us! how many fine women's heads have been turn'd upon the fame occafion!

Lord *Town.* O Manly! 'tis too true! there's the fource of my difquiet! fhe knows, and has abufed her power! nay, I am ftill fo weak (with fhame I fpeak it) 'tis not an hour ago, that in the midft of my impatience———I gave her another bill for five hundred to throw away.

Man. Well—my lord! to let you fee I am fometimes upon the fide of good-nature, I won't abfolutely blame you; for the greater your indulgence, the more you have to reproach her with.

Lady *Grace.* Ay, Mr. Manly! here now, I begin to come in with you: who knows, my lord, but you may have a good account of your kindnefs!

Man. That, I am afraid, we had not beft depend upon: but fince you have had fo much patience, my lord, even go on with it it a day or two more! and upon her ladyſhip's next ſally, be a little rounder in your expoſtulations; if that don't work——— drop her ſome cool hints of a determin'd reformation, and leave her———to breakfaſt upon 'em.

Lord Town. You are perfectly right! how valuable is a friend, in our anxiety!

Man. Therefore to divert that, my lord, I beg, for the preſent, we may call another cauſe.

Lady Grace. Ay, for goodneſs ſake let's have done with this.

Lord Town. With all my heart.

Lady Grace. Have you no news abroad, Mr. Manly?

Man. A propos———I have ſome, madam; and I believe, my lord, as extraordinary in its kind———

Lord Town. Pray let's have it.

Man. Do you know, that your country neighbour, and my wiſe kinſman, ſir Francis Wronghead, is coming to town with his whole family?

Lord Town. The fool! what can be his buſineſs here?

Man. Oh! of the laſt importance, I'll aſſure you———no leſs than the buſineſs of the nation.

Lord Town. Explain!

Man. He has carried his election———againſt ſir John Worthland.

Lord Town. The duce! what! for———for———

Man. The famous borough of Guzzledown!———

Lord Town. A proper repreſentative, indeed.

Lady Grace. Pray, Mr. Manly, don't I know him?

Man. You have din'd with him, madam, when I was laſt down with my lord, at Bellmont.

Lady Grace. Was not that he, that got a little merry before dinner, and overſet the tea-table, in making his compliments to my lady?

Man. The ſame.

Lady Grace. Pray what are his circumſtances? I know but very little of him.

Man. Then he is worth your knowing, I can tell you, madam. His eſtate, if clear, I believe, might be a good two thouſand pounds a year: though as it was left him, ſaddled with two jointures, and two weighty mortgages upon it, there is no ſaying what it is———but that he might be ſure never to mend it, he married a profuſe young huſſy, for love, without a penny of money! thus having, like his brave anceſtors, provided heirs for the family (for his dove breeds like a tame pigeon.) he now finds children and intereſt-money make ſuch a bawling about his ears, that, at laſt, he has taken the friendly advice of his kinſman, the good lord Danglecourt, to run his eſtate two thouſand pounds more in debt, and to put the whole management of what's left into Paul Pillage's hands, that he may be at leiſure himſelf to retrieve his affairs, by being a parliament man.

B   Lord

Lord Town. A moft admirable fcheme, indeed!

Man. And with this politic profpect, he's now upon his journey to London——

Lord Town. What can it end in ?

Man. Pooh ! a journey into the country again.

Lord Town. Do you think he'll ftir, 'till his money's gone ? or at leaft, 'till the feffion is over ?

Man. If my intelligence is right, my lord, he won't fit long enough to give his vote for a turnpike.

Lord Town. How fo ?

Man. O ! a bitter bufinefs ! he had fcarce a vote, in the whole town, befide the returning officer; Sir John will certainly have it heard at the bar of the houfe, and fend him about his bufinefs again.

Lord Town. Then he has made a fine bufinefs of it, indeed.

Man. Which, as far as my little intereft will go, fhall be done, in as few days as poffible.

Lady Grace. But why would you ruin the poor gentleman's fortune, Mr. Manly ?

Man. No, madam, I would only fpoil his project, to fave his fortune.

Lady Grace. How are you concern'd enough to do either ?

Man. Why——I have fome obligations to the family, madam : I enjoy, at this time, a pretty eftate, which Sir Francis was heir at law to: but——by his being a booby, the laft will of an obftinate old uncle gave it to me.

Enter a Servant.

Serv. [*to* Man.] Sir, here's one of your fervants from your houfe, defires to fpeak with you.

Man. Will you give him leave to come in, my lord ?

Lord Town. Sir——the ceremony's of your own making.

Enter Manly's *Servant.*

Man. Well, James ! what's the matter now ?

James. Sir, here's John Moody juft come to town ; he fays fir Francis, and all the family, will be here to-night, and is in a great hurry to fpeak with you.

Man. Where is he ?

James. At our houfe, Sir ; he has been gaping and ftumping about the ftreets, in his dirty boots, and afking every one he meets, if they can tell him where he may have a good lodging for a parliament-man, till he hires a handfome whole houfe, fit for all his family, for the winter.

Man. I am afraid, my lord, I muft wait upon Mr. Moody.

Lord Town. Pr'ythee ! let's have him here : he will divert us.

Man. O my lord ! he's fuch a cub ! not but he's fo near common fenfe, that he paffes for a wit in the family.

Lady Grace. I beg of all things, we may have him : I am in love with nature, let her drefs be never fo homely.

Man. Then defire him to come hither, James. [*Exit* James.

Lady Grace. Pray what may be Mr. Moody's poft ?

Man. Oh! his *Maître d' Hôtel*, his butler, his bailiff, his hind, his huntſman; and ſometimes——his companion.

Lord *Town.* It runs in my head, that the moment this knight has ſet him down in the houſe, he will get up, to give them the earlieſt proof, of what importance he is to the public, in this own country.

Man. Yes, and when they have heard him, he will find, that his utmoſt importance ſtands valued at——ſometimes being invited to dinner.

Lady *Grace.* And her ladyſhip, I ſuppoſe, will make as conſiderable a figure in her ſphere too.

Man. That you may depend upon: for (if I don't miſtake) ſhe has ten times more of the jade in her, than ſhe yet knows of: and ſhe will ſo improve in this rich ſoil, in a month, that ſhe will viſit all the ladies, that will let her into their houſes; and run in debt to all the ſhop-keepers that will let her into their books: in ſhort, before her important ſpouſe has made five pounds, by his eloquence, at Weſtminſter; ſhe will have loſt five hundred at dice and quadrille, in the pariſh of St. James's.

Lord *Town.* So that, by that time he is declared unduly elected, a ſwarm of duns will be ready for their money; and his worſhip——will be ready for a jail.

Man. Yes, yes, that I reckon will cloſe the account of this hopeful journey to London——but ſee here comes the fore-horſe of the team!

Enter John Moody.

Oh! honeſt John!

John Moody. Ad's waunds, and heart! meaſter Manly! I'm glad I ha' ſun ye. Lawd! lawd! give me a buſs! why that's friendly naw! fleſh! I thought we ſhould never ha' got hither! well! and how d'ye do, meaſter?——good lack! I beg pardon for my bawldneſs——I did not ſee, 'at his honour was here.

Lord *Town.* Mr. Moody, your ſervant: I am glad to ſee you in London; I hope all the good family is well.

John Moody. Thanks be prais'd your honour, they are all in pretty good heart; thof' we have had a power of croſſes upo' the road.

Lady *Grace.* I hope my lady has had no hurt, Mr. Moody.

John Moody. Noa, and pleaſe your ladyſhip, ſhe was never in better humour: there's money enough ſtirring now.

Man. What has been the matter, John?

John Moody. Why, we came up in ſuch a hurry, you man think, that our tackle was not ſo tight as it ſhould be.

Man. Come, tell us all——pray how do they travel?

John Moody. Why i'th the awld coach, meaſter, and 'cauſe my lady loves to do things handſom, to be ſure, ſhe would have a couple of cart horſes clapt to th' four old geldings, that neighbours might ſee ſhe went up to London in her coach and ſix: and ſo Giles Joulter, the plowman, rides poſtillion.

Man. Very well! the journey fets out as it fhould do [*Afide.*] What, do they bring all the children with them too?

John Moody. Noa, noa, only the young fquoire, and Mifs Jenny. The other foive are all out at board, at half a crown a head, a week, with John Growfe, at Smoke-Dunghill farm.

Man. Good again! a right Englifh academy for younger children!

John Moody. Anon, fir.   [*Not underftanding him.*

Lady Grace. Poor fouls! what will become of 'em?

John Moody. Nay, nay, for that matter, madam, they are in very good hands: Joan loves 'um as thof' they were all her own: for fhe was wet nurfe to every mother's babe of 'um—— ay, ay, they'll ne'er want for a belly-full there!

Lady Grace. What fimplicity!

Man. The lud 'a mercy upon all good folks! what work will thefe people make!   [*Holding up his hands.*

Lord Town. And when do you expect them here, John?

John Moody. Why we were in hopes to ha' come yefterday, an' it had no' been, that th' awld weazlebelly horfe tyr'd: and then we were fo cruelly loaden, that the two fore wheels came crafh! down at once, in Waggorrut Lane, and there we loft four hours 'fore we cou'd fet things to rights again.

Man. So they bring all their baggage with the coach, then?

John Moody. Ay, ay, and good ftore on't there is——why, my lady's geer alone were as much as fill'd four portmantel trunks, befide the great deal-box, that heavy Ralph and the monkey fit upon behind.

Lord Town. Lady *Grace,* and *Man.* Ha, ha, ha!

Lady Grace. Well, Mr. Moody, and pray how many are they within the coach?

John Moody. Why there's my lady, and his worfhip; and the young fquoire, and Mifs Jenny, and the fat lapdog, and my lady's maid, Mrs. Handy, and Doll Tripe the cook, that's all ——only Doll puked a little with riding backward, fo they hoifted her into the coach-box—and then her ftomach was eafy.

Lady Grace. Oh! I fee 'em: I fee 'em go by me. Ha! ha!   [*Laughing.*

John Moody. Then you mun think, meafter, there was fome ftowage for the belly, as well as th' back too; children are apt to be famifht upo' the road; fo we had fuch cargoes of plum-cake, and bafkets of tongues, and bifcuits, and cheefe, and cold boil'd beef——and then, in cafe of ficknefs, bottles of cherry brandy, plague water, fack, tent, and ftrong beer fo plenty as made th' owld coach crack again! Mercy upon them! and fend 'em all well to town, I fay.

Man. Ay! and well out on't again, John.

John Moody. Ods bud! meafter, you're a wife mon; and for that matter, fo am I——whoam's whoam, I fay; I'm fure we ha' got but little good, e'er fin' we turn'd our backs on't. No-

thing but mischief! some devil's trick or other plagued us, awth'
dey lung! crack! goes one thing: bawnce! goes another. Woa,
says Roger—Then sowse! we are all set fast in a slough. Whaw,
cries Miss! scream go the maids, and bawl, just as thof' they
were stuck! and so mercy on us! this was the trade from morning to night. But my lady was in such a murrain haste to be
here, that set out she would, thof' I told her, it was Childer-
mas day.

Man. These ladies, these ladies, John——

John Moody. Ah, measter! I ha' seen a little of 'em; and I
find that the best—when she's mended, won't ha' much goodness
to spare.

Lord Town. Well said, John. Ha, ha!

Man. I hope at least, you and your good woman agree still.

John Moody. Ay! ay! much of a muchness. Bridget sticks
to me: tho' as for her goodness—why, she was willing to come
to London too——but hawld a bit! noa, noa, says I, there
may be mischief enough done, without you.

Man. Why that was bravely spoken, John, and like a man.

John Moody. Ah, weast heart, were measter but hawf the
mon that I am——ods wookers! thof' he'll speak stawtly too
sometimes——but then he canno' hawld it——no! he canno'
hawld it.

Lord Town. Lady *Grace,* *Man.* Ha, ha, ha!

John Moody. Ods flesh! but I mun hye me whoam! th' coach
will be coming every hour naw——but measter charg'd me to
find your worship out; for he has hugey business with you; and
will certainly wait upon you, by that time he can put on a
clean neckcloth.

Man. O John! I'll wait upon him.

John Moody. Why you wonno' be so kind, wull ye?

Man. If you'll tell me where you lodge.

John Moody. Just i'th' street next to where your worship
dwells; at the sign of the Golden Ball——It's gold all over;
where they sell ribbons and flappits, and other sort of geer for
gentlewomen.

Man. A milliner's?

John Moody. Ay, ay, one Mrs. Motherly: waunds! she has
a couple of cleaver girls there stitching i'th' fore-room.

Man. Yes, yes, she's a woman of good business, no doubt
on't——who recommended that house to you, John?

John Moody. The greatest good fortune in the world, sure!
for as I was gaping about the streets, who should look out of
the window there, but the fine gentleman, that was always
riding by our coach side, at York races———Count——
Basset; ay, that's he.

Man. Basset? Oh, I remember; I know him by sight.

John Moody. Well! to be sure, as civil a gentleman, to see
to——

Man. As any sharper in town. 　　　　　　　　[*Afide*
　　　　　　　　　　　　　　　　　　　　　　　John

John Moody. At York, he us'd to breakfast with my lady every morning.

Man. Yes, yes, and I suppose her ladyship will return his compliment here in town.   [*Aside.*

John Moody. Well, Measter————

Lord Town. My service to sir Francis, and my lady, John.

Lady Grace. And mine, pray Mr. Moody.

John Moody. Ay, your honours, they'll be proud on't, I dare say.

Man. I'll bring my compliments myself: so, honest John————

John Moody. Dear measter Manly! the goodness of goodness bless and preserve you.   [*Exit John Moody.*

Lord Town. What a natural creature 'tis!

Lady Grace. Well! I can't but think John, in a wet afternoon in the country, must be very good company.

Lord Town. O! the Tramontane! if this were known at half the Quadrille-tables in town, they would lay down their cards to laugh at you.

Lady Grace. And the minute they took them up again they would do the same at the losers————but to let you see, that I think good company may sometimes want cards to keep them together; what think you, if we three sat soberly down, to kill an hour at Ombre?

Man. I shall be too hard for you, madam.

Lady Grace. No matter: I shall have as much advantage of my lord, as you have of me.

Lord Town. Say you so, madam? have at you then! here I get the Ombre table, and cards.   [*Exit Lord Townly.*

Lady Grace. Come, Mr. Manly————I know you don't forgive me now!

Man. I don't know whether I ought to forgive your thinking so, madam. Where do you imagine I could pass my time so agreeable?

Lady Grace. I'm sorry my lord is not here to take his share of the compliment————but he'll wonder what's become of us!

Man. I'll follow in a moment, madam————
                                     [*Exit Lady Grace.*

It must be so————she sees I love her————yet with what unoffending decency she avoids an explanation? how amiable is every hour of her conduct? what a vile opinion have I had, of the whole sex, for these ten years past, which this sensible creature has recovered in less than one? such a companion, sure, might compensate all the irksome disappointments, that pride, folly, and falshood ever gave me!

Could women regulate, like her, their lives,
What Halcyon days were in the gift of wives!
Vain rovers, then, might envy what they hate;
And only fools would mock the married state.   [*Exit.*

ACT II. SCENE I.

Mrs. Motherly's *House.*

Enter Count Basset *and Mrs.* Motherly.

Count Baf. I TELL you there is not such a family in England for you! do you think I would have gone out of your lodgings, for any body, that was not sure to make you easy for the winter?

Moth. Nay, I see nothing against it, Sir, but the gentleman's being a parliament-man; and when people may, as it were, think one impertinent, or be out of humour, you know, when a body comes to ask for one's own——.

Count Baf. Pshah! pr'ythee never trouble thy head—His pay is as good as the bank!—Why, he has above two thousand a year!

Moth. Alas-a-day! that's nothing: Your people of ten thousand a year, have ten thousand things to do with it.

Count Baf. Nay, if you are afraid of being out of your money; what do you think of going a little with me, Mrs. Motherly?——

Moth. As how?

Count Baf. Why I have a game in my hand; in which, if you'll croup me, that is, help me to play it, you shall go five hundred to nothing.

Moth. Say you so?——why then, I go, Sir——and now pray let's see your game.

Count Baf. Look you in one word, my cards lie thus—when I was down this summer at York, I happen'd to lodge in the same house with this knight's lady, that's now coming to lodge with you.

Moth. Did you so, Sir?

Count Baf. And sometimes had the honour to breakfast, and pass an idle hour with her——.

Moth. Very good! and here I suppose you would have the impudence to sup, and be busy with her.

Count Baf. Pshah! pr'ythee hear me.

Moth. Is this your game? I would not give sixpence for it: what! you have a passion for her pin-money——no, no, country ladies are not so flush of it.

Count Baf. Nay, if you won't have patience——.

Moth. One had need to have a good deal, I am sure, to hear you talk at this rate! is this your way of making my poor niece Myrtilla easy?

Count Baf. Death! I shall do it still, if the woman will but let me speak——.

Moth. Had not you a letter from her this morning?

Count Baf. I have it here in my pocket——this is it.

[*Shews it and puts it up again.*

Moth. Ay, but I don't find you have made any answer to it.

Count

Count *Baf.* How the devil can I, if you won't hear me!

Moth. What! hear you talk of another woman?

Count *Baf.* O lud! O lud! I tell you, I'll make her fortune ——'ounds! I'll marry her.

Moth. A likely matter! if you would not do it when she was a maid, your stomach is not so sharp set now, I presume.

Count *Baf.* Hey day! why your head begins to turn, my dear: the devil! you did not think I propofed to marry her myself?

Moth. If you don't, who the devil do you think will marry her?

Count *Baf.* Why, a fool——

Moth. Humph! there may be sense in that——

Count *Baf.* Very good——one for t'other, then; if I can help her to a husband, why should not you come into my scheme of helping me to a wife?

Moth. Your pardon, Sir! ay! ay! in an honourable affair, you know you may command me——but pray where is this blessed wife and husband to be had?

Count *Baf.* Now have a little patience——you must know then, this country knight, and his lady, bring up, in the coach with them, their eldest son and a daughter, to teach them to ——wash their faces, and turn their toes out.

Moth. Good!

Count *Baf.* The son is an unlick'd whelp, about sixteen, just taken from school; and begins to hanker after every wench in the family: the daughter, much of the same age, a pert, forward hussy, who having eight thousand pounds left her by an old doting grandmother, seems to have a devilish mind to be doing in her way too.

Moth. And your design is, to put her into business for life?

Count *Baf.* Look you; in short, Mrs. Motherly, we gentlemen, whose occasional chariots roll, only, upon the four aces, are liable sometimes, you know, to have a wheel out of order: which, I confess, is so much my case at present, that my dapple grays are reduc'd to a pair of ambling chairmen: now, if with your assistance I can whip up this young jade into a hackney-coach, I may chance, in a day or two after, to carry her in my own chariot, *en famille*, to an opera. Now what do you say to me?

Moth. Why, I shall not sleep——for thinking of it. But how will you prevent the family's smoaking your design?

Count *Baf.* By renewing my addresses to the mother.

Moth. And how will the daughter like that, think you?

Count *Baf.* Very well——whilst it covers her own affair.

Moth. That's true——it must do——but, as you say, one for t'other, Sir, I stick to that——if you don't do my niece's business with the son, I'll blow you with the daughter, depend upon't.

Count *Baf.* It's a bet—pay as we go, I tell you, and the five hundred shall be stak'd in a third hand.

Moth. That's honest——but here comes my niece! shall we let her into the secret?   Count.

Count Baf. Time enough! may be, I may touch upon it.

Enter Myrtilla.

Moth. So, niece, are all the rooms done out, and the beds fheeted?

Myr. Yes, madam, but Mr. Moody tells us the lady always burns wax, in her own chamber, and we have none in the houfe.

Moth. Odfo! then I muft beg your pardon, count; this is a bufy time you know. [*Exit Mrs.* Motherly.

Count Baf. Myrtilla! how doft thou do, child?

Myr. As well as a lufing gamefter can.

Count Baf. Why, what have you loft?

Myr. What I fhall never recover; and what's worfe, you that have won it, don't feem to be much the better for't.

Count Baf. Why child, doft thou ever fee any body over-joyed for winning a deep ftake, fix months after 'tis over?

Myr. Would I had never played for it!

Count Baf. Pfhah! hang thefe melancholy thoughts! we may be friends ftill.

Myr. Dull ones.

Count Baf. Ufeful ones, perhaps —— fuppofe I fhould help thee to a good hufband?

Myr. I fuppofe you'll think any one good enough, that will take me off o'your hands.

Count Baf. What do you think of the young country 'fquire, the heir of the family, that's coming to lodge here?

Myr. How fhould I know what to think of him?

Count Baf. Nay, I only give you the hint, child; it may be worth your while, at leaft, to look about you—hark! what buftle's that without?

Enter Mrs. Motherly *in hafte.*

Moth. Sir! Sir! the gentleman's coach is at the door: they are all come!

Count Baf. What, already?

Moth. They are juft getting out!——won't you ftep and lead in my lady? do you be in the way, niece! I muft run and receive them. [*Exit Mrs.* Motherly.

Count Baf. And think of what I told you. [*Exit* Count.

Myr. Ay! ay! you have left me enough to think of, as long as I live——a faithlefs fellow! I am fure, I have been true to him; and for that only reafon, he wants to be rid of me: but while women are weak, men will be rogues.

Mrs. Motherly *returns, fhewing in Lady* Wronghead, *led by* Count Baffet.

Moth. If your ladyfhip pleafes to walk into this parlour, madam, only for the prefent, till your fervants have got all your things in.

Lady Wrong. Well! dear Sir, this is fo infinitely obliging!—I proteft it gives me pain tho', to turn you out of your lodging thus!

Count Baf. No trouble in the leaft, madam; we fingle fellows are

are foon moved ; befides, Mrs. Motherly's my old acquaintance and I could not be her hindrance.

Moth. The count is fo well bred, madam, I dare fay he would do a great deal more, to accommodate your ladyfhip.

Lady *Wrong.* O dear, madam !——A good well bred fort of a woman.   [*Apart to the Count*

Count *Baf.* O, madam, fhe is very much among people of quality, fhe is feldom without them in her houfe.

Lady *Wrong.* Are there a good many people of quality in this ftreet, Mrs. Motherly ?

Moth. Now your ladyfhip is here, madam, I don't believe there is a houfe without them.

Lady *Wrong.* I am mighty glad of that : for really I think people of quality fhould always live among one another.

Count *Baf.* 'Tis what one would choofe, indeed, madam.

Lady *Wrong.* Blefs me ! but where are the children all this while ?

Moth. Sir Francis, madam, I believe, is taking care of them.

Sir *Fran.* [*Within.*] John Moody ! ftay you by the coach, and fee all our things out——Come, children.

Moth. Here they are, madam.

Enter Sir Francis, *Squire* Richard, *and Mifs* Jenny.

Sir *Fran.* Well, Count ! I mun fay it, this was koynd, indeed !

Count *Baf.* Sir Francis ! give me leave to bid you welcome to London.

Sir *Fran.* Pfhah ! how doft do, mon ?——Waunds, I'm glad to'fee thee ! A good fort of a houfe this !

Count *Baf.* Is not that mafter Richard ?

Sir *Fran.* Ey ! Ey ! that's young hopeful——why do'ft not baw, Dick ?

Squ. Rich. So I do, feyther.

Count *Baf.* Sir, I'm glad to fee you ——— I proteft Mrs. Jane is grown fo, I fhould not have known her.

Sir *Fran.* Come forward, Jenny !

Jenny. Sure, papa, do you think I don't know how to behave myfelf ?

Count *Baf.* If I have permiffion to approach her, Sir Francis.

Jenny. Lord, Sir, I'm in fuch a frightful pickle —— [*Salute.*

Count *Baf.* Every drefs that's proper muft become you, madam,——you have been a long journey.

Jenny. I hope you will fee me in a better, to-morrow, Sir.

[Lady Wrong. *whifpers* Mrs. Moth. *pointing to* Myrtilla.

Moth. Only a niece of mine, madam, that lives with me : fhe will be proud to give your ladyfhip any affiftance in her power.

Lady *Wrong.* A pretty fort of a young woman——Jenny, you two muft be acquainted.

Jenny. O, mamma ! I am never ftrange, in a ftrange place !

                    [*Salutes* Myrtilla.
                                        Myr.

Myr. You do me a great deal of honour, madam——Madam, our ladyship's welcome to London.

Jenny. Mamma! I like her prodigioufly! fhe call'd me my idyfhip.

Squ. Rich. Pray mother, mayn't I be acquainted with her too?

Lady Wrong. You! you clown! ftay 'till you learn a little iore breeding firft.

Sir Fran. Od's heart! my lady Wronghead! why do you baïk fe lad? how fhould he ever learn breeding, if he does not put imfelf forward?

Squ. Rich. Why ay, feyther, does mother think 'at I'd be un-ivil to her?

Myr. Mafter has fo much good humour, madam, he would oon gain upon any body. [*He kiffes* Myr.

Squ. Rich. Lo' you there, mother: an you would but be quiet, fhe and I fhould do well enough.

Lady Wrong. Why, how now, firrah! boys muft not be fo amiliar.

Squ. Rich. Why, an' I know no-body, haw the murrain mun pafs my time here, in a ftrange place? Naw you and I, and ifter, forfooth, fometimes, in an afternoon, may play at one and hirty bone-ace, purely.

Jenny. Speak for yourfelf, Sir! D'ye think I play at fuch lownifh games?

Squ. Rich. Why and you woant yo' ma' let it aloane; then he, and I, mayhap, will have a bawt at all-fours, without you.

Sir Fran. Noa! noa! Dick, that won't do neither; you mun earn to make one at ombre, here, child.

Myr. If mafter pleafes, I'll fhew it him.

Squ. Rich. What! the Humber! hey day! why, does our iver run to this tawn, feyther?

Sir Fran. Pooh! you filly tony! ombre is a geam at cards, hat the better fort of people play three together at.

Squ. Rich. Nay the moare the merrier, I fay; but fifter is ilways fo crofs-grain'd——

Jenny. Lord! this boy is enough to deaf people——and one ias really been ftuft up in a coach fo long, that——pray, ma-lam——could not I got a little powder for my hair?

Myr. If you pleafe to come along with me, madam.

[*Exeunt* Myr. *and* Jenny.

Squ. Rich. What has fifter taken her away naw! mefs, I'll o and have a little game with 'em. [*Ex. after them.*

Lady Wrong. Well, count, I hope you won't fo far change our lodgings, but you will come, and be at home here fome-imes?

Sir Fran. Ay! ay! pr'ythee come and take a bit of mutton rith us, naw and tan, when thouh'ft nawght to do.

Count Baf. Well, Sir Francis, you fhall find I'll make but ery little ceremony.

Sir Fran. Why ay naw, that's hearty!

Moth. Will your ladyſhip pleaſe to refreſh yourſelf, with a diſh of tea, after your fatigue ? I think I have pretty good.

Lady *Wrong.* If you pleaſe, Mrs. Motherly ; but I believe we had beſt have it above ſtairs.

Moth. Very well, madam : it ſhall be ready immediately.
[*Exit* Mrs. Motherly.

Lady *Wrong.* Won't you walk up, Sir ?

Sir *Fran.* Moody !

Count *Baſ.* Shan't we ſtay for Sir Francis, madam ?

Lady *Wrong.* Lard ! don't mind him ! he will come if he likes it.

Sir *Fran.* Ay ! ay ! ne'er heed me——I ha' things to look after. [*Exeunt Lady* Wrong. *and Count* Baſ.
Enter John Moody.

John Moody. Did your worſhip want muh ?

Sir *Fran.* Ay, is the coach clear'd ? and all our things in ?

John Moody. Aw but a few band-boxes, and the nook that's left o'the gooſe poy——but a plague on him, th' monkey has gin us the flip, I think——I ſuppoſe he's goon to ſee his relations ; for here looks to be a power of 'um in this tawn.——but heavy Ralph is ſkawer'd after him.

Sir *Fran.* Why, let him go to the devil ! no matter, and the hawnds had had him a month agoe——but I wiſh the coach and horſes were got ſafe to th' inn : this is a ſharp tawn, we mun look about us here, John ; therefore I would have you go along with Roger, and ſee that nobody runs away with them before they get to the ſtable.

John Moody. Alas-a-day, Sir, I believe our awld cattle won't yeaſily be run away with to-night——but howſomdever, we'ſt ta' the beſt care we can of 'um, poor ſawls.

Sir *Fran.* Well, well ! make haſte then——
[*Moody goes out, and returns.*

John Moody. Ods fleſh ! here's maſter Monly come to wait upo' your worſhip !

Sir *Fran.* Wheere is he ?

John Moody. Juſt coming in at threſhould.

Sir *Fran.* Then goa about your buſineſs. [*Ex.* Moody.
Enter Manly.

Couſin Manly ! Sir, I am your very humble ſervant.

Man. I heard you were come, Sir Francis—and—

Sir *Fran.* Odſheart ! this was ſo kindly done of you naw.

Man. I wiſh you may think it ſo, couſin : for, I confeſs, I ſhould have been better pleas'd to have ſeen you in any other place.

Sir *Fran.* How ſoa, Sir ?

Man. Nay, 'tis for your own ſake : I'm not concern'd.

Sir *Fran.* Look you, couſin : thof' I know you wiſh me well ; yet I don't queſtion I ſhall give you ſuch weighty reaſons for what I have done, that you will ſay, Sir, this is the wiſeſt journey that ever I made in my life.

Man.

Man. I think it ought to be, coufin ; for I believe you will find it the moft expenfive one—your election did not coft you a trifle, I fuppofe.

Sir Fran. Why ay ! it's true ! that—that did lick a little ; but if a man's wife, (and I han't fawn'd yet that I'm a fool) there are ways, coufin, to lick one's felf whole again.

Man. Nay if you have that fecret——

Sir Fran. Don't you be fearful, coufin——you'll find that I knows fomething.

Man. If it be any thing for your good, I fhould be glad to know it too.

Sir Fran. In fhort, then, I have a friend in a corner, that has let me a little into what's what, at Weftminfter——that's one, thing.

Man. Very well ! but what good is that to do you ?

Sir Fram. Why not me, as much as it does other folks ?

Man. Other people, I doubt, have the advantage of different qualifications.

Sir Fran. Why ay ! there's it naw ! you'll fay that I have lived all my days i'the country——what then——I'm o'the Quorum——I have been at feffions, and I have made fpeeches there ! ay, and at veftry too——and mayhap they may find here, ——that I have brought my tongue up to town with me ! D'ye take me, naw ?

Man. If I take your cafe right, coufin, I am afraid the firft occafion you will have for your eloquence here, will be, to fhew that you have any right to make ufe of it at all.

Sir Fran. How d'ye mean ?

Man. That Sir John Worthland has lodg'd a petition againft you.

Sir Fran. Petition ! why ay ! there let it lie—— we'll find a way to deal with that, I warrant you !—— why, you forget, coufin, Sir John's o'the wrung fide, mon !

Man. I doubt, Sir Francis, that will do you but little fervice ; for in cafes very notorious (which I take yours to be) there is fuch a thing as a fhort day, and difpatching them immediately.

Sir Fran. With all my heart ! the fooner I fend him home again, the better.

Man. And this is the fcheme you have laid down to repair your fortune ?

Sir Fran. In one word, coufin, I think it my duty ! the Wrongheads have been a confiderable family, ever fince Eng-land was England; and fince the world knows I have talents where-withal ; they fhan't fay it's my fault, if I don't make as good a figure as any that ever were at the head on't.

Man. Nay ! this project, as you have laid it, will come up to any thing your anceftors have done thefe five hundred years.

Sir Fran. And let me alone to work it : mayhap I havn't told you all, neither——

Man. You aftonifh me ! what ! and is it full as practicable as what you have told me ?

C   Sir

Sir Fran. Ay, thof' I fay it——every whit, coufin! you'll find that I have more irons i'the fire than one; I doan't come of a fool's errand!

Man. Very well.

Sir Fran. In a word, my wife has got a friend at court, as well as myfelf, and her dowghter Jenny is naw pretty well grown up——

Man. [*Afide.*]——And what in the devil's name would he do with the dowdy?

Sir Fran. Naw, if I doan't lay in for a hufband for her, may-hap, i'this tawn, fhe may be looking out for herfelf——

Man. Not unlikely.

Sir Fran. Therefore I have fome thoughts of getting her to be maid of honour.

Man. [*Afide.*] Oh! he has taken my breath away! but I muft hear him out——Pray, Sir Francis, do you think her edu-cation has yet qualified her for a court?

Sir Fran. Why, the girl is a little too mettlefome, it's true! but fhe has tongue enough: fhe wean't be dafh't! Then fhe fhall learn to daunce forthwith, and that will foon teach her how to ftond ftill, you know.

Man. Very well; but when fhe is thus accomplifht, you muft ftill wait for a vacancy.

Sir Fran. Why I hope one has a good chance for that every day, coufin! For if I take it right, that's a poft, that folks are not more willing to get into, than they are to get out of—It's like an orange-tree, upon that accawnt—it will bear bloffoms, and fruit that's ready to drop, at the fame time.

Man. Well, Sir, you beft know how to make good your pre-tenfions! But pray where is my lady, and my young coufins? I fhould be glad to fee them too.

Sir Fran. She is but juft taking a difh of tea with the count, and my landlady—I'll call her dawn.

Man. No, no, if fhe's engag'd, I fhall call again.

Sir Fran. Odfheart! but you mun fee her naw, coufin: what! the beft friend I have in the world!——here! fweetheart! [*To a Servant without*] pr'ythee defire my lady and the gentle-man to come dawn a bit; tell her here's coufin Manly come to wait upon her.

Man. Pray, Sir, who may the gentleman be?

Sir Fran. You mun know him to be fure; why it's count Baffet.

Man. Oh! is it he?—your family will be infinitely happy in his acquaintance.

Sir Fran. Troth! I think fo too: he's the civileft man that ever I knew in my life——why! here he would go out of his own lodgings, at an hour's warning, purely to oblige my family. Wafn't that kind, naw?

Man. Extremely civil——the family is in admirable hands already!

Sir *Fran.* Then my lady likes him hugely—all the time of York races, she would never be without him.

Man. That was happy indeed! and a prudent man, you know, should always take care that his wife may have innocent company.

Sir *Fran.* Why ay! that's it! and I think there could not be such another!

Man. Why truly, for her purpose, I think not.

Sir *Fran.* Only naw and tan, he—he stonds a leetle too much upon ceremony; that's his fault.

Man. O never fear! he'll mend that every day—Mercy on us! what a head he has! [*Afide.*

Sir *Fran.* So! here they come!

Enter Lady Wronghead, *Count* Baffet, *and Mrs.* Motherly.

Lady *Wrong.* Coufin Manly! this is infinitely obliging! I am extremely glad to fee you.

Man. Your moft obedient fervant, madam; I am glad to fee your ladyfhip look fo well, after your journey.

Lady *Wrong.* Why really! coming to London is apt to put a little more life in one's looks.

Man. Yet the way of living here, is very apt to deaden the complexion——and give me leave to tell you, as a friend, madam, you are come to the worst place in the world, for a good woman to grow better in.

Lady *Wrong.* Lord, coufin! how fhould people ever make any figure in life, that are always moap'd up in the country?

Count *Baf.* Your ladyfhip certainly takes the thing in a quite right light, madam: Mr. Manly, your humble fervant——a hem.

Man. Familiar puppy. [*Afide.*] Sir, your moft obedient ——I muft be civil to the rafcal, to cover my fufpicion of him. [*Afide.*

Count *Baf.* Was you at White's this morning, Sir?

Man. Yes, Sir, I juft call'd in.

Count *Baf.* Pray—what—was there any thing done there?

Man. Much as ufual, Sir; the fame daily carcafes, and the fame crows about them.

Count *Baf.* The Demoivre-baronet had a bloody tumble yefterday.

Man. I hope, Sir, you had your fhare of him.

Count *Baf.* No, faith! I came in when it was all over——I think I juft made a couple of bets with him, took up a cool hundred, and fo went to the King's Arms.

Lady *Wrong.* What a genteel, eafy manner he has! [*Afide.*

Man. A very hopeful acquaintance I have made here. [*Afide.*

Enter Squire Richard, *with a wet brown Paper on his Face.*

Sir *Fran.* How naw, Dick! what's the matter with thy forehead, lad?

Squ. *Rich.* I ha' gotten a knuck upon't.

Lady *Wrong.* And how did you come by it, you heedlefs creature?

Squ.

Squ. Rich. Why, I was but running after fister, and t'other
young woman, into a little room just naw: and so with that,
they clapt the door full in my face, and gave me such a whurr
here—— I thought they had beaten my brains out! so I gut a
dab of wet brown paper here, to swage it a while.

Lady Wrong. They serv'd you right enough! will you never
have done with your horse-play?

Sir Fran. Pooh never heed it, lad! it will be well by to-morrow——the boy has a strong head!

Man. Yes, truly, his scull seems to be of a comfortable thick-
ness.   [*Aside.*

Sir Fran. Come, Dick, here's cousin Manly——Sir, this is
your god-son.

Lady Wrong. Oh! here's my daughter too.

Enter Miss Jenny.

Squ. Rich. Honour'd godfeyther! I crave leave to ask your
blessing.

Man. Thou hast it, child——and if it will do thee any good,
may it be to make thee, at least, as wise a man as thy father.

Lady Wrong. Miss Jenny! don't you see your cousin, child?

Man. And as for thee, my pretty dear——[*Salutes her.*] may'st
thou be, at least, as good a woman as thy mother.

Jenny. I wish I may ever be so handsome, Sir.

Man. Hah! Miss Pert! Now that's a thought, that seems to
have been hatcht in the girl on this side Highgate.   [*Aside.*

Sir Fran. Her tongue is a little nimble, Sir.

Lady Wrong. That's only from her country education, Sir
Francis. You know she has been kept too long there——so I
brought her to London, Sir, to learn a little more reserve and
modesty.

Man. O, the best place in the world for it—every woman she
meets will teach her something of it——There's the good gentlewoman of the house, looks like a knowing person; even she perhaps will be so good as to shew her a little London behaviour.

Moth. Alas! Sir, Miss won't stand long in need of my instructions.

Man. That I dare say: What thou can't teach her, she will
soon be mistress of.   [*Aside.*

Moth. If she does, Sir, they shall always be at her service.

Lady Wrong. Very obliging indeed, Mrs. Motherly.

Sir Fran. Very kind and civil truly—I think we are got into a
mighty good hawse here.

Man. O yes, and very friendly company.

Count Bas. Humph! I'gad I don't like his looks—he seems a
little smoky——I believe I had as good brush off——If I stay, I
don't know but he may ask me some odd questions.   [*Aside.*

Man. Well, Sir, I believe you and I do but hinder the family——

Count Bas. It's very true, Sir—I was just thinking of going—
He don't care to leave me, I see: but it's no matter, we have

time enough. [*Aside.*] And so, ladies, without ceremony, your humble servant. [*Exit* Count Basset, *and drops a letter.*

Lady Wrong. Ha! what paper's this? Some billet-doux I'll lay my life, but this is no place to examine it. [*Puts it in her pocket.*

Sir Fran. Why in such haste, cousin?

Man. O! my Lady must have a great many affairs upon her hands, after such a journey.

Lady Wrong. I believe, Sir, I shall not have much less every day, while I stay in this town, of one sort or other.

Man. Why truly, ladies seldom want employment here, madam.

Jenny. And mamma did not come to it to be idle, Sir.

Man. Nor you neither, I dare say, my young mistress.

Jenny. I hope not, Sir.

Man. Ha! Miss Mettle!——Where are you going, Sir?

Sir Fran. Only to see you to the door, Sir.

Man. Oh! Sir Francis, I love to come and go, without ceremony.

Sir Fran. Nay, Sir, I must do as you will have me—your humble servant. [*Exit* Manly.

Jenny. This cousin Manly, pappa, seems to be but of an odd sort of a crusty humour——I don't like him half so well as the count.

Sir Fran. Pooh! that's another thing, child——Cousin is a little proud, indeed! but, however, you must always be civil to him, for he has a deal of money; and no-body knows who he may give it to.

Lady Wrong. Pshah; a fig for his money, you have so many projects of late about money, since you are a parliament man: What! we must make ourselves slaves to his impertinent humours, eight or ten years perhaps, in hopes to be his heirs, and then he will be just old enough to marry his maid.

Moth. Nay, for that matter, madam, the town says he is going to be married already.

Sir Fran. Who? Cousin Manly?

Lady Wrong. To whom, pray?

Moth. Why, is it possible your ladyship should know nothing of it!——to my Lord Townly's sister, Lady Grace.

Lady Wrong. Lady Grace!

Moth. Dear Madam, it has been in the News-Papers!

Lady Wrong. I don't like that neither.

Sir Fran. Now, I do; for then it's likely it mayn't be true.

Lady Wrong. [*Aside.*] If it is not too far gone, at least it may be worth one's while to throw a rub in his way.

Squ. Rich. Pray, feyther, haw long will it be to supper?

Sir Fran. Odso! that's true! step to the cook, lad, and ask what she can get us.

Moth. If you please, Sir, I'll order one of my maids to shew her where she may have any thing you have a mind to.

Sir Fran. Thank you kindly, Mrs. Motherly.

C 3   Squ.

Squ. Rich. Ods-fleſh! what is not it i'the hawſe yet——I ſhall be famiſht——but hawld! I'll go and aſk Doll, an ther's none o'the gooſe-poy left.

Sir Fran. Do ſo, and do'ſt hear, Dick——ſee if ther's e'er a bottle o'the ſtrong beer that came i'th' coach with us——if there be, clap a toaſt in it, and bring it up.

Squ. Rich. With a little nutmeg and ſugar, ſhawn't I, feyther?

Sir Fran. Ay! ay! as thee and I always drink it for breakfaſt—Go thy ways!—and I'll fill a pipe i'the mean while. [*Takes one from a pocket-caſe, and fills it.*]   [*Exit Squ.* Rich.

Lady Wrong. This boy is always thinking of his belly!

Sir Fran. Why, my dear, you may allow him to be a little hungry after his journey.

Lady Wrong. Nay, ev'n breed him your own way—He has been cramming in or out of the coach all this day, I am ſure——I wiſh my poor girl could eat a quarter as much.

Jenny. O as for that I could eat a great deal more, mamma; but then, mayhap, I ſhould grow coarſe, like him, and ſpoil my ſhape.

Lady Wrong. Ay, ſo thou would'ſt, my dear.

Enter Squire Richard *with a full tankard.*

Squ. Rich. Here, feyther, I ha' browght it—it's well I went as I did; for our Doll had juſt bak'd a toaſt, and was going to drink it herſelf.

Sir Fran. Why then, here's to thee, Dick!   [*Drinks.*

Squ. Rich. Thonk yow, feyther.

Lady Wrong. Lord! Sir Francis! I wonder you can encourage the boy to ſwill ſo much of that lubberly liquor——it's enough to make him quite ſtupid.

Squ. Rich. Why it never hurts me, mother; and I ſleep like a hawnd after it.   [*Drinkt.*

Sir Fran. I am ſure I ha' drunk it theſe thirty years, and by your leave, madam, I don't know that I want wit: ha! ha!

Jenny. But you might have had a great deal more, papa, if you would have been governed by my mother.

Sir Fran. Daughter, he that is governed by his wife, has no wit at all.

Jenny. Then I hope I ſhall marry a fool, Sir; for I love to govern dearly.

Sir Fran. You are too pert, child; it don't do well in a young woman.

Lady Wrong. Pray, Sir Francis, don't ſnub her! ſhe has a fine growing ſpirit, and if you check her ſo, you will make her as dull as her brother there.

Squ. Rich. [*After a long draught.*] Indeed, mother, I think my ſiſter is too forward.

Jenny. You—you think I'm too forward! ſure! brother mud! your head's too heavy to think of any thing but your belly.

Lady Wrong. Well ſaid, Miſs, he's none of your maſter,

Squ. Rich. No, nor the fhawn't be my miftrefs, while fhe's younger fifter.

Sir Fran. Well faid, Dick! fhew 'em that ftawt liquor makes a ftawt heart, lad!

Squ. Rich. So I will! and I'll drink ageen, for all her! [*Drinks.*

Enter John Moody.

Sir Fran. So John! how are the horfes?

John Moody. Troth, Sir, I ha' noa good opinion o' this tawn, it's made up o' mifchief, I think!

Sir Fran. What's the matter naw?

John Moody. Why I'll tell your worfhip——before we were gotten to th' ftreet end, with the coach, here, a great lugger-headed cart with wheels as thick ay a brick wall, laid hawld on't, and has poo'd it aw to bits; crack! went the perch! down goes the coach! and whang fays the glaffes, all to fhievers! marcy upon us! and this be London! would we were aw weell in the country ageen!

Jenny. What have you to do, to wifh us all in the country again, Mr. Lubber? I hope we fhall not go into the country again thefe feven years, mamma; let twenty coaches be pull'd to pieces.

Sir Fran. Hold your tongue, Jenny!——was Roger in no fault in all this?

John Moody. Noa, Sir, nor I, noather, are not yow afham'd, fays Roger to the carter, to do fuch an unkind thing by ftrangers? noa, fays he, you bumkin. Sir, he did the thing on very purpofe! and fo the folks faid that ftood by—very well, fays Roger, yow fhall fee what our meyfter will fay to ye! Your meyfter, fays he; your meyfter may kifs my—and fo he clapp'd his hand juft there, and like your worfhip. Fleth! I thought they had better breeding in this tawn.

Sir Fran. I'll teach this rafcal fome, I'll warrant him! Odfbud! if I take him in hand, I'll play the devil with him.

Squ. Rich. Ay, do, feyther; have him before the parliament.

Sir Fran. Odfbud! and fo I will——I will make him know who I am! Where does he live?

John Moody. I believe in London, Sir.

Sir Fran. What's the rafcal's name?

John Moody. I think I heard fomebody call him Dick.

Squ. Rich. What, my name!

Sir Fran. Where did he go?

John Moody. Sir, he went home.

Sir Fran. Where's that?

John Moody. By my troth, Sir, I doan't know! I heard him fay he would crofs the fame ftreet again to-morrow; and if we had a mind to ftand in his way, he wou'd pooll us over and over again.

Sir Fran. Will he fo? Odfzooks! get me a conftable.

Lady Wrong. Pooh! get you a good fupper. Come, Sir Francis, don't put yourfelf in a heat for what can't be helpt. Accidents

will

will happen to people that travel abroad to fee the world——For my part, I think it's a mercy it was not over-turn'd before we were all out on't.

Sir Fran. Why, ay, that's true again, my dear.

Lady Wrong. Therefore fee to-morrow if we can buy one at fecond hand, for prefent ufe; to befpeak a new one, and then all's eafy.

John Moody. Why troth, Sir, I doan't think this could have held you above a day longer.

Sir Fran. Dye think fo, John?

John Moody. Why you ha' had it, ever fince your worfhip were high fheriff.

Sir Fran. Why then go and fee what Doll has got us for fupper——and come and get off my boots.   [*Exit Sir* Fran.

Lady Wrong. In the mean time, Mifs, do you ftep to Handy, and bid her get me-fome frefh night-clothes.

[*Exit Lady* Wrong.

Jenny. Yes, mamma, and fome for myfelf too. [*Exit* Jenny.

Squ. Rich. Odsflefh! and what mun I do all alone?
I'll e'en feek out where t'other pratty Mifs is,
And fhe and I'll go and play at cards for kiffes.   [*Exit.*

ACT III. SCENE. I.

SCENE, *the Lord* Townly's *Houfe.*

Enter Lord Townly, *a Servant attending.*

Lord Town. WHO's there?

Serv. My Lord.

Lord Town. Bid them get dinner ——Lady Grace, your fervant.

Enter Lady Grace.

Lady Grace. What, is the houfe up already? My lady is not dreft yet!

Lord Town. No matter—it's three o'clock—fhe may break my reft, but fhe fhall not alter my hours.

Lady Grace. Nay you need not fear that now, for fhe dines abroad.

Lord Town. That, I fuppofe, is only an excufe for her not being ready yet.

Lady Grace. No, upon my word, fhe is engaged in company.

Lord Town. Where, pray?

Lady Grace. At my lady Revel's; and you know they never dine 'till fupper-time.

Lord Town. No truly —— fhe is one of thofe orderly ladies, who never let the fun fhine upon any of their vices! ——But pr'ythee, fifter, what humour is fhe in to-day?

Lady

Lady Grace. O! in tip-top spirits, I can assure you——she won a good deal last night.

Lord Town. I know no difference between her winning or losing, while she continues her course of life.

Lady Grace. However, she is better in good humour than bad.

Lord Town. Much alike: when she is in good humour, other people only are the better for it: when in a very ill humour, then, indeed, I seldom fail to have my share of her.

Lady Grace. Well, we won't talk of that now——Does any body dine here?

Lord Town. Manly promis'd me—by the way, madam, what do you think of his last conversation?

Lady Grace.——I am a little at a stand about it.

Lord Town. How so?

Lady Grace. Why——I don't know how he can ever have any thoughts of me, that could lay down such severe rules upon wives, in my hearing.

Lord Town. Did you think his rules unreasonable?

Lady Grace. I can't say I did: but he might have had a little more complaisance before me, at least.

Lord Town. Complaisance is only a proof of good breeding: but his plainness was a certain proof of his honesty; nay, of his good opinion of you: for he would never have open'd himself so freely, but in confidence that your good sense could not be disobliged at it.

Lady Grace. My good opinion of him, brother, has hitherto been guided by yours: but I have receiv'd a letter this morning that shews him a very different man from what I thought him.

Lord Town. A letter from whom?

Lady Grace. That I don't know, but there it is.

[*Gives a letter.*

Lord Town. Pray let's see.   [*Reads.*

The inclos'd, madam, fell accidentally into my hands; if it no way concerns you, you will only have the trouble of reading this, from your sincere friend and humble servant, Unknown, &c.

Lady Grace. And this was the inclos'd.   [*Giving another.*

Lord Town. [*Reads.*] *To Charles Manly, Esq;*

Your manner of living with me of late, convinces me, that I now grow as painful to you, as to myself: but, however, though you can love me no longer, I hope you will not let me live worse than I did before I left an honest income for the vain hopes of being ever yours,

Myrtilla Dupe.

P. S. *'Tis above four months since I receiv'd a shilling from you.*

Lady Grace. What think you now?

Lord Town. I am considering——

Lady Grace. You see it's directed to him——

Lord Town. That's true: but the postscript seems to be a reproach, that I think he is not capable of deserving.

Lady Grace. But who could have concern enough, to send it

Lord

Lord Town. I have obferved that thefe fort of letters from unknown friends, generally come from fecret enemies.

Lady Grace. What would you have me do in it?

Lord Town. What I think you ought to do—fairly fhew it him, and fay I advis'd you to it.

Lady Grace. Will not that have a very odd look, from me?

Lord Town. Not at all, if you ufe my name in it; if he is innocent, his impatience to appear fo, will difcover his regard to you. If he is guilty, it will be your beft way of preventing his addreffes.

Lady Grace. But what pretence have I to put him out of countenance?

Lord Town. I can't think there's any fear of that.

Lady Grace. Pray what is it you think then?

Lord Town. Why certainly, that it's much more probable this letter may be all an artifice, than that he is in the leaft concerned in it——

Enter a Servant.

Serv. Mr. Manly, my lord.

Lord Town. Do you receive him; while I ftep a minute in, to my lady.   [*Exit* Lord Townly.

Enter Manly.

Man. Madam, your moft obedient; they told me, my lord was here.

Lady Grace. He will be here prefently; he is but juft gone in to my fifter.

Man. So! then my lady dines with us.

Lady Grace. No; fhe is engag'd.

Man. I hope you are not of her party, madam?

Lady Grace. Not till after dinner.

Man. And pray how may fhe have difpos'd of the reft of the day?

Lady Grace. Much as ufual! fhe has vifits 'till about eight; after that, 'till court-time, fhe is to be at quadrille, at Mrs. Idle's: after the drawing-room, fhe takes a fhort fupper with my lady Moonlight: and from thence, they go together to my lord Noble's affembly.

Man. And are you to do all this with her, madam?

Lady Grace. Only a few of the vifits; I would indeed have drawn her to the play; but I doubt we have fo much upon our hands, that it will not be practicable.

Man. But how can you forbear all the reft of it?

Lady Grace. There's no great merit in forbearing, what one is not charm'd with.

Man. And yet I have found that very difficult in my time.

Lady Grace. How do you mean?

Man. Why, I have pafs'd a great deal of my life in the hurry of the ladies, though I was generally better pleas'd when I was at quiet without 'em.

Lady Grace. What induc'd you, then, to be with them?

                                                        Man.

Man. Idleness, and the fashion.

Lady Grace. No mistresses in the case?

Man. To speak honestly——Yes——being often in the toy-shop, there was no forbearing the bawbles.

Lady Grace. And of course, I suppose sometimes you were tempted to pay for them twice as much as they were worth.

Man. Why really, where fancy only makes the choice, madam, no wonder if we are generally bubbled in those sort of bargains, which I confess has been often my case: for I had constantly some coquette, or other, upon my hands, whom I could love perhaps just enough, to put it in her power to plague me.

Lady Grace. And that's a pow'r, I doubt, commonly made use of.

Man. The amours of a coquette, madam, seldom have any other view! I look upon them, and prudes, to be nuisances, just alike; tho' they seem very different: the first are always plaguing the men; and the other are always abusing the women.

Lady Grace. And yet both of them do it for the same vain ends; to establish a false character of being virtuous.

Man. Of being chaste, they mean; for they know no other virtue: and, upon the credit of that, they traffick in every thing else, that's vicious: they (even against nature) keep their chastity, only because they find they have more power to do mischief with it, than they could possibly put in practice without it.

Lady Grace. Hold! Mr. Manly: I am afraid this severe opinion of the sex, is owing to the ill choice you have made of your mistresses.

Man. In a great measure it may be so; but, madam, if both these characters are so odious; how vastly valuable is that woman, who has attain'd all they aim at without the aid of the folly or vice of either!

Lady Grace. I believe those sort of women to be as scarce, Sir, as the men that believe there are any such; or that allowing such have virtue enough to deserve them.

Man. That could deserve them then——had been a more favourable reflection!

Lady Grace. Nay, I speak only from my little experience: for (I'll be free with you, Mr. Manly) I don't know a man in the world, that, in appearance, might better pretend to a woman of the first merit, than yourself: and yet I have a reason, in my hand, here, to think you have your failings.

Man. I have infinite, madam; but I am sure, the want of an implicit respect for you, is not among the number——pray what is in your hand, madam?

Lady Grace. Nay, Sir, I have no title to it; for the direction is to you.   [*Gives him a letter.*

Man. To me! I don't remember the hand——*Reads to himself.*

Lady Grace. I can't perceive any charge of guilt in him! and his surprise seems natural! [*Aside.*]——Give me leave to tell you one thing by the way, Mr. Manly; that I should never have shewn you this, but that my brother enjoin'd me to it.

Man. I take that to proceed from my lord's goo
me, madam.

Lady Grace. I hope, at leaſt, it will ſtand as a
my taking this liberty.

Man. I never yet ſaw you do any thing, madam
ted an excuſe ; and, I hope, you will net give me
to the contrary, by refuſing the favour I am going

Lady Grace. I don't believe I ſhall refuſe any, th
proper to aſk.

Man. Only this, madam; to indulge me ſo far,
know how this letter came into your hands.

Lady Grace. Inclos'd to me in this, without a n

Man. If there be no ſecret in the contents, mada

Lady Grace. Why——there is an impertinent i
it : . but as I know your good ſenſe will think it ſo
venture to truſt you.

Man. You'll oblige me, madam.

[*He takes the other lett*

Lady Grace. [*Aſide.*] Now am I in the oddeſt ſr
thinks our converſation grows terribly critical! Th
duce ſomething :———O lud l would it were ove

Man. Now, madam, I begin to have ſome light i
project, that is at the bottom of all this.

Lady Grace. I have no notion of what could be pr

Man. A little patience, madam———Firſt, as to th
you mention———

Lady Grace. O ! what is he going to ſay now l

Man. Tho' my intimacy with my lord may have
viſits to have been very frequent here of late ; yet
talking town as this, you muſt not wonder, if a g
thoſe viſits are plac'd to your account : and this taker
I ſuppoſe has been told to my lady Wronghead, a
news, ſince her arrival, not improbably without mar
aginary circumſtances.

Lady Grace. My lady Wronghead!

Man. Ay, madam, for I am poſitive this is her h

Lady Grace. What view could ſhe have in writin

Man. To interrupt any treaty of marriage, ſhe ma
I am engaged in : becauſe, if I die without heirs, he
pects that ſome part of my eſtate may return to them
I hope, ſhe is ſo far miſtaken, that if this letter ha
the leaſt uneaſineſs———I ſhall think that the happ
of my life.

Lady Grace. That does not carry your uſual c
Mr. Manly.

Man. Yes, madam, becauſe I am ſure I cannot c
of my innocence.

Lady Grace. I am ſure I have no right to inquire

Man. Suppoſe you may not, madam ; yet you ma
cently have ſo much curioſity.

With what an artful gentleness he steals in
[*Aside.*] Well, Sir, I won't pretend to have so
man in me, as to want curiosity——but pray do
then, this Myrtilla, is a real, or a fictitious

I recollect, madam, there is a young woman, in
re my lady Wronghead lodges, that I heard some-
illa: this letter may be written by her——but
rected to me, I confess is a mystery; that before
to see your ladyship again, I think myself obliged,
id out.   [*Going.*
Mr. Manly——you are not going?
ut to the next street, madam; I shall be back in

Nay! but dinner's just coming up.
m, I can neither eat, nor rest, till I see an end

But this is so odd! why should any silly curiosity
you away?
you won't suffer it to be yours, madam; then it
satisfy my own curiosity——[*Exit* Manly.
Well——and now, what am I to think of; all
se an indifferent person had heard every word we
e another, what would they have thought on't?
een very absurd to conclude, he is seriously in-
he rest of his life with me?——I hope not——
the case is terribly clear on my side! and why
ithout vanity, suppose my——unaccountable
has done as much execution upon him?——why—
er told me so—nay, he has not so much as men-
I love, or ever said one civil thing to my person—
as said a thousand to my good opinion, and has
——had he spoke first to my person, he had paid a
ment to my understanding—I should have thought
it, and never have troubled my head about him;
manag'd the matter, at least I am sure of one thing,
eights be what they will, I shall never trouble my
other man, as long as I live.
    Enter Mrs. Trusty.
usty, is my sister dress'd yet?
, madam; but my lord has been courting her so, I
y are both out of humour.
How so?   A
y, it began, madam, with his lordship's desiring her
e at home to-day——upon which my lady said she
ady; upon that, my lord ordered them to stay the
th my lady ordered the coach; then my lord took
said, he had order'd the coachman to set up; then
him a great curtesy, and said, she would wait 'till
orses had din'd; and was mighty pleasant; but for

D   feat

fear of the worst, madam, she whisper'd me —— to get her chair
ready. 　　　　　　　　　　　　　　　[*Exit* Trusty,

Lady *Grace.* O here they come; and, by their looks, seem a
little unfit for company. 　　　　　　　　[*Exit Lady* Grace.

　　　Enter Lady Townly, *Lord* Townly *following.*

Lady *Town.* Well! look you, my lord; I can bear it no
longer! nothing still but about my faults, my faults! an agreeable subject truly!

Lord *Town.* Why, madam, if you won't hear of them; how
can I ever hope to see you mend them?

Lady *Town.* Why, I don't intend to mend them—I can't mend
them——you know I have try'd to do it an hundred times, and
—it hurts me so—I can't bear it!

Lord *Town.* And I, madam, can't bear this daily licentious
abuse of your time and character.

Lady *Town.* Abuse! astonishing! when the universe knows,
I am never better company, than when I am doing what I have
a mind to! but to see this world! that men can never get over
that silly spirit of contradiction——why but last Thursday now,
——there you wisely amended one of my faults as you call them
——you insisted upon my not going to the masquerade——and
pray, what was the consequence! was not I as cross as the devil,
all the night after? was not I forc'd to get company at home?
and was not it almost three o'clock in the morning, before I
was able to come to myself again? and then the fault is not
mended neither,————for next time, I shall only have twice
the inclination to go: so that all this mending, and mending,
you see, is but dearning an old ruffle, to make it worse than it
was before.

Lord *Town.* Well, the manner of womens living, of late,
is unsupportable; and one way or other——

Lady *Town.* It's to be mended, I suppose! why so it may:
but then, my dear lord, you must give one time——and when
things are at worst, you know, they may mend themselves! ha!
ha!

Lord *Town.* Madam! I am not in a humour, now, to trifle.

Lady *Town.* Why then, my lord, one word of fair argument
—to talk with you, your own way now——you complain of
my late hours, and I of your early ones——so far are we even,
you'll allow——but pray which gives us the best figure in the
eye of the polite world? my active, spirited three in the morning, or your dull drowsy eleven at night? Now, I think, one
has the air of a woman of quality, and t'other of a plodding mechanic, that goes to bed betimes, that he may rise early, to open
his shop!—Faugh!

Lord *Town.* Fy, fy, madam! is this your way of reasoning?
'tis time to wake you then——'tis not your ill hours alone, that
disturb me, but as often the ill company, that occasion those ill
hours.

Lady *Town.* Sure I don't understand you now, my lord; what
ill company do I keep? 　　　　　　　　　　　　　Lord

Lord Town. Why, at best, women that lose their money, and men that win it! Or, perhaps, men that are voluntary bubbles at one game, in hopes a lady will give them fair play at another. Then that unavoidable mixture with known rakes, conceal'd thieves, and sharpers in embroidery——or what, to me, is still more shocking, that herd of familiar chattering crop-ear'd cox-combs, who are so often like monkeys, there would be no know-ing them asunder, but that their tails hang from their head, and the monkey's grows where it should do.

Lady Town. And a husband must give eminent proof of his sense, that thinks their powder-puffs dangerous.

Lord Town. Their being fools, madam, is not always the husband's security: or if it were, fortune, sometimes, gives them advantages might make a thinking woman tremble.

Lady Town. What do you mean?

Lord Town. That women, sometimes, lose more than they are able to pay; and if a creditor be a little pressing, the lady may be reduc'd to try if, instead of gold, the gentleman will accept of a trinket.

Lady Town. My lord, you grow scurrilous; you'll make me hate you. I'll have you to know, I keep company with the politest people in town, and the assemblies I frequent are full of such.

Lord Town. So are the churches——now and then.

Lady Town. My friends frequent them too, as well as the assemblies.

Lord Town. Yes, and would do it oftner, if a groom of the chambers were there allowed to furnish cards to the company.

Lady Town. I see what you drive at all this while; you would lay an imputation on my fame, to cover your own avarice! I might take any pleasures, I find, that were not expensive.

Lord Town. Have a care, madam; don't let me think you only value your chastity, to make me reproachable for not indulg-ing you in every thing else, that's vicious——I, madam, have a reputation too, to guard, that's dear to me, as yours——The follies of an ungovern'd wife may make the wisest man uneasy; but 'tis his own fault if ever they make him contemptible.

Lady Town. My lord——you would make a woman mad!

Lord Town. You'd make a man a fool.

Lady Town. If heav'n has made you otherwise, that won't be in my power.

Lord Town. Whatever may be in your inclination, madam; I'll prevent you making me a beggar at least.

Lady Town. A beggar! Croesus! I'm out of patience! I won't come home 'till four to-morrow morning.

Lord Town. That may be, madam; but I'll order the doors to be lock'd at twelve.

Lady Town. Then I won't come home 'till to-morrow night.

D 2 *Lord*

Lord Town. Then, madam;———you shall never come home again.   [*Exit Lord* Town.

Lady Town. What does he mean! I never heard such a word from him in my life before! the man always us'd to have manners in his worst humours! there's something, that I don't see, at the bottom of all this——but his head's always upon some impracticable scheme or other, so I won't trouble mine any longer about him. Mr. Manly, your servant.

Enter Manly.

Man. I ask pardon for intrusion, madam; but I hope my business with my lord will excuse it.

Lady Town. I believe you'll find him in the next room, Sir.

Man. Will you give me leave, madam?

Lady Town. Sir—you have my leave, tho' you were a lady.

Man. [*Aside.*] What a well-bred age do we live in!
                                                 [*Exit* Manly.

Enter Lady Grace.

Lady Town. O! my dear lady Grace! how could you leave me so unmercifully alone all this while?

Lady Grace. I thought my lord had been with you.

Lady Town. Why yes—and therefore I wanted your relief; for he has been in such a fluster here——

Lady Grace. Bless me! for what?

Lady Town. Only our usual breakfast; we have each of us had our dish of matrimonial comfort this morning! we have been charming company!

Lady Grace. I am mighty glad of it! sure it must be a vast happiness, when a man and a wife can give themselves the same turn of conversation!

Lady Town. O! the prettiest thing in the world!

Lady Grace. Now I should be afraid, that where two people are every day together so, they must often be in want of something to talk upon.

Lady Town. O my dear, you are the most mistaken in the world! married people have things to talk of, child, that never enter into the imagination of others.——Why, here's my lord and I now; we have not been married above two short years, you know, and we have already eight or ten things constantly in bank, that whenever we want company, we can take up any one of them for two hours together, and the subject never the flatter! nay, if we have occasion for it, it will be as fresh next day too, as it was the first hour it entertain'd us.

Lady Grace. Certainly that must be vastly pretty.

Lady Town. O! there's no life like it! why t'other day for example, when you din'd abroad; my lord and I, after a pretty chearful tête à tête meal, sat us down by the fire-side, in an easy, indolent, pick-tooth way, for about a quarter of an hour, as if we had not thought of any other's being in the room——at last, stretching himself and yawning——My dear, says he,—

a w

aw——you came home very late, laſt night——'Twas but juſt
turn'd of two, ſays I——I was in bed—aw——by eleven,
ſays he ; ſo you are every night, ſays I——Well, ſays he, I
am amaz'd you can ſit up ſo late——how can you be amaz'd,
ſays I, at a thing that happens ſo often ?——upon which we
enter'd into a converſation——and tho' this is a point has entertain'd us above fifty times already, we always find ſo many pretty
new things to ſay upon it, that I believe in my ſoul, it will laſt
as long as we live.

Lady *Grace.* But pray ! in ſuch ſort of family dialogues (tho'
extremely well for paſſing the time) don't there, now and then,
enter ſome little witty ſort of bitterneſs ?

Lady *Town.* O yes ! which does not do amiſs at all ! A ſmart
repartee, with a zeſt of recrimination at the head of it, makes the
prettieſt ſherbet ; ay, ay ! if we did not mix a little of the acid
with it, a matrimonial ſociety would be ſo luſcious, that nothing
but an old liquoriſh prude would be able to bear it.

Lady *Grace.* Well,——certainly you have the moſt elegant
taſte——

Lady *Town.* Tho' to tell you the truth, my dear, I rather
think we ſqueez'd a little too much lemon into it, this bout ; for
it grew ſo four at laſt, that—I think——I almoſt told him, he
was a fool——and he again——talk'd ſomething oddly of——
turning me out of doors.

Lady *Grace.* O ! have a care of that !

Lady *Town.* Nay, if he ſhould, I may thank my own wiſe
father for that——

Lady *Grace.* How ſo ?

Lady *Town.* Why——when my good lord firſt open'd his
honourable trenches before me, my unaccountable papa, in whoſe
hands I then was, gave me up at diſcretion.

Lady *Grace.* How do you mean ?

Lady *Town.* He ſaid, the wives of this age were come to that
paſs, that he would not deſire even his own daughter ſhould be
truſted with pin-money ; ſo that my whole train of ſeparate inclinations are left entirely at the mercy of an huſband's odd
humours

Lady *Grace.* Why, that, indeed, is enough to make a woman of ſpirit look about her !

Lady *Town.* Nay, but to be ſerious, my dear ; what would
you really have a woman do in my caſe ?

Lady *Grace.* Why——if I had a ſober huſband as you
have, I would make myſelf the happieſt wife in the world by
being as ſober as he.

Lady *Town.* O ! you wicked thing ! how can you teize one at this
rate ? when you know he is ſo very ſober, that (except giving me
money) there is not one thing in the world he can do to pleaſe me !
and I at the ſame time, partly by nature, and partly, perhaps, by
keeping the beſt company, do with my ſoul love almoſt every thing
he hates ! I dote upon aſſemblies ! my heart bounds at a ball ;

and at an opera——I expire! then I love play to diftraction! cards inchant me! and dice—put me out of my little wits! dear! dear bazard! oh! what a flow of fpirits it gives one! do you never play at hazard, child?

Lady *Grace.* Oh! never! I don't think it fits well upon women; there's fomething fo mafculine, fo much the air of a rake in it; you fee how it makes the men fwear and curfe! and when a woman is thrown into the fame paffion——why——

Lady *Town.* That's very true! one is a little put to it, fometimes, not to make ufe of the fame words to exprefs it.

Lady *Grace.* Well—and, upon ill luck, pray what words are you really forc'd to make ufe of?

Lady *Town.* Why upon a very hard cafe, indeed, when a fad wrong word is rifing, juft to one's tongue's end, I give a great gulp——and fwallow it.

Lady *Grace.* Well——and is not that enough to make you forfwear play, as long as you live?

Lady *Town.* O yes: I have forfworn it.

Lady *Grace.* Serioufly?

Lady *Town.* Solemnly! a thoufand times; but then one is conftantly forfworn.

Lady *Grace.* And how can you anfwer that?

Lady *Town.* My dear, what we fay, when we are lofers, we look upon to be no more binding than a lover's oath, or a great man's promife. But I beg pardon, child; I fhould not lead you fo far into the world; you are a prude, and defign to live foberly.

Lady *Grace.* Why, I confefs, my nature, and my education do, in a good degree, incline me that way.

Lady *Town.* Well! how a woman of fpirit (for you don't want that, child) can dream of living foberly, is to me inconceivable! for you will marry, I fuppofe.

Lady *Grace.* I can't tell but I may.

Lady *Town.* And won't you live in town?

Lady *Grace.* Half the year, I fhould like it very well.

Lady *Town.* My ftars! and you would really live in London half the year to be fober in it?

Lady *Grace.* Why not?

Lady *Town.* Why can't you as well go, and be fober in the country?

Lady *Grace.* So I would————t'other half year.

Lady *Town.* And pray, what comfortable fcheme of life would you form now, for your fummer and winter fober entertainments?

Lady *Grace.* A fcheme that I think might very well content us.

Lady *Town.* O! of all things let us hear it.

Lady *Grace.* Why, in fummer, I could pafs my leifure hours in riding, in reading, walking by a canal, or fitting at the end of it under a great tree; in dreffing, dining, chatting with an agreeable friend; perhaps, hearing a little mufic, taking a difh of tea, or a game of cards, foberly! managing my family, looking

ing

ng into its accounts, playing with my children (if I had any)
or in a thousand other innocent amusements————soberly!
and possibly, by these means, I might induce my husband to be
as sober as myself.——

Lady *Town.* Well, my dear, thou art an astonishing creature!
for sure such primitive antediluvian notions of life, have not been
in any head these thousand years————under a great tree! O' my
soul!————but I beg we may have the sober town-scheme too——
for I am charm'd with the country one!————

Lady *Grace.* You shall, and I'll try to stick to my sobriety
there too.

Lady *Town.* Well, tho' I'm sure it will give me the vapours,
I must hear it however.

Lady *Grace.* Why then, for fear of your fainting, madam,
I will first so far come into the fashion, that I would never be
dress'd out of it————but still it should be soberly. For I can't
think it any disgrace to a woman of my private fortune, not to
wear her lace as fine as the wedding-suit of a first duchess. Tho'
there is one extravagance I would venture to come up to.

Lady *Town.* Ay now for it——

Lady *Grace.* I would every day be as clean as a bride.

Lady *Town.* Why the men say, that's a great step to be made
one——Well now you are drest—pray let's see to what purpose?

Lady *Grace.* I would visit—that is, my real friends; but as
little for form as possible.————I would go to court; sometimes
to an assembly, nay, play at quadrille—soberly: I would see all
the good plays; and, (because 'tis the fashion) now and then an
opera—but I would not expire there, for fear I should never go
again: and lastly, I can't say, but for curiosity, if I lik'd my
company, I might be drawn in once to a masquerade! And this,
I think, is as far as any woman can go—soberly.

Lady *Town.* Well! if it had not been for that last piece of
sobriety, I was just going to call for some surfeit-water.

Lady *Grace.* Why, don't you think, with the farther aid of
breakfasting, dining, taking the air, supping, sleeping, not to say
a word of devotion, the four and twenty hours might roll over in
a tolerable manner?

Lady *Town.* Tolerable? Deplorable! Why, child, all you
propose, is but to indure life, now I want to enjoy it————

Enter Mrs. Trusty.

Trust. Madam, your ladyship's chair is ready.

Lady *Town.* Have the footmen their white flambeaux yet? for
last night I was poison'd.

Trust. Yes, madam: there were some come in this morning.
[*Exit* Trusty.

Lady *Town.* My dear, you will excuse me; but you know
my time is so precious——

Lady *Grace.* That I beg I may not hinder your least enjoyment
of it.

Lady *Town.* You will call on me at lady Revel's?

Lady

Lady Grace. Certainly.

Lady Town. But I am so afraid it will break into your scheme, my dear!

Lady Grace. When it does, I will—soberly break from you.

Lady Town. Why then, 'till we meet again, dear sister, I wish you all tolerable happiness.   [*Exit Lady* Town.

Lady Grace. There she goes—Dash! into her stream of pleasures! poor woman! she is really a fine creature! and sometimes infinitely agreeable! nay, take her out of the madness of this town, rational in her notions, and easy to live with: but she is so borne down by this torrent of vanity in vogue, she thinks every hour of her life is lost that she does not lead at the head of it. What it will end in, I tremble to imagine!——Ha! my brother, and Manly with him! I guess what they have been talking of—I shall hear it in my turn, I suppose, but it won't become me to be inquisitive.   [*Exit Lady* Grace.

Enter Lord Townly *and* Manly.

Lord Town. I did not think my lady Wronghead had such a notable brain: tho' I can't say she was so very wise, in trusting this silly girl you call Myrtilla, with the secret.

Man. No, my lord, you mistake me, had the girl been in the secret, perhaps I had never come at it myself.

Lord Town. Why I thought you said the girl writ this letter to you, and that my lady Wronghead sent it inclos'd to my sister?

Man. If you please to give me leave, my lord——the fact is thus——this inclos'd letter to lady Grace was a real original one, written by this girl, to the count we have been talking of: the count drops it, and my lady Wronghead finds it: then only changing the cover, she seals it up as a letter of business, just written by herself, to me; and pretending to be in a hurry, gets this innocent girl to write the direction, for her.

Lord Town. Oh! then the girl did not know she was superscribing a billet-doux of her own to you?

Man. No, my lord; for when I first question'd her about the direction, she own'd it immediately: but when I shew'd her that her letter to the count was within it, and told her how it came into my hands, the poor creature was amaz'd, and thought herself betray'd both by the count and my lady—in short, upon this discovery the girl and I grew so gracious, that she has let me into some transactions, in my lady Wronghead's family, which, with my having a careful eye over them, may prevent the ruin of it.

Lord Town. You are very generous, to be solicitous for a lady that has given you so much uneasiness.

Man. But I will be most unmercifully revenged of her; for I will do her the greatest friendship in the world—against her will.

Lord Town. What an uncommon philosophy art thou master of! to make even thy malice a virtue!

Man. Yet, my lord, I assure you, there is no one action of my life gives me more pleasure than your approbation of it.

Lord Town. Dear Charles! my heart's impatient, 'till thou

and as a proof that I have long wish'd thee fo,
indeed has chofen rather to deferve than afk
I have been as fecretly induftrious to make her
erit : and fince on this occafiou you have open'd
o me, 'tis now with equal pleafure, I affure you,
eeded——fhe is as firmly yours——
e ! you flatter me !
o glad you think it flattery : but fhe herfelf
: fhe dines with us alone : when the fervants
l open a converfation, that fhall excufe my leav-
O ! Charles ! had I, like thee, been cautious in
elancholy hours had this heart avoided !
of that, I beg, my lord——
t 'twill, at leaft, be fome relief to my anxiety
f content the ftate has been to me) to fee fo near
happy in it : your harmony of life will be a
i the choice of temper is preferable to beauty,
oft hours in mutual kindnefs move,
iy virtue what I loft by love.   [Exeunt,

T. IV. SCENE I.

N E, *Mrs.* Motherly's *Houfe.*
Irs. Motherly, *meeting* Myrtilla.
e ! where is it poffible you can have been thefe
irs ?
m ! I have fuch a terrible ftory to tell you !
. ods my life ! what have you done with the
hundred pound, I fent you about ? is it fafe
urity ?
t is fafe : but for its goodnefs——mercy on us !
ir way to be hang'd about it !
ens ! has the rogue of a count play'd us ano-

hear, madam ; when I came to Mr. Cafh,
hewed him his note for five hundred pounds,
t, or order, in two months——he look'd ear-
defired me to ftep into the inner room, while
oks——after I had ftaid about ten minutes,
——claps to the door, and charges me with a
y.
foul ! and how didft thou get off ?
vas ready to fink in this condition, I begg'd
patience, 'till I could fend for Mr. Manly,
be a gentleman of worth and honour, and
vould convince him, whatever fraud might
I was myfelf an innocent abus'd woman——
ould have it, in lefs than half an hour Mr.
, without mincing the matter, I fairly told
                                              him

him upon what defign the count had, lodg'd that note in you hands, and in fhort, laid open the whole fcheme he had draw us into, to make our fortune.

Moth. The devil you did!

Myr. Why, how do you think it was poffible, I could any otherwife make Mr. Manly my friend, to help me out of the fcrape I was in? to conclude, he foon made Mr. Cafh eafy, and fent away the conftable: nay farther he promis'd me, if would truft the note in his hands, he would take care it fhould be fully paid before it was due, and at the fame time would give me an ample revenge upon the count; fo that all you have to confider now, madam, is, whether you think yourfelf fafe in the count's hands, or Mr. Manly's.

Moth. Nay, nay, child; there is no choice in the matter Mr. Manly may be a friend indeed, if any thing in our powe can make him fo.

Myr. Well, madam, and now pray, how ftand matters a home here? what has the count done with the ladies?

Moth. Why every thing he has a mind to do, by this time I fuppofe. He is in as high favour with Mifs, as he is with my lady.

Myr. Pray, where are the ladies?

Moth. Rattling abroad in their own coach, and the well-bre count along with them: they have been fcouring all the fhop in town over, buying fine things and new clothes from morning to night: they have made one voyage already, and have brought home fuch a cargo of bawbles and trumpery——mercy on the poor man that's to pay for them!

Myr. Did not the young fquire go with them?

Moth. No, no; Mifs faid, truly he would but difgrace their party: fo they even left him afleep by the kitchen fire.

Myr. Has not he afked after me all this while? for I had a fort of an affignation with him.

Moth. O yes! he has been in a bitter taking about it. At laft his difappointment grew fo uneafy, that he fairly fell a crying fo to quiet him, I fent one of the maids and John Moody abroad with him, to fhew him the lions, and the monument. [*Exeun*

Enter Sir Francis Wronghead *and Mrs.* Motherly.

Sir Fran. What! my wife and daughter abroad, fay you?

Moth. O dear Sir, they have been mighty bufy all the day long; they juft come home to fnap up a fhort dinner, and f went out again.

Sir Fran. Well, well, I fhan't ftay fupper for 'em, I can tell 'em that: for ods-heart! I have had nothing in me, but a toaf and tankard, fince morning.

Moth. I am afraid, Sir, thefe late parliament hours won' agree with you.

Sir Fran. Why, truly, Mrs. Motherly, they don't do righ with us country gentlemen; to lofe one meal out of three, is hard tax upon a good ftomach.

Moth. It is so, indeed, Sir.

Sir Fran. But, howsoever, Mrs. Motherly, when we consider, that what we suffer is for the good of our country——

Moth. Why truly, Sir, that is something.

Sir Fran. Oh! there's a great deal to be said for't——the good of one's country, is above all things——a true hearted Englishman thinks nothing too much for it——I have heard of some honest gentlemen so very zealous, that for the good of their country—— they would sometimes go to dinner at midnight.

Moth. O! the goodness of 'em! sure their country must have a vast esteem for them?

Sir Fran. So they have, Mrs. Motherly; they are so respected when they come home to their boroughs, after a session, and so belov'd——that their country will come and dine with them every day in the week.

Moth. Dear me! what a fine thing 'tis to be so populous!

Sir Fran. It is a great comfort, indeed! and I can assure you you are a good sensible woman, Mrs. Motherly.

Moth. O dear Sir, your honour's pleas'd to compliment.

Sir Fran. No, no, I see you know how to value people of consequence.

Moth. Good lack! here's company, Sir; will you give me leave to get you a little something, 'till the ladies come home, Sir?

Sir Fran. Why troth, I don't think it would be amiss.

Moth. It shall be done in a moment, Sir. [*Exit*

Enter Manly.

Man. Sir Francis, your servant.

Sir Fran. Cousin Manly.

Man. I am come to see how the family goes on here.

Sir Fran. Troth! all as busy as bees; I have been upon the wing ever since eight o'clock this morning.

Man. By your early hour, then, I suppose you have been making your court to some of the great men.

Sir Fran. Why, faith! you have hit it, Sir——I was advis'd to lose no time; so I e'en went straight forward, to one great man I had never seen in my life before.

Man. Right! that was doing business: but who had you got to introduce you?

Sir Fran. Why, no body——I remember'd I had heard a wise man say——My son, be bold—so troth! I introduc'd myself.

Man. As how, pray?

Sir Fran. Why, thus—Look ye—Please your lordship, says I, I am Sir Francis Wronghead of Bumper-Hall, and member of parliament for the borough of Guzzledown——Sir, your humble servant, says my lord; tho' I have not the honour to know your person, I have heard you are a very honest gentleman; and I am glad your borough has made choice of so worthy a representative; and so, says he, Sir Francis, have you any service to command me? Now, cousin! those last words, you may be sure, gave me

no

no small encouragement. And that I know, Sir, you have low contemporary opinion of my plan, yet I believe, you won't say I miss it now ...

Man. Well, I hope I shall have no cause.

Sir Fran. So when I found him so conceited——My lord, says I, I did not think to ha' troubled your lordship with so much upon my first visit: but since your lordship is pleased not to stand upon ceremony——why truly, says I, I think now is as good as another time.

Man. Right! there you push'd him home.

Sir Fran. Ay, ay, I had a mind to let him see that I was none of your mealy-mouth'd ones.

Man. Very good!

Sir Fran. So, in short, my lord, says I, I have a good estate but—a—it's a little out at elbows: and as I desire to serve my king, as well as my country, I shall be very willing to accept of a place at court.

Man. So, this was making short work on't.

Sir Fran. I'cod! I shot him flying, cousin! Some of your hard-witted ones now, would ha' hemm'd and haw'd, and dangled a month or two after him, before they durst open their mouths about a place, and may-hap, not ha' got it at last neither.

Man. Oh! I'm glad you're so sure on't———

Sir Fran. You shall hear, cousin———Sir Francis, says my lord, pray what sort of a place may you ha' turn'd your thoughts upon? My lord, says I, beggars must not be choosers; but any place, says I, about a thousand a year, will be well enough to be doing with 'til something better falls in——for I thought it would not look well to stand haggling with him at first.

Man. No, no, your business was to get footing any way.

Sir Fran. Right! there's it! ay, cousin, I see you know the world!

Man. Yes, yes, one sees more of it every day——well! but what said my lord to all this?

Sir Fran. Sir Francis, says he, I shall be glad to serve you any way that lies in my power; so he gave me a squeeze by the hand, as much as to say, give yourself no trouble, I'll do your business; with that he rose up, and went to a gentleman with a colour'd ribbon a-cross here, that look'd, in my conscience, as if he came for a place too.

Man. Ha? so, upon these hopes, you are to make your fortune!

Sir Fran. Why, do you think there's any doubt of it, Sir?

Man. Oh no, I have not the least doubt of it at all——for just as you have done, I made my fortune ten years ago.

Sir Fran. Why, I never knew that had a place, cousin.

Man. Nor I neither, upon my faith, cousin. But you, perhaps, may have better fortune! for I suppose my lord has told you of what importance you were in the debate to-day——You have been down at the House, I presume!

Sir Fran. O yes!, I would not neglect the house, for ever so much.

Man. Well, and pray what have they done there?

Sir Fran. Why, doth? I can't well tell you what they have done, but I can tell you what I did, and I think pretty well too, only I happen'd to make a little mistake at last, indeed.

Man. How was that?

Sir Fran. Why, they were all got there, into a sort of a puzzling debate, about the good of the nation——and I were always for that, you know——but in short, the arguments were so long-winded o' both sides, that, wounds! I did not well understand 'em; howsobe'it, I was concern'd, and so resolv'd to vote right, according to my conscience——so when they came to put the question, as they call it,——I don't know how 'twas that I cry'd ay! when I should ha' cry'd no!

Man. How came that about?

Sir Fran. Why, by a mistake, as I tell you——for there was a good honest sort of a gentleman, one Mr. Tosserfaie, I think they call him, that sit next me, as soon as I had cry'd ay——gives me a hearty shake by the hand! Sir, says he, you are a man of honour, and a true Englishman, and I should be proud to be better acquainted with you——and so, with that, he takes me by the sleeve, along with the crowd into the lobby——so I knew how 'twas——but plague! I was got o' the wrong side the post——for I were told, afterwards, I should have staid where I was.

Man. [Aside.] And so, if you had not quite made your fortune before, you have clench'd it now!——no! thou head of the Wrong-head.   [Aside.

Sir Fran. Odso! here's my lady come home at last——I hope, cousin, you will be so kind, as to take a family supper with us?

Man. Another time, Sir Francis; but to-night, I am engag'd!

Enter Lady Woodford, Miss Jenny, and Count Basset.

Lady Wrong. Cousin! your servant; I hope you will pardon my rudeness: but we have really been at such a christened hurry here, that we have not had a leisure moment to return your last visit.

Man. O madam! I am a man of no ceremony; you see that has not hinder'd my coming again.

Lady Wrong. Yes, we should certainly—— but I'll redeem my credit with you.

Man. At your own time, madam.

Count Baf. I must say that for Mr. Manly, madam; if making people easy is the rule of good-breeding, he is certainly the best-bred man in the world.

Man. Soh! I am not to keep my acquaintance, I find——
[Aside.] I am afraid, Sir, I shall grow vain upon your good opinion.

with fifty more to it, that I was forc'd to borrow of the count here.

Jenny. Yes, indeed, papa, and that would hardly do neither ———There's th' account.

Sir Fran. [*Turning over the bills.*] Let's see! let's see! what the devil have we got here?

Man. Then you have founded your aunt, you say, and she readily comes into all I propos'd to you?

Myr. Sir, I'll answer, with my life, she is most thankfully yours in every article: she mightily desires to see you, Sir.   *Apart.*

Man. I am going home, directly: bring her to my house in half an hour; and if she makes good what you tell me, you shall both find your account in it.

Myr. Sir, she shall not fail you.

Sir Fran. Ods-life! Madam, here's nothing but toys and trinkets, and fans, and clock-stockings, by wholesale.

Lady Wrong. There's nothing but what's proper, and for your credit, Sir Francis—Nay, you see I am so good a housewife, that in necessaries for myself, I have scarce laid out a shilling.

Sir Fran. No, by my troth, so it seems; for the devil o'one thing's here, that I can see you have any occasion for!

Lady Wrong. My dear! do you think I came hither to live out of the fashion! why, the greatest distinction of a fine lady in this town is in the variety of pretty things that she has no occasion for.

Jenny. Sure, papa, could you imagine, that women of quality wanted nothing but stays and petticoats?

Lady Wrong. Now, that is so like him!

Man. So! the family comes on finely.   [*Aside.*

Lady Wrong. Lard, if men were always to govern, what dowdies would they reduce their wives to!

Sir Fran. An hundred pound in the morning, and want another afore night! Waunds and fire! the Lord Mayor of London could not hold it at this rate!

Man. O! do you feel it, Sir?   [*Aside.*

Lady Wrong. My dear, you seem uneasy; let me have the hundred pound, and compose yourself.

Sir Fran. Compose the devil, madam! why, do you consider what a hundred pound a day comes to in a year?

Lady Wrong. My life, if I account with you from one day to another, that's really all my head is able to bear at a time—But I'll tell you what I consider—I consider that my advice has got you a thousand pound a year this morning——That now methinks you might consider, Sir.

Sir Fran. A thousand a year? waunds, madam, but I have not touch'd a penny of it yet!

Man. Nor ever will, I'll answer for him.   [*Aside.*

Enter Squire Richard.

Squ.

Squ. Rich. Feyther, an you doan't come quickly, the meat will be coal'd : and I'd fain pick a bit with you.

Lady Wrong. Bleſs me, Sir Francis ! you are not going to ſup by yourſelf !

Sir Fran. No, but I'm going to dine by myſelf, and that's pretty near the matter, madam.

Lady Wrong. Had not you as good ſtay a little, my dear ? we ſhall all eat in half an hour ; and I was thinking to aſk my couſin Manly to take a family morſel with us.

Sir Fran. Nay, for my couſin's good company, I don't care if I ride a day's journey without baiting.

Man. By no means, Sir Francis. I am going upon a little buſineſs.

Sir Fran. Well, Sir, I know you don't love compliments.

Man. You'll excuſe me, madam———

Lady Wrong. Since you have buſineſs, Sir———[*Exit* Manly.
Enter Mrs. Motherly.

O, Mrs. Motherly ! you were ſaying this morning, you had ſome very fine lace to ſhew me———can't I ſee it now ?
[*Sir* Francis *ſtarts.*

Moth. Why really, madam, I had made a ſort of a promiſe to let the counteſs of Nicely have the firſt ſight of it for the birth-day : but your ladyſhip———

Lady Wrong. O ! I die if I don't ſee it before her.

Squ. Rich. Woan't you goa, feyther ?

Sir Fran. Waunds ! Lad, I ſhall ha' noa ſtomach } *Apart.*
at this rate !

Moth. Well, madam, though I ſay it, 'tis the ſweeteſt pattern that ever came over———and for fineneſs———no cobweb comes up to it !

Sir Fran. Ods guts and gizard, madam ! lace as fine as a cobweb ! why, what the devil's that to coſt now ?

Moth. Nay, Sir Francis does not like it, madam———

Lady Wrong. He like it ! dear Mrs. Motherly, he is not to wear it.

Sir Fran. Fleſh, madam, but I ſuppoſe I am to pay for it.

Lady Wrong. No doubt on't ! think of your thouſand a year, and who got it you ; go, eat your dinner, and be thankful, go. [*Driving him to the door.*]. Come, Mrs. Motherly.
[*Exit Lady* Wronghead *with Mrs.* Motherly.

Sir Fran. Very fine ! ſo here I mun faſt, till I am almoſt famiſh'd for the good of my country ; while madam is laying me out an hundred pound a day in lace, as fine as a cobweb, for the honour of my family ! Ods-fleſh ! things had need go well at this rate !

Squ. Rich. Nay, nay———come, feyther. [*Exit Sir* Francis.
Enter Mrs. Motherly.

Moth. Madam, my lady deſires you and the count will pleaſe to come and aſſiſt her fancy in ſome of the new laces.

Count Baſ. We'll wait upon her———[*Exit Mrs.* Motherly.

Jenny.

Jenny. So! I told you how it was! you see f
leave us together.

Count *Baf.* No matter, my dear: you know f
to ftay fupper: fo, when your papa and fhe are a-
tilla will let me into the houfe again; then yo
her chamber, and we'll have a pretty fneaker of p

Myr. Ay, ay, madam, you may command me

Jenny. Well! that will be pure!

Count *Baf.* But you had beft go to her alone,
look better if I come after you.

Jenny. Ay, fo it will: and to-morrow you kr
querade. And then!—hey! *Oh, I'll have a buf*
&c.

Myr. So,-Sir! am not I very *commode* to you?

Count *Baf.* Well, child! and don't you find
it?-d d not I tell you we might fill be of ufe to c

Myr. Well, but how ftands your affair wit
main?

Count *Baf.* O fhe's mad for the mafquerade!
nail; we want nothing now but a parfon, to clin
your aunt fay fhe could get one at a fhort warning

Myr. Yes, yes, my lord Townly's chaplain is
know; he'll do your bufinefs and mine, at the f

Count *Baf.* O! it's true! but where fhall we

My.. Why, you know my lady Townly's hou
to the mafques upon a ball-night, before they
market.

Count *Baf.* Good.

Myr. Now the doctor propofes we fhould all
our habits, ar s when the rooms are full, we may
chamber, he fays, and there——crack——he'll g
nical commiffion to go to-bed together.

Count *Baf.* Admirable! Well, the devil fetch
not be heartily glad to fee thee well fettled, child.

Myr. And may the black gentleman tuck me
the fame time, if I fhall not think myfelf oblig'd
as I live.

Count *Baf.* One kifs for old acquaintance f
fhall want to be bufy again!

Myr. O you'll have one fhortly will find you er
I muft run to my fquire.

Count *Baf.* And I to the ladies——fo your
fweet Mrs. Wronghead.

Myr. Yours, as in duty bound, moft noble cu

'Count *Baf.* Why! ay! count! that title has
ufe to me indeed! not that I have any more pret
I have to a blue ribband. Yet, I have made a
able figure in life with it: I have loll'd in m
dealt at affemblies, din'd with ambaffadors; and

quadrille, with the firſt women of quality——but——*Tempora mutantur*——ſince that damn'd ſquadron at White's have loſt me out of their laſt ſecret, 1 am reduced to trade upon my own ſtock of induſtry, and make my laſt puſh upon a wife: if my card comes up right (which I think cannot fail) I ſhall once more cut a figure, and cock my hat in the face of the beſt of them; for ſince our modern men of fortune are grown wiſe enough to be ſharpers, I think ſharpers are fools that don't take up the airs of men of quality.   [*Exit.*

ACT V. SCENE I.

Manly meeting Sir Francis.

SIR Francis, your ſervant; how came I by the favour of this extraordinary viſit?

Sir Fran. Ah! Couſin!

Man. Why that ſorrowful face, man?

Sir Fran. I have no friend alive but you——

Man. I am ſorry for that——but what's the matter?

Sir Fran. I have play'd the fool by this journey, I ſee now —for my bitter wife——

Man. What of her?

Sir Fran. Is playing the devil!

Man. Why, truly, that's a part that moſt of your fine ladies begin with, as ſoon as they get to London.

Sir Fran. If I am a living man, couſin, ſhe has made away with above two hundred and fifty pounds ſince yeſterday morning!

Man. Hah! I ſee a good houſewife will do a great deal of work in a little time.

Sir Fran. Work do they call it! Fine work indeed!

Man. Well, but how do you mean made away with it? what, ſhe has laid it out, may be — but I ſuppoſe you have an account of it.

Sir Fran. Yes, yes, I have had the account indeed; but I mun needs ſay, it's a very ſorry one.

Man. Pray, let's hear.

Sir Fran. Why, firſt I let her have an hundred and fifty, to get things handſome about her, to let the world ſee that I was ſomebody! and I thought that ſum was very genteel.

Man. Indeed I think ſo; and in the country, might have ſerv'd her a twelve-month.

Sir Fran. Why, ſo it might — but here in this fine town, forſooth! it could not get through four and twenty hours—— for in half that time, it was all ſquander'd away in bawbles, and new-faſhion'd trumpery.

Man.

Man. O! for ladies in London, Sir Francis, all this might be necessary.

Sir *Fran.* Noa! there's the plague on't! the devil o' one useful thing do I see for it, but two pair of lac'd shoes, and those stond me in three pound three shillings a pair too.

Man. Dear Sir! this is nothing! Why, we have city wives here, that while their good man is selling three pennyworth of sugar, will give you twenty pound for a short apron.

Sir *Fran.* Mercy on us! What a mortal poor devil is a husband!

Man. Well, but I hope you have nothing else to complain of?

Sir *Fran.* Ah! would I could say so too—but there's another hundred behind yet, that goes more to my heart, than all that went before it.

Man. And how might that be disposed of?

Sir *Fran.* Troth I am almost asham'd to tell you.

Man. Out with it.

Sir *Fran.* Why, she has been at an assembly.

Man. What, since I saw you! I thought you had all supt at home last night?

Sir *Fran.* Why, so we did—and all as merry as grigs——I'cod! my heart was so open, that I tofs'd another hundred into her apron, to go out early this morning with —— But the cloth was no sooner taken away, than in comes my lady Townly here, (—— who between you and I—mum! has had the devil to pay yonder——) with another rantipole dame of quality, and out they must have her, they said, to introduce her at my lady Noble's assembly forsooth——a few words, you may be sure, made the bargain——so, bawnce! and away they drive as if the devil had got into the coach-box—so about four or five in the morning—— home comes madam, with her eyes a foot deep in her head—— and my poor hundred pound left behind her at the hazard-table.

Man. All lost at dice!

Sir *Fran.* Every shilling—— among a parcel of pig-tail puppies, and pale-fac'd women of quality.

Man. But pray, Sir Francis, how came you, after you found her so ill an housewife of one sum, so soon to trust her with another?

Sir *Fran.* Why, truly, I mun say that was partly my own fault: for if I had not been a blab of my tongue, I believe that last hundred might have been sav'd.

Man. How so?

Sir *Fran.* Why, like an owl as I was, out of good-will, for-

Man. Sir Francis, I have heard you with a great deal of patience, and I really feel compassion for you.

Sir Fran. Truly, and well you may, cousin, for I don't see that my wife's goodness is a bit the better, for bringing to London.

Man. If you remember I gave you a hint of it.

Sir Fran. Why, ay, it's true you did so: but the devil himself could not have believ'd she would have rid post to him.

Man. Sir, if you stay but a fortnight in this town, you will every day see hundreds as fast upon the gallop, as she is.

Sir Fran. Ah! this London is a base place, indeed——waunds, if things should happen to go wrong with me at Westminster, at this rate, how the devil shall I keep out of a jail?

Man. Why, truly, there seems to me but one way to avoid it.

Sir Fran. Ah! would you could tell me that, cousin.

Man. The way lies plain before you, Sir; the same road that brought you hither will carry you safe home again.

Sir Fran. Odsflesh! Cousin, what! and leave a thousand pound a year behind me?

Man. Pooh! pooh! leave any thing behind you, but your family, and you are a saver by it.

Sir Fran. Ay, but consider, cousin, what a scurvy figure shall I make in the country, if I come dawn withawt it!

Man. You will make a much more lamentable figure in a jail without it.

Sir Fran. Mayhap 'at yow have no great opinion of it then, cousin?

Man. Sir Francis, to do you the service of a real friend, I must speak very plainly to you: you don't yet see half the ruin that's before you.

Sir Fran. Good-lack! how may yow mean, cousin?

Man. In one word, your whole affairs stand thus——In a week you'll lose your seat at Westminster; in a fortnight my lady will run you into jail, by keeping the soft company——In four and twenty hours, your daughter will run away with a sharper, because she han't been us'd to better company: and your son will steal into marriage with a cast mistress, because he has not been used to any company at all.

Sir Fran. I' th' name o'goodness why should you think all this?

Man. Because I have proof of it; in short, I know so much of their secrets, that if all this is not prevented to-night, it will be out of your power to do it to-morrow morning.

Sir Fran. Mercy upon us! you frighten me——Well, Sir, I will be govern'd by yow; but what am I to do in this case?

Man. I have not time here to give you proper instructions: but about eight this evening, I'll call at your lodgings; and there you shall have full conviction, how much I have it at heart to serve you.

Enter a Servant.

Serv. Sir, my lord desires to speak with you.

Man. I'll wait upon him.

Sir

Sir *Fran.* Well then, I'll go ſtraight home,.
Man. At eight depend upon me.
Sir *Fran.* Ah! dear couſin! I ſhall be bou
as I live. Mercy deliver us! what a terrible
made on't!

The SCENE *opens to a Dreſſing Room.*
    juſt up, walks to her Toilet, leaning on M
Truſt. Dear madam, what ſhould make you
of order?

Lady *Town.* How is it poſſible to be well, w
for want of ſleep?

Truſty. Dear me! it was ſo long before you
was in hopes your ladyſhip had been finely comp

Lady *Town.* Compos'd! why I have lain in
houſe is worſe than an inn, with ten ſtage-coa
tween my lord's impertinent people of buſineſs i
the intolerable thick ſhoes of footmen at noon, (
all night.

Truſty. Indeed, madam, it's a great pity
perſuaded into the hours of people of quality——
ſay that, madam, your ladyſhip is certainly the
manager in town.

Lady *Town.* Oh! you are quite miſtaken, I
very ill! for notwithſtanding all the power I h
ing over-fond of my lord——yet I want money
than he is willing to give it me.

Truſty. Ah, if his lordſhip could but be brou
ſelf, madam, then he might feel what it is to 5

Lady *Town.* Oh! don't talk of it! do you kno
done, Truſty?

Truſty. Mercy forbid, madam!

Lady *Town.* Broke! ruin'd! plunder'd!——
a confiſcation of my laſt guinea.

Truſty. You don't tell me ſo, madam!

Lady *Town.* And where to raiſe ten pound h
What is to be done, Truſty?

Truſty. Truly, I wiſh I were wiſe enough to t
but may be your ladyſhip may have a run of bet
ſome of the good company that comes here to-r

Lady *Town.* But I have not a ſingle guinea
tune!

Truſty. Ha!—that's a bad buſineſs, indeed, m
I have a thought in my head, madam, if it is no

Lady *Town.* Out with it quickly, then, I be

Truſty. Has not the ſteward ſomething of fift
that you left in his hands, to pay ſomebody abou

Lady *Town.* O! ay! I had forgot—'twas
his filthy name?

Truſty. Now I remember, madam, 'twas t

hat your ladyfhip turn'd off about a year ago,
uft you no longer.

he very wretch! if he has not paid it, run
fty, and bid him bring it hither immediately
rufty.] Well! fure mortal woman never had
e! five, and nine, againft poor feven for
er that horrid bar of my chance, that lady.
red fift upon the table, I faw it was impoffi-
another ftake———fit up all night! lofe all
im of winning thoufands! wake without a
———how like a hag I look! In fhort———
e, are not worth this diforder! if it were not
:ould almoft think lady Grace's fober fcheme
ous———if my wife lord could but hold
:ek, 'tis odds, but I fhould hate the town in a
will not be driven out of it, that's pofitive!

[Trufty *returns.*

m! there's no bearing of it! Mr. Lute.tring
he door, as I came to the ftair foot; and the
ually paying him the money in the hall.
in to the ftair-cafe head, again———and fcream
ft fpeak with him this inftant.

[Trufty *runs out, and fpeaks.*

indage———a hem! Mr. Poundage,
uickly.
] I'll come to you prefently.
y won't do, man, you muft come
: juft paying a little money, here.
y-life! paying money? is the man
here, I tell you, to my lady, this

without.

[Trufty *returns.*

ill the monfter come or no?———
eat him now, madam, he is hobbling up as faft

on't let him come in———for he will keep fuch
s accounts,———my brain is not able to bear him.
mes to the door with a money-bag in his hand.
well you are come, Sir! where's the fifty

ere it is; if you had not been in fuch hafte, I,
by this time———the man's now writing a re-

ter! my lady fays, you muft not pay him with
is not enough, it feems; there's a piftole, and
iot good in it———befides there is a miftake in
—[*Twitching the bag from him.*] But fhe is not
ie it now; fo you muft bid Mr. What-d'ye-
er time.

Lady

Lady Town. What is all that noise there?

Pound. Why and it please your ladyship——

Lady Town. Pr'ythee! don't plague me now, were order'd.

Pound. Nay, what your ladyship pleases, mad

Trusty. There they are, madam——[*Pours the bag.*] The pretty things——were so near falli tradesman's hands, I protest it made me tremble fancy your ladyship had as good give me, that luck's sake—thank you, madam.

Lady Town. Why, I did not bid you take i

Trusty. No, but your ladyship look'd as if yo to bid me, and so I was willing to save you the ing, madam.

Lady Town. Well! thou hast deserv'd it, an but hark! don't I hear the man making a noise I think now we may compound for a little of hi

Trusty. I'll listen.

Lady Town. Pr'ythee do.   [*Trusty*

Trusty. Ay! they are at it, madam——he's i with poor Poundage——bless me! I believe he' mercy on us; how the wretch swears!

Lady Town. And a sober citizen too! that's

Trusty. Ha! I think all's silent, of a sudde porter has knock'd him down—I'll step and see—

Lady Town. Those trades-people are the tro tures! No words will satisfy them!

Trusty. O madam! undone! undone! my lo out upon the man, and is hearing all his pitiful your ladyship pleases to come hither, you may he

Lady Town. No matter: it will come round have it from my lord, without losing a word l warrant you.

Trusty. O lud! madam! here's my lord just

Lady Town. Do you get out of the way Trusty.] I am afraid I want spirits! but h 'em me.

Enter Lord Townly.

Lord Town. How comes it, madam, that a be clamorous in my house, for money due to hi

Lady Town. You don't expect, my lord, that for other people's impertinence!

Lord Town. I expect, madam, you should own extravagances, that are the occasion of it— had given you money three months ago, to sat of people!

Lady Town. Yes, but you see they never a

Lord Town. Nor am I, madam, longer to what's become of the last five hundred I gave

Lady *Town.* Gone.

Lord *Town.* Gone! what way, madam?

Lady *Town.* Half the town over, I believe, by this time.

Lord *Town.* 'Tis well! I see ruin will make no impreffion, ill it falls upon you.

Lady *Town.* In fhort, my lord, if money is always the fub-ject of our converfation, I fhall make you no anfwer.

Lord *Town.* Madam! madam, I will be heard, and make you anfwer.

Lady *Town.* Make me! then I muft tell you, my lord, this is a language I have not been us'd to, and I won't bear it.

Lord *Town.* Come! come, madam, you fhall hear a great deal more, before I part with you.

Lady *Town.* My lord, if you infult me, you will have as much to bear, on your fide, I can affure you.

Lord *Town.* Pooh! your fpirit grows ridiculous—you have neither honour, worth, or innocence, to fupport it!

Lady *Town.* You'll find, at leaft, I have refentment! and do you look well to the provocation!

Lord *Town.* After thofe you have given me, madam, 'tis almoft infamous, to talk with you.

Lady *Town.* I fcorn your imputation, and your menaces! the narrownefs of your heart's your monitor! 'tis there! there, my lord, you are wounded; you have lefs to complain of than many hufbands of an equal rank to you.

Lord *Town.* Death, madam! do you prefume upon your corporal merit! that your perfon's lefs tainted, than your mind! is it there! there alone an honeft hufband can be injured? have you not every other vice that can debafe your birth, or ftain the heart of woman? is not your health, your beauty, hufband, fortune, family, difclaim'd for nights confum'd in riot and extravagance? the wanton does no more; if fhe conceals her fhame, does lefs; and fure the diffolute avow'd, as forely wrongs my honour, and my quiet.

Lady *Town.* I fee, my lord, what fort of wife might pleafe you.

Lord *Town.* Ungrateful woman! could you have feen yourfelf, you in yourfelf had feen her——I am amaz'd our legiflature has left no precedent of a divorce for this more vifible injury, this adultery of the mind, as well as that of the perfon! when a woman's whole heart is alienated to pleafures I have no fhare in; what is't to me, whether a black-ace, or a powder'd coxcomb has poffeffion of it?

Lady *Town.* If you have not found it yet, my lord, this is not the way to get poffeffion of mine, depend upon it.

Lord *Town.* That, madam, I have long defpair'd of; and fince our happinefs cannot be mutual, 'tis fit that with our hearts, our perfons too fhould feparate.——This houfe you fleep no more in! tho' your content might grofly feed upon the difhonour

of a hufband, yet my defires would ftarve upon t
a wife.

Lady *Town.* Your ftile, my lord, is much of
ficacy with your fentiments of honour.

Lord *Town.* Madam, madam! this is no time
ments——I have done with you.

Lady *Town.* If we had never met, my lord, I
my heart for it! but have a care! I may not, p
eafily recall'd as you may imagine.

Lord *Town.* Recall'd!—Who's there! [*Enter*
Defire my fifter and Mr. Manly to walk up.

Lady *Town.* My lord, you may proceed as yo
pray what indifcretions have. I committed, that a
practis'd by a hundred other women of quality

Lord *Town.* 'Tis not the number of ill wives,
makes the patience of a hufband lefs contemptib
a ha ne may be the beft man's lot, yet he'll m
figure in the world, that keeps his misfortunes c
than he that tamely keeps them within.

Lady *Town.* I don't know what figure you ma
lord, but I fhall have no reafon to be afham'd of m
ever company I may meet you.

Lord *Town.* Be fparing of your fpirit, madam,
to fupport you.

Enter Lady Grace *and* Manly.

Mr. Manly, I have an act of friendfhip to t
which wants more apologies, than words can make

Man. Then pray make none, my lord, that I m
greater merit in obliging you.

Lord *Town.* Sifter, I have the fame excufe to in
too.

Lady *Grace.* To your requeft, I beg, my lord.

Lord *Town.* Thus then—as you both were prefe
confider'd marriage, I now defire you each will be
my determin'd feparation——I know, Sir, your
and my fifter's muft be fhock'd at the office I imp
but, as I don't afk your juftification of my caufe
you are confcious——that an ill woman can't repro
you are filent, upon her fide.

Man. My lord, I never thought, 'till now, it c
ficult to oblige you.

Lady *Grace.* [*Afide.*] Heavens! how I tremble!

Lord *Town.* For you, my lady Townly, I need
peat the provocations of my parting with you—the w
is too well inform'd of them——for the good lord,
father's fake, I will ftill fupport you, as his daughte
lord Townly's wife, you have had every thing a fo
could beftow, and (to our mutual fhame I fpeak it)
happy wives defire—but thofe indulgences muft end

page, and splendor, but ill become the vices that misuse 'em—the decent necessaries of life shall be supply'd—but not one article to luxury! not even the coach, that waits to carry you from hence, shall you ever use again! Your tender aunt, my lady Lovemore, with tears, this morning, has consented to receive you; where if time, and your condition, brings you to a due reflection, your allowance shall be increas'd—but, if you still are lavish of your little, or pine for past licentious pleasures, that little shall be less! nor will I call that soul my friend that names you in my hearing!

Lady Grace. My heart bleeds for her!　　　　[*Aside.*

Lord Town. O Manly! look there! turn back thy thoughts with me, and witness to my growing love! there was a time when I believ'd that form incapable of vice or of decay! there I propos'd the partner of an easy home! there I, for ever, hoped to find, a chearful companion, an agreeable intimate, a faithful friend, a useful help-mate, and a tender mother——but oh! how bitter now the disappointment!

Man. The world is different in its sense of happiness: offended as you are, I know you will still be just.

Lord Town. Fear me not.

Man. This last reproach, I see, has struck her.　　[*Aside.*

Lord Town. No, let me not (though I this moment call her from my heart for ever) let me not urge her punishment beyond her crimes——I know the world is fond of any tale that feeds its appetite of scandal: and as I am conscious, severities of this kind seldom fail of imputations too gross to mention, I here, before you both, acquit her of the least suspicion rais'd against the honour of my bed: therefore, when abroad her conduct may be questioned, do her fame that justice.

Lady Town. O sister!　　　[*Turns to lady Grace weeping.*

Lord Town. When I am spoken of, where, without favour, this action may be canvass'd, relate but half my provocations, and give me up to censure.　　　　[*Going.*

Lady Town. Support me! save me! hide me from the world!
　　　　　　　　[*Falls on lady Grace's neck.*

Lord Town. [*Returning.*] —— I had forgot me—you have no share in my resentment; therefore, as you have liv'd in friendship with her, your parting may admit of gentler terms than suit the honour of an injur'd husband.　　　[*Offers to go out.*

Man. [*Interposing.*] My lord, you must not, shall not leave her thus! one moment's stay can do your cause no wrong! If looks can speak the anguish of the heart, I'll answer with my life, there's something labouring in her mind, that, would you bear the hearing, might deserve it.

Lord Town. Consider! since we no more can meet; press not my staying to insult her.

Lady Town. Yet stay, my lord—the little I would say, will not deserve an insult; and undeserv'd, I know your nature gives

E 2

of a husband, yet my desires would starve
a wife.

Lady *Town.* Your stile, my lord, is mu
licacy with your sentiments of honour.

Lord *Town.* Madam, madam! this is r
ments——I have done with you.

Lady *Town.* If we had never met, my lc
my heart for it! but have a care! I may
easily recall'd as you may imagine.

Lord *Town.* Recall'd!——Who's there! [
Desire my sister and Mr. Manly to walk up

r Lady *Town.* My lord, you may proceed
pray what indiscretions have I committed,
practis'd by a hundred other women of quali

Lord *Town.* 'Tis not the number of ill
makes the patience of a husband less
a ha be may be the best man's lot, yet t
figure in the world, that keeps his misfor
than he that tamely keeps them within.

Lady *Town.* I don't know what figure y
lord, but I shall have no reason to be asham'
ever company I may meet you.

Lord *Town.* Be sparing of your spirit, ma
to support you.

Enter Lady Grace *and* Man

Mr. Manly, I have an act of friendsh
which wants more apologies, than words can

Man. Then pray make none, my lord, th
greater merit in obliging you.

Lord *Town.* Sister, I have the same excuse
too.

Lady *Grace.* To your request, I beg, my

Lord *Town.* Thus then——as you both wer
consider'd marriage, I now desire you each w
my determin'd separation——I know, Sir,
and my sister's must be shock'd at the office
but, as I don't ask your justification of my
you are conscious——that an ill woman can
you are silent, upon her side.

Man. My lord, I never thought, 'till now
ficult to oblige you.

Lady Grace. [*Aside.*] Heavens! how I tre

Lord *Town.* For you, my lady Townly,
peat the provocations of my parting with you
is too well inform'd of them——for the goo
father's sake, I will still support you, as his c
lord Townly's wife, you have had every thin
could bestow, and (to our mutual shame I spe
happy wives desire——but those indulgences you

, but ill become the vices that misuse 'em——

—— of life shall be supply'd——but not one

—— even the coach, that waits to carry you

you ever use again! Your tender aunt, inv

—— ith tears, this morning, has consented to re-

if time, and your condition, brings you to a

—— r allowance shall be increas'd——but, if you

—— our little, or pine for past licentious pleasures,

less! nor will I call that soul my friend that

hearing!

—— v heart bleeds for her!   [Aside.

Manly! look there! turn back thy thoughts

—— s to my growing love! there was a time when

—— incapable of vice or of decay! there I pro-

—— f an easy home! there! I, for ever, hoped

—— l companion, an agreeable intimate, a faith-

—— al help-mate, and a tender mother——but

—— v the disappointment!

—— is different in its sense of happiness: offend-

—— ow you will still be just.

—— r me not.

—— eproach, I see, has struck her.   [Aside.

—— let me not (though I this moment call her

—— ver), let me not urge her punishment beyond

—— ow the world is fond of any tale that feeds its

—— and as I am conscious, severities of this kind

—— atious too gross to mention, I here, before you

—— he least suspicion rais'd against the honour of

—— when abroad her conduct may be questioned,

—— tice.

—— ster!   [Turns to lady Grace weeping.

—— I am spoken of, where, without favour, this

—— s'd, relate but half my provocations, and give

[Going.

—— ort me! save me! hide me from the world!

[Falls on lady Grace's neck,

—— eeping.]—— I had forgot me—you have no

—— ient; therefore, as you have liv'd in friend-

—— arring may admit of gentler terms than suit

—— r'd husband.   [Offers to go out

—— .] My lord, you must not, shall not leave her;

—— stay can do your cause no wrong! If looks,

—— th of the heart, I'll answer with my life;

—— suring in her mind, that, would you bear

—— eserve it.

—— der! since we no more can meet; press not

—— her.

—— stay, my lord——the little I would say, will

—— and undeserv'd, I know your nature giv

it not. But as you've call'd in friends, to witness your resentment, let them be equal hearers of my last reply.

Lord *Town.* I shan't refuse you that, madam——be it so.

Lady *Town.* My lord, you ever have complain'd I wanted
love; but as you kindly have allowed I never gave it to another;
so when you hear the story of my heart, though you may still
complain, you will not wonder at my coldness.

Lady *Grace.* This promises a reverse of temper.   [*Apart.*

Man. This, my lord, you are concern'd to hear!

Lord *Town.* Proceed, I am attentive.

Lady *Town.* Before I was your bride, my lord, the flattering
world had talk'd me into beauty; which, at my glass, my youthful vanity confirm'd: wild with that fame, I thought mankind
my slaves, I triumph'd over hearts, while all my pleasure was
their pain: yet was my own so equally insensible to all, that
when a father's firm commands enjoin'd me to make choice of
one, I even there declin'd the liberty he gave, and to his own
election yielded up my youth——his tender care, my lord, directed him to you——Our hands were join'd! but still my heart
was wedded to its folly! My only joy was power, command,
society, profuseness, and to lead in pleasures! The husband's right
to rule, I thought a vulgar law, which only the deform'd or
meanly-spirited obey'd! I knew no directors, but my passions;
no master, but my will! Even you, my lord, some time o'ercome
by love, was pleas'd with my delights; nor, then, foresaw this
mad misuse of your indulgence ——And, though I call myself
ungrateful, while I own it, yet, as a truth, it cannot be deny'd——
That kind indulgence has undone me! it added strength to my
habitual failings, and in a heart thus warm, in wild unthinking
life, no wonder if the gentler sense of love was lost.

Lord *Town.* O Manly! where has this creature's
heart been buried?   }*Apart.*

Man. If yet recoverable——how vast a treasure? }

Lady *Town.* What I have sa'd, my lord, is not my excuse,
but my confession! my errors (give 'em, if you please, a harder
name) cannot be defended! No! What's in its nature wrong,
no words can palliate, no plea can alter! What then remains in
my condition, but resignation to your pleasure? Time only can
convince you of my future conduct: therefore, 'till I have liv'd
an object of forgiveness, I dare not hope for pardon——The penance of a lonely contrite life were little to the innocent; but to
have deserv'd this separation, will strow perpetual thorns upon my
pillow.

Lady *Grace.* O happy, heavenly hearing!

Lady *Town.* Sister, farewell! [*Kissing her.*] Your virtue needs
no warning from the shame that falls on me; but when you
think I have aton'd my follies past——persuade your injur'd
brother to forgive them.

Lord *Town.* No, madam! Your errors thus renounc'd, this
                                                   instant

inſtant are forgotten I ſo deep, ſo due a ſenſe of them, has made you, what my utmoſt wiſhes form'd, and all my heart has ſigh'd for.

Lady Town. [*Turning to Lady Grace.*] How odious does this goodneſs make me!

Lady Grace. How amiable your thinking ſo!

Lord Town. Long parted——————— through eaſy voyages of life, receive but common—————— their meeting: but from a ſhipwreck ſav'd, we mingle tears with our embraces!

[*Embracing Lady* Townly.

Lady Town. What words! what loved what duty can repay ſuch obligations?

Lord Town. Preſerve but this deſire to pleaſe, your power is endleſs!

Lady Town. Oh!—— till this moment, never did I know, my lord, I had a heart to give you!

Lord Town. By heav'n, this yielding hand, when firſt it gave you to my wiſhes, preſented not a treaſure more deſirable! O Manly! Siſter! as you have often ſhar'd in my diſquiet, partake of my felicity! my new-born joy! ſee here the bride of my deſires! This may be called my wedding-day!

Lady Grace. Siſter! (for now methinks that name is dearer to my heart than ever) let me congratulate the happineſs that opens to you.

Man. Long, long, and mutual may it flow——

Lord Town. To make our happineſs compleat, my dear, join here with me to give a hand, that amply will repay the obligation.

Lady Town. Siſter, a day like this——

Lady Grace. Admits of no excuſe againſt the general joy.

[*Gives her hand to* Manly.

Man. A joy like mine——deſpairs of words to ſpeak it.

Lord Town. O Manly! how the name of friend endears the brother!

[*Embracing him.*

Man. Your words, my lord, will warm me, to deſerve them.

Enter a Servant.

Serv. My lord, the apartments are full of maſquefaders—— And ſome people of quality there deſire to ſee your lordſhip, and my lady.

Lady Town. I thought, my lord, your orders had forbid their receiving?

Lord Town. No, my dear, Manly has deſir'd their admittance to-night, it ſeems, upon a particular occaſion——Say we will wait upon them inſtantly.

[*Exit Servant.*

Lady Town. I ſhall be but ill company to them.

Lord Town. No matter! not to ſee them, would on a ſudden be too particular. Lady Grace will aſſiſt you to entertain them.

Lady Town. With her, my lord, I ſhall be always eaſy——

F 3   Siſter,

Sister, to your unerring virtue, I now commit the guidance of
my future days——

> Never the paths of pleasure more to tread,
> But where your guarded innocence shall lead,
> For in the marriage-state the world must own,
> Divided happiness was ne'er known,
> To make it mutual, nature points the way,
> Let husbands govern, gentle wives obey. [*Exeunt.*]

Manly *re-enters with* Sir Francis Wronghead.

Sir *Fran.* Well, cousin, you have made my very hair stand on
end! wauns! if what you tell me be true, I'll huff my whole
family into a stage-coach, and trundle them into the country again
on Monday morning.

Man. Stick to that, Sir, and we may yet find a way to redeem
all: In the mean time, place yourself behind this screen, and for
the truth of what I have told you, take the evidence of your own
senses: but be sure you keep close till I give you the signal.

Sir *Fran.* Sir! I'll warrant you——Ah! my lady, my lady
Wronghead! What a bitter business have you drawn me into!

Man. Hush! to your post; here comes one couple already.
Sir Francis *retires behind the Screen.*   [*Exit* Manly.

Enter Myrtilla *with Squire* Richard.

Squ. *Rich.* What! is this the doctor's chamber?
Myr. Yes, yes, speak softly.
Squ. *Rich.* Well, but where is he?
Myr. He'll be ready for us presently, but he says he can't do us
the good turn without witnesses: so, when the count and your
sister come, you know he and you may be fathers for one another.

Squ. *Rich.* Well, well, tit for tat! ay, ay, that will be
friendly.

Myr. And see! here they come.

Enter Count Basset, *and Miss* Jenny.

Count *Bas.* So, so, here's your brother, and his bride, before
us, my dear.

Jenny. Well, I vow my heart's at my mouth still! I thought
I should never have got rid of mamma! but, while she stood
gaping upon the dance, I gave her the slip! lawd! do but feel
how it beats here.

Count *Bas.* O the pretty flutterer! I protest, my dear, you
have put mine into the same palpitation!

Jenny. Ah! you say so——but let's see now——O lud! I
vow it thumps purely——well, well, I see, it will do, and so where's
the parson?

Count *Bas.* Mrs. Myrtilla, will you be so good as to see if
the doctor's ready for us?

Myr. He only staid for you, Sir: I'll fetch him immediately.

Jenny. Pray, Sir, am not I to take place of mamma, when I'm a countess?

Count *Baſ.* No doubt on't, my dear.

Jenny. O lud! how her back will be up then, when she meets me at an assembly! or you and I in our coach and six, at Hyde-Park together!

Count *Baſ.* Ay, or when she hears the box-keepers, at an opera, call out.—The Countess of Ballet's servants!

Jenny. Well, I say it, that will be delicious! and then, may-hap, to have a fine gentleman with a star and what-d'ye-call-um ribbon, lead me to my chair, with his hat under his arm all the way! hold up, says the chairman, and so, says I, my lord, your humble servant, I suppose, madam, says he, we shall see you at my lady Quadrille's! ay, ay, to be sure my lord, says I ——so in swops me, with my hoop stuff'd up to my fore-head! and away they trot, swing! swang! with my tassels dangling, and my flambeaux blazing, and——oh! it's a charming thing to be a woman of quality!

Count *Baſ.* Well, I see that plainly, my dear, there's ne'er a duchess of 'em all will become an equipage like you.

Jenny. Well, well, do you find equipage, and I'll find airs, I warrant you. [*Sings.*

Squ. Rich. Troth! I think this masquerading's the merriest game that ever I saw in my life; thof, in my mind, and there were but a little wrestling, or cudgel-playing now, it would help it hugely. But what a-rope makes the parson stay so?

Count *Baſ.* Oh! here he comes, I believe.

Enter Myrtilla, *with a Constable.*

Conſt. Well, madam, pray which is the party that wants a spice of my office here?

Myr. That's the gentleman. [*Pointing to the Count.*

Count *Baſ.* Hey-day! what in masquerade, doctor?

Conſt. Doctor! Sir, I believe you have mistaken your man: but if you are called Count Ballet, I have a Billet-doux in my hand for you, that will set you right presently.

Count *Baſ.* What the devil's the meaning of all this?

Conſt. Only my lord chief justice's warrant against you for forgery, Sir.

Count *Baſ.* Blood and thunder!

Conſt. And so, Sir, if you please to pull off your fool's frock there, I'll wait upon you to the next justice of peace immediately.

Jenny. O dear me! what's the matter? [*Trembling.*

Count *Baſ.* O! nothing, only a masquerading frolic, my dear.

Squ. Rich. Oh ho! is that all?

Sir Fran. No, sirrah! that is not all.

[*Sir Francis coming softly behind the Squire, knocks him down with his Cane.*

Enter

Enter Manly.

Squ. *Rich.* O lawd! O lawd! he has beaten my brains out!
Man. Hold, hold, Sir Francis, have a little mercy upon my
poor godson, pray Sir.

Sir *Fran.* Waunds, coufin, I han't patience.

Count *Baf.* Manly! nay, then, I'm blown to the devil. [*Afide.*

Squ. *Rich.* O my head! my head!

Enter Lady Wronghead.

Lady *Wrong.* What's the matter here, gentlemen? for hea-
v'ns fake! What are you murd'ring my children?

Conf. No, no, madam! no murder! only a little fufpicion of
felony, that's all.

Sir *Fran.* [*To* Jenny.] And for you, Mrs. Hot-upon't, I could
find in my heart to make you wear that habit, as long as you live,
you jade you. Do you know, huffy, that you were within two
minutes of marrying a pickpocket?

Count *Baf.* So, fo, all's out I find. [*Afide.*

Jenny. O the mercy! why, pray, papa, is not the count a
man of quality then?

Sir *Fran.* O yes! one of the unhang'd ones, it feems.

Lady *Wrong.* [*Afide.*] Married! O the confident thing!
There was his urgent bufinefs then——flighted for her! I han't
patience!——and for ought I know, I have been all this while
making a friendfhip with a highwayman.

Man. Mr. Conftable, fecure there.

Sir *Fran.* Ah, my lady! my lady! this comes of your journey to London! but now I'll have a frolic of my own, madam;
therefore pack up your trumpery this very night; for the moment my horfes are able to crawl, you and your brats fhall make
a journey into the country again.

Lady *Wrong.* Indeed you are miftaken, Sir Francis——I fhall
not ftir out of town yet, I promife you.

Sir *Fran.* Not ftir! waunds! madam——

Man. Hold, Sir!——if you'll give me leave a little——I fancy
I fhall prevail with my lady to think better on't.

Sir *Fran.* Ah! Coufin, you are a friend indeed!

Man. [*Apart to my Lady*] Look you, madam, as to the favour you defign'd me, in fending this fpurious letter inclofed to
my lady Grace, all the revenge I have taken, is, to have fav'd
your fon and daughter from ruin——Now if you will take them
fairly and quietly into the country again, I will fave your ladyfhip from ruin.

Lady *Wrong.* What do you mean, Sir?

Man. Why, Sir Francis——fhall never know what is in this
letter; look upon it. How it came into my hands you fhall know
at leifure.

Lady *Wrong.* Ha! my billet-doux to the count! and an appointment in it! I fhall fink with confufion!

Man.

Man. What shall I say to Sir Francis, madam?

Lady Wrong. Dear Sir, I am in such a trembling! preserve my honour and I am all obedience! [*Apart to* Manly.

Man. Sir Francis————my lady is ready to receive your commands for her journey, whenever you please to appoint it.

Sir Fran. Ah cousin! I doubt I am obliged to you for it.

Man. Come, come, Sir Francis! take it as you find it. Obedience in a wife is a good thing, though it were never so wonderful!————and now, Sir, we have nothing to do but to dispose of this gentleman.

Count Baf. Mr. Manly! Sir, I hope you won't ruin me.

Man. Did not you forge this note for five hundred pounds, Sir?

Count Baf. Sir————I see you know the world, and therefore I shall not pretend to prevaricate————but it has hurt nobody yet, Sir! I beg you will not stigmatize me! since you have spoil'd my fortune in one family, I hope you won't be so cruel to a young fellow, as to put it out of my power, Sir, to make it in another, Sir!

Man. Look you, Sir, I have not much time to waste with you: but if you expect mercy yourself, you must shew it to one you have been cruel to.

Count Baf. Cruel, Sir!

Man. Have you not ruin'd this young woman?

Count Baf. I, Sir!

Man. I know you have————therefore you can't blame her, if, in the fact you are charg'd with, she is a principal witness against you. However, you have one, and one only chance to get off with. Marry her this instant————and you take off her evidence.

Count Baf. Dear Sir!

Man. No words, Sir; a wife or a mittimus.

Count Baf. Lord, Sir! this is the most unmerciful mercy!

Man. A private penance, or a public one————constable.

Count Baf. Hold, Sir, since you are pleas'd to give me my choice; I will not make so ill a compliment to the lady, as not to give her the preference.

Man. It must be done this minute, Sir: the chaplain you expected is still within call.

Count Baf. Well, Sir,————since it must be so————come, spouse————I am not the first of the fraternity, that has run his head into one noose, to keep it out of another.

Myr. Come, Sir, don't repine: marriage is, at worst, but playing upon the square.

Count Baf. Ay, but the worst of the match, too, is the devil.

Man. Well, Sir, to let you see it is not so bad as you think it is, as a reward for her honesty, in detecting your practices, instead of the forged bill, you would have put upon her, there's

a real

a real one of five hundred pounds, to begin a new honey-moon
with.   [*Gives it to* Myrtilla.

Count *Baf.* Sir, this is fo generous an act——

Man. No compliments, dear Sir——I am not, at leifure now
to receive them: Mr. Conftable, will you be fo good as to wait
upon this gentleman into the next room, and give this lady in
marriage to him?

Conft. Sir, I'll do it faithfully.

Count *Baf.* Well! five hundred will ferve to make a handfome
pufh with, however.   [*Exeunt Count,* Myrtilla, *and Conftable.*

Sir *Fran.* And that I may be fure my family's rid of him for
ever——come, my lady, let's e'en take our children along with
us, and be all witnefs of the ceremony.

            [*Exeunt Sir* Francis, *Lady* Wronghead, *Mifs and Squire.*

Man. Now, my lord, you may enter.

Enter Lord and Lady Townly, *and Lady* Grace.

Lord *Town.* So, Sir, I give you joy of your negotiation.

Man. You overheard it all, I prefume?

Lady *Grace.* From firft to laft, Sir.

Lord *Town.* Never were knaves and fools better difpos'd of.

Man. A fort of poetical juftice, my lord, not much above the
judgment of a modern comedy.

Lord *Town.* To heighten that refemblance, I think, fifter, there
only wants your rewarding the hero of the fable, by naming the
day of his happinefs.

Lady *Grace.* This day, to-morrow, every hour, I hope, of
life to come, will fhew I want not inclination to complete it.

Man. Whatever I may want, madam, you will always find
endeavours to deferve you.

Lord *Town.* Then all are happy.

Lady *Town.* Sifter, I give you joy! confummate as the happieft pair can boaft.

In you, methinks, as in a glafs, I fee
The happinefs, that once advanc'd to me.
So vifible the blifs, fo plain the way.
How was it poffible my fenfe could ftray?
But now, a convert, to this truth, I come,
That married happinefs is never found from home.

Sung by Mrs. CIBBER in the Fourth ACT.

OH, I'll have a hufband! ay, marry;
   For why fhould I longer tarry,
For why fhould I longer tarry,
   Than other brifk girls have done?
For if I ftay, 'till I grow gray;
They'll call me old maid, and fufty old jade;
   So I'll no longer tarry;
But I'll have a hufband, ay, marry,
   If money can buy me one.

My mother fhe fays I'm too coming;
And ftill in my ears fhe is drumming,
And ftill in my ears fhe is drumming,
   That I fuch vain thoughts fhou'd fhun;
My fifters they cry, oh fy! and oh fy!
But yet I can fee, they're as coming as me;
   So let me have hufbands in plenty:
   I'd rather have twenty times twenty,
   Than die an old madi undone.

Sung by Mrs. CIBBER, in the Fifth ACT.

I.

WHAT tho' they call me country lass,
    I read it plainly in my glass,
That for a duchess I might pass ;
    Oh, could I see the day !
Would fortune but attend my call,
At park, at play, at ring and ball,
I'd brave the proudest of them all,
    With a *stand by——clear the way.*

II.

Surrounded by a crowd of beaux,
With smart toupees, and powder'd clothes,
At rivals I'd turn up my nose ;
    Oh, could I see the day !
I'd dart such glances from these eyes,
Should make some lord or duke my prize ;
And then, oh ! how I'd tyrannize,
    With a *stand by——clear the way.*

III.

Oh ! then for ev'ry new delight,
For equipage and diamonds bright,
Quadrille, and plays, and balls at night ;
    Oh, could I see the day !
Of love and joy I'd take my fill,
The tedious hours of life to kill,
In ev'ry thing I'd have my will,
    With a *stand by——clear the way.*

F I N I S.

The FIRST PART of

HENRY IV.

WITH THE

LIFE and DEATH

OF

HENRY *Sirnamed* HOT-SPUR.

By Mr. WILLIAM SHAKESPEAR.

LONDON:

Printed for J. TONSON, and the reſt of the
PROPRIETORS; and ſold by the Bookſellers
of *London* and *Weſtminſter.*

MDCCXXXIV.

ADVERTISEMENT.

WHEREAS R. *Walker*, with his Accomplices, have printed and publifh'd feveral of *Shakefpear's* Plays; and to fcreen their innumerable Errors, advertife, That they are Printed as they are acted, and Induftrioufly report, that the faid Plays are printed from Copies made ufe of at the Theatres: I therefore declare, in Juftice to the Proprietors, whofe Right is bafely invaded, as well as in Defence of Myfelf, That no Perfon ever had, directly or indirectly from me, any fuch Copy or Copies; neither wou'd I be acceffary on any Account in Impofing on the Publick fuch Ufelefs, Pirated, and Maim'd Editions, as are publifh'd by the faid R. *Walker*.

W. CHETWOOD, Prompter to His Majefty's Company of Comedians at the Theatre-Royal in *Drury-Lane*.

Dramatis Personæ.

KING Henry *the Fourth*,
Henry, *Prince of* Wales, } *Sons to the King.*
John, *Prince of* Lancaster, }

Worcester,
Northumberland,
Hot-spur,
Mortimer,
Archbishop of York, } *Enemies to the King.*
Dowglas,
Owen Glendower,
Sir Richard Vernon,
Sir Mitchell,

Westmorland, } *of the King's Party.*
Sir Walter Blunt, }

Sir John Falstaff.

Poins,
Gads-hill, } *Companions of Falstaff.*
Peto,
Bardolph,

Lady Percy, *Wife to* Hot-spur.
Lady Mortimer, *Daughter to* Glendower, *and Wife to*
    Mortimer.
Hostess,

Sheriff, Vintner, Chamberlain, Drawers, two Carriers,
    Travellers, and Attendants.

SCENE, *ENGLAND*.

The

The FIRST PART of

HENRY IV.

ACT I. SCENE I.

LONDON.

Enter King Henry, Lord John of Lancaster, Earl of Westmorland and others.

King HENRY.

O ſhaken as we are, ſo wan with care,
Find we a time for frighted peace to pant,
And breathe ſhort-winded accents of new
broils
To be commenc'd in ſtronds afar remote.
No more the thirſty entrance of this ſoil
Shall * dawb her lips with her own children's blood:
No more ſhall trenching war channel her fields,
Nor bruiſe her flowrets with the armed hoofs
Of hoſtile paces. Thoſe oppoſed eyes
Which like the meteors of a troubled heav'n,
All of one nature, of one ſubſtance bred,

Did

* *damp.*   A 3

Did lately meet in the in estine shock
And furious close of civil butchery,
Shall now in mutual well beseeming ranks
March all one way, and be no more oppos'd
Against acquaintance, kindred, and allies:
The edge of War, like an ill-sheathed knife,
No more shall cut his Master. Therefore, friends,
As far as to the sepulchre of Christ,
(Whose soldier now, under whose blessed cross
We are impressed, and engag'd to fight)
Forthwith a power of *English* shall we levy;
Whose arms were moulded in their mother's **womb,**
To chase these Pagans, in those holy fields
Over whose acres walk'd those blessed feet
Which fourteen hundred years ago, were nail'd
For our advantage on the bitter Cross.
But this our purpose is a twelvemonth old,
And bootless 'tis to tell you we will go:
Therefore we meet not now. Then let me hear,
Of you my gentle cousin *Westmorland*;
What yesternight our council did decree,
In forwarding this dear expedience.

West. My Liege, this haste was hot in question,
And many limits of the charge set down
But yesternight: when all athwart there came
A post from *Wales*, loaden with heavy news;
Whose worst was, that the noble *Mortimer*,
Leading the men of *Herefordshire* to fight
Against th' irregular and wild *Glendower*,
Was by the rude hands of that *Welshman* taken;
A thousand of his people butchered,
Upon whose dead corps there was such misuse,
Such beastly, shameless transformation,
By those *Welshwomen* done, as may not be
Without much shame, † re-told or spoken of.

K. Henry. It seems then that the tidings of this broil
Brake off our business for the holy land.

West. This, matcht with other like, my gracious lord;
Far more uneven and unwelcome news

Came

† *be told.*

Came from the North, and thus it did * import.
On holy-rood day, the gallant *Hot-ſpur* there
Young *Harry Percy*, and brave *Archibald*
That ever valiant and approved *Scot*,
At *Holmedon* ſpent a ſad and bloody hour.
As by diſcharge of their artillery
And ſhape of likelihood, the news was told;
For he that brought it, in the very heat
And pride of their contention, did take horſe,
Uncertain of the iſſue any way.

    K. Henry. Here is a dear and true induſtrious friend,
Sir *Walter Blunt*, new lighted from his horſe,
Stain'd with the variation of each ſoil,
Betwixt that *Holmedon*, and this feat of ours:
And he hath brought us ſmooth and welcome news,
The Earl of *Dowglas* is diſcomfited,
Ten thouſand bold *Scots*, two and twenty Knights
Balk'd in their own blood did Sir *Walter* ſee
On *Holmedon*'s plains. Of priſoners, *Hot-ſpur* took
Mordake the Earl of *Fife*, and eldeſt ſon
To beaten *Dowglas*, and the Earls of *Athol*,
Of *Murry*, *Angus*, and *Menteith*.
And is not this an Honourable ſpoil?
A gallant prize? ha, couſin, is it not?

    Weſt. In faith, a conqueſt for a Prince to boaſt of.
    K. Henry. Yea, there thou mak'ſt me ſad, and mak'ſt
      me ſin,
In envy, that my lord *Northumberland*
Should be the father of ſo bleſt a ſon:
A ſon, who is the theam of honour's tongue:
Amongſt a grove, the very ſtraighteſt plant,
Who is ſweet fortune's minion, and her Pride:
Whilſt I by looking on the praiſe of him,
See riot and diſhonour ſtain the brow
Of my young *Harry*. O could it be prov'd,
That ſome night-tripping Fairy had exchang'd
In cradle clothes, our children where they lay,
And call'd mine *Percy*, his *Plantagenet*;
Then would I have his *Harry*, and he mine.

              A 4   Buc.

    * *report.*

But let him from my thoughts. What think you cou-
    sin,
Of this young *Percy*'s Pride? the prisoners
Which he in this adventure hath surpriz'd,
To his own use he keeps, and sends me word
I shall have none but *Mordake* Earl of *Fife*.

   West This is his uncle's teaching, this is *Worcester*,
Malevolent to you in all aspects;
Which makes him prune himself, and bristle up
The crest of youth against your dignity.

   K. *Henry*. But I have sent for him to answer this;
And for this cause a while we must neglect
Our holy purpose to *Jerusalem*.
Cousin, on *Wednesday* next, our council we
Will hold at *Windsor*, so inform the lords:
But come your self with speed to us again;
For more is to be said, and to be done,
Than out of anger can be uttered.

   West. I will, my Liege.   *[Exeunt.*

SCENE II.

Enter Henry *Prince of* Wales, *and Sir* John Falstaff.

   Fal. NOW *Hal*, what time of day is it, lad?

   P. *Henry*. Thou art so fat-witted with drinking old sack, and unbuttoning thee after supper, and
sleeping upon benches in the afternoon, that thou hast
forgotten to demand that truly which thou would'st truly know. What a devil hast thou to do with the time of
the Day? Unless hours were cups of sack, and minutes
capons, and clocks the tongues of bawds, and dials the
signs of leaping-houses, and the blessed Sun himself a fair
hot wench in flame-colour'd taffata. I see no reason
why thou should'st be so superfluous, to demand the time
of th: day.

   Fal. Indeed you come near me now, *Hal*: For we that
take purses, go by the Moon and seven stars, and not by
                         Phœbus,

Phœbus, he, that wandring knight fo fair. And I pray thee, fweet wag, when thou art King —— as God fave thy grace, (Majefty I fhould fay, for grace thou wilt have none.) ——

P. Henry. What! none?

Fal. No, by my troth, not fo much as will ferve to be Prologue to an egg and butter.

P. Henry. Well, how then? come roundly, roundly.

Fal. Marry then, fweet wag, when thou art King, let not us that are fquires of the night's body, be call'd thieves of the day's beauty. Let us be *Diana's* forefters, gentlemen of the fhade, minions of the Moon; and let men fay, we be men of good government, being governed as the fea is, by our noble and chafte miftrefs the Moon, under whofe countenance we —— fteal.

P. Henry. Thou fayft well, and it holds well too; for the fortune of us that are the Moon's men, doth ebb and flow like the fea, being govern'd as the fea is, by the Moon. As for proof, now: A purfe of gold moft refolutely fnatch'd on *Monday* night, and moft diffolutely fpent on *Tuefday* morning; got with fwearing, *lay by*; and fpent with crying, *bring in*: now in as low an ebb as the foot of the ladder; and by and by in as high a flow as the † ridge of the gallows.

Fal. By the lord thou fay'ft true, lad; and is not mine hoftefs of the Tavern a moft fweet wench?

P. Henry. As the honey of *Hibla*, my old lad of the caftle; and is not a buff-jerkin a moft fweet robe of durance?

Fal. How now, how now mad wag, what, in thy quips and thy quiddities? what a plague have I to do with a buff-jerkin?

P. Henry. Why, what a pox have I to do with my hoftefs of the tavern?

Fal. Well, thou haft call'd her to a reckoning many a time and oft.

P Henry. Did I ever call thee to pay thy part?

Fal. No, I'll give thee thy due, thou haft paid all there.

A 5 *P Henry.*

* *laid by.* † *fide.*

P. Henry. Yea and elsewhere, so far as my coin would stretch, and where it would not I have us'd my credit.

Fal. Yea, and so us'd it, that were it not here apparent, that thou art heir apparent —— But I pr'ythee sweet wag, shall there be gallows standing in *England* when thou art King? and resolution thus fobb'd as it is, with the rusty curb of old father antick, the law? Do not thou when thou art a King, hang a thief.

P. Henry. No; thou shalt.

Fal. Shall I? O rare! I'll be a brave judge.

P. Henry. Thou judgest false already: I mean thou shall have the hanging of thieves, and so become a rare hangman.

Fal. Well, *Hal*, well; and in some sort it jumps with my humour, as well as waiting in the court, I can tell you.

P. Henry. For obtaining of suits?

Fal. Yea, for obtaining of suits, whereof the hangman hath no lean wardrobe. 'Sblood I am as melancholy as a gib-cat, or a lugg'd bear.

P. Henry. Or an old Lion, or a lover's lute.

Fal. Yea, or the drone of a *Lincolnshire* bagpipe.

P. Henry. What say'st thou to a Hare or the melancholy of Moor-ditch?

Fal. Thou hast the most unsavoury similies, and art indeed the most comparative, rascalest, sweet young Prince — But *Hal*, I pr'ythee trouble me no more with vanity, I would to God thou and I knew where a commodity of good names were to be bought: an old lord of the council rated me the other day in the street about you, Sir; but I mark'd him not, and yet he talk'd very wisely, and in the street too.

P. Henry. * Thou didst well, for wisdom cries out in the street, and no man regards it.

Fal. O, thou hast damnable iteration, and art indeed able to corrupt a saint. Thou hast done much harm unto me, *Hal*, God forgive thee for it. Before I knew thee, *Hal*, I knew nothing, and now I am, if a man

should

---

* *thou didst well, for no man regards it.*

should speak truly, little better than one of the wicked. I must give over this life, and I will give it over by the lord ; an I do not, I am a villain. I'll be damn'd for never a King's son in christendom.

P. Henry. Where shall we take a purse to-morrow, *Jack ?*

Fal. Where thou wilt, lad, I'll make one; an I do not, call me villain, and baffle me.

P. Henry. I see a good amendment of life in thee, from praying to purse-taking.

Fal. Why *Hal,* 'tis my vocation, *Hal.* 'Tis no sin for a man to labour in his vocation.

S C E N E III.

Enter Poins.

Poins. Now shall we know if *Gads-hill* have set a match. O, if men were to be saved by merit, what hole in hell were hot enough for him ? this is the most omnipotent villain that ever cry'd, stand, to a true man.

P. Henry. Good morrow, *Ned.*

Poins. Good morrow, sweet *Hal.* What says Monsieur remorse ? what says Sir *John* sack and sugar ? *Jack!* how agree the devil and thou about thy soul, that thou soldest him on *Good Friday* last, for a cup of *Madera,* and a cold capon's leg.

P. Henry. Sir *John* stands to his word, the devil shall have his bargain, for he was never yet a breaker of proverbs ; He *will give the devil his due.*

Poins. Then art thou damn'd for keeping thy word with the devil.

P. Henry. Else he had been damn'd for cozening the devil.

Poins. But my lads, my lads, to-morrow morning, by four a clock early at *Gads-hill*; there are pilgrims going to *Canterbury* with rich offerings, and traders riding to *London* with fat purses. I have vizards for you all; you have horses for your selves : *Gads-hill* lies to-night in *Rochester,*

I have

I have befpoke fupper to-morrow in *Eaft-cheap*; we may do it as fecure as fleep: if you will go, I will ftuff your purfes full of crowns; if you will not, tarry at home and be hang'd.

Fal. Hear ye *Tedward*, if I tarry at home, and go not, I'll hang you for going.

Poins. You will, chops?

Fal. Hal, wilt thou make one?

P. Henry. Who? I rob? I a thief? not I, by my faith.

Fal. There's neither honefty, manhood, nor good fellowfhip in thee; thou cam'ft not of the blood-royal, if thou dar'ft not cry, ftand for ten fhillings.

P. Henry. Well then, once in my days I'll be a madcap.

Fal. Why that's well faid.

P. Henry. Well come what will, I'll tarry at home.

Fal. By the lord I'll be a traitor then, when thou art King.

P. Henry. I care not.

Poins. Sir *John*, I pr'ythee leave the Prince and me alone, I will lay him down fuch reafons for this adventure, that he fhall go.

Fal. Well, may'ft thou have the fpirit of perfuafion, and he the ears of profiting, that what thou fpeak'ft may move, and what he hears may be believ'd; that the true Prince may, for recreation's fake, prove a falfe thief; for the poor abufes of the time want countenance. Farewel, you fhall find me in *Eaft-cheap.*

P. Henry. Farewel † thou latter fpring. Farewel allhallown fummer.   [*Exit* Fal.

Poins. Now, my good fweet honey lord, ride with us to-morrow. I have a jeft to execute, that I cannot manage alone. *Falftaff, Harvey, Roffil,* and *Gads-hill,* fhall rob thefe men that we have already way-laid; your felf and I will not be there; and when they have the booty, if you and I do not rob them, cut this head from my fhoulders.

                                        P. Henry.

        † *the.*

P. Henry. But how shall we part with them in setting forth ?

Poins. Why, we will set forth before or after them, and appoint them a place of meeting, wherein it is at our pleasure to fail ; and then will they adventure upon the exploit themselves, which they shall have no sooner atchiev'd, but we'll set upon them.

P. Henry. Ay but 'tis like they will know us by our horses, by our habits, and by every other appointment, to be our selves.

Poins. Tut, our horses they shall not see, I'll tie them in the wood; our Vizards we will change after we leave them; and sirrah, I have cases of buckram for the nonce, to immask our noted outward garments.

P. Henry. But I doubt they will be too hard for us.

Poins. Well, for two of them, I know them to be as true-bred cowards as ever turn'd back; and for the third, if he fights longer than he sees reason, I'll forswear arms. The virtue of this jest will be, the incomprehensible lies that this same fat rogue will tell us when we meet at supper; how thirty at least he fought with, what † wards, what blows, what extremities he endured; and in the reproof of this, lies the jest.

P. Henry. Well, I'll go with thee; provide us all things necessary, and meet me to-morrow night in *Eastcheap*; there I'll sup. Farewel.

   Poins. Farewel, my lord.   [*Exit* Poins.

   P. Henry. I know you all, and will a while uphold
The unyok'd humour of your idleness;
Yet herein will I imitate the sun,
Who doth permit the base contagious clouds
To smother up his beauty from the world;
That when he please again to be himself,
Being wanted, he may be more wondred at,
By breaking through the foul and ugly mists
Of vapours, that did seem to strangle him.
If all the year were playing holidays,
To sport would be as tedious as to work;
But when they seldom come, they wisht-for come,

                        And

   † *words.*

And nothing pleaseth but rare accidents;
So when this loose behaviour I throw off,
And pay the debt I never promised;
By how much better then my word I am,
By so much shall I falsify mens hopes;
And, like bright metal on a sullen ground,
My reformation glittering o'er my fault
Shall shew more goodly, and attract more eyes,
Than that which hath no * foil to set it off.
I'll so offend, to make offence a skill,
Redeeming time, when men think least I will.   [*Exit.*

SCENE IV.

Enter King Henry, Northumberland, Worcester, Hot-
spur, *Sir* Walter Blunt, *and others.*

K. *Henry.* MY blood hath been too cold and tem-
                   perate.
Unapt to stir at these indignities;
And you have found me; for accordingly
You tread upon my patience: but be sure,
I will from henceforth rather be my self,
Mighty, and to be fear'd, than my Condition,
Which hath been smooth as oyl, soft as young down,
And therefore lost that title of respect,
Which the proud soul ne'er pays, but to the proud.
    Wor. Our house, my sovereign Liege, little deserves
The scourge of greatness to be used on it,
And that same Greatness too, which our own hands
Have help'd to make so portly.
    North. My good lord ———
    K. *Henry.* *Worcester* get thee gone, for I do see
Danger and disobedience in thine eye.
O Sir, your presence is too bold and peremptory,
And Majesty might never yet endure
The moody frontier of a servant brow,
You have good leave to leave us. When we need
                                              Your

                    * *foil.*

Your ufe and counfel, we fhall fend for you.

[*Exit* Worcefter.

You were about to fpeak.   [*To* Northumberland.

North. Yes, my good Lord.

Thofe prifoners in your highnefs' name demanded,
Which *Harry Percy* here at *Holmedon* took,
Were, as he fays, not with fuch ftrength deny'd
As was deliver'd to your Majefty.
* Or envy therefore, or mifprifion,
Is guilty of this fault, and not my fon.

Hot. My Liege, I did deny no prifoners.
But I remember, when the fight was done,
When I was dry with rage, and extream toil,
Breathlefs and faint, leaning upon my fword;
' Came there a certain lord, neat, trimly drefs'd :
' Frefh as a bridegroom, and his chin new-reap'd
' Shew'd like a ftubble-land at harveft-home.
' He was perfumed like a milliner,
' And 'twixt his Finger and his Thumb, he held
' A pouncet-box, which ever and anon
' He gave his nofe : ‡ and ftill he fmil'd and talk'd;
' And as the foldiers bare dead bodies by,
' He call'd them untaught Knaves, unmannerly,
' To bring a flovenly, unhandfome coarfe
' Betwixt the wind, and his nobility.
' With many holiday and lady terms
' He queftion'd me : amongft the reft, demanded
' My prifoners, in your Majefty's behalf;
' I, then all-fmarting with my wounds being cold,
' To be fo pefter'd with a popinjay,
' Out of my grief, and my impatience,
' Anfwer'd, negleftingly, I know not what;

' He

---

*   ――― nofe, and took't away again ;
Who therewith angry, when it next came there,
Took it in fnuff. ――― And ftill he fmil'd, &c.

‡ *Whoever through envy or mifprifion*
Was guilty of this fault, 'twas not my fon.

‘ He ſhould or ſhould not; for he made me mad,
‘ To ſee him ſhine ſo brisk, and ſmell ſo ſweet,
‘ And talk ſo like a waiting-gentlewoman,
‘ Of guns, and drums, and wounds; (God ſave the
    mark!)
‘ And telling me, the ſoveraign'ſt thing on earth
‘ Was Parmacity, for an inward bruiſe;
‘ And that it was great pity, ſo it was,
‘ This villainous ſalt-petre ſhould be digg'd
‘ Out of the bowels of the harmleſs earth,
‘ Which many a good, tall Fellow had deſtroy'd
‘ So cowardly: And but for theſe vile guns,
‘ He would himſelf have been a ſoldier.
This bald, unjointed chat of his, my lord,
I anſwer'd indirectly, as I ſaid;
And I beſeech you, let not this report
Come currant for an accuſation,
Betwixt my love and your high Majeſty.

    Blint. The circumſtance conſider'd, good my lord,
Whatever *Harry Percy* then had ſaid,
To ſuch a Perſon, and in ſuch a place,
At ſuch a time, with all the reſt retold,
May reaſonably die and never riſe
To do him wrong, or any way impeach
What then he ſaid, ſo he unſay it now.

    K. Henry. Why yet he doth deny his priſoners,
But with proviſo and exception,
That we at our own charge ſhall ranſom ſtrait
His brother-in-law, the fooliſh *Mortimer,*
Who, on my ſoul, hath wilfully betray'd
The lives of thoſe, that he did lead to fight,
Againſt the great magician, damn'd *Glendower;*
Whoſe daughter, as we hear, the Earl of *March*
Hath lately marry'd. Shall our coffers then
Be empty'd, to redeem a traitor home?
Shall we buy treaſon? and * indent with ſears,
When they have loſt and forfeited themſelves?
No; on the barren mountains let him ſtarve;
For I ſhall never hold that man my friend,
                           Whoſe

* *indent,* for *article, bargain.*

Whofe tongue fhall ask me for one penny coft
To ranfom home revolted *Mortimer*.

　Hot. Revolted *Mortimer?*
He never did fall off, my foveraign Liege,
But by the chance of war; to prove that true,
Needs no more but one tongue, for all thofe wounds,
Thofe mouthed wounds, which valiantly he took,
When on the gentle *Severn's* fedgy Bank,
In fingle oppofition hand to hand,
He did confound the beft part of an hour
In changing hardiment with great *Glendower* :
Three times they breath'd, and three times did they
　　drink,
Upon agreement, of fwift *Severn's* flood ;
Who then affrighted with their bloody looks,
Ran fearfully among the trembling reeds,
And hid his crifp'd head in the hollow bank,
Blood-ftained with thefe valiant combatants,
Never did bafe and rotten policy
Colour her working with fuch deadly wounds;
Nor ever could the noble *Mortimer*
Receive fo many and all willingly.
Then let him not be flander'd with revolt.

　K. Henry. Thou doft bely him, *Percy*, thou belieft
　　him;
He never did encounter with *Glendower*;
He durft as well have met the Devil alone,
As *Owen Glendower* for an Enemy.
Art not afham'd? but firrah, from this hour
Let me not hear you fpeak of *Mortimer*.
Send me your prifoners with the fpeedieft means,
Or you fhall hear in fuch a kind from me
As will difpleafe you. Lord *Northumberland*,
We licence your departure with your fon.
Send us your prifoners, or you'll hear of it.
　　　　　　　　　　[*Exit K. Henry.*

　Hot. And if the devil come and roar for them,
I will not fend them. I will after ftrait,
And tell him fo; for I will eafe my heart.
　　　　　　　　　　　　　Although

Although it be with hazard of my head.   [a-while,
   North. What, drunk with choler? stay, and pause
Here comes your uncle.

Enter Worcester.

   Hot. Speak of *Mortimer?*
Yes, I will speak of him, and let my soul
Want mercy, if I do not join with him.
In his behalf, I'll empty all these veins,
And shed my dear blood drop by drop in dust,
But I will lift the downfall'n *Mortimer*
As high i'th'Air as this unthankful King,
As this ingrate and cankred *Bolingbroke.*
   North. Brother, the King hath made your Nephew
         mad.   [*To* Worcester.
   Wor. Who struck this heat up after I was gone?
   Hot. He will, forsooth, have all my Prisoners:
And when I urg'd the ransom once again
Of my wife's brother, then his cheek look'd pale,
And on my face he turn'd an eye of death,
Trembling ev'n at the name of *Mortimer.*
   Wor. I cannot blame him; was he not proclaim'd
By *Richard* that dead is, the next of blood?
   North. He was: I heard the proclamation;
And then it was, when the unhappy King
(Whose wrongs in us, God pardon) did set forth
Upon his *Irish* expedition;
From whence he intercepted did return
To be depos'd, and shortly murthered.
   Wor. And for whose death, we in the world's wide
         mouth,
Live scandaliz'd, and foully spoken of.
   Hot. But soft, I pray you; did King *Richard* then
Proclaim my brother *Mortimer*
Heir to the Crown?
   North. He did; my self did hear it.
   Hot. Nay, then I cannot blame his cousin King,
That wish'd him on the barren mountains starv'd.
But shall it be, that you that set the crown
                                        Upon

Upon the head of this forgetful man,
And for his fake wear the detefted blot
Of murd'rous † fubornation? fhall it be,
That you a world of curfes undergo,
Being the agents or bafe fecond means,
The cords, the ladder, or the hangman rather?
O pardon me, that I defcend fo low,
To fhew the line and the predicament
Wherein you range under this fubtle King.
Shall it for fhame be fpoken in thefe days,
Or fill up chronicles in time to come,
That men of your nobility and power
Ingag'd them both in an unjuft behalf;
(As both of you, God pardon it, have done,)
To put down *Richard*, that fweet lovely rofe,
And plant this thorn, this Canker *Bolinbroke*?
And fhall it in more fhame be further fpoken,
That you are fool'd, difcarded, and fhook off
By him, for whom thefe fhames ye underwent?
No; yet time ferves, wherein you may redeem
Your banifh'd honours, and reftore your felves
Into the good thoughts of the world again.
Revenge the jeering and difdain'd contempt
Of this proud King, who ftudies day and night
To anfwer all the debt he owes unto you,
Ev'n with the bloody payments of your deaths:
Therefore I fay ―――――

   Wor. Peace, Coufin, fay no more,
And now I will unclafp a fecret book,
And to your quick * conceiving difcontents,
I'll read you matter, deep and dangerous,
As full of peril and adventrous fpirit,
As to o'er-walk a current roaring loud,
On the unftedfaft footing of a fpear.

   Hot. If he fall in, good-night, or fink or fwim:
Send Danger from the eaft unto the weft,
So Honour crofs it from the north to fouth;
And let them grapple. O! the blood more ftirs
To roufe a Lion, than to ftart a Hare.

   † *fubordinations.*   * *conveying.*

North. Imagination of some great exploit
Drives him beyond the bounds of Patience.

Hot. By heav'n, methinks it were an easy leap,
To pluck bright honour from the pale-fac'd Moon,
Or dive into the bottom of the deep,
Where fadom-line could never touch the ground,
And pluck up drowned honour by the locks;
So he that doth redeem her thence, might wear
Without co-rival, all her dignities.
But out upon this half-fac'd fellowship!

Wor. He apprehends a world of figures here,
But not the form of what he should attend.
Good cousin, give me audience for a while.

Hot. I cry you mercy.

Wor. Those same noble-*Scots*
That are your prisoners——

Hot. I'll keep them all.
By heav'n, he shall not have a *Scot* of them:
No, if a *Scot* would save his Soul, he shall not,
I'll keep them by this hand.

Wor. You start away,
And lend no ear unto my purposes,
Those prisoners you shall keep.

Hot. I will; that's flat:
He said he would not ransom *Mortimer*:
Forbad my tongue to speak of *Mortimer*:
But I will find him when he lies asleep,
And in his ear I'll holla, *Mortimer!*
Nay, I will have a Starling taught to speak
Nothing but *Mortimer*, and give it him,
To keep his anger still in motion.

Wor. Hear you, cousin: a word.

Hot. All studies here I solemnly defy,
Save how to gall and pinch this *Bolingbroke:*
And that same sword-and-buckler-Prince of *Wales;*
(But that I think his father loves him not,
And would be glad he met with some mischance,)
I'd have him poison'd with a pot of ale.

Wor. Farewel, my kinsman; I will talk to you
When you are better temper'd to attend.

North.

North. Why what a wafp-tongu'd and impatient fool
Art thou, to break into this woman's mood,
Tying thine ear to no tongue but thine own?

Hot. Why look you, I am whipt and fcourg'd with
  rods,
Nettled and ftung with pifmires, when I hear
Of this vile politician *Bolingbroke:*
In *Richard's* time — what do ye call the place? —
A plague upon't — it is in *Glo'fterfhire* ——
'Twas where the mad-cap Duke his uncle kept ——
His uncle *York* — where I firft bow'd my knee
Unto this King of fmiles this *Bolingbroke:*
When you and he came back from *Ravenfprug.*

North. At *Barkley* caftle.-

Hot. You fay true:
Why what a deal of † candied courtefy
This fawning greyhound then did proffer me! ·
Look, when his *infant fortune came to age* ——
And *gentle Harry Percy* — and *kind coufin* ———
The devil take fuch cozeners — God forgive me —
Good uncle tell your tale, for I have done.

Wor. Nay, if you have not, to't again,
We'll ftay your leifure.

Hot. I have done i'faith.

Wor. Then once more to your *Scotifh* prifoners,
Deliver them without their ranfom ftrait,
And make the *Dowglas'* fon your only mean
For pow'rs in *Scotland?* which for divers reafons
Which I fhall fend you written, be affured
Will eafily be granted you, my lord,
Your fon in *Scotland* being thus employ'd
Shall fecretly into the bofom creep
Of that fame noble prelate, well-belov'd,
Th' Archbifhop.

Hot. York, is't not?

Wor. True, who bears hard
His brother's death at *Briftol,* the lord *Scroop.*
I fpeak not this in eftimation,
As what I think might be, but what I know

† *gaudy.*

Is

Is ruminated, plotted and fet down,
And only ftays but to behold the face
Of that occafion that fhall bring it on.

   Hot. I fmell it : on my life it will do well.

   North. Before the Game's a-foot, thou ftill lett'ft flip.

   Hot. It cannot choofe but be a noble Plot,
And then the power of *Scotland*, and of *York*
To join with *Mortimer*; ha !

   Wor. So they fhall,

   Hor. In faith it is exceedingly well aim'd.

   Wor. And 'tis no little reafon bids us fpeed
To fave our heads, by raifing of a head :
For bear our felves as even as we can,
The King will always think him in our debt,
And think we deem our felves unfatisfy'd
Till he hath found a time to pay us home.
And fee already, how he doth begin
To make us ftrangers to his looks of love.

   Hot. He does, he does; we'll be reveng'd on him.

   Wor. Coufin, farewel. No further go in this
Than I by Letters fhall direct your courfe;
When time is ripe, which will be fuddenly,
I'll fteal to *Glendower*, and Lord *Mortimer*,
Where you, and *Dowglas*, and our powers at once,
(As I will fafhion it) fhall happily meet,
To bear our Fortunes in our own ftrong arms,
Which now we hold at much uncertainty.

   North. Farewel, good brother, we fhall thrive, I truft.

   Hor. Uncle, adieu: O let the hours be fhort,
Till fields, and blows, and groans applaud our fport.

                         [*Exeunt.*

ACT II. SCENE I.

An *INN*.

Enter a Carrier with a Lanthorn in his Hand.

1 CARRIER.

HEIGH ho, an't be not four by the day I'll be hang'd. *Charles's wain* is over the new chimney, and yet our horfe not packt. What, Oftler?

Oft. Anon, anon.

1 *Car.* I pr'ythe *Tom*, beat *Cutts'* faddle, put a few flocks in the point : the poor jade is wrung in the withers, out of all cefs.

Enter another Carrier.

2 *Car.* Peafe and beans are as ‡ dank here as a dog, and that is the next way to give poor jades the bots : this houfe is turn'd upfide down, fince *Robin* Oftler dy'd.

1 *Car.* Poor fellow never joy'd fince the price of oats rofe, it was the death of him.

2 *Car.* I think this is the moft villainous houfe in all *London* road for Fleas : I am ftung like a Tench.

1 *Car.* Like a Tench ? by th'Mafs there's ne'er a King in Chriftendom could be better bit, than I have been fince the firft cock.

2 *Car.* Why, they will allow us ne'er a jourden, and then we leak in your chimney : and your chamberlie breeds fleas like a Loach.

1 *Car*

‡ *dank, i, e. wet and rotten.*

1 *Car.* What, oftler, come away, and be hang'd, come away.

2 *Car.* I have a gammon of bacon, and two razes of ginger, to be deliver'd as far as *Charing-Cross.*

1 *Car.* 'Odsbody, the Turkies in my panniers are quite ftarv'd. What oftler? a plague on thee; haft thou never an eye in thy head? canft not hear? an't were not as good a deed as drink, to break the pate of thee, I am a very villain. Come and be hang'd, haft thou no faith in thee?

Enter Gads-hill.

Gads. Good-morrow carriers. What's a clock?

Car. I think it be two a clock.

Gads. I pr'ythee lend me thy lanthorn, to fee my gelding in the ftable.

1 *Car.* Nay, foft I pray ye, I know a trick worth two of that i'faith.

Gads. I pr'ythee lend me thine.

2 *Car.* Ay, when? can'ft tell? lend me thy lanthorn quoth a! marry, I'll fee thee hang'd firft.

Gads. Sirrah, carrier, what time do you mean to come to *London?*

2 *Car.* Time enough to go to bed with a candle, I warrant thee. Come, neighbour *Mugges,* we'll call up the gentlemen, they will along with company, for they have great charge. [*Exe. Carriers.*

S C E N E II.

Enter Chamberlain.

Gads. What ho, chamberlain?

Chamb. At hand, quoth pick-purfe.

Gads. That's even as fair, as at hand, quoth the chamberlain; for thou varieft no more from picking of purfes, than giving directions doth from labouring. Thou lay'ft the plot how?

          Chamb.

Chamb. Good-morrow mafter *Gads-hill*, it holds currant, that I told you yefternight.   There's a Franklin
in the wild of *Kent*, hath brought three hundred marks
with him in gold; I heard him tell it to one of his company laft night at fupper; a kind of auditor, one that
hath abundance of charge too, God knows what: they
are up already, and call for eggs and butter. They will
away prefently.

Gads. Sirrah, if they meet not with † St. *Nicholas'*
clarks, I'll give thee this neck.

Chamb. No, I'll none of it: I pr'ythee keep that for
the hangman, for I know thou worfhipp'ft St. *Nicholas* as
truly as a man of falfhood may.

Gads. What talkft thou to me of the hangman? if I
hang, I'll make a fat pair of gallows. For if I hang,
old Sir *John* hangs with me, and thou know'ft he's no
ftarveling. Tut, there are other *Trojans* that thou dream'ft
not of, the which, for fport-fake, are content to do the
profeffion fome grace; that would, if matters fhould be
look'd into, for their own credit fake, make all whole.
I am join'd with no foot-land-rakers, no long-ftaff fix-
penny-ftrikers, none of thofe mad Muftachio-purple-hu'd
malt-worms; but with nobility and tranquillity; bur-
gomafters, and great * one-eyers, fuch as can hold in,
fuch as will ftrike fooner than fpeak; and fpeak fooner
than drink; and drink fooner than pray; and yet I lye,
for they pray continually unto their faint the common-
wealth: or rather, not pray to her, but prey on her;
for they ride up and down on her, and make her their
boots.

Chamb. What, the common-wealth their boots? will
fhe hold out water in foul way?

Gads. She will, fhe will; juftice hath liquor'd her.
We fteal, as in a caftle, cock-fure; we have the receipt
of Fern-feed, we walk invifible.

B   *Chamb.*

† *A cant-word for the devil,* old-nick.
* *Perhaps,* Oneraries, Trufees or Commiffioners. *Or cunning men that look fharp, and aim well,* Metaph.

Chamb. Nay, I think rather, you are more beholden to the night, than the Fern-feed, for your walking invisible.

Gads. Give me thy hand : thou shalt have a share in our purchase, as I am a true man.

Chamb. Nay, rather let me have it, as you are a false thief.

Gads. Go to, *Homo* is a common name to all men; Bid the ostler bring my gelding out of the stable. Farewel, ye muddy knave.   [*Exeunt.*

S C E N E III.

The High-way.

Enter *Prince* Henry, Poins *and* Peto.

Poins. COME, shelter, shelter; I have removed *Falstaff*'s horse, and he frets like a gumm'd velvet.

P. Henry. Stand close.

Enter Falstaff.

Fal. Poins, Poins, and be hang'd, *Poins!*

P. Henry. Peace ye fat-kidney'd rascal, what a bawling dost thou keep ?

Fal. What, *Poins ? Hal.*

P. Henry. He is walk'd up to the top of the hill, I'll go seek him.

Fal. I am accurst to rob in that thief's company : the rascal hath remov'd my horse, and ty'd him I know not where. If I travel but four foot by the square farther afoot, I shall break my wind. Well, I doubt not but to die a fair death for all this, if I 'scape hanging for killing that rogue. I have forsworn his company hourly any time this two and twenty year, and yet I am bewitch'd with the rogue's company. If the rascal have not given me medicines to make me love him, I'll be

hang'd,

hang'd, it could not be elſe; I have drunk medicines.
Poins! Hal! a plague upon you both. *Bardolph!* Peto!
I'll ſtarve ere I'll rob a foot further. An 'twere not as
good a deed as to drink, to turn true-man, and to leave
theſe rogues, I am the verieſt varlet that ever chewed
with a tooth. Eight yards of uneven ground, is three-
ſcore and ten Miles afoot with me: and the ſtony-hearted
villains know it well enough. A plague upon't, when
thieves cannot be true to one another. [*They whiſtle*]
Whew, a plague upon you all. Give me my horſe; you
rogues, give me my horſe, and be hang'd.

P. *Henry.* Peace ye fat guts, lie down, lay thine ear
cloſe to the ground, and liſt if thou canſt hear the tread
of travellers.

Fal. Have you any leavers to liſt me up ag in, being down? 'Sblood I'll not bear mine own fleſh ſo far
afoot again, for all the coin in thy father's exchequer.
What a plague mean ye, to colt me thus?

P. *Henry,* Thou lieſt, thou art not colted, thou art
uncolted.

Fal. I pr'ythee, good Prince *Hal,* help me to my
horſe, good King's ſon.

P. *Henry.* Out you rogue, ſhall I be your oſtler?

Fal. Go hang thy ſelf in in thy own heir-apparent
garters; if I be ta'en, I'll peach for this; an I have
not ballads made on} you all. and ſung to filthy tunes,
let a cup of ſack be my poiſon; when a jeſt is ſo
forward, and afoot too! I hate it.

Enter Gads-hill *and* Bardolph.

Gads. Stand,

Fal. So I do againſt my will.

Poins, O 'tis our ſetter, I know his voice:
Bardolph, what news?

Bard. Caſe ye, caſe ye: on with your vizards; there's
money of the King's coming down the hill, 'tis going
to the King's Exchequer.]

Fal. You lie, you rogue, 'tis going to the King's tavern.

Gads. There's enough to make us all.

Fal. To be hang'd.

P. Henry. You four shall front them in the narrow lane: *Ned Poins* and I will walk lower; if they scape from your encounter, then they light on us.

Peto. But how many be of them?

Gads, Some eight or ten.

Fal, Zounds, will they not rob us?

P. Henry. What a coward, Sir *John Paunch*?

Fal. Indeed I am not *John* of *Gaunt,* your grand-father; but yet no coward, *Hal.*

P. Henry. Well, we'll leave that to the proof.

Poins. Sirrah, *Jack,* thy horse stands behind the hedge, when thou need'st him, there shalt thou find him; farewel, and stand fast.

Fal. Now cannot I strike him if I should be hang'd.

P. Henry. *Ned,* where are our disguises?

Poins. Here hard by: stand close.

Fal. Now my Masters, happy man be his dole say I : every man to this business.

S C E N E IV.

Enter Travellers.

Trav. Come, neighbour; the boy shall lead our horses down the hill; we'll walk a foot a while, and ease our legs.

Thieves. Stand,

Trav. Jesu bless us!

Fal. Strike; down with them, cut the villains throats; ah! whorson caterpillars; bacon-fed knaves, they hate us youth; down with them, fleece them.

Trav. O, we are undone, both we and ours for ever.

Fal. Hang ye gorbellied knaves, are you undone? no, ye fat chuffs, I would your store were here. On bacons, on!

on! what ye knaves? young men muſt live; you are grand jurors, are ye? we'll jure ye i'faith.

[*Here they rob and bind them: Exeunt.*

Enter Prince Henry *and* Poins.

P. *Henry.* The thieves have bound the true-men: now could thou and I rob the thieves and go merrily to *London,* it would be argument for a week, laughter for a month, and a good jeſt for ever.

Poins. Stand cloſe, I hear them coming.

Enter Thieves again.

Fal. Come my maſters, let us ſhare, and then to horſe before day; and the Prince and *Poins* be not two arrant cowards, there's no equity ſtirring. There's no more valour in that *Poins,* than in a wild Duck.

P. *Henry.* Your money.

Poins. Villains.

[*As they are ſharing, the Prince and* Poins *ſet upon them. They all run away, and* Falſtaff *after a blow or two runs away too, leaving the booty behind them.*

P. *Henry.* Got with much eaſe. Now merrily to horſe:
The Thieves are ſcatter'd and poſſeſt with fear
So ſtrongly, that they dare not meet each other;
Each takes his fellow for an officer.
Away, good *Ned.* Now *Falſtaff* ſweats to death,
And lards the lean earth as he walks along:
Wer't not for laughing, I ſhould pity him.

Poins. How the rogue roar'd! [*Exeunt.*

B 3 SCENE

S C E N E V.

Lord Percy's *House.*

Enter Hot-spur *solus, reading a letter.*

B UT *for mine own part, my lord, I could be well con-*
    tented to be there, in respect of the love I bear your
House. He could be contented to be there; why is he
not then ? *in respect of the love he bears our house:* he
shews in this, he loves his own barn better than he
loves our house. Let me see some more. *The purpose*
you undertake is dangerous. Why that's certain: 'tis dangerous to take a cold, to sleep, to drink: but I tell
you, my lord fool, out of this nettle, danger, we
pluck this flower, safely. *The purpose you u..*
dangerous, the friends you have named un...
time it self unsorted, and your whole plot too...
the counterpoize of so great an opposition. Say ...
say you so ? I say unto you again, you are a shallow
cowardly hind, and you lye. What a lack-brain is this ?
By the lord, our plot is a good plot as ever was laid;
our friends true and constant: a good plot, good
friends, and full of expectation: an excellent plot,
very good friends. What a frosty-spirited rogue is
this ? Why, my lord of *York* commends the plot, and
the general course of the action. By this hand, if I
were now by this rascal, I could brain him with his
lady's fan. Is there not my father, my uncle, and my
self, Lord *Edmond Mortimer,* my lord of *York,* and
Owen Glendower ? Is there not beside, the *Dowglas ?*
have I not all their letters, to meet me in arms by
the ninth of the next month ? and are there not some
of them set forward already ? What a Pagan rascal
is this ? an infidel. Ha! you shall see now in very sincerity of fear and cold heart, will he to the King,
and lay open all our proceedings. O, I could divide my
self, and go to buffets, for moving such a dish of skimm'd
milk with so honourable an action. Hang him, let him
                                                    tell

tell the King. We are prepared, I will set forward
 to-night.

S C E N E VI.

Enter Lady Percy.

How now, *Kate!* I must leave you within these two
   hours.
   Lady. O my good lord, why are you thus alone?
For what offence have I this fortnight been
A banish'd woman from my *Harry's* bed?
Tell me, sweet Lord, what is't that takes from thee
Thy stomach, pleasure, and thy golden sleep?
Why dost thou bend thy eyes upon the earth?
And start so often when thou sitt'st alone?
Why hast thou lost the fresh blood in thy cheeks?
And given thy treasures and my rights of thee,
To thick-ey'd musing, and curst melancholy!
In thy faint slumbers I by thee have watcht,
And heard thee murmur tales of iron wars:
Speak terms of manage to thy bounding steed;
Cry, Courage! to the field! and thou hast talk'd
Of sallies and retires; of trenches, tents,
Of palisadoes, frontiers, parapets;
Of basilisks, of cannon, culverin,
Of prisoners ransom, and of soldiers slain,
And all the current of a heady fight.
Thy spirit within thee hath been so at war,
And thus hath so bestir'd thee in thy sleep,
That Beads of sweat have stood upon thy brow,
Lik bubbles in a late disturbed stream:
And in thy face strange motions have appear'd,
Such as we see when men restrain their breath,
On some great sudden haste. O what portents are
   these?
Some heavy business hath my lord in hand,
And I must know it; else he loves me not.
   Hot. What ho, is *Gilliams* with the packet gone?

B 4   *Enter*

Enter Servant.

Serv. He is, my lord, an hour agone.

Hot. Hath *Butler* brought thoſe horſes from the Sheriff?

Serv. One horſe, my lord, he brought ev'n now.

Hot. What horſe? a roan, a crop ear, is it not?

Serv. It is, my lord.

Hot. That roan ſhall be my throne.
Well, I will back him ſtrait. O *Eſperance!*
Bid *Butler* lead him forth into the park.

Lady. But hear you, my lord.

Hot. What ſay'ſt thou, my lady?

Lady. What is it carries you away?

Hot. Why, my horſe, my love, my horſe.

Lady. Out you mad-headed ape! A weaſel hath not
Such a deal of ſpleen as you are toſt with.
In faith I'll know your buſineſs, that I will.
I fear my brother *Mortimer* doth ſtir
About his title, and hath ſent for you
To line his enterprize, but if you go ——

Hot. —— So far afoot, I ſhall be weary, love.

Lady. Come, come, you Paraquito, anſwer me
Directly to this queſtion, I ſhall aſk.
I'll break thy little finger, *Harry,*
If thou wilt not tell me true.

Hot. Away, away, you trifler: love! I love thee
not.
I care not for thee, *Kate*; this is no world
To play with † mammets, and to tilt with lips.
We muſt have bloody noſes, and crack'd crowns,
And paſs them currant too —— gods me! my horſe.
What ſay'ſt thou, *Kate!* what wouldſt thou have with
me?

Lady. Do you not love me? do you not indeed?
Well, do not then. For ſince you love me not,
I will not love my ſelf. Do you not love me?
Nay, tell me if you ſpeak in jeſt or no?

Hot.

† *Mammets,* i. e, girls.

Hot. Come, wilt thou fee me ride?
And when I am on horse-back, I will fwear
I muft not have you henceforth queftion me,
Whither I go; nor reafon where about.
Whither I muft, I muft; and to conclude,
This evening muft I leave thee, gentle *Kate.*
I know you wife, but yet no further wife
Than *Harry Percy's* wife.   Conftant you are,
But yet a woman; and for fecrefie,
No lady clofer.   For I will believe,
Thou wilt not utter what thou doft not know,
And fo far will I truft thee, gentle *Kate.*
    Lady. How fo far?
    Hot. Not an inch further.   But hark you *Kate*;
Whither I go, thither fhall you go too:
To-day will I fet forth, to-morrow you.
Will this content you, *Kate?*
    Lady. It muft of force.   [*Exeunt.*

SCENE VII.

The Tavern in Eaft-cheap.

Enter Prince Henry *and* Poins.

P. Henry. NED, pr'ythee come out of that fat room,
                and lend me thy hand to laugh a little.
    Poins. Where haft been, *Hal?*
    P. Henry. With three or four loggerheads, amongft
three or fourfcore hogfheads.   I have founded the very
bafs ftring of humility.   Sirrah, I am fworn brother to
a leafh of drawers, and can call them by their Chriften
names, as *Tom, Dick,* and *Francis.*   They take it already upon their * confcience that though I be but Prince
of *Wales,* yet I am the King of courtefie; telling me
flatly I am no proud *Jack,* like *Jack Falftaff,* but a
Corinthian, a lad of mettle, a good boy: and when I

B 5   am

* *confidence.*

am King of *England*. I ſhall command all the good lads
in *Eaſt cheap*. They call drinking deep, dying ſcarlet;
and when you * breathe in your watring, they cry hem!
and bid you play it off. To conclude, I am ſo good a
proficient in one quarter of an hour, that I can drink
with a tinker in his own language during my life. I
tell thee *Ned*, thou haſt loſt much honour, that thou
wert not with me in this action; but ſweet *Ned*, (to
ſweeten which name of *Ned*, I give thee this penny-
worth of ſugar, clapt even now into my hand by an under skinker, one that never ſpake other *Engliſh* in his
life, then *Eight Shillings and Six Pence*, and *You are welcome Sir:* with this ſhrill addition, *Anon, Sir, anon Sir;
Score a pint of baſtard in the half moon*, or ſo.) But *Ned*,
to drive away time till *Falſtaff* come, I pr'ythee do thou
ſtand in ſome bye room, while I queſtion my puny
drawer, to what end he gave me the ſugar? and do never leave caling *Francis*, that his tale to me may be
nothing but, *anon*. Step aſide, and I'll ſhew thee a
precedent.

    Poins. Francis.
    P. *Henry.* Thou art perfect.
    Poins. Francis.

S C E N E VIII.

Enter Francis *the drawer.*

Fran. Anon, anon, Sir; look down into the pomgranet,
Ralph.
    P. *Henry.* Come hither, *Francis.*
    Fran. My lord.
    P. *Henry* How long haſt thou to ſerve *Francis?*
    Fran. Forſooth, five years, and as much a to ——
    Poins. Francis.
    Fran. Anon, anon, Sir.
    P. *Henry.* Five years; by'r-lady, a long leaſe for the
clinking of pewter. But *Francis*, dareſt thou be ſo va-
                                           liant;

    * *break.*

liant, as to play the coward with thy indenture, and shew it a fair pair of heels, and run from it?

Fran. O lord, Sir, I'll be sworn upon all the books in *England,* I could find in my heart ━━━━━

Poins. Francis.

Fran. Anon, anon, Sir.

P. Henry. How old art thou, *Francis?*

Fran. Let me see, about *Michaelmas* next I shall be━━━━━

Poins. Francis.

Fran. Anon Sir; pray you stay a little, my lord.

P. Henry. Nay, but hark you *Francis,* for the sugar thou gavest me, 'twas a pennyworth, was't not?

Fran. O lord, I would it had been two.

P. Henry. I will give thee for it a thousand pound: ask me when thou wilt, and thou shalt have it.

Poins. Francis.

Fran. Anon, anon.

P. Henry. Anon, *Francis?* no, *Francis,* but to-morrow *Francis;* or *Francis,* on *Thursday;* or indeed *Francis,* when thou wilt. But *Francis.*

Fran. My lord.

P. Henry. Wilt thou rob this leathern-jerkin, christal-button, * knot-pated, agat-ring, puke-stocking, caddice-garter, smooth tongue, *Spanish* pouch.

Fran. O lord, Sir, who do you mean?

P. Henry. Why then your brown bastard is your only drink; for look you, *Francis,* your white canvas doublet will sully. In *Barbary,* Sir, it cannot come to so much.

Fran. What, Sir?

Poins. Francis.

P. Henry. Away you rogue, dost thou not hear them call?

[*Here they both call, the drawer stands amazed not knowing which way to go.*

Enter

---

* *not-pated.*

Enter Vintner.

Vint. What, ftand'ft thou ftill, and hear'ft fuch a call-ing? Look to the guefts within. My lord, old Sir *John* with half a dozen more are at the door; fha'l I let them in?

P. *Henry.* Let them alone a while, and then open the door, *Poins.*

Enter Poins.

Poins. Anon, anon, Sir.

P. *Henry.* Sirrah, *Falftaff* and the reft of the thieves are at the door; fhall we be merry?

Poins. As merry as Crickets, my lad. But hark ye what cunning match have you made with this jeft of the drawer? come, what's the iffue?

P. *Henry.* I am now of all humours, that have fhew'd themfelves humours, fince the old days of goodman *Adam,* to the pupil age of this prefent twelve a clock at midnight. What's a clock, *Francis?*

Fran. Anon, anon, Sir.

P. *Henry.* That ever this fellow fhould have fewer words than a Parrot, and yet the fon of a Woman. His induftry is up ftairs and down ftairs; his eloquence the parcel of a reckoning. I am not yet of *Percy's* mind, the hot-fpur of the north; he that kills me fome fix or feven dozen of *Scots* at a breakfaft, wafhes his hands and fays to his wife, fie upon this quiet life, I want work, O my fweet *Harry,* fays fhe, how many haft thou kill'd to day? Give my roan horfe a drench, fays he, and anfwers, fome fourteen, an hour after; a trifle, a trifle. I pr'ythee call in *Falftaff,* I'll play *Percy.* and that damn'd brawn fhall play dame *Mortimer* his wife. *Rivo,* fays the drunkard. Call in ribs, call in tallow.

SCENE IX.

Enter Falstaff.

Poins. Welcome *Jack*, where haſt thou been?

Fal. A plague of all Cowards, I ſay, and a vengeance too, marry and *Amen.* Give me a cup of ſack, boy —— Ere I lead this life long, Ill ſow nether ſocks and mend them, and foot them too. A plague of all cowards. Give me a cup of ſack, rogue. Is there no virtue extent?

[*He drinks.*

P. Henry. Didſt thou never ſee *Titan* kiſs a diſh of butter? pitiful hearted * *Titan*, that melted at the ſweet tale of the ſun? if thou didſt, then behold that compound.

Fal. You rogue, here's lime in this ſack too; there is nothing but roguery to be found in villainous Man; yet a coward is worſe than a cup of ſack with lime in it. A villainous coward —— Go thy ways old *Jack*, die when thou wilt; if manhood, good manhood be not forgot upon the face of the earth, then am I a ſhotten herring: there live not three good men unhang'd in *England*, and one of them is fat, and grows old. God help the while, a bad world I ſay. I would I were a weaver, I could ſing pſalms, and all manner of ſongs. A plague of all Cowards, I ſay ſtill.

P. Henry, How now *Woolſack*, what mutter you?

Fal. A King's ſon? if do not beat thee out of thy kingdom with a dagger of lath, and drive all thy ſubjects afore thee like a flock of wild geeſe, I'll never wear hair on my face more. You Prince of *Wales?*

P. Henry. Why you whorſon round Man! what's the matter?

Fal. Are you not a coward: anſwer me to that, and *Poins* there?

P. Henry. Ye fat paunch, an ye call me coward, I'll ſtab thee.

Fal.

_____

* *or rather,* Butter *that melted,* &c.

Fal. I call thee coward! I'll fee thee damn'd ere I'll call thee Coward; but I would give a thoufand pound I could run as faft as thou canft. You are ftrait enough in the fhoulders, you care not who fees your back: call you that backing of your friends? a plague upon fuch backing; give me them that will face me —— Give me a cup of fack, I am a rogue if I drunk to-day.

P. Henry. O villain, thy Lips are fcarce wip'd fince thou drunk'ft laft.

Fal. All's one for that.   [*He drinks.*
A plague of all cowards ftill, fay I.

P. Henry. What's the matter?

Fal. What's the matter! here be four of us, have ta'en a thoufand pound this morning.

P. Henry. Where is it? *Jack*? where is it?

Fal. Where is it? taken from us, it is; a hundred upon poor four of us.

P. Henry. What, a hundred, man?

Fal. I am a rogue if I were not at half fword with a dozen of them two hours together. I have efcap'd by miracle. I am eight times thruft through the doublet, four through the hofe, my buckler cut through and through, my fword hack'd like a hand faw, *ecce fignum.* I never dealt better fince I was a Man; all would not do. A plague of all cowards —— let them fpeak; if they fpeak more or lefs than truth, they are villains and the fons of darknefs.

P. Henry. Speak Sirs. how was it?

* *Gads.* We four fet upon fome dozen.

Fal, Sixteen, at leaft, my lord.

Gads. And bound them.

Peto. No, no, they were not bound.

Fal. You rogue they were bound, every man of them, or I am a *Jew* elfe, an *Ebrew Jew*.

Gads. As we were fharing, fome fix or feven frefh men fet upon us.
                                                            Fal.

---

* *In the old edition* Roffel *fpeaks here, and not* Gadfhill.

Fal. And unbound the reft, and then came in the other.

P. Henry. What, fought ye with them all?

Fal. All? I know not what ye call all; but if I fought not with fifty of them, I am a bunch of radifh: if there were not two or three and fifty upon poor old *Jack*, then am I no two-legg'd creature.

Poins. Pray heav'n, you have not murthered fome of them.

Fal. Nay that's paft praying for. I have pepper'd two of them; two I am fure I have pay'd, two rogues in buckram fuits. I tell thee what, *Hal*, If I tell thee a lie, fpit in my face, call me horfe; thou know'ft my old ward; here I lay, and thus I bore my point; four rogues in buckram let drive at me.

P. Henry. What four? thou faidft but two, even now.

Fal. Four, *Hal*, I told thee four.

Poins. Ay, ay, he faid four.

Fal. Thefe four came all a-front, and mainly thruft at me? I made no more ado, but took all their feven points in my target, thus.

P. Henry. Seven! why there were but four even now.

Fal. In buckram.

Poins. Ay, four in buckram Suits.

Fal. Seven, by thefe Hilts, or I am a villain elfe.

P. Henry. Pr'ythee let him alone, we fhall have more anon.

Fal. Doft thou hear me, *Hal*?

P. Henry. Ay, and mark thee too, *Jack.*

Fal. Do fo, for it is worth the liftning to: thefe nine in buckram, that I told thee of————

P. Henry. So, two more already.

Fal. Their points being broken ————

Poins. Down fell his hofe.

Fal. Began to give me ground; but I follow'd me clofe, came in foot and hand; and with a thought, feven of the eleven I pay'd.

P. Henry.

P. Hen. O monſtrous! eleven buckram men grown out of two!

Fal. But as the devil would have it, three miſ-begotten knaves in *Kendal* green, came at my back, ſnd let drive at me; (for it was ſo dark, *Hal,* that thou couldſt not ſee thy hand.)

P. Hen. Theſe lies are like the Father that begets them, groſs as a mountain, open, palpable. Why thou clay-brain'd guts, thou knotty-pated fool, thou whorſon obſcene greaſy tallow-catch ⸻

Fal. What, art thou mad? art thou mad? is not the truth, the truth?

P. Henry. Why how cou'd'ſt thou know theſe men in *Kendal* green, when it was ſo dark, thou could'ſt not ſee thy Hand? come tell us your reaſon: what ſay'ſt thou to this?

Poins. Come, your reaſon, *Jack,* your reaſon.

Fal. What, upon compulſion? no; were I at the ſtrappado, or all the racks in the world, I would not tell you on compulſion. Give you a reaſon on compulſion! if reaſons were as plenty as black-berries, I would give no man a reaſon upon compulſion: I?

P. Henry. I'll be no longer guilty of this ſin. This ſanguine coward, this bed-preſſer, this horſeback-breaker, this huge hill of fleſh.

Fal. Away you ſtarveling, you elf-ſkin, you dry'd neats-tongue, bull's pizzel, ycu ſtock-fiſh: O for breath to utter! What is like thee? You taylor's yard, you ſheath, you bow-caſe, you vile ſtanding tuck.

P. Henry. Well, breathe a while, and then to't again; and when thou haſt tir'd thy ſelf in baſe compariſons, hear me ſpeak but this.

Poins. Mark, *Jack.*

P. Henry. We two ſaw you four ſet on four, you bound them, and were maſters of their wealth: mark now how a plain tale ſhall put you down. Then did we two ſet on you four, and with a word, outfac'd you from your prize, and have it, yea, and can ſhew it you here in the houſe. And *Falſtaff,* you carry'd your guts away as nimbly, with as quick dexterity, and roar'd

for

for mercy, and ſtill ran and roar'd, as ever I heard bull-calf. What a ſlave art thou, to hack thy ſword as thou haſt done, and then ſay it was in fight. What trick? what deviſe? what ſtarting hole, can'ſt thou now find out, to hide thee from this open and apparent ſhame?

Poins. Come, let's hear, *Jack*: what trick haſt thou now?

Fal. By the Lord, I knew ye, as well as he that made ye. Why hear ye, my Maſters; was it for me to kill the heir apparent? Should I turn upon the true Prince? Why thou knoweſt I am as valiant as *Hercules*; but beware inſtinct, the Lion will not touch the true Prince: inſtinct is a great matter, I was a coward on inſtinct: I ſhall think the better of my ſelf, and thee, during my life; I, for a valiant Lion, and thou for a true Prince. But, by the lord, lads, I am glad you have the money. Hoſteſs, clap to the doors; watch to-night, pray to-morrow. Gallants, lads, boys, hearts of gold, all the titles of good fellowſhip come to you. What, ſhall we be merry? ſhall we have a play *extempore?*

P. Henry. Content, and the argument ſhall be, thy running away.

Fal. Ah, no more of that, *Hal*, if thou loveſt me.

S C E N E X.

Enter Hoſteſs.

Hoſt. O Jeſu! my lord the Prince!

P. Henry. How now, my lady the Hoſteſs, what ſay'ſt thou to me?

Hoſt. Marry, my lord, there is a nobleman of the Court at door would ſpeak with you, he ſays he comes from your father,

P. Henry. Give him as much as will make him a royal man, and ſend him back again to my mother.

Fal. What manner of man is he?

Hoſt. An old man.

Fal.

Fal. What doth gravity out of his bed at midnight? Shall I give him his anſwer?

P. Henry. Pr'ythee do, *Jack.*

Fal, Faith and I'll ſend him packing.   [*Exit.*

P. Henry. Now Sirs, by'r-lady you fought fair; ſo did you *Peto,* ſo did you *Bardolph:* you are Lions too, you ran away npon inſtinct; you will not touch the true Prince, no, fie.

Bard. 'Faith I ran when I ſaw others run.

P. Henry. Tell me now in earneſt; how came *Falſtaff's* ſword ſo hackt;

Peto. Why he hackt it with his dagger, and ſaid, he would ſwear truth out of *England,* but he would make you believe it was done in fight, and perſuaded us to do the like.

Bard. Yea, and to tickle our noſes with ſpear-graſs, to make them bleed, and then beſlubber our garments with it, and ſwear it was the blood of true men, I did that I did not theſe ſeven years before, I bluſh'd to hear his monſtrous devices.

P. Henry. O Villain, thou ſtolleſt a cup of ſack eighteen years ago, and wert taken in the manner, and ever ſince thou haſt bluſh'd *extempore;* thou hadſt fire and ſword on thy ſide, and yet thou ranneſt away; what inſtinct hadſt thou for it?

Bard. My lord do you ſee theſe meteors? do you behold theſe exhalations?

P. Henry. I do.

Bard. What think you they portend?

P, Henry. Hot livers and cold purſes.

Bard. Choler, my lord, if rightly taken.

P. Henry. No, if rightly taken.

P. Henry. No, if rightly taken; halter.

S C E N E XI.

Enter Falſtaff.

Here comes lean *Jack,* here comes bare-bone. How now my ſweet creature of bombaſt, how long is't ago, *Jack,* ſince thou ſaw'ſt thy own knee?

Fal.

Fal. My own knee? When I was about thy Year^s, *Hal*, I was not an Eagle's talon in the wafte, I could lave crept into any Alderman's thumb-ring: a plague of ighing and grief, it blows a man up like a bladder. There's villainous news abroad: here was Sir *John Braby* rom your father; you muft go to the court in the morn-ng. That fame mad fellow of the north, *Percy*; and he if *Wales*, that gave *Amamon* the baftinado, and made *Lucifer* cuck·ld, and fwore the devil his true Liegeman ipon the crofs of a *Welfh*-hook: what a plague call you iim ——

Poins. O, *Glendower*.

Fal. *Owen, Owen*; the fame, and his fon in-law *Mor-imer*, and old *Northumberland*, and the fprightly *Scot* of icots, *Dowglas*, that runs a horfeback up a hill perpendi-:ular ——

P. Henry. He that rides at high fpeed, and with a piftol kills a Sparrow flying.

Fal. You have hit it.

P. Henry. So did he never the Sparrow.

Fal. Well, that rafcal hath good mettle in him, he will not run.

P. Henry. Why, what a rafcal art thou then, to praife him for fo running?

Fal. A horfeback, ye cuckow, but afoot he will not budge a foot.

P. Henry. Yes *Jack*, upon inftinct.

Fal. I grant ye, upon inftinct: well he is there too, ind one *Mordake*, and a thoufand blue-caps more. *Wor-tefter* is ftoln away by night: thy father's beard is turn'd white with the news: you may buy land now as cheap as ftinking mackerel.

P. Henry. Then 'tis like, if there come a hot * *June*, and this civil buffeting hold, we fhall buy maidenheads as they buy hob-nails, by the hundred.

Fal. By the mafs, lad, thou fay'ft true, it is like we fhall have good trading that way. But tell me, *Hal*, are not thou horrible afeard? thou being heir apparent
                                                 could

——————

* *Jun.*

Could the world pick the out three ſuch enemies again as that fiend *Dowglas*, that ſpirit *Percy*, and that devil *Glendower*? art thou not horribly afraid? doth not thy blood thrill at it?

P. Henry. Not a whit i'faith, I lack ſome of thy inſtinct.

Fal. Well thou wilt be horribly chid to-morrow, when thou com'ſt to thy father: if thou do love me, practiſe an anſwer.

P. Henry. Do thou ſtand for my father, and examine me upon the particulars of my life.

Fal. Shall I? content: this chair ſhall be my ſtate, this dagger my ſcepter, and this cuſhion my crown.

P. Henry. Thy ſtate is taken for a joint-ſtool, thy golden ſcepter for a leaden dagger, and thy precious rich crown for a pitiful bald crown.

Fal. Well, an the fire of grace be not quite out of thee, now ſhalt thou be moved ———— Give me a cup of ſack to make mine eyes look red, that it may be thought I have wept; for I muſt ſpeak in paſſion, and I will do it in King *Cambyſes'* vein.

P. Henry. Well, here is my leg.

Fal. And here is my ſpeech ———— Stand aſide nobili'y ————

Hoſt. This is excellent ſport, i'faith.

Fal. Weep not, ſweet Queen, for trickling tears are vain.

Hoſt. O the father! how he holds his countenance?

Fal. For God's ſake, lords, convey my triſtful Queen, For tears do ſtop the flood-gates of her eyes.

Hoſt. O rare, he doth it as like one of thoſe harlotry players, as I ever ſee.

Fal. Peace, good pint-pot, peace good tickle-brain ——
' *Harry*, I do not only marvel, where thou ſpendeſt thy
' time; but alſo, how thou art accompany'd: for though
' the camomile, the more it is trodden on, the faſter it
' grows: yet youth, the more it is waſted, the ſooner
' it wears, Thou art my ſon; I have partly thy mo-
' ther's word, partly my opinion; but chiefly, a villainous
' trick of thine eye, and a fooliſh hanging of the nether

4 lin

lip, that doth warrant me. If then thou be fon to me, here lyeth the point; why, being fon to me, art thou fo pointed at? Shall the bleffed Son of heav'n prove a † micher, and eat black-berries? a queftion not to be ask'd. Shall the fon of *England* prove a thief, and take Purfes? a queftion to be ask'd. There is a thing, *Harry*, which thou haft often heard of, and it is known to many in our land by the name of pitch: this pitch, as ancient writers do report, doth defile; fo doth the company thou keep'ft; for *Harry*, now do I not fpeak to thee in drink, but in tears; not in pleafure, but in paffion; not in words only, but in woes alfo; and yet there is a virtuous man, whom I have often noted in thy company, but I know not his name.

P. *Henry.* What manner of man, an it like your Ma-ſty?

' *Fal.* A goodly portly man i'faith, and a corpulent; of a chearful look, a pleafing eye, and a moft noble carriage; and as I think, his age fome fifty, or, by'r-lady, inclining to threefcore; and now I remember me, his name is *Falftaff*: if that man fhould be lewd-ly given, he deceives me; for *Harry*, I fee virtue in his looks. If then the tree may be known by the fruit, as the fruit by the tree, then peremptorily I fpeak it, there is virtue in that *Falftaff*; keep with him, the reft banifh. And tell me now, thou naughty varlet, tell me, where haft thou been this month?

P. *Henry.* Doft thou fpeak like a King? do thou ftand for me, and I'll play my father.

Fal. Depofe me. If thou do'ft it half fo gravely, fo majeftically, both in word and matter, hang me up by the heels for a rabbet-fucker, or a poulterer's hare.

P. *Henry.* Well, here I am fet.

Fal. And here I ftand; judge, my mafters.

P. *Henry.* Now *Harry*, whence come you?

Fal. My noble lord, from *Eaft-cheap*.

P. Henry

† *a micher, i. e. a truant; to mich, is to lurk out of fight: a hedge-creeper.*

P. Henry. Tho complaints I hear of thee are grievou
Fal. 'Sblood, my lord, they are falſe.——Nay, I
tickle ye for a young Prince.

' *P. Henry.* Sweareſt thou, ungracious boy? hencefor
' ne'er look on me; thou art violently carry'd away fro
' grace; there's a devil haunts thee, in the likeneſs of
' fat old man: a tun of man is thy companion. Wl
' doſt thou converſe with that trunk of humours, th
' boulting-hu ch of beaſtlineſs, that ſwoln parcel of dro
' ſies, that huge bombard of ſack, that ſtuft clock bag
' guts, that roaſted *Manning-tree* Ox with the pudding
' his belly, that reverend vice, that grey iniquity, th
' father ruffian, that vanity in years? Wherein is he goo
' but to taſte ſack and drink it? wherein neat and clea
' ly, but to carve a capon and eat it? wherein cunnin
' but in craft? wherein crafty but in villainy? where
' villainous, but in all things? wherein worthy, but
' nothing?

Fal. I would your grace would take me with yo
whom means your grace?

P. Henry. That villainous abominable mif-leader
youth, *Falſtaff*, that old white-bearded Satan.

Fal. My lord the man I know.

P. Henry. I know thou doſt.

' *Fal.* But to ſay, I know more harm in him than i
' my ſelf, were to ſay more than I know. That he
' old, the more's the pity, his white hairs do witneſs i
' but that he is, (ſaving your reverence,) a whoremaſte
' that I utterly deny. It ſack and ſugar be a fault, Go
' help the wicked: it to be old and merry, be a ſin, the
' many an old hoſt that I know is damn'd: if to be fa
' be to be hated, then *Pharaoh's* lean kine are to be lov'
' No, my good lord, baniſh *Peto*, baniſh *Bardolph*, baniſ
' *Poins*; but for ſweet *Jack Falſtaff*, kind *Jack Falſtaj*
' true *Jack Falſtaff*, valiant *Jack Falſtaff*, and therefor
' more valiant, being as he is, old *Jack Falſtaff*; baniſ
' not him thy *Harry's* company: baniſh plump *Jack*, an
' baniſh all the world.

P. Henry. I do, I will.

Fal·le

Enter Bardolph *running.*

Bard. O, my lord, my lord, the Sheriff with a moſt monſtrous watch, is at the door.

Fal. Out you rogue, play out the play : I have much to ſay in the behalf of that *Falſtaff.*

Enter the Hoſteſs.

Hoſt. O, my lord, my lord!

Fal. Heigh, heigh, the devil rides upon a fiddel-ſtick : what's the matter?

Heſt. The Sheriff and all the watch are at the door : they are come to ſearch the houſe : ſhall I let them in ?

Fal. Doſt thou hear, *Hal ?* never call a true piece of gold a counterfeit : thou art eſſentially mad, without ſeeming ſo.

P. Henry. And thou a natural coward, without inſtinct,

Fal. I deny your *major ;* if you will deny the Sheriff, ſo ; if not, let him enter. If I become not a cart as well as another man, a plague on my bringing up ; I hope I ſhall as ſoon be ſtrangled with a halter, as another.

P. Henry. Go hide thee behind the arras, the reſt walk above. Now my maſters, for a true face and good conſcience.

Fal. Both which I have had ; but their date is out, and therefore I'll hide me.

[*Exeunt* Falſtaff, Bardolph, &c.

P. Henry. Call in the Sheriff.

S C E N E XII.

Enter Sheriff and the Carrier.

P. Henry. Now maſter Sheriff, what is your will with me?

Sher.

Sher. Firſt, pardon me, my lord.   A hue and cry
Hath follow'd certain men unto this houſe.

P. Henry. What men?

Sher. One of them is well known, my gracious lord,
A groſs fat man.

Car. As fat as butter.

P. Henry. The man, I do aſſure you, is not here,
For I my ſelf at this time have employ'd him;
And, Sheriff, I engage my word to thee,
That I will by to-morrow dinner time,
Send him to anſwer thee, or any man.
For any thing he ſhall be charg'd withal:
And ſo let me intreat you leave the Houſe.

Sher. I will, my lord: there are two gentlemen
Have in this robbery loſt three hundred marks.

P. Henry. It may be ſo; if he have robb'd theſe men,
He ſhall be anſwerable; and ſo farewel.

Sher. Good night, my noble lord.

P. Henry. I think it is good morrow, is it not?

Sher. Indeed, my lord, I think it be two a clock.
                                        [*Exit.*

P. Henry. This oily raſcal is known as well as *Paul's*;
go call him forth.

Peto. Falſtaff? faſt aſleep behind the arras, and ſnorting
like a horſe.

P. Henry. Hark, how hard he fetches his breath; ſearch
his pockets.
        [*He ſearches his pockets, and finds certain papers.*

P. Henry. What haſt thou found?

Peto. Nothing but Papers, my lord.

P. Henry. Let's ſee, what be they? read them.

Peto. Item, a capon, 2 *s.* 2 *d.*
Item, Sawce, 4 *d.*
Item, Sack, two gallons, 5 *s.* 8 *d.*
Item, Anchoves and ſack after ſupper, 2 *s.* 6 *d.*
Item, Bread a halfpenny.

P. Henry. O monſtrous, but one halfpenny-worth of
bread, to this intolerable deal of ſack? What there is
elſe, keep cloſe, we'll read it at more advantage; there
let him ſleep till day. I'll to the court in the morning:
                                        we

we muſt all to the wars, and thy place ſhall be honourable. I'll procure this fat rogue a charge of foot, and I
know his death will be a † march of twelveſcore. The
money ſhall be paid back again with advantage. Be with
me betimes in the morning; and ſo good morrow, *Peto.*
    Peto. Good-morrow, good my Lord.   [*Exeunt.*

ACT III. SCENE I.
WALES.

Enter Hot-ſpur, Worceſter, *Lord* Mortimer, *and* Owen
    Glendower.

MORTIMER.

THESE promiſes are fair, the parties ſure,
And our induction full or proſp'rous hope.
  Hot. Lord *Mortimer,* and couſin *Glen-
    dower,*
Will you ſit down?
And uncle *Worceſter*——A plague upon it.
                    [*Exeunt.*

I have forgot the map.
  Glend. No, here it is;
Sit, couſin *Percy,* ſit, good couſin *Hotſpur:*
For by that name, as oft as *Lancaſter*
Doth ſpeak of you, his cheeks look pale, and with
A riſing ſigh, he wiſheth you in heav'n.
  Hot. And you in hell, as often as he hears
Owen Glendower ſpoke of.
  Glend. I blame him not : at my nativity
The front of heav'n was full of fiery ſhapes,

                    C   Of

† *i. e. it will kill him to march ſo far as twelveſcore*
feet.

Of burning creſſets ; know that at my birth,
The frame and the foundation of the earth
Shook like a coward.

   Hot. So it wou'd have done
At the ſame ſeaſon, if your mother's cat
Had kitten'd, though your ſelf had ne'er been born.

   Glend. I ſay the earth did ſhake when I was born.

   Hot. I ſay the earth then was not of my mind ;
If you ſuppoſe, as fearing you, it ſhook.

   Glend. The heav'ns were all on fire, the earth did
    tremble.

   Hot. O, then the earth ſhook to ſee the heav'ns on
    fire,
And not in fear of your nativity.
Diſeaſed nature oftentimes breaks forth
In ſtrange eruptions ; and the teeming earth
Is with a kind of cholick pinch'd and vext,
By the impriſoning of unruly wind
Within her womb ; which for enlargement ſtriving,
Shakes the old beldam earth, and topples down
High tow'rs and moſs-grown ſteeples. At your birth,
Our grandam earth, with this diſtemperature,
In paſſion ſhook.

   Glend. Couſin, of many men
I do not bear theſe croſſings : give me leave
To tell you once again, that at my birth
The front of heav'n was full of fiery ſhapes,
The goats ran from the mountains, and the herds
Were ſtrangely clam'rous in the frighted fields :
Theſe ſigns have marked me extraordinary,
And all the courſes of my life do ſhew,
I am not in the roll of common men.
Where is he living, clipt in with the ſea
That chides the banks of *England, Wales,* or *Scotland,*
Who calls me pupil, or hath read to me ?
And bring him out, that is but woman's ſon,
Can trace me in the tedious ways of art,
Or hold me pace in deep experiments.

   Hot. I think there is no man ſpeaks better *Welſh.*
I'll to dinner⸺

                         Mort.

Mort. Peace, coufin *Percy,* you will make him mad.

Glend. I can call fpirits from the vafty deep.

Hot. Why, fo can I, or fo can any man:
But will they come, when you do call for them?

Glend. Why, I can teach thee to command the devil.

Hot. And I can teach thee, coz. to fhame the devil,
By telling truth. *Tell truth, and fhame the devil.*
If thou have pow'r to raife him, bring him hither,
And I'll be fworn, I've pow'r to fhame him hence.
Oh, while you live, tell truth, and fhame the devil.

Mort. Come, come!
No more of this unprofitable chat.

Glend. Three times hath *Henry Bolingbroke* made head
Againft my pow'r; thrice from the banks of *Wye,*
And fandy-bottom'd *Severn,* have I fent
Him bootlefs home, and weather-beaten back.

Hot. Home, without boots, and in foul weather too!
How 'fcapes he agues, in the devil's name?

Glend. Come, here's the map: fhall we divide our right,
According to our threefold order ta'en?

Mort. Th' Arch-deacon hath divided it
Into three limits, very equally:
England, from *Trent,* and *Severn* hitherto,
By fouth and eaft, is to my part affign'd:
All weftward, *Wales,* beyond the *Severn* fhore,
And all the fertile land within that bound,
To *Owen Glendower;* and dear coz. to you
The remnant northward, lying off from *Trent.*
And our indentures tripartite are drawn:
Which being fealed interchangeably,
(A bufinefs that this night may execute)
To-morrow, coufin *Percy,* you and 1
And my good lord of *Worcefter,* will fet forth,
To meet your father, and the *Scotifh* power,
As is appointed us at *Shrewsbury.*
My father *Glendower* is not ready yet,
Nor fhall we need his help thefe fourteen days:
Within that fpace, you may have drawn togeth^r
Your tenants, friends, and neighbouring gentlemen.

Glend.

Glend. A shorter time shall send me to you, Lords:
And in my conduct shall your Ladies come,
From whom you now must steal and take no leave,
For there will be a world of water shed,
Upon the parting of your wives and you.

Hot. Methinks my moiety, north from *Burton* here,
In quantity equals not one of yours:
See, how this river comes me crankling in,
And cuts me, from the best of all my land,
A huge half-moon a monstrous cantle out.
I'll have the current in this place damm'd up:
And here the smug and silver *Trent* shall run
In a new channel, fair and evenly:
It shall not' wind with so rich a deep indent,
To rob me of so rich a bottom here.

Glend. Not wind? it shall, it must, you see it doth.

Mort. But mark, he bears his course, and runs me up
With like advantage on the other side,
Gelding th'opposed continent as much,
As on the other side it takes from you.

Wor. Yes, but a little charge will trench him here,
And on this north-side win this cape of land,
And then he runs strait and even.

Hot. I'll have it so, a little charge will do it.

Glend. I will not have it alter'd.

Hot. Will not you?

Glend. No, nor you shall not.

Hot. Who shall say me nay?

Glend. Why, that will I.

Hot. Let me not understand you then,
Speak it in *Welsh.*

Glend. I can speak *English*, Lord, as well as you,
For I was train'd up in the *English* court:
Where, being young, I framed to the harp
Many an *English* ditty, lovely well,
And gave the tongue a helpful ornament;
A virtue that was never seen in you.

Hot. Marry, I'm glad of it with all my heart.
I had rather be a kitten, and cry mew,
Than one of these same meter-ballad-mongers;

I'2d

I'ad rather hear a brazen candleftick tun'd,
Or a dry wheel grate on the axle-tree.
And that would nothing fet my teeth on edge,
Nothing fo much as mincing poetry;
'Tis like the forc'd gait of a fhuffling nag.
  Glend. Come, you fhall have *Trent* turn'd.
  Hot. I do not care; I'll give thrice fo much land
To any well deferving friend;
But in the way of bargain, mark ye me,
I'll cavil on the ninth part of a hair.
Are the indentures drawn? fhall we be gone?
  Glend. The moon fhines fair, you may away by night :
(I'll hafte with the * writer) and withal,
Break with your wives of your departure hence:
I am afraid my daughter will run mad,
So much fhe doteth on her *Mortimer.*   [*Exit.*

SCENE II.

  Mort. Fie, coufin *Percy*, how you crofs my father?
  Hot. I cannot chufe; fometime he angers me,
† With telling of the Moldwarp and the Ant,
Of dreamer *Merlin*, and his prophecies;
And of a Dragon, and a finlefs Fifh,
A clipt-wing'd Griffin, and a moulting Raven;
A couching Lion, and a ramping Cat;
And fuch a deal of skimble-skamble ftuff,
As put's me from my faith. I tell you what,
He held me the laft night at leaft nine hours,
In reck'ning up the feveral devils names,
That were his lackeys: I cry'd hum, and well,
But mark'd him not a word. O, he's as tedious
As a tir'd horfe, or as a railing wife:
Worfe than a fmoaky houfe. I'ad rather live
With cheefe and garlick, in a windmill far;

C 3   Than

* *He means the writer of the articles.*

† *This alludes to an old prophecy which is faid to have
induced* O. Glendower *to take arms againft* K. Henry.
See Hall's *Chron. fol.* 20.

Than feed on cates, and have him talk to me,
In any summer-house in Christendom.

Mort. In faith he was a worthy gentleman,
Exceedingly well read, and profited
In strange concealments, valiant as a **Lion**;
And wond'rous affable; as bountiful
As mines of *India*: shall I tell you, cousin,
He holds your temper in a high respect,
And curls himself, even of his natural scope,
When you do cross his humour; faith he does.
I warrant you, that man is not alive
Might so have tempted him as you have done,
Without the taste of danger and reproof.
But do not use it oft, let me intreat you.

War. In faith, my lord, you are too wilful blame,
And since your coming here have done enough
To put him quite besides his patience:
You must needs learn, lord, to amend this fault;
Though sometimes it shews greatness, courage, blood,
And that's the dearest grace it renders you;
Yet oftentimes it doth present harsh rage,
Defect of manners, want of government,
Pride, haughtiness, opinion and disdain:
The least of which, haunting a nobleman,
Loseth men's hearts, and leaves behind a stain
Upon the beauty of all parts besides,
Beguiling them of commendation.

Hot. Well, I am school'd; good manners be your
speed;
Here come our wives, and let us take our leave.

S C E N E   III.

Enter Glendower, *with the ladies.*

Mort. This is the deadly spight that angers me,
My Wife can speak no *English*, I no *Welsh*.

Glend. My daughter weeps, she will not part with you,
She'll be a Soldier too, she'll to the wars.

Mort. Good father, tell her, she and my aunt *Percy*
Shall

Shall follow in your conduct speedily.
> [*Glendower speaks to her in* Welsh, *and she answers*
> *him in the same.*

Glend. She's desp'rate here: a peevish self-will'd harlotry,
That no persuasion can do good upon.
> [*The Lady speaks in* Welsh.

Mort. I understand thy looks; that pretty *Welsh*,
Which thou pow'r'st down from those two swelling
heavens,
I am too perfect in: and but for shame,
In such a parly should I answer thee.
> [*The Lady again in* Welsh.

Mort. I understand thy kisses; and thou mine,
And that's a feeble disputation:
But I will never be a truant, love,
'Till I have learn'd thy language; for the tongue
Makes *Welsh* as sweet as ditties highly penn'd,
Sung by a fair Queen in a summer's bower,
With ravishing division to her lute.

Glend. Nay, if thou melt, then will she run mad.
> [*The Lady speaks again in* Welsh.

Mort. O, I am ignorance it self in this.

Glend. She bids you,
All on the wanton rushes lay you down,
And rest your gentle head upon her lap,
And she will sing the song that pleaseth you,
And on your eye-lids crown the God of sleep,
Charming your blood with pleasing heaviness;
Making such diff'rence betwixt wake and sleep,
As is the diff'rence betwixt day and night,
The hour before the heav'nly harness'd team
Begins his golden progress in the east.

Mort. With all my heart I'll sit and hear her sing
By that time will our book, I think, be drawn.

Glend. Do so;
And those musicians that shall play to you,
Hang in the air a thousand leagues from hence;
Yet strait they shall be here, fit, and attend.

Hot. Come, *Kate*, thou art perfect in lying down:
Come,

come, quick, quick, that I may lay my head in thy lap.

Lady. Go, ye giddy gooſe.   [*The muſick plays.*

Hot. Now I perceive the devil underſtands *Welſh*, and 'tis no marvel he is ſo humorous: by'r-lady he's a good muſician.

Lady. Then would you be nothing but muſical, for you are altogether govern'd by humours: lie ſtill, ye thief, and hear the Lady ſing in *Welſh*.

Hot. I had rather hear *Lady*, my brach, howl in *Iriſh*.

Lady. Would'ſt have thy head broken?

Hot. No.

Lady. Then be ſtill.

Hot. Neither, 'tis a woman's fault.

Lady. Now God help thee.

Hot. To the *Welſh* lady's bed.

Lady. What's that?

Hot. Peace, ſhe ſings. [*Here the Lady ſings a* Welſh *ſong.* Come, I'll have your ſong too.

Lady. Not mine in good ſooth.

Hot. Not yours in good ſooth! you ſwear like a com-fit-maker's wife, not you, *in good ſooth*; and *as true as I love*; and, *as God ſhall mend me*; and, *as ſure as day*: and giveſt ſuch ſarcenet ſurety for thy oaths, as if thou never walk'dſt further than *Finsbury*.

Swear me, *Kate*, like a Lady, as thou art,

A good mouth filling oath, and leave inſooth,

And ſuch proteſt of pepper-ginger-bread,

To velvet-guards, and *Sunday*-citizens.

Come ſing.

Lady. I will not ſing.

Hot. 'Tis the next way to turn tailor, or be *Robin-Red-Breaſt* teacher: if the indentures be drawn, I'll away within theſe two hours: and ſo come in, when ye will.   [*Exit.*

Glend. Come, come, Lord *Mortimer*, you are as ſlow,

As hot Lord *Percy* is on fire to go.

By this, our book is drawn: we will but ſeal,

And then to horſe immediately.

Mort. With all my heart.   [*Exeunt.*

SCENE

SCENE IV.

WINDSOR.

Enter King Henry, *Prince of* Wales, *Lords and others.*

K. *Henry.* LORDS, give us leave; the Prince of
Wales, and I
Muſt have ſome private conference: but be near,
For we ſhall preſently have need of you.———
[*Exeunt Lords.*

I know not whether God will have it ſo,
For ſome diſpleaſing ſervice I have done;
That in his ſecret doom, out of my blood
He breeds revengement and a ſcourge for me:
But thou doſt in thy paſſages of life
Make me believe, that thou art only mark'd
For the hot vengeance and the rod of heav'n,
To puniſh my miſ-treadings. Tell me elſe,
Could ſuch inordinate and low deſires,
Such poor, ſuch baſe, ſuch lewd, ſuch mean attempts,
Such barren pleaſures, rude ſociety,
As thou art match'd withal and grafted to,
Accompany the greatneſs of thy blood,
And hold their level with thy princely heart?
P. *Henry.* So pleaſe your Majeſty, I wiſh I could
Quit all offences with as clear excuſe,
As well, as I am doubtleſs I can purge
My ſelf of many I am charg'd withal,
Yet ſuch extenuation let me beg,
As in reproof of many tales devis'd,
Which of the ear of greatneſs needs muſt hear;
By ſmiling pick-thanks and baſe news-mongers;
I may for ſome things true, (wherein my youth
Hath faulty wander'd, and irregular)
Find pardon, on my true ſubmiſſion.
K. *Henry.* Heav'n pardon thee: yet let me wonder,
Harry,

At thy affections which do hold a wing
Quite from the flight of all thy ancestors.
Thy place in council thou hast rudely lost,
Which by thy younger brother is supply'd;
And art almost an alien to the hearts
Of all the court and Princes of my blood.
The hope and expectation of thy time
Is ruin'd, and the soul of every man
Prophetically does fore-think thy fall.
' Had I so lavish of my presence been,
' So common-hackney'd in the eyes of men,
' So stale and cheap to vulgar company;
' Opinion, that did help me to the crown,
Had still kept loyal to possession,
' And left me in reputeless banishment,
A fellow of no mark nor likelihood.
' By being seldom seen, I could not stir
' But like a comet I was wondred at!
' That men would tell their children, this is he.
' Others wou'd say, where? which is *Bolingbroke?*
' And then I stole all courtesie from heav'n,
' And drest my self in such humility,
' That I did pluck allegiance from men's hearts,
' Loud shouts and salutations from their mouths,
' Even in the presence of the crowned King.
' Thus I did keep my person fresh and new,
' My presence like a robe pontifical,
' Ne'er seen, but wonder'd at, and so my state,
' Seldom but sumptuous, shewed like a feast,
' And won, by rareness, such solemnity.
' The skipping King, he ambled up and down
' With shallow jesters, and rash bavin wits,
' Soon kindled, and soon burnt; carded his state,
' Mingled his royalty with carping fools,
' Had his great name profaned with their scorns,
' And gave his countenance, against his name,
' To laugh at gybing boys, and stand the push
' Of every beardless vain comparative:
' Grew a companion to the common streets,
' Enfeoff'd himself to popularity:

Th

' That being daily fwallow'd by men's eyes,
' They furfeited with honey, and began
' To loath the tafte of fweetnefs, whereof little
' More than a little, is by much too much.
' So when he had occafion to be feen,
' He was but as the Cuckow is in *June*,
' Heard, not regarded ; feen, but with fuch eyes,
' As fick and blunted with community,
' Afford no extraordinary gaze ;
' Such as is bent on fun-like Majefty,
' When it fhines feldom in admiring eyes :
' But rather drowz'd, and hung their eye-lids down,
' Slept in his face, and rendred fuch afpect
' As cloudy men ufe to their adverfaries,
' Being with his prefence glutted, gorg'd and full,
And in that very line, *Harry*, ftand'ft thou;
For thou haft loft thy princely privilege
With vile participation. Not an eye,
But is a-weary of thy common fight,
Save mine, which hath defir'd to fee thee more :
Which now doth, what I would not have it do,
Make blind it felf with foolifh tendernefs.
　　P. *Henry.* I fhall hereafter, my thrice gracious lord,
Be more my felf.
　　K. *Henry.* For all the world,
As thou art at this hour, was *Richard* then,
When I from *France* fet foot at *Ravenfprug*;
And ev'n as I was then, is *Percy* now.
Now by my fcepter, and my foul to boot,
He hath more worthy Intereft to the ftate,
Than thou, the fhadow of fucceffion !
For of no right, nor colour like to right,
He doth fill fields with harnefs in the realm,
Turns head againft the Lions armed jaws ;
And being no more in debt to years than thou,
Leads ancient lords and rev'rend bifhops on,
To bloody battles, and to bruifing arms.
What never-dying honour hath he got
Againft renowned *Dowglas*, whofe high deeds,
Whofe hot incurfions, and great name in arms,

　　　　　　　　　　　　　　　　Holds

Holds from all foldiers chief majority,
And military title capital,
Through all the Kingdoms that acknowledge Chrift,
Thrice hath this *Hot-fpur Mars* in fwathing cloaths,
This infant warrior, in his enterprifes,
Difcomfited great *Dowglas*, ta'en him once,
Enlarg'd him, and made a friend of him,
To fill the mouth of deep defiance up,
And fhake the peace and fafety of our throne.
And what fay you to this? *Percy, Northumberland,*
Th' Arch-bifhop's grace of *York, Dowglas* and *Mortimer,*
Capitulate againft us, and are up.
But wherefore do I tell this news to thee?
Why, *Harry*, do I tell thee of my foes,
Which art my near'ft and deareft enemy?
Thou that art like enough, through vaffal fear,
Bafe inclination, and the ftart of fpleen,
To fight againft me under *Percy*'s pay,
To dog his heels, and curt'fie at his frowns,
To fhew how much thou art degenerate.

   P. Henry. Do not think fo, you fhall not find it fo:
And heav'n forgive them, that fo much have fway'd
Your Majefty's good thoughts away from me.
I will redeem all this on *Percy*'s head,
And in the clofing of fome glorious day,
Be bold to tell you, that I am your fon:
When I will wear a garment of all blood,
And ftain my favours in a bloody mask,
Which wafht away, fhall fcowre my fhame with it.
And that fhall be the day, whene'er it lights,
That this fame child of honour and renown,
This gallant *Hot-fpur*, this all-praifed Knight
And your unthought-of *Harry*, chance to meet.
For every honour fitting on his helm,
Would they were multitudes, and on my head
My fhames redoubled! for the time will come,
That I fhall make this northern youth exchange
His glorious deeds for my indignities.
Percy is but my factor, good my lord,

     2   T'

T'engrofs up glorious deeds on my behalf :
And I will call him to fo ftrict account,
That he fhall render every glory up,
Yea, even the flighteft worfhip of his time,
Or I will tear the reck'ning from his heart.
This, in the name of heav'n, I promife here :
The which, if I perform, and do furvive,
I do befeech your Majefty, may falve
The long-grown wounds of my intemperature ;
If not, the end of life cancels all bonds,
And I will die a hundred thoufand deaths,
Ere break the fmalleft parcel of this vow.
 K. Henry. A hundred thoufand rebels die in this!
Thou fhalt have charge, and fovereign truft herein.

Enter Blunt.

How now, good *Blunt?* thy looks are full of fpeed,
 Blunt. So is the bufinefs that I come to fpeak of.
Lord *Mortimer* of *Scotland* hath fent word,
That *Dowglas* and the *Englifh* rebels met
Th' eleventh of this month, at *Shrewsbury* :
A mighty and a fearful head they are,
If promifes be kept on every hand,
As ever offer'd foul play in a ftate.
 K. Henry. The Earl of *Weftmorland* fet forth to-day :
With him my fon, lord *John* of *Lancafter*,
For this advertifement is five days old.
On *Wednefday* next, *Harry*, thou fhalt fet forward :
On *Thurfday*, we our felves will march: our meeting
Is at *Bridgnorth*; and *Harry*, you fhall march
Through *Glo'fterfhire* : ‖ by which, fome twelve days
  hence.
Our general forces at *Bridgnorth* fhall meet.   **Exe**

‖ *by which account*
Our bufinefs valued, fome twelve days hence
Our gen'ral forces⸺

Our hands are full of buſineſs : let's away,
‡ Advantage feeds them fat, while we delay. [*Exeunt.*

S C E N E V.

Tavern in Eaſt-cheap.

Enter Falſtaff *and* Bardolph.

Fal. **B**Ardolph, am I not fall'n away vilely, ſince this
laſt action ? Do I not bate ? do I not dwindle ?
why, my skin hangs about me like an old lady's looſe
gown : I am wither'd like an old apple *John.* Well, I'll
repent, and that ſuddenly, while I am in ſome liking :
I ſhall be out of heart ſhortly, and then I ſhall have no
ſtrength to repent. An I have not forgotten what the
inſide of a church is made of, I am a pepper-corn, a
brewer's horſe; the inſide of a church! company, villainous company hath been the ſpoil of me.

Bard. Sir *John*, you are ſo fretful, you cannot live
long.

Fal. Why there is it; come ſing me a bawdy ſong,
to make me merry : I was as virtuouſly given, as a
gentleman need to be; virtuous enough; ſwore little ;
diced not above ſeven times a week; went to a bawdy-
houſe not above once in a quarter of an hour; paid mony that I borrow'd, three or four times; liv'd well, and
in good compaſs; and now I live out of all order, out of
all compaſs.

Bard. Why, you are ſo fat, Sir *John*, that you muſt
needs be out of all compaſs, out of all reaſonable compaſs, Sir *John:*

Fal. Do thou amend thy face, and I'll amend my life.
Thou art our Admiral, thou beareſt the lanthorn in the
poop, but 'tis in the noſe of thee; thou art the knight of
the burning lamp.   *Bard.*

‡ *Advantage feeds him fat, while men delay.* Firſt edition.
                                                     Bard.

Bard. Why, Sir *John*, my face does you no harm.

Fal. No, I'll be sworn; I make as good use of it, as many a man doth of a death's head, or a *memento mori*. I never see thy face, but I think upon hell-fire, and *Dives* that liv'd in purple; for there he is in his robes burning. If thou wert any way given to virtue, I would swear by thy face; my Oath should be, by this fire: but thou art altogether given over; and wert indeed, but for the light in thy face, the son of utter darkness. When thou rann'st up *Gad's-Hill* in the night to catch my horse, if I did not think thou hadst been an *ignis fatuus*, or a ball of wild-fire, there's no purchase in mony. O thou art a perpetual triumph, an everlasting bonfire light; thou hast sav'd me a thousand marks in links and torches, walking with thee in the night, betwixt tavern and tavern; but the sack that thou hast drank me, would have bought me lights as good cheap, at the dearest chandler's in *Europe*. I have maintain'd that *Salamander* of yours with fire, any time this two and thirty years, heaven reward me for it.

Bard. 'Sblood, I would my face were in your belly.

Fal. God-a-mercy! so should I be sure to be heart-burn'd.

Enter Hostess.

How now, dame *Partlet* the hen, have you enquir'd yet who pick'd my pocket?

Host. Why, Sir *John*, what do you think, Sir *John*? do you think I keep thieves in my house? I have search'd, I have enquir'd, so has my husband, man by man, boy by boy, servant by servant: the tythe of a hair was never lost in my house before.

F.l. Ye lye, hostess; *Bardolph* was shav'd and lost many a hair; and I'll be sworn my pocket was pick'd; go to, you are a woman, go.

Host. Who I? I defie thee; I was never call'd so in mine own house before.

Fal. Go to, I know you well enough.

Host. No, Sir *John*: you do not know me, Sir *John*;

A

I know you, Sir *John*; you owe me money, Sir *John*, and now you pick a quarrel to beguile me of it. I bought you a dozen of ſhirts to your back.

Fal. Dowlas, filthy dowlas: I have given them a-way to baker's wives, and they have made boulters of them.

Hoſt. Now as I am a true woman, *Holland* of eight ſhillings an ell : you owe money here beſides, Sir *John*, for your diet, and by-drinkings, and money lent you, four and twenty pounds.

Fal. He had his part of it, let him pay.

Hoſt. He ? alas! he is poor, he hath nothing.

Fal. How! poor : look upon his face ; what call you rich ? let him coin his noſe, let him coin his cheeks: I'll not pay a denier.   What, will you make a yonker of me ? ſhall I not take mine eaſe in mine inn, but I ſhall have my pocket pick'd ? I have loſt a ſeal-ring of my grandfather's worth forty mark.

Hoſt. O Jeſu! I have heard the Prince tell him, I know not how oft, that the ring was copper.

Fal. How ? the Prince is a *Jack*, a ſneak-cup ; and if he were here, I would cudgel him like a dog, if he would ſay ſo.

SCENE VI.

Enter Prince Henry *marching, and* Falſtaff *meets him, playing on his Truncheon like a Fife.*

Fal. How now, lad ? is the wind in that door ? muſt we all march ?

Bard. Yea, two and two, *Newgate* faſhion.

Hoſt. My lord, I pray you hear me.

P. Henry. What ſay'ſt thou, Miſtreſs *Quickly* ? how does thy husband ? I love him well, he is an honeſt man.

Hoſt. Good, my Lord, hear me.

Fal. Pr'ythee let her alone, and liſt to me.

P. Henry. What ſay'ſt thou, *Jack* ?

Fal.

Fal. The other night I fell afleep here behind the arras, and had my pocket pickt: this houfe is turn'd bawdy-houfe, they pick pockets.

P. Henry. What didft thou lofe, *Jack?*

Fal. Wilt thou believe me, *Hal?* three or four bonds of forty pounds a-piece, and a feal-ring of my grand-father's.

P. Henry. A trifle, fome eight-penny matter.

Hoft. So I told him, my lord; and I faid, I heard your grace fay fo: and my lord, he fpeaks moft vilely of you, like a foul-mouth'd man as he is, and faid he would cudgel you.

P. Henry, What! he did not?

Hoft. There's neither faith, truth, nor woman-hood in me elfe.

Fal. There's no more faith in thee than in a ftew'd pruen; no more truth in thee than in a drawn Fox; and for woman-hood, Maid-*Marian* may be the deputy's wife of the ward to thee. Go you thing, go.

Hoft. Say, what thing? what thing?

Fal. What thing? why a thing to thank God on.

Hoft. I am nothing to thank God on, I would thou fhould'ft know it: I am an honeft man's wife; and fetting thy knighthood afide, thou art a knave to call me fo.

Fal. Setting thy woman-hood afide, thou art a beaft to fay otherwife.

Hoft. Say, what beaft, thou knave thou?

Fal. What beaft? why an Otter.

P. Henry. An Otter, Sir *John,* why an Otter?

Fal. Why? fhe's neither fifh nor flefh; a man knows not where to have her.

Hoft. Thou art an unjuft man in faying fo: thou or any man knows where to have me; thou knave thou.

P. Henry. Thou fay'ft true, hoftefs, and he flanders thee moft grofly.

Hoft. So he doth you, my lord, and faid this other day, you ow'd him a thoufand pound.

P. Henry. Sirrah, do I owe you a thoufand pound?

Fal. A thousand pound, *Hal?* a million; thy love is worth a million: thou ow'st me thy love.

Host. Nay, my lord, he call'd you *Jack,* and said he would cudgel you.

Fal. Did I, *Bardolph?*

Bard. Indeed, Sir *John,* you said so.

Fal. Yea, if he said my ring was copper.

P. Henry. I say 'tis copper. Dar'st thou be as good as thy word now?

Fal. Why, *Hal,* thou know'st, as thou art but a man I dare; but as thou art a Prince, I fear thee, as I fear the roaring of the Lion's whelp.

P. Henry. And why not as the Lion?

Fal. The King himself is to be fear'd as the Lion; dost thou think I'll fear thee, as I fear thy father? nay, if I do, let my girdle break.

P. Henry. O, if it should, how would thy guts fall about thy knees! But sirrah, there's no room for faith, truth, nor honesty, in this bosom of thine; it is all fill'd up with guts and midriff. Charge an honest woman with picking thy pocket! why thou whoreson, impudent, imbost rascal, if there were any thing in thy pocket but tavern reckonings, *Memorandums* of bawdy-houses, and one poor penny-worth of sugar-candy to make thee long-winded; if thy pocket were enrich'd with any other injuries but these, I am a villain; and yet you will stand to it, you will not pocket up wrongs. Art thou not asham'd?

Fal. Dost thou hear, *Hal?* thou know'st in the state of innocency, *Adam* fell: And what should poor *Jack Falstaff* do, in the days of villany? thou seest, I have more flesh than another man, and therefore more frailty. You confess then you pickt my pocket?

P. Henry. It appears so by the story.

Fal. Hostess, I forgive thee: go make ready breakfast; love thy husband, look to thy servants, and cherish thy guests: thou shalt find me tractable to any honest reason: thou seest, I am pacify'd still. Nay, I pr'ythee be gone, *[Exit Hostess.*

Now,

Now, *Hal,* to the news at court for the robbery, lad;
how is that anſwered?

P. Henry. O my ſweet beef; I muſt ſtill be good angel
to thee. The money is paid back again.

Fal. O, I do not like that paying back; 'tis a double
labour.

P. Henry. I am good friends with my father, and may
do any thing.

Fal. Rob me the exchequer the firſt thing thou do'ſt,
and do it with unwaſh'd hands too.

Bard. Do, my lord.

P. Henry. I have procur'd thee, *Jack,* a charge of foot.

Fal. I would it had been of horſe. Where ſhall I find
one that can ſteal well? O, for a fine thief, of two and
twenty, or thereabout; I am heinouſly unprovided. Well,
God be thanked for theſe rebels, they offend none but
the virtuous, I laud them, I praiſe them.

P. Henry. Bardolph!

Bard. My lord.

P. Henry. Go bear this Letter to lord *John* of *Lancaſter,*
to my brother *John.* This to my lord of *Weſtmorland,*
go *Peto,* to horſe; for thou and I have thirty miles to
ride yet ere dinner-time. *Jack,* meet me to-morrow
in the *Temple-Hall* at two o' clock in the afternoon, there
ſhalt thou know thy charge, and there receive money
and order for their furniture.

The land is burning, *Percy* ſtands on high,
And either they, or we, muſt lower lie.

Fal. Rare words! brave world! hoſteſs my breakfaſt,
 come:

Oh, I could wiſh this tavern were my drum! [*Exeunt.*

ACT IV. SCENE I.

At SHREWSBURY.

Enter Hot-fpur, Worcefter, and Dowglas.

Hot-spur.

ELL faid, my noble *Scot*; if fpeaking truth
In this fine age, were not thought flattery,
Such attribution fhould the *Dowglas* have,
As not a Soldier of this feafon's ftamp
Should go fo gen'ral current through the
      World.
By heav'n, I cannot flatter: I defy
The Tongues of foothers. But a braver place
In my heart's love hath no man than your felf.
Nay, task me to my word; approve me, lord.
   Dow. Thou art the King of honour:
No man fo potent breathes upon the ground,
But I will beard him.

Enter a Meffenger.

   Hot. Do, and 'tis well—What letters haft thou there—
I can but thank you.
   Meff. Thefe come from your father.
   Hot. Letters from him? why comes he not himfelf?
   Meff. He cannot come, my lord, he's grievous fick.
   Hot. Heavn's! how has he the leifure to be fick
In fuch a juftling time? Who leads his power:

Under whofe government come they along?

Meff. His letters bear his mind, not I his mind.

Wor. I pr'ythee tell me, doth he keep his bed?

Meff. He did, my lord, four days ere I fet forth:
And at the time of my departure thence,
He was much fear'd by his phyfician.

Wor. I would the ftate of time had firft been whole,
Ere he by ficknefs had been vifited;
His health was never better worth than now.

Hot. Sick now? droop now? this ficknefs doth in-
     fect
The very life-blood of our enterprize;
'Tis catching hither, even to our camp.
He writes me here, that inward ficknefs————
And that his friends by deputation
Could not fo foon be drawn: nor thought he meet
To lay fo dangerous and dear a truft
On any foul remov'd, but on his own:
Yet doth he give us bold advertifement,
That with our fmall conjunction we fhould on,
To fee how fortune is difpofed to us:
For, as he writes, there is no quailing now,
Becaufe the King is certainly poffeft
Of all our purpofes, what fay you to it?

Wor. Your father's ficknefs is a maim to us.

Hot. A perilous gafh, a very limb lopt off:
And yet, in faith, 'tis not; his prefent want
Seems more than we fhall find it. Were it good,
To fet the exact wealth of all our ftates
All at one caft? to fet fo rich a * main
On the nice hazard of one doubtful hour,
It were not good; for therein fhould we read
The very bottom, and the foul of hope,
The very lift, the very utmoft bound
Of all our fortunes.

Dow. Faith, and fo we fhould;
Where now remains a fweet reverfion.
We now may boldly fpend upon the hope
Of what is to come in:

A

* *mine.*

A comfort of retirement lives in this.

Hot. A rendezvous, a home to fly unto,
If that the devil and mischance look big
Upon the maidenhead of our affairs.

Wor. But yet I would your father had been here :
The quality and † hair of our attempt
Brooks no division, it will be thought
By some, that know not why he is away,
That wisdom, loyalty, and meer dislike
Of our proceedings, kept the Earl from hence.
And think, how such an apprehension
May turn the tide of fearful faction,
And breed a kind of question in our cause :
For well you know we of th' * offending side,
Must keep aloof from strict arbitrement,
And stop all sight-holes, every loop, from whence
The eye of reason may pry in upon us :
This absence of your Father draws a curtain,
That shews the ignorant a kind of fear
Before not dreamt upon.

Hot. You strain too far.
I rather of his absence make this use :
It lends a lustre, and more great opinion,
A larger ‡ glare to your great enterprise,
Than if the Earl were here : for men must think,
If we without his help can make a head,
To push against the Kingdom ; with his help,
We shall o'erturn it topsie-turvy down.
Yet all goes well, yet all our joints are whole.

Dow. As heart can think ; there is not such a word
Spoke of in *Scotland,* as this ‖ term of fear.

SCENE II.

Enter *Sir* Richard Vernon.

Hot. My cousin *Vernon,* welcome by my soul.
Ver. Pray God my news be worth a welcome, lord.
The Earl of *Westmorland,* sev'n thousand strong,

† *heir.*　　* *offering.*　　‡ *dare.*　　‖ *dream.*

Is marching hither, with Prince *John* of *Lancaster*.
  Hot. No harm; what more?
  Ver. And further I have learn'd,
The King himself in person hath set forth,
Or hitherwards intended speedily,
With strong and mighty preparation.
  Hot. He shall be welcome too : Where is his son?
The nimble-footed mad-cap Prince of *Wales*,
And his comrades, that daft the world aside
And bid it pass?
  Ver. All furnish'd, all in arms,
All plum'd like Estridges, that with the wind
|| Baited like Eagles, having lately bath'd :
Glittering in golden coats like images,
As full of spirit as the month of *May*,
And gorgeous as the sun at *Midsummer*,
Wanton as youthful goats, wild as young bulls.
I saw young *Harry* with his beaver on,
His ‡ cuisses on his thighs, gallantly arm'd,
Rise from the ground like feather'd *Mercury*;
And vaulted with such ease into his seat,
As if an Angel dropt down from the Clouds,
To turn and wind a fiery *Pegasus*,
And * witch the world with noble horsemanship.
  Hot. No more, no more; Worse than the sun in *March*,
This praise doth nourish agues; let them come.
They come like sacrifices in their trim,
And to the fire-ey'd maid of smoaky war,
All hot, and bleeding, will we offer them.
The mailed *Mars* shall on his altar sit
Up to the ears in blood. I am on fire,
To hear this rich reprisal is so nigh,
And yet not ours. Come, let me take my horse,
Who is to bear me like a thunder-bolt,
Against the bosom of the Prince of *Wales*.
Harry to *Harry* shall, and horse to horse

                       Meet;

  || Baited, i.e. *flutter'd the wings*.
  ‡ cuisses, *fr. armour for the thighs*.
  * witch, for *bewitch, charm*.

Meet, and ne'er part, till one drop down a coarſe.
Oh, that *Glendower* were come.
Ver. There is more news:
I learnt in *Worceſter*, as I rode along,
He cannot draw his Pow'r this fourteen days.
Dow. That's the worſt tidings that I hear of, yet.
Wor. Ay, by my faith, that bears a froſty ſound.
Hot. What may the King's whole battle reach unto?
Ver. To thirty thouſand.
Hot. Forty let it be,
My Father and *Glendower* being both away,
The pow'r of us may ſerve ſo great a day.
Come, let us take a muſter ſpeedily:
Dooms-day is near; die all, die merrily.
Dow. Talk not of dying, I am out of fear
Of death, or death's hand, for this one half year. [*Exeunt.*

SCENE III.

Enter Falſtaff *and* Bardolph.

Fal. BArdolph, get thee before to *Coventry*: fill me a bottle of ſack: our ſoldiers ſhall march through: we'll to *Sutton-cop-hill* to-night.

Bard. Will you give me money, captain?

Fal. Lay out, lay out.

Bard. This bottle makes an angel.

Fal. And if it do, take it for thy labour; and if it make twenty, take them all, I'll anſwer the coynage. Bid my lieutenant *Peto* meet me at the town's end.

Bard. I will, captain: farewel. [*Exit.*

Fal. If I be not aſham'd of my ſoldiers, I am a ſowc'd gurnet: I have miſ-us'd the King's preſs damnably. 'I have got, in exchange of an hundred and 'fifty ſoldiers, three hundred and odd pounds. I preſs 'me none but good houſholders, yeomens ſons: en'quire me out contracted batchelors, ſuch as have been 'ask'd twice on the banes: mmodity of warm
' ſlaves,

‘ flaves, as had as lieve hear the devil, as a drum; fuch
‘ as fear the report of a culverin, worfe than a ftruck-
‘ fowl, or a hurt wild-duck. I prefs me none but fuch
‘ toafts and butter, with hearts in their bellies no bigger
‘ than pins heads, and they have bought out their fervi-
‘ ces: and now my whole charge confifts of ancients,
‘ corporals, lieutenants, gentlemen of companies, flaves
‘ as ragged as *Lazarus* in the painted cloth, where the
‘ glutton's dogs licked his fores; and fuch as indeed
‘ were never foldiers, but difcarded unjuft fervingmen,
‘ younger fons to younger brothers: revolted tapfters,
‘ and oftlers trade-fall'n, the cankers of a calm world
‘ and long peace: ten times more difhonourably ragged,
‘ than an old fac'd ancient; and fuch have I to fill up
‘ the rooms of them that have bought out their fer-
‘ vices; that you would think I had a hundred and fifty
‘ tatter'd prodigals, lately come from fwine-keeping, from
‘ eating draff and husks. A mad fellow met me on the
‘ way, and told me, I had unloaded all the gibbits, and
‘ preft the dead bodies. No eye hath feen fuch skare-
‘ crows: I'll not march through *Coventry* with them,
‘ that's flat. Nay, and the villians march wide betwixt
‘ the legs, as if they had † gyves on: for indeed, I had
‘ the moft of them out of prifon. There's but a fhirt
‘ and a half in all my company; and the half fhirt is
‘ two napkins tack'd together, and thrown over the
‘ fhoulders like a herald's coat without fleeves; and the
‘ fhirt, to fay the truth, ftoll'n from my hoft of *St.*
‘ *Albans*; or the red-nos'd Inn-keeper of *Daintry*.
‘ But that's all one, they'll find linnen enough on every
‘ hedge.

Enter Prince Henry, *and* Weftmorland.

P. *Henry.* How now, blown *Jack*? how now, quilt?
Fal. What, *Hal*? How now mad wag, what a devil do'ft thou in *Warwickfhire*? My good lord of *Weft-*
          D   *morland,*

† *fhackles.*

morland, I cry you mercy, I thought your honour had already been at *Shrewsbury.*

Weſt. 'Faith, Sir *John,* 'tis more than time that I were there, and you too; but my powers are there already. The King, I can tell you, looks for us all; we muſt away all to-night.

Fal. Tut, never fear me, I am as vigilant as a Cat, to ſteal Cream.

P. Henry. I think to ſteal cream indeed, for thy theft hath already made thee butter; but tell me, *Jack,* whoſe fellows are theſe that come after?

Fal. Mine, *Hal,* mine.

P. Henry. I did never ſee ſuch pitiful raſcals.

Fal. Tut, tut, good enough to toſs: food for powder, food for powder; they'll fill a pit, as well as better; tuſh man, mortal men, mortal men.

Weſt. Ay, but, Sir *John,* methinks they are exceeding poor and bare, too beggarly.

Fal. Faith, for their poverty, I know not where they had that; and for their bareneſs, I am ſure they never learn'd that of me.

P. Henry. No, I'll be ſworn, unleſs you call three fingers on the ribs, bare. But, Sirrah, make haſte. *Percy* is already in the field.

Fal. What is the King encamp'd?

Weſt. He is, Sir *John:* I fear we ſhall ſtay too long.

Fal. Well,
The latter end of a fray, and beginning of a feaſt,
Fits a dull fighter, and a keen gueſt.

[*Exeunt.*

SCENE

SCENE IV.

At SHREWSBURY.

Enter Hot-spur, Worcester, Dowglas, *and* Vernon.

Hot. WE'll fight with him to-night.
  Wor. It may not be.
Dow. You give him then advantage.
Ver. Not a whit.
Hot. Why say you so? looks he not for supply?
Ver. So do we.
Hot. His is certain, ours is doubtful.
Wor. Good cousin be advis'd, stir not to-night.
Ver. Do not, my lord.
Dow. You do not counsel well;
You speak it out of fear, and from cold heart.
 Ver. Do me no slander, *Dowglas* : by my life,
And I dare well maintain it with my life,
If well-respected honour bid me on,
I hold as little counsel with weak fear,
As you, my lord, or any *Scot* that lives.
Let it be seen to-morrow in the battel,
Which of us fears.
 Dow. Yea, or to-night.
 Ver. Content.
 Hot. To-night, say I.
 Ver. Come, come, it may not be : I wonder much,
Being men of such great leading as you are,
That you foresee not what impediments
Drag back our expedition ; certain horse
Of my cousin *Vernon's* are not yet come up,
Your uncle *Worcester's* horse came but to-day,
And now their pride and mettle is asleep,
Their courage with hard labour tame and dull,
That not a horse is half, half of himself.
 Hot. So are the horses of the enemy
In gen'ral, journey-bated, and brought low:

         The

The better part of ours are full of reſt.

Wor. The number of the King's exceedeth ours:
For God's ſake, couſin, ſtay till all come in.

[*The Trumpet ſounds a parley.*

S C E N E   V.

Enter Sir Walter Blunt.

Blunt. I come with gracious offers from the King,
If you vouchſafe me hearing, and reſpect.

Hot. Welcome, Sir *Walter Blunt :* and would to God
You were of our determination ;
Some of us love you well ; and ev'n thoſe ſome
Envy your great deſervings, and good name,
Becauſe you are not of our quality ;
But ſtand againſt us like an Enemy.

Blunt. And heav'n defend, but ſtill I ſhould ſtand ſo,
So long as out of limit and true rule
You ſtand againſt anointed Majeſty.
But to my charge.——The King hath ſent to know
The nature of your griefs, and whereupon
You conjure from the breaſt of civil peace
Such bold hoſtility, teaching his dutious land
Audacious cruelty. If that the King
Have any way your good deſerts forgot,
Which he confeſſeth to be manifold,
He bids you name your griefs, and with all ſpeed
You ſhall have your deſires, with intereſt:
And pardon abſolute for yourſelf, and theſe,
Herein miſ-led by your ſuggeſtion.

Hot. The King is kind: and well we know, the King
Knows at what time to promiſe, when to pay.
My father and my uncle, and myſelf,
Did give him that ſame royalty he wears :
And when he was not ſix and twenty ſtrong,
Sick in the world's regard, wretched and low,
A poor unminded out-law, ſneaking home,

My

My father gave him welcome to the shore:
And when we heard him swear and vow to God,
He came to be but Duke of *Lancaster*,
To sue his livery and beg his peace,
With tears of innocence and terms of zeal;
My father, in kind heart and pity mov'd,
Swore him assistance, and perform'd it too.
Now, when the lords and barons of the realm
Perceiv'd *Northumberland* did lean to him,
They more and less came in with cap and knee,
Met him in boroughs, cities, villages,
Attended him on bridges, stood in lanes,
Laid gifts before him, proffer'd him their oaths,
Gave him their heirs, as pages * following him
Even at the heels, in golden multitudes.
He presently, as greatness knows itself,
Steps me a little higher than his vow
Made to my father, while his blood was poor,
Upon the naked shore at *Ravenspurg:*
And now, forsooth, takes on him to reform
Some certain edicts, and some strait decrees,
That lay too heavy on the common-wealth;
Cries out upon abuses, seems to weep
Over his country's wrongs; and by this face,
This seeming brow of justice, did he win
The hearts of all that he did angle for:
Proceeded further, cut me off the heads
Of all the fav'rites that the absent King
In deputation left behind him here,
When he was personal in the *Irish* war.
   Blunt. I came not to hear this.
   Hot. Then to the point.
In short time after, he depos'd the King,
Soon after that, depriv'd him of his life:
And in the neck of that, task'd the whole state.
To make that worse, suffer'd his kinsman *March,*
(Who is, if every owner were right plac'd,
Indeed his King) to be engag'd in *Wales,*
There without ransom, to lie forefeited:

                    D 3   Disgrac'd

* *follow'd.*

Diſgrac'd me in my happy victories,
Sought to intrap me by intelligence,
Rated my uncle from the council-board,
In rage diſmiſs'd my father from the court,
Broke oath on oath, committed wrong on wrong,
And in concluſion drove us to ſeek out
This head of ſafety; and withall to pry
Into his title too, the which we find .
Too indirect, for long continuance.

 Blunt. Shall I return this anſwer to the King?

 Hot. Not ſo, Sir *Walter*; we'll withdraw a while:
Go to the King, and let there be impawn'd
Some ſurety for a ſafe return again;
And in the morning early ſhall my uncle
Bring him our purpoſes: and ſo farewel.

 Blunt. I would you would accept of grace and love.

 Hot. It may be ſo we ſhall.

 Blunt. Pray heav'n you do.   [*Exeunt.*

SCENE VI.

Enter the Archbiſhop of York, *and Sir* Michell.

York. HIE, good Sir *Michell*, bear this ſealed brief
    With winged haſte to the Lord Mareſhal.
This to my couſin *Scroop*, and all the reſt
To whom they are directed: if you knew
How much they do import, you wou'd make haſte.

 Sir Mich. My lord, I gueſs their tenour.

 York. Like enough.
To-morrow, good Sir *Michell*, is a day
Wherein the fortune of ten thouſand men
Muſt bide the touch. For, Sir, at *Shrewsbury*,
As I am truly given to underſtand,
The King, with mighty and quick-raiſed power,
Meets with lord *Harry*; and I fear, Sir *Michell*,
What with the ſickneſs of *Northumberland*,
Whoſe pow'r was in the firſt proportion;
And what with *Owen Glendower's* abſence thence,
         Who

Who with them was † a ᶠ rated finew too,
And comes not in, o'er-rul'd by prophecies ;
I fear the pow'r of *Percy* is too weak
To wage an inftant tryal with the King.

 Sir *Mich.* Why, my good lord, there's *Dowglas,*
And lord *Mortimer.*

 York. No, *Mortimer* is not there.

 Sir *Mich.* But there is *Mordake, Vernon, Harry Percy,*
And there's my lord of *Worcefter,* and a head
Of gallant warriors, noble gentlemen.

 York. And fo there is : but yet the King hath drawn
The fpecial head of all the land together :
The prince of *Wales,* lord *John* of *Lancafter* ;
The noble *Weftmorland,* and warlike *Blunt,*
And many more corrivals, and dear men
Of eftimation and command in arms.

 Sir *Mich.* Doubt not, my lord, they fhall be well
        oppos'd.

 York. I hope no lefs : yet needful 'tis to fear.
And to prevent the worft, Sir *Michell,* fpeed ;
For if lord *Percy* thrive not, e'er the King
Difmifs his power, he means to vifit us ;
For he hath heard of our confederacy,
And 'tis but wifdom to make ftrong againft him :
Therefore make hafte, I muft go write again
To other friends ; and fo farewel, Sir *Michell.*

[Exeunt.

 ᶠ *rated firmly.*

 †-a rated finew, *fo the firft edition,* i, e. *accounted* a
ftrong aid.

ACT V. SCENE I.

SHREWSBURY.

Enter King Henry, *Prince of* Wales, *Lord* John *of Lancaster,* Earl *of* Weſtmorland, *Sir* Walter Blunt, *and* Falſtaff.

K. HENRY.

OW bloodily the fun begins to peer
Above yon busky hill: the day looks pale
At his diſtemperature.
    P. *Henry.* The fouthern wind
Doth play the trumpet to his purpofes,
    And by his ho'low whiftling in the leaves,
Foretels a tempeſt, and a bluſt'ring day.
    K. *Henry.* Then with the lofers let it fympathize,
For nothing than feem foul to thofe that win.
                    [*The Trumpet founds.*

Enter Worceſter.

    K. *Henry.* How, now, my lord of *Wor'ſter?* 'tis not well,
That you and I ſhould meet upon fuch terms
As now we meet. You have deceiv'd our truſts,
And made us doff our eafie robes of peace,
To cruſh our old limbs in ungentle ſteel:
This is not well, my lord, this is not well.
What fay you to't? will you again unknit
This churlish knot of all-abhorred war,
And move in that obedient orb again,
Where you did give a fair and natural light;
And be no more an exhal'd meteor,

                               A

A prodigy of fear, and a portent
Of broached mifchief, to the unborn times?
  Wor. Hear me, my Liege:
For mine own part, I could be well content
To entertain the lag-end of my life
With quiet hours: for I do proteſt,
I have not fought the day of this diſlike.
  K. *Henry.* You have not fought it, Sir? how comes
    it then?
  Fal. Rebellion lay in his way, and he found it.
  P. *Henry.* Peace, * *Chevet*, peace.
  Wor. It pleas'd your Majeſty, to turn your looks
Of favour, from myſelf and all our houſe;
And yet I muſt remember you, my lord,
We were the firſt and deareſt of your friends:
For you, my ſtaff of office did I break
In *Richard*'s time, and poſted day and night
To meet you on the way, and kiſs your hand,
When yet you were in place and in account
Nothing ſo ſtrong and fortunate, as I:
It was myſelf, my brother, and his ſon,
That brought you home, and boldly did out-dare
The dangers of the time. You ſwore to us,
And you did ſwear that oath at *Doncaſter*,
That you did nothing purpoſe 'gainſt the ſtate,
Nor claim no further than your new-fall'n right,
The ſeat of *Gaunt*, Dukedom of *Lancaſter*.
To this, we ſware our aid: but in ſhort ſpace
It rain'd down fortune ſhow'ring on your head,
And ſuch a flood of greatneſs fell on you,
What with our help, what with the abſent King,
What with the injuries of a wanton time,
The ſeeming ſuff'rances that you had borne
And the contrarious winds that held the King
So long in the unlucky *Iriſh* wars,
That all in *England* did repute him dead:
And from this ſwarm of fair advantages
You took occaſion to be quickly woo'd,
To gripe the gen'ral ſway into your hand;
              D 5   Forgot

   * *Chevet, ſr. a bolſter.*

Forgot your oath to us at *Doncaſter* ;
And being fed by us, you us'd us ſo,
As that ungentle gull, the Cuckow's bird,
Uſeth the Sparrow ; did oppreſs our neſt,
Grew by our feeding to ſo great a bulk,
That ev'n our love durſt not come near your ſight
For fear of ſwallowing; but with nimble wing
We were inforc'd for ſafety's ſake to fly
Out of your ſight, and raiſe this preſent head:
Whereby we ſtand·oppoſed by ſuch means
As you yourſelf have forg'd againſt yourſelf,
By unkind uſage, dangerous countenance,
And violation of all faith and troth,
Sworn to us in your younger enterprize.

    K. *Henry*. Theſe things indeed you have articulated,
Proclaim'd at market-croſſes, read in churches,
To face the garment of rebellion
With ſome fine colour, that may pleaſe the eye
Of fickle changelings and poor diſcontents ;
Which gape, and rub the elbow at the news
Of hurly-burly innovation ?
And never yet did Inſurrection want
Such water-colours, to impaint his cauſe ;
Nor moody beggars, ſtarving for a time
Of pell-mell havock and confuſion.

    P. *Henry*. In both our armies, there is many a ſoul
Shall pay full dearly for this bold encounter,
If once they join in tryal. Tell your nephew,
The Prince of *Wales* doth join with all the world
In praiſe of *Harry Percy*: By my hopes,
(This preſent enterprize ſet off his head)
I do not think a braver gentleman,
More active, valiant, or more valiant young,
More daring, or more bold, is now alive,
To grace this latter age with noble deed.
For my part, I may ſpeak it to my ſhame,
I have a truant been to chivalry,
And ſo, I hear, he doth account me too.
Yet this before my father's Majeſty,
I am content that he ſhall take the odds.

                                     Of

Of his great name and eftimation,
And will, to fave the blood on either fide,
Try fortune with him, in a fingle fight.

K. *Henry*. And, Prince of *Wales*, fo dare we ventur
thee,
Albeit, confiderations infinite,
Do make againft it: No, good *Wor'fter*, no,
We love our people well; even thofe we love
That are mif-led upon your coufin's part:
And will, they take the offer of our grace;
Both he, and they, and you, yea, every man
Shall be my friend again, and I'll be his.
So tell your coufin, and return me word
What he will do. But if he will not yield,
Rebuke and dread correction wait on us,
And they fhall do their office. So be gone,
We will not now be troubled with reply;
We offer fair, take it advifedly.   [*Exit* Worcefter.

P. *Henry*. It will not be accepted, on my life.
The *Dowglas* and the *Hot-fpur* both together
Are confident againft the world in arms.

K. *Henry*. Hence therefore, every leader to his charge.
For on their anfwer will we fet on them:
And God befriend us, as our caufe is juft.   [*Exeunt*.

SCENE II.

Manent Prince Henry *and* Falftaff.

Fal. *Hal*, if thou fee me down in the battel, and be-
ftride me, fo; 'tis a point of friendfhip.

P. *Henry*. Nothing but a Coloffus can do thee that
friendfhip: Say thy prayers, and farewel.

Fal. I would it were bed-time, *Hal*, and all well.

P. *Henry*. Why, thou oweft heav'n a death.

Fal. 'Tis not due yet: I would be loth to pay him
before his day. What need I be fo forward with him
that calls not on me? Well, 'tis no matter, honour
pricks me on. But how if honour prick me off when I
come on? ' how then? can honour fet to a leg? no,

‘or

' or an arm ? no. or take away the grief of a wound ?
' no. Honour hath no skill in surgery then? no. What
' is honour? a word. what is that word honour? Air;
' a trim reckoning. who hath it? he that dy'd a *Wed-*
' *nesday*, doth he feel it? no. doth he hear it? no. is
' it insensible then? yea, to the dead. but will it not live
' with the living ? no. why? Detraction will not suffer
' it, therefore I'll none of it. honour is a meer scutcheon,
' and so ends my catechism.   [*Exit.*

SCENE III.

Enter Westmorland, *and Sir* Richard Vernon.

Wor. O no, my nephew must not know, Sir *Richard,*
The liberal kind offer of the King.
   Ver. 'Twere best he did.
   Wor. Then we are all undone.
It is not possible, it cannot be,
The King shou'd keep his word in loving us;
He will suspect us still, and find a time
To punish this offence in other faults:
Suspicion all our lives, shall be stuck full of eyes;
For treason is but trusted like the Fox,
Who ne'er so tame, so cherish'd, and lock'd up,
Will have a wild trick of his ancestors.
Look how we can, or sad or merrily,
Interpretation will misquote our looks;
And we shall feed like Oxen at a stall,
The better cherish'd, still the nearer death.
My nephew's trespass may be well forgot,
It hath th' excuse of youth and heat of blood,
And an adopted name of privilege,
A hare-brain'd *Hot-spur*, govern'd by a spleen:
All his offences live upon my head.
And on his father's. We did train him on,
And his corruption being ta'en from us,
We as the spring of all, shall pay for all.
                         Therefore,

Therefore, good coufin, let not *Harry* know
In any cafe the offer of the King.
  Ver. Deliver what you will, I'll fay 'tis fo.
Here comes your coufin.

SCENE IV.

Enter Hot-fpur *and* Dowglas.

  Hot. My uncle is return'd :
Deliver up my lord of *Weftmorland.*
Uncle, what news ?
  Wor. The King will bid you battel prefently.
  Dow. Defie him by the lord of *Weftmorland.*
  Hot. Lord *Dowglas,* go you then and tell him fo.
  Dow. Marry I fhall, and very willingly.
                              [*Exit* Dowglas.
  Wor. There is no feeming mercy in the King.
  Hot. Did you beg any? God forbid.
  Wor. I told him gently of our grievances,
Of his oath-breaking; which he mended thus,
By now forfwearing that he is forfworn.
He calls us rebels, traitors, and will fcourge
With haughty arms, this hateful name in us.

Enter Dowglas.

  Dow. Arms, gentlemen, to arms; for I have thrown
A brave defiance in King *Henry*'s teeth :
And *Weftmorland* that was ingag'd did bear it,
Which cannot chufe but bring him quickly on.
  Wor. The Prince of *Wales* ftept forth before the King,
And, nephew, challeng'd you to fingle fight.
  Hot. O, would the quarrel lay upon our heads,
And that no man might draw fhort breath to-day,
But I and *Harry Monmouth.* Tell me, tell me,
How fhew'd his talking? feem'd it in contempt?
  Ver. No, by my foul: I never in my life
Did hear a challenge urg'd more modeftly,
Unlefs a brother fhould a brother dare,

                                        To

To gentle exercife and proof of arms.
He gave you all the duties of a man,
Trim'd up your praifes with a princely tongue,
Spoke your defervings like a chronicle,
Making you ever better than his praife :
And which became him like a Prince indeed,
He made a blufhing * cital of himfelf,
And chid his truant youth with fuch a grace,
As if he mafter'd there a double fpirit,
Of teaching, and of learning inftantly.
There did he paufe ; but let me tell the world,
If he out-live the envy of this day,
England did never owe fo fweet a hope,
So much mifconftrued in his wantonnefs.

Hot. Coufin, I think thou art enamoured
Upon his follies ; never did I hear
Of any Prince fo wild a liberty.
But be he as he will, yet once e'er night
I will embrace him with a foldier's arm,
That he fhall fhrink under my courtefie.
Arm, arm with fpeed. And fellows, foldiers, friends,
Better confider what you have to do,
Than I, that have not well the gift of tongue,
Can lift your blood up with perfuafion.

SCENE V.

Enter a Meffenger.

Meff. My lord, here are letters for you.
Hot. I cannot read them now.
O Gentlemen, the time of life is fhort :
To fpend that fhortnefs bafely were too long,
Tho' life did ride upon a dial's point,
Still ending at th' arrival of an hour.
And if we live, we live to tread on Kings :
If die ; brave death, when Princes die with us.
Now for our confciences, the arms are fair,
When the intent for bearing them is juft.

Enter

* cital, *for* taxation.

Enter another Meſſenger.

Meſſ. My lord, prepare, the King comes on apace.

Hot. I thank him, that he cuts me from my tale,
For I profeſs not talking : only this,
Let each man do his beſt. And here draw I
A ſword, whoſe temper I intend to ſtain
With the beſt blood that I can meet withal,
In the adventure of this perilous day.
Now * *Eſperance ! Percy,* and ſet on :
Sound all the lofty inſtruments of war;
And by that muſick let us all embrace :
For (heav'n to earth) ſome of us never ſhall
A ſecond time do ſuch a courteſie.

[*They embrace, then* exeunt. *The Trumpets ſound*

S C E N E VI.

The King entreth with his power ; Alarm to the battel.

Then enter Dowglas *and Sir* Walter Blunt.

Blunt. What is thy name, that thus in battel croſſeſ
me ?
What honour doſt thou ſeek upon my head ?

Dow. Know then, my name is *Dowglas.*
And I do haunt thee in the battel thus,
Becauſe ſome tell me that thou art a King.

Blunt. They tell thee true.

Dow. The lord of *Stafford* dear to-day hath bought
Thy likeneſs; for inſtead of thee, King *Harry,*
This Sword hath ended him, ſo ſhall it thee,
Unleſs thou yield thee as my priſoner.

Blunt. I was not born to yield, thou haughty *Scot,*
And thou ſhalt find a King that will revenge
Lord *Stafford's* death.

Fight

* *This was the word of battel on* Percy's *ſide.* Se
Hall's *Chron. fol.* 22.

Fight, Blunt *is slain: then enter* Hot-spur.

Hot. O *Dowglas*, hadst thou fought at *Holmedon* thus
I never had triumphed o'er a *Scot*.

Dow. All's done, all's won, here breathless lies the King.

Hot. Where?

Dow. Here.

Hot. This, *Dowglas*? no: I know this face full well:
A gallant knight he was, his name was *Blunt*,
Semblably furnish'd like the King himself.

Dow. Ah! fool go with thy soul whither it goes,
A borrow'd title hast thou bought too dear.
Why didst thou tell me that thou wert a King?

Hot. The King hath many marching in his coats.

Dow. Now by my sword, I will kill all his coats.
I'll murder all his wardrobe piece by piece,
Until I meet the King.

Hot. Up and away,
Our soldiers stand full fairly for the day.   [*Exeunt.*

S C E N E VII.

Alarm, enter Falstaff *solus.*

Fal. Though I could scape shot-free at *London*, I fear
the shot here: here's no scoring, but upon the pate. Soft,
who art thou? Sir *Walter Blunt*? there's honour for you;
here's no vanity: I am as hot as moulten lead, and as
heavy too: heaven keep lead out of me, I need no more
weight than mine own bowels. I have led my rag-e-
muffians where they are pepper'd; there's not three of
my hundred and fifty left alive; and they are for the
town's end, to beg during life. But who comes here!

Enter

Enter Prince Henry.

P. *Henry.* What, ftand'ft thou idle here? lend me thy
· fword,
Many a noble man lies ftark and ftiff
Under the hoofs of vaunting enemies,
Whofe deaths are unreveng'd. Lend me thy fword.

Fal. O *Hal,* I pr'ythee give me leave to breathe a
while. Turk *Gregory* never did fuch deeds in arms, as
I have done this day. I have paid *Percy,* I have made
him fure.

P. *Henry.* He is indeed, and living to kill thee:
I pi'ythee lend me thy fword.

Fal. Nay *Hal,* if *Percy* be alive, thou get'ft not my
fword: but take my piftol if thou wilt.

P. *Henry.* Give it me: what, is it in the cafe?

Fal. Ay *Hal,* 'tis hot. There's that will fack a city.
·   [*The Prince draws out a bottle of fack.*

P. *Henry.* What, is it a time to jeft and dally now?
[*Throws it at him, and exit.*

Fal. If *Percy* be alive, I'll pierce him; if he do come
in my way, fo; if he do not, if I come in his, willingly, let him make a carbonado of me. I like not fuch
grinning honour as Sir *Walter* hath: give me life, which
if I can fave, fo; if not, honour comes unlook'd for,
and there's an end.   [*Exit.*

S C E N E VIII.

Alarum, Excurfions, Enter the King, the Prince, Lord John
of Lancafter, *and the Earl of* Weftmorland.

K. *Henry.* I pr'ythee, *Harry,* withdraw thy felf, thou
bleedeft too much: Lord *John* of *Lancafter,* go you with
him.

Lan. Not I, my Lord, unlefs I did bleed too.

P. *Henry.* I do befeech your Majefty make up,
Left your retirement do amaze your Friends.

K. *Henry.*

K. Henry. I will do ſo:
My lord of *Weſtmorland,* lead him to his tent.
Weſt. Come, my lord, I'll lead you to your tent.
P. Henry. Lead me, my Lord! I do not need your help,
And heav'n forbid a ſhallow ſcratch ſhould drive
The Prince of *Wales* from ſuch a field as this,
Where ſlain'd nobility lies trodden on,
And rebels arms triumph in maſſacres.
Lan. We breathe too long; come couſin *Weſtmorland,*
Our duty this way lies, for heaven's ſake come.
P. Henry. By heav'n thou haſt deceiv'd me, *Lancaſter,*
I did not think thee lord of ſuch a ſpirit:
Before, I lov'd thee as a brother, *John;*
But now, I do reſpect thee as my ſoul.
K. Henry. I ſaw him hold lord *Percy* at the point,
With luſtier maintenance than I did look for
Of ſuch an ungrown warrior.
P. Henry. Oh this boy
Lends mettle to us all.   [*Ex.*

Manet King Henry.   *Enter* Dowglas.

Dow. Another King? they grow like *Hydra's* heads:
I am the *Dowglas* fatal to all thoſe
That wear thoſe colours on them. What art thou
That counterfeit'ſt the perſon of a King?
K. Henry. The King himſelf, who, *Dowglas,* grieves
    at heart
So many of his ſhadows thou haſt met,
And not the very King, I have two boys
Seek *Percy* and thyſelf about the field;
But ſeeing thou fall'ſt on me ſo luckily
I will aſſay thee: ſo defend thyſelf.
Dow. I fear thou art another counterfeit;
And yet in faith thou bear'ſt thee like a King;
But mine I'm ſure thou art, who e'er thou be,
And thus I win thee.

[*They fight, the King being in danger.*

Enter

Enter Prince Henry.

P. Henry. Hold up thy head, vile *Scot*, or thou art like
Never to hold it up again : the fpirits
Of *Sherly, Stafford, Blunt,* are in my arms ;
It is the Prince of *Wales* that threatens thee,
Who never promifeth, but means to pay.
　　　　　　　　　[*They fight,* Dowglas *flyeth.*
Chearly, my lord ; how fares your grace ?
Sir *Nicholas Gawfey* hath for fuccour fent,
And fo hath *Clifton :* I'll to *Clifton* ſtrait.
　K. Henry. Stay, and breathe a while.
Thou haſt redeem'd my loſt opinion,
And ſhew'd thou mak'ſt ſome tender of my life,
In this fair refcue thou haſt brought to me.
　P. Henry. O heav'n, they did me too much injury,
That ever faid I hearken'd for your death.
If it were fo, I might have let alone
Th' infulting hand of *Dowglas* over you,
Which would have been as fpeedy in your end,
As all the pois'nous portions in the world,
And fav'd the treach'rous labour of your fon.
　K. Henry. Make up to *Clifton*, I'll to Sir *Nicholas Gawfey.*
　　　　　　　　　　　　　　　[*Exit.*

SCENE IX.

Enter Hot-fpur.

Hot. If I miftake not, thou art *Harry Monmouth.*
P. Henry. Thou fpeak'ſt as if I would deny my name.
Hot. My name is *Harry Percy.*
　P. Henry. Then I fee
A very valiant rebel of that name.
I am the Prince of *Wales* ; and think not, *Percy*,
To fhare with me in glory any more :
Two ſtars keep not their motion in one fphere,

　　　　　　　　　　　　　　Nor

Nor can one *England* brook a double reign,
Of *Ha.ry Percy* and the Prince of *Wales*.

    Hot. Nor shall it, *Harry*, for the hour is come
To end the one of us: and would to heav'n
Thy name in arms were now as great as mine.

    P. Henry. I'll make it greater ere I part from thee;
And all the budding honours on thy crest
I'll crop to make a garland for my head:

    Hot. I can no longer brook thy vanities.   [*Fight.*

Enter Falstaff.

    Fal. Well said, *Hal*; to it, *Hal.* Nay, you shall find
no boys play here, I can tell you.

Enter Dowglas, *he fights with* Falstaff, *who falls down as if
he were dead. The Prince kills* Percy.

    Hot. Oh, *Harry*, thou hast robb'd me of my youth:
I better brook the loss of brittle life,
Than those proud titles thou hast won of me;
They wound my thoughts worse than thy sword my
    flesh:
But thought's the slave of life, and life time's fool;
And time, that takes survey of all the world,
Must have a stop. O, I could prophesie,
But that the ‡ earthy and cold hand of death,
Lies on my tongue: no, *Percy*, thou art dust,
And food for——————   [*Dies.*

    P. Henry. Worms, brave *Percy*, Fare thee well!
Ill-weav'd ambition, how much art thou shrunk!
When that this body did contain a spirit,
A kingdom for it was too small a bound:
But now two paces of the vilest earth
Is room enough! this earth that bears thee dead,
Bears not alive so stout a gentleman.
If thou art sensible of courtesie,
I should not make so great a show of zeal.
But let my favours hide thy mangled face,
                              And

    ‡ *earth, and the*

And ev'n in thy behalf, I'll thank my felf
For doing thefe fair rites of tendernefs.
Adieu, and take thy praife with thee to heav'n,
Thy ignominy fleep with thee in the grave,
But not remember'd in thy epitaph.   [*He fees* Falftaff.
——What! old acquaintance! could not all this flefh
Keep in a little life? poor *Jack*, farewel.
I could have better fpar'd a better man.
O, I fhould have a heavy mifs of thee,
If I were much in love with vanity.
Death hath not ftruck fo fat a Deer to-day,
Though many a dearer in this bloody fray:
Imbowell'd will I fee thee by and by,
Till then, in blood by noble *Percy* lie.   [*Exit.*

SCENE X.

Falftaff *rifes.*

Fal. Imbowell'd! if thou imbowel me to-day, I'll
give you leave to powder me, and eat me to-morrow.
'Sblood, 'twas time to counterfeit, or that hot termagant
Scot had paid me fcot and lot too. Counterfeit? I lye, I
am no counterfeit; to die, is to be a counterfeit, for he
is but the counterfeit of a man, who hath not the life of
a man: but to counterfeit dying, when a man thereby
liveth, is to be no counterfeit, but the true and perfect
image of life indeed. The better part of valour is
difcretion, in the which better part, I have faved my
life. I am afraid of this gun-powder *Percy*, though he
be dead. How if he fhould counterfeit too, and rife? I
am afraid he would prove the better counterfeit; therefore
I'll make him fure: yea, and I'll fwear I kill'd him. Why
may not he rife as well as I? nothing confutes me but
eyes, and nobody fees me. Therefore, firrah, with a
new wound in your thigh, come you along with me.
                    [*Takes* Hot-fpur *on his back.*

SCENE

SCENE XI.

Enter Prince Henry *and* John *of* Lancaſter.

P. Henry. Come, brother *John,* full bravely haſt thou fleſht
Thy maiden ſword.

Lan. But ſoft, whom have we here?
Did you not tell me this fat man was dead?

P. Henry. I did, I ſaw him dead,
And breathleſs on the ground: art thou alive,
Or is it fancy plays upon our eye-ſight?
I pr'ythee ſpeak, we will not truſt our eyes
Without our ears: thou art not what thou ſeem'ſt.

Fal. No, that's certain; I am not a double man; but if I am not *Jack Falſtaff,* then am I a *Jack* : there is *Percy,* if your father will do me any honour, ſo; if not, let him kill the next *Percy* himſelf. I look either to be Earl or Duke, I can aſſure you.

P. Henry. Why, *Percy* I kill'd my ſelf, and ſaw thee dead.

Fal. Didſt thou? lord, lord, how the world is given to lying! I grant you I was down, and out of breath, and ſo was he; but we roſe both at an inſtant, and fought a long hour by *Shrew.bury* clock : If I may be believed, ſo; if not, let them that ſhould reward valour bear the ſin upon their own heads. I'll take't on my death I gave him this wound in the thigh: if the man were alive, and would deny it, I would make him eat a piece of my Sword.

Lan. This is the ſtrangeſt tale that e'er I heard.

P. Henry. This is the ſtrangeſt fellow, brother *John.*
Come, bring your luggage nobly on your back:
For my part, if a lye may do thee grace,
I'll gild it with the happieſt terms I have.

                      [A Retreat is ſounded.

The trumpets ſound retreat, the day is ours:
Come, brother, let's to th'higheſt of the field.
To ſee what friends are living, who are dead. *[Exeunt.*
                                 Fal.

Fal. I'll follow, as they fay, for reward. He that rewards me, heav'n reward him. If I do grow great, I'll grow lefs ; for I'll purge, and leave fack, and live cleanly, as a noble-man fhould do.   [*Exit.*

S C E N E XII.

The Trumpets found : Enter King Henry, *Prince of* Wales, *Lord* John *of* Lancafter, *Earl of* Weftmorland, *with* Worcefter *and* Vernon *Prifoners.*

K. Henry. Thus ever did rebellion find rebuke.
Ill-fpirited *Wor'fter,* did we not fend grace,
Pardon, and terms of love to all of you?
And wouldft thou turn our offers contrary?
Mifufe the tenor of thy kinfman's truft?
Three knights upon our party flain to-day,
A noble Earl, and many a creature elfe,
Had been alive this hour,
If like a chriftian thou had'ft truly born
Betwixt our armies true intelligence.
    Wor. What I have done, my fafety urg'd me to,
And I embrace this fortune patiently,
Since not to be avoided it falls on me.
    K. Henry. Bear *Worcefter* to death, and *Vernon* too.
Other offenders we will paufe upon.
                    [*Exeunt* Worcefter *and* Vernon.
How goes the field?
    P. Henry. The gallant *Scot,* lord *Dowglas,* when he faw
The fortune of the day quite turn'd from him,
The noble *Percy* flain, and all his men
Upon the foot of fear, fled with the reft :
And falling from a hill, he was fo bruis'd
That the purfuers took him.   At my tent
The *Dowglas* is, and I befeech your grace,
I may difpofe of him.
    K. Henry. With all my heart.
    P. Henry. Then brother *John* of *Lancafter,* to you
This honourable bounty fhall belong:

G

Go to the *Dowglas*, and deliver him
Up to his pleasure, ransomless and free:
His valour shewn upon our crests to-day,
Hath taught us how to cherish such high deeds,
Ev'n in the bosom of our adversaries.

**Lan.* I thank your grace for this high courtesie,
Which I shall give away immediately.

   K. *Henry.* Then this remains; that we divide our
     power.
You Son *John*, and my Cousin *Westmorland*,
Tow'rds *York* shall bend you, with your dearest speed,
To meet *Northumberland* and Prelate *Scroop*,
Who, as we hear, are busily in arms.
My self and my son *Harry* will tow'rds *Wales*,
To fight with *Glendower* and the Earl of *Marche*.
Rebellion in this land shall lose his sway,
Meeting the check of such another day;
And since this business so far fair is done,
Let us not leave 'till all our own be won.   [*Exeunt.*

* *These two lines added out of the first edition.*

F I N I S.

The Second Part of

HENRY IV.

Containing his DEATH:

AND THE

CORONATION

OF

King HENRY V.

By Mr. WILLIAM SHAKESPEAR.

LONDON:

Printed for J. TONSON, and the reſt of the
PROPRIETORS; and ſold by the Bookſellers
of *London* and *Weſtminſter.*

M DCC XXXIV.

ADVERTISEMENT.

WHEREAS R. *Walker*, with his Accomplices, have printed and publish'd several of *Shakespear's* Plays; and to screen their innumerable Errors, advertise, That they are Printed as they are acted, and Industriously report, that the said Plays are printed from Copies made use of at the Theatres: I therefore declare, in Justice to the Proprietors, whose Right is basely invaded, as well as in Defence of Myself, That no Person ever had, directly or indirectly from me, any such Copy or Copies; neither wou'd I be accessary on any Account in Imposing on the Publick such Useless, Pirated, and Maim'd Editions, as are publish'd by the said R. *Walker.*

> W. CHETWOOD, Prompter to His Majesty's Company of Comedians at the Theatre-Royal in *Drury-Lane.*

JOHN LEVER, Bookſeller, Sta-
tioner and Printſeller, at *Little
Moorgate*, near *Moorfields*.

Dramatis Perſonæ,

KING Henry *the Fourth.*

Prince Henry, *afterwards crowned King* Henry *the Fifth.*

Prince John, *of* Lancaſter, ⎫
Humphry *of* Gloucester, ⎬ *Sons to* Henry *the Fourth,*
Thomas *of* Clarence, ⎭ *and Brethren to* Henry *the Fifth.*

Northumberland, ⎫
Archbiſhop of York, ⎪
Mowbray, ⎪
Haſtings, ⎬ *Oppoſites againſt King* Henry *the Fourth.*
Lord Bardolph, ⎪
Travers, ⎪
Moreton, ⎪
Colvile, ⎭

Warwick, ⎫
Weſtmorland, ⎪
Surrey, ⎬ *of the King's Party.*
Gower, ⎪
Harcourt, ⎪
Lord Chief Juſtice, ⎭

Falſtaff, ⎫
Poins, ⎪
Bardolph, ⎬ *Irregular Humouriſts.*
Piſtol, ⎪
Peto, ⎪
Page, ⎭

Shallow *and* Silence, *Country Juſtices.*

Davy, *Servant to* Shallow.

Phang *and* Snare, *two Serjeants.*

Mouldy, ⎫
Shadow, ⎪
Wart, ⎬ *Country Soldiers.*
Feeble, ⎪
Bulcalf. ⎭

Lady Northumberland.
Lady Percy.
Hoſteſs Quickly.
Dol Tear-ſheet.

Drawers, Beadles, Grooms, &c.

The

The SECOND PART of.

HENRY IV.

ACT I.

INDUCTION.

Enter RUMOUR, * *painted full of Tongues.*

PEN your ears: for which of you will stop
The vent of hearing, when loud *Rumour* speaks?
I from the orient to the drooping west
Making the wind my post horse, still unfold
The acts commenced on this ball of earth.
Upon my tongues continual slanders ride,
The which in every language I pronounce,
Stuffing the ears of † men with false reports:
I speak of peace, while covert enmity,
Under the smile of safety, wounds the world:
And who but *Rumour*, who but only I,
Make fearful musters and prepar'd defence,
Whilst the big year, swoln with some other griefs,
Is thought with child by the stern tyrant war,

A 3   And

* *This direction, which is only to be found in the first edition in quarto of* 1600, *explains a passage in what follows, otherwise obscure.* † *them.*

And no such matter? *Rumour* is a pipe
Blown by surmifes, jealoufies, conjectures;
And of fo eafy and fo plain a ftop,
That the blunt monfter with uncounted heads,
The ftill-difcordant wavering multitude
Can play upon it. But what need I thus
My well-known body to anatomize
Among my houfhold? Why is *Rumour* here?
I run before King *Harry's* victory,
Who in a bloody field by *Shrewsbury*
Hath beaten down young *Hot-fpur* and his troops;
Quenching the flame of bold rebellion
Even with the rebels blood. But what mean I
To fpeak † fo true at firft? my office is
To noife abroad that *Harry Monmouth* fell
Under the wrath of noble *Hot-fpur's* fword;
And that the King before the *Douglas'* rage
Stoop'd his anointed head as low as death.
This have I rumour'd through the peafant towns;
Between that royal field of *Shrewsbury*,
And this worm-eaten hole of ragged ftone,
Where *Hot-fpur's* father, old *Northumberland*
Lies crafty-fick. The pofts come tiring on,
And not a man of them brings other news
Than they have learn'd of me From *Rumour's* tongues,
They bring fmooth comforts falfe, worfe than true
     wrongs.   [*Exit.*

SCENE I.

Northumberland's Caftle.

Enter Lord Bardolph, *and the Porter at one door.*

Bard. Who keeps the gate here, hoa? where is the
    Earl?

Port. What fhall I fay you are?

Bard. Tell thou the Earl,
That the lord *Bardolph* doth attend him here.

  Port. His lordfhip is walk'd forth into the orchard;
Pleafe it your honour knock but at the gate,
And he himfelf will anfwer.

                       Enter

† *of truth.*

Enter Northumberland.

Bard. Heie's the Earl.

North. What news, lord *Bardolph?* ev'ry minute now
Should be the father of some stratagem.
The times are wild: Contention like a horse
Full of high feeding, madly hath broke loose,
And bears down all before him.

Bard. Noble Earl,
I bring you certain news from *Shrewsbury.*

North. Good, if heav'n will!

Bard. As good as heart can wish :
The King is almost wounded to the death :
And in the fortune of my lord your son,
Prince *Harry* slain outright ; and both the *Blunts*
Kill'd by the hand of *Dowglas*; young Prince *John,*
And *Westmerland,* and *Stafford,* fled the field.
And *Harry Monmouth's* brawn, the hulk, Sir *John,*
Is prisoner to your son. O, such a day,
So fought, so follow'd, and so fairly won,
Came not till now, to dignify the times
Since *Cæsar's* fortunes.

North. How is this deriv'd ?
Saw you the field? came you from *Shrewsbury?*

Bard. I spake with one, my lord, that came from
thence,
A gentleman well-bred, and of good name,
That freely render'd me these news for true.

North. Here comes my servant *Travers,* whom I sent
On *Tuesday* last, to listen after news.

Bard. My lord, I over-rode him on the way.
And he is furnish'd with no certainties,
More than he, haply, may retail from me.

SCENE II.

Enter Travers.

North. Now *Travers,* what good tidings come with you?

Tra. My lord, Sir *John Umfrevil* turn'd me back
With joyful tidings ; and being better hors'd.
Out-rode me. After him came spurring hard
A gentleman, almost fore-spent with speed,
That stopp'd by me to breathe his bloodied horse :

A 4　　　　He

He ask'd the way to *Chester*; and of him
I did demand what news from *Shrewsbury*?
He told me, that rebellion had ill luck,
And that young *Harry Percy*'s spur was cold.
With that he gave his able horse the head,
And bending forward, struck his * agile heels
Against the panting sides of his poor jade
Up to the rowel-head, and starting so,
He seem'd in running to devour the way,
Staying no longer question.

North. Ha! again:
Said he young *Harry Percy*'s spur was cold?
Rebellion had ill luck?

Bard. My lord, I'll tell you.
If my young lord your son have not the day,
Upon mine honour, for a silken point
I'll give my barony.   Ne'er talk of it.

North. Why should the gentleman that rode by *Travers*
Give then such instances of loss?

Bard. Who he?
He was some † hilding fellow, that had stol'n,
The horse he rode on; and upon my life
Spake at adventure. Look, here comes more news.

SCENE III.
Enter Morton.

North. Yea, this man's brow, like to a title-leaf,
Foretells the nature of a tragick volume:
So looks the strond, ‡ whereon th' imperious flood
Hath left a witnefs'd ufurpation.
Say, *Morton*, did'st thou come from *Shrewsbury*?

Mort. I ran from *Skrewsbury*, my noble lord,
Where hateful death put on his uglieft mask
To fright our party.

North. How doth my son and brother?
Thou tremblest; and the whiteness in thy cheek
Is apter than thy tongue to tell thy errand.
Even such a man, fo faint, fo fpiritlefs,
So dull, fo dead in look, fo woe-be-gone,
Drew *Priam*'s curtain in the dead of night,

And

* able. † hilding, *for* hinderling; *i. e. bafe, degenerate.*
‡ *when the*

have told him, half his *Troy* was burn'd:
found the fire, ere he his tongue:
Percy's death, ere thou report it ir.
would'st say: your son did thus and thus,
er, thus: so fought the noble *Douglas*:
y greedy ear with their bold deeds.
nd, to stop mine ear indeed,
 sigh to blow away this praise,
 brother, son, and all, are dead!
wglas is living, and your brother, yet:
lord, your son ————
hy, he is dead.
ready tongue suspicion hath;
fears the thing he would not know,
ftinct, knowledge from other eyes,
he fear'd is chang'd. Yet *Morton*, speak:
y Earl, his divination lies;
take it as a sweet disgrace,
hee rich, for doing me such wrong.
u are too great, to be by me gainsaid:
is too true, your fears too certain.
et for all this, say not that *Percy*'s dead.
ge confession in thine eye:
t thy head, and hold'st it fear, or sin,
truth. If he be slain, say so:
offends not, that reports his death:
 sin that doth bely the dead,
ich says the dead is not alive.
 bringer of unwelcome news
losing office: and his tongue
after as a sullen bell,
, tolling a departing friend.
annot think, my lord, your son is dead.
 sorry I should force you to believe
 I would to heav'n I had not seen.
ine eyes saw him in bloody state,
int quittance, wearied and out-breath'd,
Monmouth; whose swift wrath beat down
launted *Percy* to the earth,
ce, with life, he never more sprung up,
 death, whose spirit lent a fire
 dullest peasant in his camp,

A 5   Being

Being bruited once; took fire and heat away
From the beſt-temper'd courage in his troops.
For from his metal was his party ſteel'd;
Which once in him abated, all the reſt
Turn'd on themſelves, like dull and heavy lead.
And as the thing that's heavy in it ſelf,
Upon enforcement, flies with greateſt ſpeed;
So did our men, heavy in Hotſpur's loſs,
Lend to this weight ſuch lightneſs with their fear,
That arrows fl.d not ſwifter toward their aim,
Than did our ſoldiers aiming at their ſafety,
Fly from the field.   Then was that noble Wor'ſter,
Too ſoon ta'en priſoner: and that furious Scot,
The bloody Douglas, whoſe well-labouring ſword
Had three times ſlain th' appearance of the King,
'Gan vail his ſtomach, and did g ace the ſhame
Of thoſe that turn'd their backs, and in his flight
Stumbling in fear, was took.   The ſum of all
Is, tha the King hath w.n: and hath ſent out
A ſpeedy pow'r t'encounter you, my lord,
Un er the conduct of young Lancaſter
And Weſtmorland.   T is is the news at full.

   North. For this, I ſhall have time e ough to mourn.
In poiſon there is phyſick: and this news,
That would, had I been well, have made me ſick,
Bei g ſick, hath in ſome meaſure made me well.
And as the wretch whoſe fever-weaken'd joints,
Like ſtreagthleſs hinges, buckle under life,
Impatient of his fi breaks like a fire
Out of his keeper's arms; even ſo my limbs
Weaken'd with grief, being now inrag'd with grief,
Are thrice themſelves. Hence therefore thou nice crutch,
A ſcaly gaun let now with joints of ſteel
Muſt glove this hand. And hence thou ſickly quoif,
Thou art a guard too wanton for the head
Which princes fleſh'd with conqueſt aim to hit.
Now bind my brows with iron, and approach
The ragged'ſt hour that time and ſpight dare bring,
To frown upon th' enrag'd Northumberland!
' Let heav'n kiſs earth! now let not nature's hand
' Keep t' e wild flood confin'd; let order die,
' And let this World no longer be a ſtage

                                                        To

' To feed contention in a lingring act:
' But let one spirit of the first-born *Cain*
' Reign in all bosoms, that each heart being set
' On bloody courses, the rude scene may end,
' And-darkness be the burier of the dead !

   * *Bard.* This strained passion doth you wrong, my
    lord ;
Sweet Earl, divorce not wisdom from your honour.

   Mort. The lives of all your loving complices
Lean on your health, the which if you give o'er
To stormy passion, must perforce decay.
†You cast th' event of war, my noble lord,
And summ'd th' account of chance, before you said
Let us make head : it was your presurmise,
That in the dole of blows, your son might drop :
You knew he walk'd o'er perils, on an edge
More likely to fall in, than to get o'er :
You were advis'd his flesh was capable
Of wounds and scars ; and that his forward spirit
Would lift him where most trade of danger rang'd :
Yet did you say, Go forth. And none of this,
Though strongly apprehended, could restrain
The stiff-born action. What hath then befall'n,
Or what hath this bold enterprize brought forth,
More than that being, which was like to be ?

   Bard. We all, that are engaged to this loss,
Knew that we ventur'd on such dangerous seas,
That if we wrought out life, was ten to one :
And yet we ventur'd for the gain propos'd,
Choak'd the respect of likely peril fear'd ;
And since we are o'er-set, venture again.
Come, we will all put forth, body and goods.

                      Mort.

---

   * *This line is only in the first edition, where it is spoken
by* Umfr ville, *who speaks no where else. It seems necessary to the connection.*

   † *The fourteen lines from hence to* Bardolph's *next speech,
are not to be found in the first editions, till that in folio of
1623. A very great number of other lines in this play are
inserted after the first edition in like manner, but of such
spirit and mastery, generally, that the insertions are plainly, by* Shakespear *himself.*

Mort. 'Tis more than time; and my most noble lord,
I hear for certain, and do speak the truth:
† The gentle Arch-bishop of *York* is up
With well-appointed Powers; he is a man
Who with a double surety binds his followers.
My lord, your son, had only but the corps,
But shadows, and the shews of men to fight.
For that same word, rebellion did divide
The action of their bodies from their souls;
And they did fight with queasiness, constrained
As men drink potions, that their weapons only
Seem'd on our side: but for their spirits and souls,
This word, rebellion, it had froze them up,
As fish are in a pond. But now the bishop
Turns insurrection to religion;
Suppos'd sincere and holy in his thoughts,
He's follow'd both with body and with mind:
And doth enlarge his rising with the blood
Of fair King *Richard*, scrap'd from *Pomfret* stones,
Derives from heav'n his quarrel and his cause;
Tells them, he doth bestride a bleeding land
Gasping for life, under great *Bolingbroke*:
And more, and less, do flock to follow him.
    North. I knew of this before: but to speak truth,
This present grief hath wip'd it from my mind.
Go in with me, and counsel every man
The aptest way for safety and revenge:
Get posts, and letters, and make friends with speed,
Never so few, nor never yet more need.   [*Exeunt.*

† *All the following lines to the end of this speech are*
not in the first edition.

SCENE IV.

A Street in London.

Enter Sir John Falstaff, *with his Page bearing his sword and buckler.*

Fal. Sirrah, you giant, what says the doctor to my water?

Page. He said, Sir, the water it self was a good † healthy water. But for the party that own'd it, he might have more diseases than he knew for.

Fal. Men of all sorts take a pride to gird at me. The brain of this foolish compounded-clay, Man, is not able to invent any thing that tends to laughter, more than I invent, or is invented on me. I am not only witty in my self, but the cause that wit is in other men. I do here walk before thee, like a Sow, that hath overwhelmed all her litter, but one. If the Prince put thee into my service for any other reason than to set me off, why then I have no judgment. Thou whorson mandrake, thou art fitter to be worn in my cap, than to wait at my heels. I was never mann'd with an agot till now: but I will set you neither in gold nor silver, but in vile apparel, and send you back again to your master for a jewel. The *Juvenil*, the Prince your master, whose chin is not yet fledg'd; I will sooner have a beard grow in the palm of my hand, than he shall get one on his cheek: yet he will not stick to say, his face is a face-royal. Heav'n may finish it when it will, it is not a hair amiss yet: he may keep it still as a face-royal, for a barber shall never earn sixpence out of it; and yet he will be crowing, as if he had writ man ever since his father was a batchelor. He may keep his own grace, but he is almost out of mine, I can assure him. What said Mr. *Dombledon*, about the satten for my short cloak and slops?

Page. He said, Sir, you should procure him better assurance than *Bardolph*: he would not take his bond and yours; he lik'd not the security.

Fal.

† *healing.*

Fal. Let him be damn'd like the glutton, may his tongue be hotter, a whorfon *Achitophel*, a rafcally yea-forfooth-knave, to bear a gentleman in hand, and then ftand upon *security?* the whorfon-fmooth-pates do now wear nothing but high fhoes; and bunches of keys at their girdles; and if a man is thorough with them in honeft taking up, then they muft ftand upon *security*: I had as lief they would put rats-bane in my mouth as offer to ftop it with fecurity. I looked he fhould have fent me two and twenty yards of fatten, as I am a true knight, and he fends me *security*. Well, he may fleep in fecurity, for he hath the horn of abundance. And the lightnefs of his wife fhines through it, and yet cannot he fee. though he have his own lanthorn to light him. Where's *Bardolph?*

Page. He's gone into *Smithfield* to buy your worfhip a horfe.

Fal. I bought him in *Pauls*, and he'll buy me a horfe in *Smithfield*. If I could get me but a wife in the ftews, I were mann'd, hors'd, and wiv'd.

SCENE V.

Enter Chief Juftice and Servants.

Page. Sir, here comes the nobleman that committed the Prince for ftriking him, about *Bardolph*.

Fal. Wait clofe, I will not fee him.

Ch. Juft. What's he that goes there?

Serv. Falftaff, and't pleafe your lordfhip.

Ch. Juft. He that was in queftion for the robbery?

Serv. He, my lord. But he hath fince done good fervice at *Shrewsbury* and, as I hear, is now going with fome charge to the lord *John of Lancafter*.

Ch. Juft. What to *York?* call him back again.

Serv. Sir *John Falftaff*.

Fal. Boy, tell him, I am deaf.

Page. You muft fpeak louder, my mafter is deaf.

Ch. Juft. I am fure he is, to the hearing of any thing good. Go pluck him by the elbow. I muft fpeak with him.

Serv. Sir *John*.

Fal.

Fal. Whàt! a young knave and beg! are there not wars? is there not employment? doth not the King lack subjects? do not the rebels need soldiers? though it be a shame to be on any side but one, it is worse shame to beg, than to be on the worst side, were it worse than the name of rebellion can tell how to make it.

Serv. You mistake me, Sir.

Fal. Why, Sir, did I say you were an honest man? setting my knight-hood and my soldiership aside, I had lied in my throat, if I had said so.

Serv. I pray you, Sir, then set your knight-hood and your soldiership aside, and give me leave to tell you, you lie in your throat, if you say I am any other than an honest man.

Fal. I give thee leave to tell me so? I lay aside that which grows to me? if thou gett'st any leave of me, hang me; if thou tak'st leave, thou wer't better be hang'd: you hunt counter, hence; avaunt.

Serv. Sir, my lord would speak with you.

Ch. Just. Sir *John Falstaff*, a word with you.

Fal. My good lord! God give your lordship good time of day. I am glad to see your lordship abroad; I heard say, your lordship was sick. I hope your lordship goes abroad by advice. Your lordship, though not clean past your youth, hath yet some smack of age in you: some relish of the saltness of time; and I most humbly beseech your lordship, to have a reverend care of your health.

Ch. Just. Sir *John*, I sent for you before your expedition to *Shrewsbury*.

Fal. If it please your lordship, I hear his Majesty is retur'n'd with some discomfort from *Wales*.

Ch. Just. I talk not of his Majesty: you would not come when I sent for you?

Fal. And I hear moreover, his Highness is fall'n into this same whorson apoplexy.

Ch. Just. Well, heav'n mend him. I pray let me speak with you.

Fal. This apoplexy is, as I take it, a kind of lethargy, an't please your lordship, a kind of sleeping in the blood, a whorson tingling.

Ch. Just. What tell you me of it? be it as it is.

Fal.

Fal. It hath its original from much grief; from ſtudy and perturbation of the brain. I have read the cauſe of it in *Galen.* It is a kind of deafneſs.

Ch. Juſt. I think you are fall'n into that diſeaſe : for you hear not what I ſay to you.

Fal. Very well, my lord, very well : rather, an't pleaſe you, it is the diſeaſe of not liſt'ning, the malady of not marking, that I am troubled with.

Ch. Juſt. To puniſh you by the heels, would amend the attention of your ears; and I care not if I be your phyſician.

Fal. I am as poor as *Job,* my lord; but not ſo patient : your lordſhip may miniſter the potion of impriſonment to me, in reſpect of poverty; but how I ſhould be your patient to follow your preſcriptions, the wiſe may make ſome dram of a ſcruple, or indeed, a ſcruple it ſelf.

Ch. Juſt. I ſent for you, when there were matters againſt you for your life, to ſpeak with me.

Fal. As I was then advis'd by my counſel learned in the laws of this land-ſervice, I did not come.

Ch. Juſt. Well, the truth is, Sir *John,* you live in great infamy.

Fal. He that buckles him in my belt, cannot live in leſs.

Ch. Juſt. Your means are very ſlender, and your waſte great.

Fal. I would it were otherwiſe : I would my means were greater, and my waſte ſlenderer.

Ch. Juſt. You have miſ-led the youthful Prince.

Fal. The young Prince hath miſ-led me. I am the fellow with the great belly, and he my dog.

Ch. Juſt. Well, I am loth to gall a new-heal'd wound; your day's ſervice at *Shrewsbury* hath a little gilded over your night's exploit on *Gads-hill.* You may thank the unquiet time, for your quiet over poſting that action.

Fal. My lord ?

Ch. Juſt. But ſince all is well, keep it ſo : wake not a ſleeping Wolf.

Fal. To wake a Wolf, is as bad as to ſmell a Fox.

Ch. Juſt. What ? you are as a candle, the better part burnt out.

Fal. A waſſel candle, my lord; all tallow; but if I did ſay of wax, my growth would approve the truth.

.*Ch.*

Ch. Juſt. There is not a white hair on your face, but ſhould have his effect of gravity.

Fal. His effect of gravy, gravy, gravy.

Ch. Juſt. You follow the young Prince up and down, like his evil angel.

Fal. Not ſo, my lord, your ill angel is light; but I hope he that looks upon me, will take me without weighing; and yet, in ſome reſpects I grant, I cannot go ;————— I cannot tell; Virtue is of ſo little regard in theſe coſtor-monger days, that true valour is turned bear-herd. Pregnancy is made a tapſter, and hath his quick wit waſted in giving recknings; all the other gifts appertinent to man, as the malice of this age ſhapes them, are not worth a gooſe-berry. You that are old, conſider not the capacities of us that are young; you meaſure the heat of our livers, with the bitterneſs of ⌐your galls; and we that are in the † va-ward of our youth, I muſt confeſs are wags too.

Ch. Juſt. Do you ſet down your name in the ſcrowl of youth, that are written down old, with all the characters of age ? have you not a moiſt eye ? a dry hand? a yellow cheek ? a white beard ? a decreaſing leg? an increaſing belly ? is not your voice broken ? your wind ſhort ? ˙* your chin double ? your wit ſingle ? and every part about you blaſted with antiquity ? and will you yet call your ſelf young ? fy, fy, fy, Sir *John.*

Fal. My lord, I was ‡ born about three of the clock in the afternoon, with a white head; and ſomething a round belly. For my voice, I have loſt it with hallow-ing and ſinging of Anthems. To approve my youth further, I will not. The truth is, I am only old in judgment and underſtanding, and he that will caper with me for a thouſand marks, let him lend me the money, and have at him. For the box o'th' ear that the Prince gave you, he gave it like a rude Prince, and you took it like a ſenſible lord. I have checkt him for it, and the young Lion repents : marry not in aſhes and ſack-cloth, but in new ſilk and old ſack.

Ch. Juſt. Well, heav'n ſend the Prince a better com-panion.　　　　　　　　　　　　　　　　　　*Fal.*

† va-ward, *i. e.* vanguard.

* *your wind ſhort, your wit ſingle,*

‡ *added from the firſt edition.*

Fal. Heav'n send the companion a better Prince : I cannot rid my hands of him.

Ch. Juſt. Well, the King hath ſever'd you and Prince *Harry.* I hear you are going with lord *John* of *Lancaſter*, againſt the Archbiſhop and the Earl of *Northumberland.*

Fal. Yes, I thank your pretty ſweet wit for it ; but look you, pray, all you that kiſs my lady peace at home, that our armies join not in a hot day: for I take but two ſhirts out with me, and I mean not to ſweat extraordinarily: if it be a hot day, if I brandiſh any thing but a bottle, would I might never ſpit white again. There is not a dangerous action can peep out his head, but I am thruſt upon it. Well, I cannot laſt ever.— ‡ but it was always the trick of our *Engliſh* nation, if they have a good thing to make it too common. If ye will needs ſay I am an old man, you ſhou'd give me reſt : I would to God my name were not ſo terrible to the enemy as it is! I were better to be eaten to death with a ruſt, than to be ſcour'd to nothing with perpetual motion.

Ch. Juſt. Well, be honeſt, be honeſt, and heav'n bleſs your expedition.

Fal. Will your lordſhip lend me a thouſand pound to furniſh me forth ?

Ch. Juſt. Not a penny, not a penny; you are too impatient to bear croſſes. Fare you well. Commend me to my couſin *Weſtmorland.*   [*Exit.*

Fal. If I do, fillip me with a * three-man-beetle. A man can no more ſeparate age and covetouſneſs, than he can part young limbs and letchery : but the gout galls the one, and the pox pinches the other, and ſo both the degrees prevent my curſes. Boy.

Page. Sir.

Fal. What money is in my purſe ?

Page. Seven groats, and two pence.

Fal. I can get no remedy againſt this conſumption of the purſe. Borrowing only lingers and lingers it out, but the diſeaſe is incurable. Go bear this letter to my

                                                      lord

‡ *Theſe following periods are reſtor'd from the firſt edition.*

* three-man-beetle, *i. e. a rammer big enough to re-*

after, this to the Prince, this to the Earl of
, and this to old Mrs. *Ursula*, whom I have
n to marry since I.perceived the first white
chin. About it ; you know where to find
of this gout, or a gout of this pox ; for
h'other plays the rogue with my great toe :
tter, if I do halt, I have the wars for my
my pension shall seem the more reasonable:
will make use of any thing, I will turn di-
nmodity.   [*Exeunt.*

S C E N E VI.

Y O R K.

ishop of York, Hastings, Thomas Mowbray
r*l Marshal) and Lord* Bardolph.

is have you heard our cause, and know our
is :
oft noble friends, I pray you all
ly your opinions of our hopes.
ord Marshal, what say you to it ?
well allow th' occasion of our arms,
would be better satisfied
means we should advance our selves
h forehead bold and big enough
ow'r and puissance of the King?
present musters grow upon the file
twenty thousand men of choice :
plies live largely in the hope
rthumberland, whose bosom burns
ensed fire of injuries.
e question then, lord *Hastings*, standeth thus;
r present five and twenty thousand
p head without *Northumberland* ?
th him we may.
marry there's the point :
out him we be thought too feeble,
nt is, we should not step too far
his assistance by the hand.
eam so bloody-fac'd as this,
        Conjecture,

Conjecture, expectation, and surmise
Of aids uncertain, should not be admitted.

York. 'Tis very true, lord *Bardolph*; for indeed
It was young *Hot-spur's* case at *Shrewsbury.*

Bard. It was, my lord, who lin'd himself with hope,
Eating the air, on promise of supply,
Flatt'ring himself with project of a power
Much smaller than the smallest of his thoughts;
And so, with great imagination,
Proper to madmen, led his pow'rs to death,
And, winking, leap'd into destruction.

Hast. But by your leave, it never yet did hurt
To lay down likelihoods and forms of hope.

Bard. Yes, if this present quality of war
* Impede the instant act; a cause on foot
Lives so in hope, as in an early spring
We see th' appearing buds; which to prove fruit,'
Hope gives not so much warrant as despair
That frosts will bite them. When we mean to build,
We first survey the plot, then draw the model,
And when we see the figure of the house,
Then must we rate the cost of the erection;
Which if we find out-weighs ability,
What do we then, but draw a-new the model
In fewer offices? at least, desist
To build at all? much more in this great work,
(Which is almost to pluck a kingdom down,
And set another up) should we survey
The plot of situation and the model;
Consent upon a sure foundation,
Question surveyors, know our own estate,
How able such a work to undergo,
To weigh against his opposite? or else,
We fortify in paper and in figures,
Using the names of men instead of men:
Like one that draws the model of a house
Beyond his pow'r to build it; who, half through,
Gives o'er, and leaves his part-created cost
A naked subject to the weeping clouds,
And waste, for churlish winter's tyranny.

Hast. Grant that our hopes, yet likely of fair birth,
Should be still-born; and that we now possest

* * Indeed.*   The

The utmoſt man of expectation:
I think we are a body ſtrong enough,
Ev'n as we are, to equal with the King.

Bard. What is the King but five and twenty thouſand?

Haſt. To us no more; nay not ſo much, lord *Bardolph.*
For his diviſions, as the times do brawl,
Are in three heads; one pow'r againſt the *French*,
And one againſt *Glendower*; perforce a third
Muſt take up us: ſo is the unfirm King
In three divided; and his coffers ſound
With hollow poverty and emptineſs.   [ther,

York. That he ſhould draw his ſev'ral ſtrengths toge-
And come againſt us in full puiſſance,
Need not be dreaded.

Haſt. If he ſhould do ſo,
He leaves his back unarm'd, the *French* and *Welſh*
Baying him at his heels; never fear that.

Bard. Who is it like ſhould lead his forces hither?

Haſt. The Duke of *Lancaſter* and *Weſtmorland*:
Againſt the *Welſh*, himſelf and *Harry Monmouth*.
But who is ſubſtituted 'gainſt the *French*,
I have no certain notice.

  * *York.* Let us on:
And publiſh the occaſion of our Arms.
The commonwealth is ſick of their own choice;
Their over-greedy love hath ſurfeited.
An habitation giddy and unſure
Hath he that buildeth on the vulgar heart.
O thou fond many! with what loud applauſe
Didſt thou beat heav'n with bleſſing *Bolingbroke*,
Before he was what thou would'ſt have him be?
And now being trim'd up in thine own deſires,
Thou, beaſtly feeder, art ſo full of him,
That thou provok'ſt thy ſelf to caſt him up.
So, ſo thou common dog, didſt thou diſgorge
Thy glutton boſom of the royal *Richard*,
And now thou would'ſt eat thy dead vomit up,
And howl'ſt to find it. What truſt in theſe times?
They, that when *Richard* liv'd, would have him die,
                                            Are

  * *This excellent ſpeech of* York, *was one of the paſſages added by* Shakeſpear *after his firſt edition.*

Are now become enamour'd on his grave:
Thou that threw'ft duft upon his goodly head,
When through proud *London* he came fighing on
After th' admired heels of *Bolingbroke*,
Cry'ft now, O Earth yield us that King again,
And take thou this. O thoughts of men accurs'd,
Paft, and to come, feem beft; things prefent, worft.

Mowb. Shall we go draw our numbers, and fet on?
Haft. We are time's fubjects, and time bids, be gone.

ACT II.   SCENE I.

L O N D O N.

Enter Hoftefs, with two Officers, Fang *and* Snare.

Hoft. MR. *Fang*, have you enter'd the action?

Fang. It is enter'd.

Hoft. Where's your yeoman? is he a lufty yeoman?
Will he ftand to it?

Fang. Sirrah, where's *Snare*?

Hoft. Ay, ay, good Mr. *Snare*.

Snare. Here, here.

Fang. Snare, we muft arreft Sir *John Falftaff*.

Hoft. Ay, good Mr. *Snare*, I have enter'd him and all.

Snare. It may chance coft fome of us our lives: he
will ftab.

Hoft. Alas-the-day; take heed of him; he ftab'd me
in mine own houfe, and that moft beaftly; he cares
not what mifchief he doth, if his weapon be out. He
will foin like any devil, he will fpare neither man,
woman, nor child.

Fang. If I can clofe with him, I care not for his thruft.

Hoft. No, nor I neither; I'll be at your elbow.

Fang. If I but fift him once; if he come but within
my * vice.

Hoft. I am undone by his going; I warrant you he is
an infinitive thing upon my fcore. Good Mr. *Fang*, hold
him

* vice, *or* grafp, *a metaphor taken from a fmith's*
vice; *there is another reading in the old edition,* view,
which I think not fo good.

him fure; good Mr. *Snare*, let him not fcape. He comes
continually to *Pie-corner*, faving your manhoods, to buy
a faddle: and he is indited to dinner to the *Lubbar's-
head* in *Lombard-ftreet* to Mr. *Smooth's* the *Silkman*. I
pray ye, fince my action is enter'd, and my cafe fo
openly known to the world, let him be brought in to
his anfwer. A hundred mark is a long one, for a poor
lone woman to bear; and I have born, and born, and
born: and have been fub'd off, and fub'd off, from this day
to that day, that it is a fhame to be thought on. There
is no honefty in fuch dealing, unlefs a woman fhould
be made an Afs and a beaft, to bear every knave's
wrong.

Enter Falftaff, Bardolph, *and the Boy.*
Yonder he comes, and that arrant malmfey-nofe knave,
Bardolph with him. Do your offices, do your offices:
Mr. *Fang* and Mr. *Snare*, do me, do me, do me your
offices.

Fal. How now? whofe mare's dead? what's the
matter?

Fang. Sir *John*, I arreft you at the fuit of Mrs. *Quickly*.

Fal. Away varlets; draw, *Bardolph*: cut me off the
villain's head: throw the quean in the kennel.

Hoft. Throw me in the kennel? I'll throw thee in the
kennel. Wilt thou? wilt thou? thou baftardly rogue.
Murder, murder! O thou hony-fuckle villain, wilt thou
kill God's officers and the King's? O thou hony-feed
rogue, thou art a hony-feed, a man-queller, and a wo-
man-queller.

Fal. Keep them off, *Bardolph*.

Fang. A refcue, a refcue!

Hoft. Good people, bring a refcue or two; thou
wo't, wo't thou, thou wo't, wo't thou rogue; do, thou
hempfeed.

Fal. Away you fcullion, you rampallian, you fuftila-
rian: I'll tickle your cataftrophe.

S C E N E II.
Enter Chief Juftice.

Ch. Juft. What's the matter? keep the peace here, hoa.

Hoft. Good my lord, be good to me. I befeech you
ftand to me.

Ch. Juft.

Ch. Juſt. How now, Sir *John?*
brawling here?
Does this become your place, your time,
You ſhould have been well on your wa
Stand from him fellow, wherefore hang'ſ

Hoſt. O my moſt worſhipful lord, an
grace I am a poor widow of *Eaſtcheap,*
reſted at my ſuit.

Ch. Juſt. For what ſum?

Hoſt. It is more than for ſome, my lo
all I have; he hath eaten me out of hou
he hath put all my ſubſtance into that fa
but I will have ſome of it out again, o
o'nights, like the mare.

Fal. I think I am as like to ride the
any vantage of ground to get up,

Ch. Juſt. How comes this, Sir *John?*
of good temper would endure this tempe
tion? are you not aſham'd to inforce a p
ſo rough a courſe to come by her own?

Fal. What is the groſs ſum that I ow

Hoſt. Marry, if thou wert an honeſt ma
the money too. Thou didſt ſwear to m
gilt goblet, ſitting in my *Dolphin*-chamb
table, by a ſea-coal fire, on *Wedneſday* in
when the Prince broke thy head for like
ſinging-man of *Windſor;* thou didſt ſwear
I was waſhing thy wound, to marry me,
my lady thy wife. Canſt thou deny it;
wife *Keech* the butcher's Wife come in th
goſſip *Quickly?* coming in to borrow a m
telling us ſhe had a good diſh of prawns,
did deſire to eat ſome; whereby I told the
for a green wound? and didſt not thou,
gone down ſtairs, deſire me to be no m
ſity with ſuch poor people, ſaying that
ſhould call me Madam? and didſt thou n
bid me fetch thee thirty-ſhillings? I pu
thy book-oath, deny it if thou canſt.

Fal. My lord, this is a poor mad ſoul; a
and down the town, that her eldeſt ſon is
hath been in good caſe, and the truth is

diſtracted her; but for theſe fooliſh Officers, I beſeech you, I may have redreſs againſt them.

Ch. Juſt. Sir *John,* Sir *John.* I am well acquainted with your manner of wrenching the true cauſe the falſe way. It is not a confident brow, nor the throng of words, that come with ſuch more than impudent ſawcineſs from you, can thruſt me from a level conſideration. I know you have practis'd upon the eaſy-yielding ſpirit of this woman. ————

Hoſt. Yes in troth, my lord.

Ch. Juſt. Pr'ythee, peace; pay her the debt you owe her, and unpay the villany you have done her: the one you may do with ſterling money, and the other with currant repentance.

Fal. My lord I will not undergo this * ſneap without reply. You call honourable-boldneſs impudent ſawcineſs: If a man will court'ſy and ſay nothing, he is virtuous. No, my lord, my humble duty remember'd, I will not be your ſuitor: I ſay to you, I deſire deliverance from theſe Officers, being upon haſty employment in the King's affairs.

Ch. Juſt. You ſpeak, as having power to do wrong: but anſwer in the effect your reputation, and ſatisfy the poor woman.

Fal. Come hither, hoſteſs.   [*Aſide.*

S C E N E III.

Enter Mr. Gower.

Ch. Juſt. Maſter *Gower,* what news?

Gower. The King, my lord, and *Henry* Prince of *Wales* Are near at hand; the reſt the paper tells.

Fal. As I am a gentleman ————

Hoſt. Nay, you ſaid ſo before.

Fal. As I am a gentleman, come, no more words of it.

Hoſt. By this heav'nly ground I tread on, I muſt be fain to pawn both my plate and the tapeſtry of my dining chambers.

Fal. Glaſſes, glaſſes is the only drinking; and for thy walls, a pretty ſlight drollery, or the ſtory of the prodigal,

B   *or*

———————————

* ſneap, *a yorkſhire word for* rebuke.

or the *German* hunting in water work is worth a thousand of these bed-hangings, and these fly-bitten tapestries:
let it be ten pound, if thou canst. Come, if it were not
for thy humours, there is not a better wench in *England.*
Go, wash thy face, and draw thy action, come, thou
must not be in this humour with me; come, I know
thou wast set on to this.

Host. Pr'ythee, Sir *John,* let it be but twenty nobles,
I am loth to pawn my plate, in good earnest la.

Fal. Let it alone, I'll make other shift; you'll be a fool
still.

Host. Well, you shall have it, though I pawn my gown.
I hope you'll come to supper: you'll pay me all together.

Fal. Will I live? go with her, with her; hook on,
hook on.

Host. Will you have *Doll Tear-Sheet* meet you at supper?

Fal. No more words. Let's have her.

[*Exeunt* Host. *and Serjeant.* ?

Ch. Just. I have heard better news.

Fal. What's the news, my good lord?

Ch. Just. Where lay the King last night?

Goxer. At *Basingstoke,* my lord.

Fal. I hope, my lord, all's well. What is the news,
my lord?

Ch. Just. Come all his forces back?

Gower. No; fifteen hundred foot, five hundred horse,
'Are march'd up to my lord of *Lancaster,*
Against *Northumberland* and the Arch-bishop.

Fal. Comes the King back from *Wales,* my noble lord?

Ch. Just. You shall have letters of me presently.
Come, go along with me, good Mr. *Gower.*

Fal. My lord.

Ch. Just. What's the matter?

Fal. Master *Gower,* shall I entreat you with me to
dinner?

Gower. I must wait upon my good lord here,
I thank you good Sir *John.*

Ch. Just. Sir *John,* you loiter here too long, being you
are to take soldiers up in the countreys as you go.

Fal. Will you sup with me, master *Gower?*

Ch. Just. What foolish master taught you these manners, Sir *John?*

Fal.

Fal. Mafter *Gower*, if they become me not, he was a fool that taught them me.   This is the right fencing grace, my lord, tap for tap, and fo part fair.

Ch. Juft. Now the lord lighten thee, thou art a great fool.   [*Exeunt.*

S C E N E IV.

Continues in London.

Enter Prince Henry *and* Poins.

P. Henry. Truft me, I am exceeding weary.

Poins. Is it come to that? I had thought wearinefs durft not have attach'd one of fo high blood.

P. Henry. It doth me, though it difcolours the complexion of my greatnefs to acknowledge it.   Doth it not fhew vilely in me, to defire fmall beer?

Poins. Why a Prince fhould not be fo loofely ftudied, as to remember fo weak a compofition.

P. Henry. Belike then my Appetite was not princely got; for in troth, I do now remember the poor creature, fmall beer.   But indeed thefe humble confiderations make me out of love with my greatnefs.   What a difgrace is it to me to remember thy name? or to know thy face to morrow? or to take note how many pair of filk ftockings thou haft? (*viz.* thefe, and thofe that were the peach-colour'd ones;) or to bear the inventory of thy fhirts, as one for fuperfluity, and one other for ufe; but that the tennis-court-keeper knows better than I, for it is a low ebb of linnen with thee, when thou keepeft not racket there, as thou haft not done a great while, becaufe the reft of thy low countries have made a fhift to eat up thy holland. * And God knows whether thofe that bawl out of the Ruins of thy linnen fhall inherit his kingdom: but the midwives fay the children are not in the fault, whereupon the world increafes, and kindreds are mightily ftrengthened.

Poins. How ill it follows, after you have labour'd fo hard, you fhould talk fo idly? tell me how many good young Princes fhould do fo, their fathers lying fo fick as yours is.

B 2   ) *P. Henry.*

---

* *This period is fupply'd out of the old edition.*

P. Henry. Shall I tell thee one thing, *Poins*?

Poins. Yes, and let it be an excellent good thing.

P. Henry. It shall serve among wits of no higher breeding than thine.

Poins. Go to; I stand the push of your one thing, that you'll tell.

P. Henry. Why I tell thee, it is not meet that I should be sad now my father is sick; albeit I could tell to thee, (as to one it pleases me for fault of a better, to call my friend) I could be sad and sad indeed too.

Poins. Very hardly upon such a subject.

P. Henry. Thou think'st me as far in the devil's book, as thou and *Falstaff*, for obduracy and persistency. Let the end try the man. But I tell thee, my heart bleeds inwardly that my father is sick: and keeping such vile company as thou art hath in reason taken from me all ostentation of sorrow.

Poins. The reason?

P. Henry. What would'st thou think of me if I should weep?

Poins. I would think thee a most princely hypocrite.

P. Henry. It would be every man's thought; and thou art a blessed fellow, to think as every man thinks; never a man's thought in the world keeps the road-way better than thine; every man would think me an hypocrite indeed. And what excites your most worshipful thought to think so?

Poins. Why, because you have * seemed so lewd, and so much ingrafted to *Falstaff*.

P. Henry. And to thee.

Poins. Nay by this light I am well spoken of, I can hear it with mine own ears; the worst they can say of me is, that I am a second brother, and that I am a proper fellow of my hands: and those two things I confess I cannot help. Look, look, here comes *Bardolph*.

P. Henry. And the boy that I gave *Falstaff*; he had him from me christian, and see if the fat villain have not transform'd him ape.

* *been.*

SCENE V.

Enter Bardolph *and* Page.

Bard. Save your grace.

P. *Henry.* And yours, moſt noble *Bardolph.*

Poins. Come you * virtuous aſs, you baſhful fool, muſt you be bluſhing? wherefore bluſh you now? what a maidenly man at arms are you become? Is it ſuch a matter to get a pottle-pot's maiden-head?

Page. He call'd me even now, my lord, through a red lattice; and I could diſcern no part of his face from the window; at laſt I ſpy'd his eyes, and methought he had made two holes in the ale-wive's new petticoat, and peep'd through.

P. *Henry.* Hath not the boy profited?

Bard. Away, you whorſon upright rabbet, away.

Page. Away you raſcally *Althea's* dream, away.

P. *Henry.* Inſtruct us, boy, what dream, boy?

Page. Marry, my lord, *Althea* dream'd ſhe was deliver'd of a firebrand, and therefore I call him her dream.

P. *Henry.* A crowns-worth of good interpretation; there it is boy. [*Gives him money.*

Poins. O that this good bloſſom could be kept from cankers: well, there is ſix-pence to preſerve thee.

Bard. If you do not make him be hang'd among you, the gallows ſhall be wrong'd.

P. *Henry.* And how doth thy maſter, *Bardolph?*

Bard. Well, my good lord; he heard of your grace's coming to town! There's a letter for you.

P. *Henry.* Deliver'd with good reſpect; and how doth the *Martlemas,* your maſter?

Bard. In bodily health, Sir.

Poins. Marry the immortal part needs a phyſician; but that moves not him; though that be ſick, it dies not.

P. *Henry.* I do allow this wen to be as familiar with me as my dog; and holds his place: for look you how he writes.

Poins reads. *John Falſtaff, knight:* —————— every man muſt know that, as oft as, he hath occaſion to name

himſelf:

* *pernicious.*

himself: even like those that are kin to the King, for they never prick their finger but they say *there is some of the King's blood spilt.* How comes that? says he that takes upon him not to conceive: the answer is as ready as a borrowed cap; *I am the King's poor Cousin, Sir.*

P. *Henry.* Nay, they will be kin to us, but they will fetch it from *Japhet.* But to the letter :———— Sir John Falstaff, *knight, to the son of the King nearest his father,* Harry *Prince of* Wales, *greeting.*

Poins. Why this is a certificate.

P. *Henry.* Peace.

I will imitate the honourable Romans *in brevity.*

Poins. Sure he means brevity in breath; short-winded. *I commend me to thee, I commend thee and I leave thee. Be not too familiar with* Poins, *for he misuses thy favours so much, that he swears thou art to marry his Sister* Nell. *Repent at idle times as thou may'st, and so farewel. Thine, by yea and no : which is as much as to say, as thou usest him,* Jack Falstaff *with my familiars:* John *with my brothers and sisters: and Sir* John *with all* Europe.

My lord, I will steep this letter in sack, and make him eat it.

P. *Henry.* That's to make him eat twenty of his words. But do you use me thus, *Ned*? must I marry your sister?

Poins. May the wench have no worse fortune. But I never said so.

P. *Henry.* Well, thus we play the fool with the time, and the spirits of the wife sit in the clouds and mock us: is your master here in *London*?

Bard. Yes, my lord.

P. *Henry.* Where sups he? doth the old Boar feed in the old * frank?

Bard. At the old place, my lord, in *East-cheap.*

P. *Henry.* What company?

Page. Ephesians, my lord, of the old church.

P. *Henry.* Sup any women with him?

Page, None, my lord, but old Mrs. *Quickly,* and Mrs. *Dol Tear-sheet.*

P. *Henry.* What Pagan may that be?

Page. A proper gentlewoman, Sir, and a kinswoman of my master's.

P. *Henry.*

---

* frank, *i. e. a* hogsty.

P. Henry. Even fuch kin, as the parifh heifers are to the town Bull. Shall we fteal upon them, *Ned*, at fupper?

Poins. I am your fhadow, my lord, I'll follow you.

P. Henry. Sirrah, you boy, and *Bardolph*, no word to your mafter that I am yet come to town. There's for your filence.

Bard. I have no tongue, Sir.

Page. And for mine, Sir, I will govern it.

P. Henry. Fare ye well: go. This *Doll Tear-fheet* fhould be fome road.

Poins. I warrant you, as common as the way between St. *Albans* and *London.*

P. Henry. How might we fee *Falftaff* beftow himfelf to-night in his true colours, and not our felves be feen?

Poins. Put on two leather jerkins and aprons, and wait upon him at his table, like drawers.

P. Henry. From a God to a Bull? a heavy * defcenfi-on. It was *Jove's* cafe. From a Prince to a prentice, a low transformation; that fhall be mine: for in every thing, the purpofe muft weigh with the folly. Follow me, *Ned.*

[*Exeunt.*

SCENE VI.

Northumberland.

Enter Northumberland, *Lady* Northumberland, *and* Lady Percy.

North. I pr'ythee loving wife, and gentle daughter,
Give even way unto my rough affairs.
Put not you on the vifage of the times,
And be like them to *Percy*, troublefome.

L. North. I have giv'n over, I will fpeak no more:
Do what you will: your wifdom be your guide.

North. Alas, fweet wife, my honour is at pawn,
And, but my going, nothing can redeem it.

L. Percy. O yet for heav'ns fake, go not to thefe wars:
The time was, father, that you broke your word,
When you were more endear'd to it, than now;
When your own *Percy*, when my Heart-dear *Harry*
Threw many a northward look, to fee his father
Bring up his pow'rs: but he did long in vain!

* *declenfion.*   B 4   Who

Who then perſuaded you to ſtay at home?
There were two honours loſt; yours and your ſon's
For yours, may heav'nly glory brighten it!
For his, it ſtuck upon him as the ſun
In the grey vault of heav'n: and by his light
Did all the chivalry of *England* move
To do brave acts.   He was indeed the glaſs
Wherein the noble Youth did dreſs themſelves.
' He had no legs, that practis'd not his gait:
And ſpeaking thick, which nature made his blemiſh,
Became the accents of the valiant:
For thoſe that could ſpeak low and tardily,
Would turn their own perfection to abuſe,
To ſeem like him.   So that in ſpeech, in gait,
In diet, in affections of delight,
In military rules, humours of blood,
He was the mark and glaſs, copy and book,
That faſhion'd others.   And him, wond'rous him!
O miracle of men! him did you leave
To look upon the hideous God of war
In diſadvantage, to abide a field
Where nothing but the ſound of *Hot-ſpur's* name
Did ſeem defenſible: ſo you left him.
Never, O never do his ghoſt the wrong,
To hold your honour more preciſe and nice
With others, than with him.   Let them alone:
The Marſhal and the Arch-biſhop are ſtrong.
Had my ſweet *Harry* had but half their numbers,
To-day might I (hanging on *Hot-ſpur's* neck)
Have talk'd of *Monmouth's* grave.
  North. Beſhrew your heart,
Fair daughter, you do draw my ſpirits from me,
With new lamenting ancient over-ſights.
But I muſt go and meet with danger there;
Or it will ſeek me in another place,
And find me worſe provided.
  L. North. Fly to *Scotland*,
Till that the nobles and the armed commons
Have of their puiſſance made a little taſte.

L. Percy.

* *The twenty two following lines, are of thoſe added by*
Shakeſpear *after his firſt edition.*

L. Percy. If they get ground and vantage of the King
Then join you with them, like a rib of steel,
To make strength stronger. But for all our loves,
First let them try themselves. So did your son:
He was so suffer'd; so came I a widow:
And never shall have length of life enough,
To rain upon remembrance with mine eyes,
That it may grow and sprout as high as heav'n,
For recordation to my noble husband.

North. Come, come, go in with me: 'tis with my mind
As with the tide swell'd up unto his height,
That makes a still-sand, running neither way.
Fain would I go to meet the Archbishop,
But many thousand reasons hold me back:
I will resolve for *Scotland*; there am I,
Till time and vantage crave my company.   [*Exeunt.*

S C E N E VII.

Tavern in Eastcheap,

Enter two Drawers.

1 *Draw.* What the devil hast thou brought there? Apple-*Johns?* thou knowest Sir *John* cannot endure an Apple-*John.*

2 *Draw.* Mass! thou sayest true; the Prince once set a dish of Apple-*Johns* before him, and told him there were five more Sir *Johns;* and putting off his hat, said, I will now take my leave of these six dry, round, old wither'd knights. It anger'd him to the heart; but he hath forgot that.

1 *Draw.* Why then cover, and set them down; and see if thou canst find out *Sneak's* noise; Mrs. *Tear-sheet* would fain hear some musick, † Dispatch! the room where they supt is too hot, they'll come in strait.

2 *Draw.* Sirrah, here will be the Prince, and Master *Poins* anon; and they will put on two of our jerkins and aprons, and Sir *John* must not know of it. *Bardolph* hath brought word.

B 5   1 *Draw.*

† *This period is from the first edition.*

1 *Draw.* Then here will be old * *Utis:* it will be an excellent ftratagem.

2 *Draw.* I'll fee if I can find out *Sneak.*   [*Exeunt.*

SCENE VIII.

Enter Hoftefs *and* Dol.

Hoft. Sweet heart, methinks now you are in an excellent good temperality; your pulfidge beats as extraordinarily as heart would defire; and your colour, I warrant you, is as red as any rofe: but you have drank too much canary, and that's a marvellous fearching wine; and it perfumes the blood ere we can fay what's this. How do you now?

Dol. Better than I was: hem.

Hoft. Why, that was well faid: a good heart's worth gold. Look, here comes Sir *John.*

Enter Falftaff.

Fal. When Arthur *firft in court* ———— empty the jordan ———— *and was a worthy King:* how now, Mrs. *Dol?*

Hoft. Sick of a calm: yea, good footh,

Fal. So is all her fect, if they be once in a calm, they are fick.

Dol. You muddy rafcal, is that all the comfort you give me?

Fal. You make fat rafcals, Mrs. *Dol.*

Dol. I make them! gluttony and difeafes make them, I make them not.

Fal. If the cook make the gluttony, you help to make the difeafes, *Dol;* we catch of you, *Dol,* we catch of you; grant that, my poor vertue, grant that.

Dol. Ay, marry, our chains and our jewels.

Fal. Your † brooches, pearls and owches, for to ferve bravely, is to come halting off, you know; to come off the breach with his pike bent bravely, and to furgery bravely; to venture upon the charg'd chambers bravely ————
                                                                    Dol.

* Utis, *an old word yet in ufe in fome counties, fignifying a merry feftival, from the French* Huit; *octo, ab A* S. Ɛahꞇa.

Dol, Hang your felf, you muddy Conger, hang your felf!

Hoſt. By my troth, this is the old faſhion; you two never meet but you fall to ſome diſcord; you are both, in good troth, as rheumatick as two dry toaſts, you cannot one bear with another's confirmities. What the good-year? one muſt bear, and that muſt be you: you are the weaker veſſel, as they ſay, the emptier veſſel. [*To Dol.*

Dol. Can a weak empty veſſel bear ſuch a huge full hogſhead? there's a whole merchant's venture of *Bourdeaux* ſtuff in him; you have not ſeen a hulk better ſtuft in the hold. Come, I'll be friends with thee, *Jack:* thou art going to the wars, and whether I ſhall ever ſee thee again or no, there is no body cares.

S·C E N·E IX.

Enter Drawer.

Draw. Sir, ancient *Piſtol* is below, and would ſpeak with you.

Dol. Hang him, ſwaggering raſcal, let him not come hither; it is the foul-mouth'd rogue in *England.*

Hoſt. If he ſwagger, let him not come here: no by my faith: I muſt live amongſt my neighbours, I'll no ſwaggerers: I am in good name and fame with the very beſt: ſhut the door, there comes no ſwaggerers here: I have not liv'd all this while to have ſwaggering now; ſhut the door, I pray you.

Fal. Doſt thou hear, hoſteſs ————

Hoſt. Pray you pacify your ſelf, Sir *John,* there comes no ſwaggerers here.

Fal. Doſt thou hear —— it is mine Ancient.

Hoſt. Tilly-fally, Sir *John,* never tell me, your antient ſwaggerers comes not in my doors. I was before maſter *Tiſick* the deputy the other day; and as he ſaid to me —— it was no longer ago than *Wedneſday* laſt —— neighbour *Quickly,* ſay he; —— maſter *Domb* our miniſter was by then; —— neighbour *Quickly,* ſays he, receive thoſe that are civil; for faith he, you are in an ill name: now he ſaid ſo, I can tell whereupon; for, ſays he, you are an honeſt woman, and well thought on, therefore take heed what gueſts you receive: receive, ſays he, no
ſwaggering.

fwaggering companions ——— There come none here. You would blefs you to hear what he faid. No, I'll no fwaggerers.

Fal. He's no fwaggerer, hoftefs; a tame cheater, i' faith; you may ftroke him as gently as a puppey-grey-hound; he will not fwagger with a *Barbary* hen, if her feathers turn back in any fhew of refiftance. Call him up, drawer.

Hoft. Cheater, call you him? I will bar no honeft man my houfe, nor no cheater; but I do not love fwaggering; I am the worfe when one fays fwagger; feel, mafters, how I fhake, look you, I warrant you.

Dol. So you do, hoftefs.

Hoft. Do I? yea, in very truth do I, as if it were an afpen leaf: I cannot abide fwaggerers.

S C E N E X.

Enter Piftol, Bardolph *and* Page.

Pift. Save you, Sir *John.*

Fal. Welcome, ancient *Piftol.* Here, *Piftol,* I charge you with a cup of fack: do you difcharge upon mine hoftefs.

Pift. I will difcharge upon her, Sir *John,* with two bullets.

Fal. She is piftol proof, Sir, you fhall hardly offend her.

Hoft. Come, I'll drink no proofs, nor no bullets: I will drink no more than will do me good, for no man's pleafure, I.

Pift. Then to you, Miftrefs *Dorothy,* I will charge you.

Dol. Charge me! I fcorn you, fcurvy companion! what? you poor, bafe, rafcally, cheating, lack-linnen mate; away, you mouldy rogue, away, I am meat for your mafter,

Pift. I know you, miftrefs *Dorothy.*

Dol. Away, you cut-purfe rafcal, you filthy bung a-way: by this wine, I'll thruft my knife in your mouldy chaps if you play the faucy cuttle with me. Away you bottle-ale rafcal, you basket-hilt ftale jugler you. Since when, I pray you, Sir? what, with two points on your fhoulder? much.

B. I will murder your ruff for this.

Fal.

* *Fal.* No more, *Piſtol*; I wou'd not have you go off here: diſcharge your ſelf of our company, *Piſtol.*

Hoſt. No, good captain *Piſtol:* not here, ſweet captain.

Dol. Captain! thou abominable damn'd cheater, art thou not aſham'd to be call'd captain? if captains were of my mind they would truncheon you out + of taking their names upon you, before you have earn'd them. You a captain! you ſlave! for what? for tearing a poor whore's ruff in a bawdy houſe? he a captain! hang him, rogue; he lives upon mouldy ſtew'd prunes and dry'd cakes. A captain! theſe villains will make the word captain! †as odious as the word occupy ; which was an excellent good word before it was ill ſorted: therefore captains had need look to it.

Bard. Pray thee go down, good Ancient.

Fal. Hark thee hither, miſtreſs *Dol.*

Piſt. Not I: I tell thee what, corporal *Bardolph,* I could tear her : I'll be reveng'd on her.

Page. Pray thee go down.

Piſt. I'll ſee her damn'd firſt, to *Pluto's* damned lake, to the infernal deep, where *Erebus* and tortures vile alſo. Hold hook and line, I ſay: down! down dogs, down fates: have we not *Hiren* here?

Hoſt. Good captain *Peeſel* be quiet, it is very late: I beſeech you now, aggravate your choler.

Piſt. Theſe be good humours indeed. Shall packhorſes And hollow-pamper'd jades of *Aſia,* Which cannot go but thirty miles a day, Compare with *Caſar,* and with *Cannibal,* And *Trojan Greeks*? nay, rather damn them with King *Cerberus,* and let the welkin roar: Shall we fall foul for toys?

Hoſt. By my troth, captain, theſe are very bitter words.

Bard. Be gone, good Ancient: this will grow to a brawl anon.

Piſt. Die men, like dogs; give crowns like pins: have we not *Hiren* here?

Hoſt. On my word, captain, there's none ſuch here. What the good-year? do you think I would deny her? I pray be quiet.

Piſt.

* *This is from the old edition,* 1600.   † *for.*

‡ *out of the old edition.*

Pist. Then feed, and be fat, my fair *Calipolis*; come, give me some sack. *Si fortuna me tormente, sperato me contente.*

Fear we broad-sides? no, let the fiend give fire: Give me some sack: and sweet-heart, lye thou there: Come we to full points here; and are *& cetera*'s nothing?

Fal. *Pistol*, I would be quiet.

Pist. Sweet knight, I kiss thy * neif: what! we have seen the seven stars.

Dol. Thrust him down stairs, I cannot endure such a fustian rascal.

Pist. Thrust him down stairs, know we not galloway nags?

Fal. Quoit him down, *Bardolph*, like a shove-groat shilling: nay, if he do nothing but speak nothing, he shall be nothing here.

Bard. Come, get you down stairs.

Pist. What shall we have incision? shall we embrew? then death rock me asleep, abridge my doleful days: why then let grievous, ghastly, gaping wounds, untwine the sisters three: come, *Atropos*, I say.   [*Drawing his sword.*

Host. Here's goodly stuff toward.

Fal. Give me my rapier, boy.

Dol. I pr'ythee, *Jack*, I pr'ythee do not draw.

Fal. Get you down stairs.

[*Drawing, and driving* Pistol *out.*

Host. Here's a goodly tumult; I'll forswear keeping house, before I'll be in these tirrits and frights. So murther, I warrant now. Alas, alas, put up your naked weapons, put up your naked weapons.

Dol. I pr'ythee, *Jack*, be quiet, the rascal is gone: ah you whorson, little valiant villain you.

Host. Are you not hurt i'th' groin? methought he made a shrewd thrust at your belly.

Fal. Have you turn'd him out of doors?

Bard. Yes, Sir, the rascal's drunk: you have hurt him, Sir, in the shoulder.

Fal. A rascal to brave me!

Dol. Ah, you sweet little rogue you! alas, poor ape, how thou sweat'st? come, let me wipe thy face——
come

* neif, *from* nativa, *i. e. a woman slave that is born in one's house   He would kiss* Dol.

come on you whorſon chops — ah rogue, I love thee — thou art as valorous as *Hector* of Troy, worth five of *Agamemnon*; and ten times better than the nine worthies: a villain!

Fal. A raſcally ſlave! I will toſs the rogue in a blanket.

Dol. Do if thou dar'ſt for thy heart : if thou doſt, I'll canvaſs thee between a pair of ſheets.

Enter Muſick.

Page. The muſick is come, Sir.

Fal. Let them play; play, Sirs. Sit on my knee, *Dol.* A raſcal, bragging ſlave! the rogue fled from me like quick-ſilver.

Dol. I'faith and thou follow'dſt him like a church: thou whorſon little tydie *Bartholomew* Boar-pig, when wilt thou leave fighting on days, and foyning on nights, and begin to patch up thine old body for heaven?

S C E N E XI.

Enter Prince Henry *and* Poins *diſguis'd.*

Fal. Peace. good *Dol*, do not ſpeak like a death's-head: do not bid me remember mine end.

Dol. Sirrah, what humour is the Prince of?

Fal. A good ſhallow young fellow: he would have made a good pantler, he would have chipp'd bread well.

Dol. They ſay *Poins* hath a good wit.

Fal. He a good wit? hang him, baboon, his wit is as thick as *Tewkſbury* muſtard: there is no more conceit in him, than is in a mallet.

Dol. Why doth the Prince love him ſo then?

Fal. Becauſe their legs are both of a bigneſs: and he plays at quoits well, and eats conger and fennel, and drinks off candles end for flap-dragons, and rides the wild mare with the boys, and jumps upon joint ſtools, and ſwears with a good grace, and wears his boot very ſmooth like unto the ſign of the leg, and breeds no bate with telling of diſcreet ſtories; and ſuch other gambol faculties he hath, that ſhew a weak mind and an able body; for the which the Prince admits him: for the Prince himſelf is ſuch another: the weight of an hair will turn the ſcales between their *Averdupois.*

P. Henry.

P. Henry. Would not this nave of a wheel have his ears cut off?

Poins. Let us beat him before his whore.

P. Henry Look, if the wither'd elder hath not his poll claw'd like a Parrot.

Poins. Is it not strange that defire fhould fo many years cut-live performance?

Fal. Kifs me, *Dol.*

P. Henry. Saturn and *Venus* this year in conjunction! what fays the almanack to that?

Poins. And look; whether the fiery *Trigon* his man be not lifping to his mafter's old tables, his note-book, his counfel-keeper?

Fal. Thou doft give me flattering buffes.

Dol. By my troth I kifs thee with a moft conftant heart.

Fal. I am old, I am old.

Dol. I love thee better than I love e'er a fcurvy young boy of them all.

Fal. What ftuff wilt thou have a kirtle of? I fhall receive mony on *Thurfday:* Thou fhalt have a cap to-morrow. A merry fong. come: it grows late, we will to bed. Thou wilt forget me when I am gone.

Dol. By my troth thou wilt fet me a weeping if thou fay'ft fo: prove that ever I dreft my felf handfom till thy return ———— Well, hearken the end.

Fal. Some fack, *Francis.*

P. Henry. Poins. Anon, anon, Sir.

Fal. Ha! a baftard fon of the King's! and art not thou *Poins* his brother?

P. Henry. Why, thou globe of finful continents, what a life doft thou lead?

Fal. A better than thou: I am a gentleman, thou art a drawer.

P. Henry. Very true, Sir; and I am come to draw you out by the ears.

Hoft. Oh, the lord preferve thy good grace. Welcome to *London.* Now heav'n blefs that fweet face of thine; what, are you come from *Wales?*

Fal. Thou whorfon-made compound of majefty, by this light flefh and corrupt blood, thou art welcome.

[Leaning his hand upon Dol.

Dol.

Dol. How! you fat-fool, I scorn you.

Poins. My lord, he will drive you out of your revenge, and turn all to a merriment, if you take not the heat.

P. Henry. You whorfon candle-myne you, how vilely did you fpeak of me even now, before this honeft, virtuous, civil gentlewoman?

Hoft. Bleffing on your good heart, and fo fhe is by my troth.

Fal. Didft thou hear me?

P. Henry. Yes; and you knew me as you did when you ran away by *Gads hill*, you knew I was at your back, and fpoke it on purpofe to try my patience.

Fal. No, no, no; not fo; I did not think thou waft within hearing.

P. Henry. I fhall drive you then to confefs the wilful abufe, and then I know how to handle you.

Fal. No abufe, *Hal*, on my honour, no abufe.

P. Henry. Not to difpraife me, and call me pantler, and bread-chipper, and I know not what?

Fal. No abufe, *Hal*.

Poins. No abufe!

Fal. No abufe, *Ned*, in the world; honeft *Ned*, none. I difprais'd him before the wicked, that the wicked might not fall in love with him; in which doing, I have done the part of a careful friend, and true fubject, and thy father is to give me thanks for it. No abufe, *Hal*. none, *Ned*, none; no, boys, none.

P. Henry. See now whether pure fear and entire cowardife doth not make thee wrong this virtuous gentlewoman, to clofe with us? Is fhe of the wicked? is thine hoftefs here of the wicked? or is the boy of the wicked? or honeft *Bardolph*, whofe zeal burns in his nofe, of the wicked?

Poins. Anfwer, thou dead Elm, anfwer.

Fal. The fiend hath prickt down *Bardolph* irrecoverable, and his face is *Lucifer*'s privy-kitchen, where he doth nothing but roaft mault-worms: for the boy, there is a good angel about him, but the devil * out-bids him too.

P. Henry. For the women?

Fal.

* *In the firft Edition it is* the devil *blinds* him too.

Fal. For one of them, fhe is in hell already, and burns, poor foul: for the other, I owe her mony; and whether fhe be damn'd for that I know not.

Hoſt. No, I warrant you.

Fal. No, I think thou art not: I think thou art quit for that. Marry, there is another indictment upon thee, for fuffering flefh to be eaten in thy houfe, contrary to the law, for the which I think thou wilt howl.

Hoſt. All victuallers do fo: what is a joint of mutton or two in a whole *Lent*?

P. Henry. You, gentlewoman.

Dol. What fays your grace?

Fal. His grace fays that which his flefh rebels againſt.

Hoſt. Who knocks fo loud at door? look to the door there, *Francis.*

SCENE XII.

Enter Peto.

P. Henry. Peto, how now? what News?

Peto. The King your father is at *Weſtminſter*, And there are twenty weak and wearied poſts
Come from the north; and as I came along,
I met and overtook a dozen captains,
Bare-headed, fweating, knocking at the taverns,
And asking every one for Sir *John Falſtaff.*

P. Henry. By heaven, *Poins,* I feel me much to blame,
So idly to profane the precious time;
When tempeſt of commotion, like the South
Born with black vapour doth begin to melt
And drop upon our bare unarmed heads.
Give me my fword, and cloak: *Falſtaff,* good night.

       [*Exeunt Prince and* Poins.

Fal. Now comes in the fweeteſt morfel of the night, and we muſt hence, and leave it unpickt. More knocking at the door? how now? what's the matter?

Bard. You muſt away to court, Sir, prefently: a dozen captains ſtay at door for you.

Fal. Pay the muficians, Sirrah: farewel hoſtefs, farewel *Dol.* You fee, my good wenches, how men of merit are fought after; the undeferver may fleep, when the

man of action is called on. Farewel, good wenches; if
I be not sent away post, I will see you again, ere I go.

Dol. I cannot speak, if my heart be not ready to burst
—— well, sweet *Jack*, have a care of thy self.

Fal. Farewel, farewel.   [*Exit.*

Host. Well, fare thee well: I have known thee these
twenty nine years, come pescod-time; but an honester
and truer-hearted man —— well, fare thee well.

Bard. Mrs. *Tear-sheet.*

Host. What's the matter?

Bard. Bid Mistress *Tear-sheet* come to my master.

Host. O run, *Dol*, run; run, good *Dol*.   [*Exeunt.*

A C T III. S C E N E I.

L O N D O N.

Enter King Henry *in his night-gown, with a* Page.

K. *Henry.* GO, call the Earls of *Surrey* and of *Warwick*;
But ere they come, bid them o'er-read
these letters,
And well consider of them: make good speed.[*Exit Page.*
How many thousands of my poorest subjects;
Are at this hour asleep! ' O gentle Sleep,
' Nature's soft nurse, how have I frighted thee,
' That thou no more wilt weigh my eye-lids down;
' And steep my senses in forgetfulness?
' Why rather, Sleep, ly'st thou in smoaky cribs,
' Upon uneasie pallets stretching thee,
' And hush't with buzzing night-flies to thy slumber,
' Than in the perfum'd chambers of the great,
' Under the canopies of costly state,
' And lull'd with sounds of sweetest melody?
' O thou dull God, why ly'st thou with the vile
' In loathsom beds, and leav'st the kingly couch.
' A watch-case, or a common larum-bell?
' Wilt thou upon the high and giddy mast,
' Seal up the ship-boy's eyes, and rock his brains,
' In cradle of the rude imperious surge;
' And in the visitation of the winds,

‘ Who take the ruffian billows by the top,
‘ Curling their monſtrous heads, and hanging them
‘ With deaf 'ning clamours in the ſlip'ry ſhrouds,
‘ That with the hurley, death it ſelf awakes?
‘ Can'ſt thou, O partial Sleep, give thy repoſe
‘ To the wet ſea-boy in an hour ſo rude?
‘ And in the calmeſt and the ſtilleſt night,
‘ With all appliances and means to boot,
‘ Deny it to a King? then happy low! lye down;
Uneaſie lyes the head that wears a crown.

SCENE II

Enter Warwick *and* Surrey.

War. Many good-morrows to your Majeſty.
K. Henry. Is it good-morrow, lords?
War. 'Tis one a clock, and paſt.
K. Honry. Why then good-morrow to you all, my lords;
Have you read o'er the letters that I ſent you?
War. We have, my Liege.
K. Henry. Then you perceive the body of our kingdom;
How foul it is; what rank diſeaſes grow,
And with what danger, near the heart of it.
War. It is but as a body, yet diſtemper'd,
Which to its former ſtrength may be reſtor'd,
With good advice and little medicine;
My lord *Northumberland* will ſoon be cool'd.
K. Henry. Oh heav'n that one might read the book
                    of fate,
And ſee the revolution of the times
Make mountains level, and the continent
Weary of ſolid firmneſs, melt it ſelf
Into the ſea; and other times, to ſee
The beachy girdle of the ocean
Too wide for *Neptune's* hips: how chances mock
And changes fill the cup of alteration
With divers liquors. O, if this were ſeen,
The happieſt youth viewing his progreſs through,
What perils paſt, what croſſes to enſue,
Wou'd ſhut the book, and ſit him down and die.

'Ti

* *Theſe four verſes are ſupply'd from the edition of* 1600.

'Tis not ten years fince. *Richard* and *Northumberland*
Did feaft together; and in two years after
Were they at wars. It is but eight years fince
This *Percy* was the man neareft my foul,
Who like a brother toil'd in my affairs,
And laid his love and life under my foot;
Yea for my fake ev'n to the eyes of *Richard*
Give him defiance. Which of you was by?
(You, coufin *Nevil*, as I may remember) (*To* Warwick.
When *Richard* with his eye brim-full of tears,
Then check'd and rated by *Northumberland*,
Did fpeak thefe words, now prov'd a prophecy.
' *Northumberland*, thou ladder by the which
'' My coufin *Bolingbroke* afcends my throne :
(Though then, heav'n knows, I had no fuch intent,
But that neceffity fo bow'd the ftate,
That I and greatnefs were compell'd to kifs)
' The time fhall come, (thus did he foilow it,)
' The time will come, that foul fin gathering head,
' Shall break into corruption; fo went on,
Fore-telling this fame time's condition;
And the divifion of our amity.
  War. There is a hiftory in all men's lives,
Figuring the nature of the times deceas'd;
The which obferv'd, a man may prophefie
With a near aim, of the main chance of things
As yet not come to life, which in their feeds
And weak beginnings lie intreafured.
Such things become the hatch and brood of time;
And by the neceffary form of this,
King *Richard* might create a perfect guefs,
That great *Northumberland*, then falfe to him,
Would of that feed grow to a greater falfenes,
Which fhould not find a ground to root upon,
Unlefs on you.
  K. Henry. Are thefe things then neceffities?
Then let us meet them like neceffities;
And that fame word even now cries out on us :
They fay the Bifhop and *Northumberland*
Are fifty thoufand ftrong.

War. It cannot be:
Rumour doth double, like the voice and echo,
The numbers of the fear'd.   Please it your grace
To go to bed. Upon my life, my lord,
The pow'rs that you already have sent forth
Shall bring this prize in very easily.
To comfort you the more, I have receiv'd
A certain instance that *Glendower* is dead.
Your Majesty hath been this fortnight ill,
And these unseason'd hours perforce must add
Unto your sickness.

  K. Henry. I will take your counsel:
And were these inward wars once out of hand,
We would, dear lords, unto the holy-land.   [*Exeunt.*

SCENE III.

The COUNTRY.

Enter Shallow *and* Silence, *Justices; with* Mouldy,
  Shadow, Wart, Feeble, *and* Bull-calf.

  Shal. Come on, come on, come on; give me your
hand, Sir ; an early stirrer, by the * rood. And how
doth my good cousin *Silence?*
  Sil. Good morrow, good cousin *Shallow.*
  Shal. And how doth my cousin, your bed-fellow ?
and your fairest daughter, and mine, my god-daughter
Ellen?
  Sil. Alas, a black ouzel, cousin *Shallow.*
  Shal. By yea and nay, Sir; I dare say my cousin *William* is become a good scholar : he is at *Oxford* still, is he
not ?
  Sil. Indeed, Sir, to my cost.
  Shal. He must then to the Inns of court shortly : I
was once of *Clement's*-Inn; where, I think, they will talk
of mad *Shallow* yet.
  Sil. You were call'd lusty *Shallow* then, cousin.
  Shal. I was call'd any thing, and I would have done
any thing indeed too, and roundly too. There was I,

and

  * *the* rood, i. e. *the* cross.

and little *John Dott* of *Staffordshire*, and black *George Bure*, and *Francis Pickbone*, and *Will. Squeele a Cot'swold* man, you had not four such swing-bucklers in all the Inns of court again; and I may say to you, we knew where the *Bona-Roba's* were, and had the best of them all at commandment. Then was *Jack Falstaff* (now Sir *John*, boy) a page to *Thomas Mowbray*, Duke of *Norfolk*.

Sil. This Sir *John*, cousin, that comes hither anon about Soldiers?

Shal. The same Sir *John*, the very same: I saw him break *Schoggan's* head at the court-gate, when he was a crack, not thus high; and the very same day I did fight with one *Sampson Stockfish*, a fruiterer, behind *Grays-Inn*. O the mad days that I have spent! and to see how many of mine old acquaintance are dead?

Sil. We shall all follow, cousin.

Shall. Certain, 'tis certain, very sure, very sure: death * (as the Psalmist saith) is certain to all, all shall die. How a good yoke of Bullocks at *Stamford* fair?

Sil. Truly, cousin, I was not there.

Shal. Death is certain. Is old *Double* of your town living yet?

Sil. Dead, Sir:

Shal. Dead! see, see, he drew a good bow: and dead? he shot a fine shoot. *John* of *Gaunt* loved him well, and betted much money on his head. Dead! he would have clapt in the clowt at twelve score, and carried you a forehand shaft a fourteen and fourteen and a half, that it would have done a man's heart good to see. How a score of ewes now?

Sil. Thereafter as they be: a score of good ewes may be worth ten pounds.

Shal. And is old *Double* dead?

SCENE IV.

Enter Bardolph *and Page.*

Sil. Here come two of Sir *John Falstaff's* men, as I think.

Shal. Good-morrow, honest gentlemen.

Bard.

Bard. I befeech you, which is Juftice *Shallow?*

Shal. I am *Robert Shallow,* Sir, a poor Efquire of this county, one of the King's Juftices of the peace: what is your good pleafure with me?

Bard. My captain, Sir, commends him to you: my captain Sir *John Falstaff;* a tall gentleman by heav'n! and a moft gallant leader.

Shal. He greets me well: Sir, I knew him a good back-fword man. How doth the good knight? may I ask how my lady his wife doth?

Bard. Sir, pardon, a foldier is better accommodated than with a wife.

Shal. It is well faid, Sir; and it is well faid indeed, too: better accommodated —— it is good, yea indeed is it; good Phrafes furely are, and * ever were, very commendable. Accommodated —— it comes of *Accommodo;* very good, a good phrafe.

Bard. Pardon me, Sir, I have heard the word. Phrafe, call you it? by this day, I know not the Phrafe: but I will maintain the word with my fword, to be a foldier-like word, and a word of exceeding good command. Accommodated, that is, when a man is, as they fay, accommodated; or, when a man is, being whereby he may be thought to be accommodated, which is an excellent thing.

S C E N E V.

Enter Falstaff.

Shal. It is very juft: look, here comes good Sir *John.* Give me your hand, give me your worfhip's good hand: truft me, you look well, and bear your years very well. Welcome, good Sir *John.*

Fal. I am glad to fee you well, good mafter *Robert Shallow:* Mafter *Sure-card;* as I think?

Shal. No, Sir *John,* it is my coufin *Silence;* in commiffion with me.

Fal. Good mafter *Silence,* it well befits you fhall be of the peace.

Sil. Your good worfhip is welcome.

Fal. Fy, this is hot weather, gentlemen, have you provided me here half a dozen of fufficient men?

Shal.

———————

* *every where.*

Shal. Marry have we, Sir: will you fit?

Fal. Let me fee them, I befeech you.

Shal. Where's the roll? where's the roll? where's the roll? let me fee, let me fee, let me fee: fo, fo, fo, fo: yea, marry, Sir. *Ralph Mouldy:* let them appear as I call: let them do fo, let them do fo. Let me fee, where is *Mouldy?*

Moul. Here, if it pleafe you.

Fal. What think you, Sir *John?* a good limb'd fellow: young, ftrong, and of good friends.

Fal. Is thy name *Mouldy?*

Moul. Yea, if it pleafe you.

Fal. 'Tis the more time thou wert us'd.

Shal. Ha, ha, ha, moft excellent i' faith. Things that are mouldy, lack ufe: very fingular good. Well faid, Sir *John,* very well faid.

Fal. Prick him.

Moul. I was prickt well enough before, if you could have let me alone: my old dame will be undone now for one to do her hufbandry, and her drudgery; you need not to have prickt me, there are other men fitter to go out than I.

Fal. Go to: peace *Mouldy,* you fhall go, *Mouldy,* it is time you were fpent.

Moul. Spent?

Shal. Peace, fellow, peace: ftand afide: know you where you are? for the other, Sir *John.* Let me fee: *Simon Shadow.*

Fal. Ay marry, let me have him to fit under: he's like to be a cold foldier.

Shal. Where's *Shadow?*

Shad. Here, Sir.

Fal. Shadow, whofe fon art thou?

Shad. My mother's fon, Sir.

Fal. Thy mother's fon! like enough; and thy father's fhadow: fo the fon of the female is the fhadow of the male: it is often fo indeed, but not of the father's fubftance.

Shal. How do you like him, Sir *John?*

Fal. Shadow will ferve for a fummer; prick him, for we have a number of fhadows to fill up the mufter-book.

C *Shal.*

Shal. Thomas Wart.

Fal. Where's he?

Wart. Here, Sir.

Fal. Is thy name *Wart?*

Wart. Yea, Sir.

Fal. Thou art a very ragged wart.

Shal. Shall I prick him down, Sir *John?*

Fal. It were superfluous; for his apparel is built upon his back, and the whole frame stands upon pins: prick him no more.

Shal. Ha, ha, ha, you can do it, Sir; you can do it: I commend you well. *Francis Feeble.*

Feeble. Here, Sir.

Shal. What trade art thou, *Feeble?*

Feeble. A woman's tailor, Sir.

Shal. Shall I prick him, Sir?

Fal. You may: but if he had been a man's tailor he would have prick'd you. Wilt thou make as many holes in an enemy's battel, as thou hast done in a woman's petticoat?

Feeble. I will do my good will, Sir; you can have no more.

Fal. Well said, good woman's tailor; well said, courageous *Feeble:* thou wilt be as valiant as the wrathful Dove, or most magnanimous Mouse. Prick the woman's tailor well, master *Shallow*, deep, master *Shallow.*

Feeble. I would *Wart* might have gone, Sir.

Fal. I would thou wert a man's tailor, that thou might'st mend him, and make him fit to go. I cannot put him to be a private soldier, that is the leader of so many thousands. Let that suffice, most forcible *Feeble.*

Feeble. It shall suffice.

Fal. I am bound to thee, reverend *Feeble.* Who is the next?

Shal. Peter Bulcalf of the green.

Fal. Yea, marry, let us see *Bulcalf.*

Bul. Here, Sir.

Fal. Trust me, a likely fellow. Come, prick me Bulcalf till he roar again.

Bul. Oh good my lord captain.

Fal. What, dost thou roar before th'art prick't?

Bul.

Bul. Oh, Sir, I am a diseased man.

Fal. What disease hast thou?

Bul. A whorson cold, Sir; a cough, Sir, which I caught with ringing in the King's affairs, upon his coronation day, Sir.

Fal. Come, thou shalt go to the Wars in a gown: we will have away thy cold; and I will take such order that thy friends shall sing for thee. Is here all?

Shal. There is two more called than your number, you must have but four here, Sir; and so, I pray you, go in with me to dinner.

Fal. Come, I will go drink with you, but I cannot tarry dinner. I am glad to see you, in good troth, master *Shallow*.

Shal. O, Sir *John*, do you remember since we lay all night in the wind-mill in Saint *George's* fields?

Fal. No more of that, good master *Shallow*, no more of that.

Shal. Ha! it was a merry night. And is *Jane Nightwork* alive?

Fal. She lives, master *Shallow*.

Shal. She never could away with me.

Fal. Never, never: she would always say she could not abide master *Shallow*.

Shal. By the mass I could anger her to the heart: she was then a *Bona-roba*. Doth she hold her own well?

Fal. Old, old, master *Shallow*.

Shal. Nay, she must be old, she cannot chuse but be old; certain she's old, and had *Robin Night-work* by old *Night-work*, before I came to *Clement's*-Inn.

Sil. That's fifty five years ago.

Shal. Hah, cousin *Silence*, that thou hadst seen that, that this knight and I have seen: hah, Sir *John*, said I well?

Fal. We have heard the chimes at midnight, Master *Shallow*.

Shal. That we have, that we have, in faith Sir *John* we have: our watch-word was hem boys. Come, let's to dinner; Oh the days that we have seen! come, come.

Bul. Good master corporate *Bardolph* stand my Friend, and here is four *Harry* ten shillings in *French* crowns

for

for you: in very truth, Sir, I had as lief be hang'd,
Sir, as go; and yet for mine own part, Sir, I do not care,
but rather because I am unwilling, and for mine own
part, have a defire to ftay with my friends, elfe, Sir,
I did not care for mine own part fo much.

Bard. Go to; ftand afide.

Mould. And good mafter corporal captain, for my old
dame's fake ftand my friend: fhe hath no body to do any
thing about her when I am gone, and fhe's old and cannot help her felf: you fhall have forty, Sir.

Bard. Go to; ftand afide.

Feeble. I care not, a man can die but once; we owe
God a death, I will never bear a bafe mind: if it be my
deftiny, fo: if it be not, fo. No man is too good to
ferve his Prince; and let it go which way it will, he that
dies this year is quit f r the next.

Bard. Well faid, thou art a good fellow.

Feeble. 'Faith I will bear no bafe mind.

Fal. Come, Sir, which men fhall I have?

Shal. Four of which you pleafe.

Bard. Sir, a word with you: I have three pound to
free *Mouldy* and *Bulcalf.*

Fal. Go to; well.

Shal. Come, Sir *John,* which four will you have?

Fal. Do you chufe for me.

Shal. Marry then, *Mouldy, Bulcalf, Feeble* and *Shadow.*

Fal. Mouldy and *Bulcalf:* for you, *Mouldy,* ftay at
home till you are paft fervice: and for your part, *Bulcalf,* grow till you come unto it: I will none of you.

Shal. Sir *John,* Sir *John,* do not your felf wrong, they
are your likelieft men, and I would have you ferv'd with
the beft.

Fal. Will you tell me, mafter *Shallow,* how to chufe a
man? care I for the limb, the thewes, the ftature, bulk
and big femblance of a man? give me the fpirit, mafter
Shallow. Here's *Wart,* you fee what a ragged appearance
it is: he fhall charge you and difcharge you with the motion of a pewterer's hammer; co ne off and on, fwifter
than he their gibbets or the brewer's bucket. And this
fame half-fac'd fellow *Shadow,* give me this man, he pre-
fents no mark to the enemy, the fo-man may with as
                                                great

great aim level at the edge of a penknife : and, for a retreat, how fwiftly will this *Feeble*, the woman's tailor, run
off. O give me the fpare men, and fpare me the great
ones. Put me a † caliver into *Wart*'s hand, *Bardolph*.

Bard. Hold *Wart*, traverfe; thus, thus.

Fal. Come, manage me your caliver: fo, very well,
go to, very good, exceeding good. O give me always a
little, lean, old, chopt, bald fhot. Well faid, *Wart*, thou
art a good fcab; hold, there's a tefter for thee.

Shal. He is not his craft-mafter, he doth not do it right.
I remember at *Mile-End-Green*, when I lay at *Clement's*
Inn, I was then Sir *Dagenet* in *Arthur's* fhow, there was
a little quiver fellow, and he would manage you his piece
thus; and he would about, and about, and come you in,
and come you in: rah, tah, tah, would he fay : bounce,
would he fay, and away again would he go, and again
would he come : I fhall never fee fuch a fellow.

Fal. Thefe fellows wil do well, Mafter *Shallow*, God
keep you; farewel, mafter *Silence*. I will not ufe many
words with you, fare you well, gentlemen both. I thank
you, I muft a dozen mile to-night. *Bardolph* give the
foldiers coats.

Shal. Sir *John*, heaven blefs you, and profper your affairs, and fend us peace. As you return, vifit my houfe,
Let our old acquaintance be renewed: peradventure I
will with you to the court.

Fal. I would you would, mafter *Shallow*.

Fal. Go to : I have fpoke at a word. Fare you well.
　　　　　　　　　　　　　　　　　　　　　　　[Exit.

Fal. Fare you well, gentlemen. On, *Bardolph*; lead the
men away. As I return, I will fetch off thefe Juftices :
I do fee the bottom of Juftice *Shallow*. How fubjeƈt we
old men are to this vice of lying ! this fame ftarv'd Juftice
hath done nothing but prated to me of the wildnefs of
his youth, and the feats he hath done about *Turnbal-ftreet*;
and every third word a lye, more duly paid to the hearer
than the *Turk's* tribute. I do remember him at *Clement's*
Inn, like a man made after fupper of a cheefe-paring.
When he was naked he was for all the world like a fork-
　　　　　　　　　　　C 3　　　　　　　　　　　　　ed

† *a large gun.*

ed radish, with a head fantastically carved upon it with a
knife. He was fo forlorn, that his dimensions, to any
thick fight were invisible. He was the very *Genius* of
famine, * yet lacherous as a Monkey, and the whores
call'd him Mandrake: he came ever in the rereward of
the fashion, and sung those tunes to the over † schutcht
hufwives that he heard the carmen whistle, and sware
they were his *Fancies*, or his *Good-nights*. And now is
this vice's dagger become a Squire, and talks as familiar-
ly of *John of Gaunt*, as if he had been sworn brother to
him: and I'll be sworn he never saw him but once in
the Tilt-yard, and then he broke his head for crouding
among the Marshal's men. I saw it, and told *John of
Gaunt* he beat his own name, for you might have truss'd
him and all his apparel into an Eel-skin: the case of a
treble hoboy was a mansion for him; and now hath he
land and beeves. Well. I will be acquainted with
him, if I return; and it shall go hard but I will make
him a philosopher's two stones to me. If the young
Dace be a bait for the old Pike, I see no reason in the
law of nature but I may snap at him, Let time shape,
and there's an end.   [*Exeunt.*

ACT IV. SCENE I.

In YORKSHIRE.

Enter the Archbishop of York, Mowbray, Hastings, *and*
Colevile.

York. WHAT is this foreft call'd?
    Haft. 'Tis *Gaultree* foreft.
  York. Here ftand my lords, and fend difcoverers forth,
To know the numbers of our enemies.
  Haft. We have fent forth already.
  York. 'Tis well done,
My friends and brethren in thefe great affairs,

                                                        I

* *added from the edition of* 1600.
‡ *fchutcht*, i. e. *whipt*, *over-fwitch'd*, i. e. *carted*.

I muſt acquaint you, that I have receiv'd
New dated letters from *Northumberland*;
Their cold intent, tenure and ſubſtance thus:
How he doth wiſh his perſon, with ſuch powers
As might hold ſortance with his quality,
The which he could not levy; whereupon
He is retir'd, to ripe his growing fortunes,
To *Scotland*: and concludes in hearty prayers,
That your attempts may over live the hazard
And fearful meeting of their oppoſite.

   Mowb. Thus do the hopes we have in him touch
  ground,
And daſh themſelves to pieces.

        Enter a Meſſenger.

   Haſt. Now, what news?
   Meſſ. Weſt of this foreſt, ſcarcely off a mile,
In goodly form comes on the enemy:
And by the ground they hide, I judge their number
Upon, or near, the rate of thirty thouſand.
   Mowb. The juſt proportion that we gave them out.
Let us ſway on, and face them in the field.

S C E N E II.

Enter Weſtmorland.

   York. What well appointed leader fronts us here?
   Mowb. I think it is my lord of *Weſtmorland*.
   Weſt. Health and fair greeting from our general,
The Prince, lord *John*, and Duke of *Lancaſter*.
   York. Say on, my lord of *Weſtmorland*, in peace,
What doth concern your coming?
   Weſt. Then, my lord,
Unto your grace do I in chief addreſs
The ſubſtance of my ſpeech. If that rebellion
Came like it ſelf, in baſe and abject routs,
Led on by bloody youth, * goaded with rage,
And countenanc'd by boys and beggary;
I ſay, if damn'd Commotion ſo appear'd
In his true, native, and moſt proper ſhape.
You, reverend father, and theſe noble lords,

                                            Had

* *guarded.*

Had not been here to dress the ugly form
Of base and bloody insurrection
With your fair honours. You, my lord Archbishop,
Whose see is by a civil peace maintain'd,
Whose beard the silver hand of peace hath touch'd,
Whose learning and good letters peace hath tutor'd,
Whose white investments figure innocence,
The dove and very blessed spirit of peace;
Wherefore do you so ill translate your self,
Out of the speech of peace, that bears such grace,
Into the harsh and boist'rous tongue of war?
Turning your books to graves, your ink to blood,
Your pens to launces, and your tongue divine
To a loud trumpet and a point of war?

   † *York.* Wherefore do I this? so the question stands.
Briefly to this end: we are all diseas'd,
And with our surfeiting and wanton hours,
Have brought our selves into a burning fever,
And we must bleed for it: of which disease
Our late King *Richard* being infected, dy'd.
But, my most noble lord of *Westmorland*,
I take not on me here as a physician:
Nor do I as an enemy to peace,
Troop in the throngs of military men:
But rather shew a while like fearful war,
To diet rank minds, sick of happiness,
And purge th' obstructions which begin to stop
Our very veins of life. Hear me more plainly,
I have in equal balance justly weigh'd
What wrongs our arms may do, what wrongs we suffer,
And find our griefs he vier than our offences.
We see which way the stream of time doth run,
And are enforc'd from our most quiet there,
By the rough torrent of occasion;
And have the summary of all our griefs,
When time shall serve, to shew in articles;
Which long ere this we offer'd to the King,
And might by no suit gain our audience.
When we are wrong'd and would unfold our griefs,
                              We

---

† *Most of this speech inserted since the first edition.*

We are deny'd acceſs unto his perſon,
Ev'n by thoſe men that moſt have done us wrong.
The danger of the day's but newly gone,
Whoſe memory is written on the earth
With yet-appearing blood; and the examples
Of every minute's inſtance, preſent now,
Hath put us in theſe ill-beſeeming arms:
Not to break peace, or any branch of it,
But to eſtabliſh here a peace indeed,
Concurring both in name and quality.

Weſt. Whenever yet was your appeal deny'd?
Wherein have you been galled by the King?
What Peer hath been ſuborn'd to grate on you,
That you ſhould ſeal this lawleſs bloody book
Of forg'd rebellion, with a ſeal divine?

York. My brother General, the commonwealth,
I make my quarrel in particular.

Weſt. There is no need of any ſuch redreſs;
Or if there were, it not belongs to you.

Mowb. Why not to him in part, and to us all,
That feel the bruiſes of the days before,
And ſuffer the condition of theſe times
To lay an heavy and unequal hand
Upon our honours?

* *Weſt.* O my good lord *Mowbray,*
Conſtrue the times to their neceſſities,
And you ſhall ſay, indeed, it is the time,
And not the King, that doth you injuries.
Yet for your part, it not appears to me,
Or from the King, or in the preſent time,
That you ſhould have an inch of any ground
To build a grief on. Were you not reſtor'd
To all the Duke of *Norfolk's* ſeigniories,
Your noble and right-well-remember'd father's?

Mowb. What thing, in honour, had my father loſt,
That need to be reviv'd and breath'd in me?
The King that lov'd him, as the ſtate ſtood then,
Was forc'd, perforce compell'd to baniſh him.
And then when *Henry Bolingbroke* and he

C 5   Being

* *The two or three next ſpeeches were alſo of thoſe inſerted.*

Being mounted and both rowfed in their feats,
Their neighing courfers daring of the fpur,
Their armed ftaves in charge, their beavers down,
Their eyes of fire fparkling through fights of fteel,
And the loud trumpet blowing them together;
Then, then, when there was nothing could have ftaid
My father from the breaft of *Bolingbroke*;
O, when the King did throw his warder down,
His own life hung upon the ftaff he threw,
Then threw he down himfelf, and all their lives,
That by indictment or by dint of fword
Have fince mifcarried under *Bolingbroke*.

   Weft. You fpeak, lord *Mowbray*, now you know not
The Earl of *Hereford* was reputed then   [what,
In *England*, the moft valiant Gentleman.
Who knows on whom fortune would then have fmil'd?
But if your father had been victor there,
He ne'er had born it out of *Coventry*,
For all the country in a general voice
Cry'd hate upon him; all their prayers and love
Were fet on *Hereford*, whom they doted on;
And blefs'd and grac'd more than the King himfelf.
But this is mere digreffion from my purpofe.
Here come I from our princely General,
To know your griefs, to tell you from his grace,
That he will give you audience; and wherein
It fhall appear that your demands are juft,
You fhall enjoy them; every thing fet off
That might fo much as think you enemies.

   Mowb. But he hath forc'd us to compel this offer,
And it proceeds from policy, not love.

   Weft. Mowbray, you over-ween to take it fo:
This offer comes from mercy, not from fear.
For lo within a ken our army lies;
Upon mine honour, all too confident
To give admittance to a thought of fear.
Our battle is more full of names than yours,
Our men more perfect in the ufe of arms,
Our armour all as ftrong, our caufe the
Then reafon wills, our hearts fhould be as good,
Say you not then our offer is compell'd,

                            Mowb.

Mowb. Well, by my will we ſhall admit no parley.
Weſt. That argues but the ſhame of your offence:
A rotten caſe abides no handling.
Haſt. Hath the Prince *John* a full commiſſion,
In very ample virtue of his father,
To hear and abſolutely to determine
Of what conditions we ſhall ſtand upon?
Weſt. That is intended in the General's name:
I muſe you make ſo ſlight a queſtion.
York. Then take, my lord of *Weſtmorland*, this ſchedule,
For this contains our general grievances:
Each ſeveral article herein redreſs'd,
All members of our cauſe, both here and hence,
That are inſinewed to this action,
Acquitted by a true ſubſtantial form;
And preſent executions of our wills,
To us, and to our purpoſes confin'd;
We come within our awful banks again;
And knit our powers to the arm of peace.
Weſt This will I ſhew the General. Pleaſe you, lords,
In ſight of our battles, we may meet
At either end in peace; which heav'n ſo frame!
Or to the place of difference call the ſwords
Which muſt decide it:
York. My lord, we will do ſo.   [*Exit* Weſt.

SCENE III.

Mowb. There is a thing within my boſom tells me,
That no conditions of our peace can ſtand.
Haſt. Fear you not that: if we can make our peace
Upon ſuch large terms and ſo abſolute,
As our conditions ſhall inſiſt upon,
Our peace ſhall ſtand as firm as rocky mountains:
Mowb. Ay, but our valuation ſhall be ſuch,
That ev'ry ſlight and falſe-derived cauſe,
Yea, ev'ry idle, nice and wanton reaſon,
Shall to the King taſte of this action.
That, were our royal faiths, martyrs in love,
We ſhall be winnow'd with ſo rough a wind,
Tha   r corn ſhall ſeem as light as chaff,
And   rom bad find no partition.

York. No, no, my lord, note this; the King is weary
Of dainty and such picking grievances:
For he hath found, to end one doubt by death
Revives two greater in the heirs of life.
And therefore will he wipe his tables clean,
And keep no tell-tale to his memory,
That may repeat and history his loss
To new remembrance. For full well he knows,
He cannot so precisely weed this land,
As his misdoubts present occasion;
His foes are so enrooted with his friends,
That plucking to unfix an enemy,
He doth unfasten so and shake a friend.
So that this land, like an offensive wife,
That hath enrag'd him on to offer strokes,
And hangs resolv'd correction in the arm
That was uprear'd to execution.

Hast. Besides, the King hath wasted all his rods
On late offenders, that he now doth lack
The very instruments of chastisement:
So that his pow'r, like to a fangless Lion,
May offer, but not hold.

York. 'Tis very true:
And therefore be assur'd, my good lord Marshal,
If we do now make our atonement well,
Our peace will like a broken limb united,
Grow stronger for the breaking.

Mowb. Be it so.
Here is return'd my lord of *Westmorland.*

       Enter Westmorland.

West. The prince is here at hand: pleaseth your lordship
To meet his grace, just distance 'tween our armies?

Mowb. Your Grace of *York* in God's name then set
   forward.

York. Before, and greet his Grace, my lord, we come.

S

SCENE IV.

Enter Prince John *of* Lancaster.

Lan. You're well encountred here, my coufin *Mowbray*;
Good day to you, my gentle lord Arch-bifhop,
And fo to you, lord *Haftings*, and to all.
My lord of *York*, it better fhew'd with you,
When that your flock aff-mbled by the bell
Encircled you, to hear with reverence
Your expofition on the holy text ;
Than now to fee you here an iron man,
Cheering a rout of rebels with your drum,
Turning the word to fword, and life to death.
That man that fi's within a monarch's heart,
And ripens in the fun fhine of his favour,
Would he abufe the count'nance of the King,
Alack, what mifchiefs might he fet abroach,
In fhadow of fuch greatnefs ? With you, lord Bifhop,
It is ev'n fo. Who hath not heard it fpoken,
How deep you were within the books of heav'n ?
To us, the fpeaker in his parliament :
To us, th' imagin'd voice of heav'n it felf;
The very opener and intelligencer
Between the grace, the fanctities of heav'n,
And our dull workings. O, who fhall believe
But you mifufe the rev'rence of your place,
Employ the countenance and grace of heav'n,
As a falfe favourite doth his Prince's name,
In deeds difhon'rable ? you've taken up,
Under the counterfeited zeal of God
The fubjects of his fubftitute, my father ;
And both againft the peace of heav'n and him
Have here upfwarm'd them.
  York. Good my lord of *Lancafter*,
I am not here againft your father's peace :
But, as I told my lord of *Weftmorland*,
The time ſ·····'d doth in common fenfe
Croud ···· ···· us to this monftrous form,
To hol· ···· ·· y up. I fent your grace
The parcels and particulars of our grief,

The

The which hath been with ſcorn ſhov'd from the court:
Wheron this *Hydra*-ſon of war is born,
Whoſe dangerous eyes may well be charm'd aſleep
With grant of our moſt juſt and right deſire;
And true obedience, of this madneſs cur'd,
Stoop tamely to the foot of majeſty.

Mowb. If not, we ready are to try our fortunes
To the laſt man.

Haſt. And though we here fall down,
We have ſupplies to ſecond our attempt:
If they miſcarry, theirs ſhall ſecond them.
And ſo ſucceſs of miſchief ſhall be borne,
And heir from heir ſhall hold this quarrel up,
While *England* ſhall have generation.

Lan. You are too ſhallow, *Haſtings*, much too ſhallow,
To ſound the bottom of the after times.

Weſt. Pleaſeth your grace, to anſwer them directly,
How far forth you do like their articles?

Lan. I like them all, and do allow them well:
And ſwear here, by the honour of my blood,
My father's purpoſes have been miſtook,
And ſome about him have too laviſhly
Wreſted his meaning and authority.
My lord, theſe griefs ſhall be with ſpeed redreſt;
Upon my life they ſhall. If this may pleaſe you,
Diſcharge your pow'rs into their ſeveral counties,
As we will ours; and here between the armies
Let's drink together friendly and embrace;
That all their eyes may bear thoſe tokens home,
Of our reſtored love and amity.

York. I take your princely word for theſe redreſſes.]

Lan. I give it you; and will maintain my word;
And thereupon I drink unto your grace.

Haſt. Go, captain, and deliver to the army
This news of peace; let them have pay, and part:
I know it will well pleaſe them. Hie thee, captain.
                                        [*Exit* Colevile.

York. To you, my noble lord of *Weſtmerland.*

Weſt. I pledge your Grace; and if I knew what
    pains
I have beſtow'd, to breed this preſent peace,

                                        You

You would drink freely ; but my love to ye
Shall fhew it felf more openly hereafter.

York. I do not doubt you.

Weft. I am glad of it.
Health to my lord, and gentle coufin *Mowbray.*

Mowb. You wifh me health in very happy feafon,
For I am on the fudden fomething ill.

York. Againft ill chances men are ever merry,
But heavinefs fore-runs the good event.

Weft. Therefore be merry Coz. fince fudden forrow
Serves to fay thus ; fome good thing comes to-morrow.

York. Believe me, I am paffing light in fpirit.

Mowb. So much the worfe, if your own rule be true.

Lan. The word of peace is render'd ; hark ! they fhout.

Mowb. This had been chearful after victory.

York. A peace is of the nature of a conqueft ;
For then both parties nobly are fubdu'd;
And neither party lofer.

Lan. Go, my lord,
And let our army be difcharged too;   [*Exit* Weft.
And good my lord, fo pleafe you, let our trains
March by us, that we may perufe the men
We fhould have cop'd withal.

York. Go, good lord *Haftings :*
And ere they be difmifs'd, let them march by.

                            [*Exit* Haftings.

Lan. I truft, lords, we fhall lie to-night together.

S C E N E V.

Enter Weftmorland.

Now, coufin, wherefore ftands our army ftill ?

Weft. The leaders having charge from you to ftand,
Will not go off until they hear you fpeak.

Lan. They know their duties.

Re-enter Haftings.

Haft. My lord, our army is difpers'd already :
Like youthful fteers unyoak'd, they took their courfe
Eaft, weft, north, fouth : or like a fchool broke up,
Each hurries towards his home and fporting-place.

Weft. Good tidings, my lord *Haftings*; for the which
I do arreft thee, traitor, of high treafon.

                            And

And you Lord Arch-bishop, and you lord *Mowbray*,
Of capital treason I attach you both.
  Mowb. Is this proceeding just and honourable?
  West. Is your assembly so?
  York. Will you thus break your faith?
  Lan. I pawn'd you none:
I promis'd you redress of these same grievances
Whereof you did complain; which by mine honour
I will perform with a most christian care.
But for you, rebels, look to taste the due
Meet for rebellion and such acts as yours.
Most shallowly did you these arms commence,
Fondly brought here, and foolishly sent hence.
Strike up our drums, pursue the scatter'd stray,
Heav'n and not we have safely fought to day.
Some guard these traitors to the block of death,
Treason's true bed and yielder up of breath. [*Exeunt-*

SCENE VI.

Enter Falstaff *and* Colevile.

  Fal. What's your name, Sir? of what condition are
you? and of what place, I pray?
  Cole. I am a Knight, Sir: and my name is *Colevile*
of the dale.
  Fal. Well then, *Colevile* is your name, a Knight is
your degree, and your place, the dale. *Colevile* shall
still be your name, a traitor your degree, and the dun-
geon your place, a place deep enough: so shall you
still be *Colevile* of the dale.
  Cole. Are you not Sir *John Falstaff?*
  Fal. As good a man as he, Sir, whoe'er I am: do ye
yield, Sir, or shall I sweat for you? if I do sweat, they
are the drops of thy lovers, and they weep for thy death,
therefore rouse up fear and trembling, and do obser-
vance to my mercy.
  Cole. I think you are Sir *John Falstaff,* and in that
thought yield me.
  Fal. I have a whole school of tongues in this belly
of mine, and not a tongue of them all speaks any other
word but my name: an I had but a belly of any indif-
ferency.

fetency, I were fimply the moſt active fellow in *Europe:* my womb, my womb, my womb undoes me. Here comes our General.

Enter Prince John *of* Lancaſter, *and* Weſtmorland.

Lan. The heat is paſt, follow no farther now, Call in the pow'rs, good couſin *Weſtmorland.* [*Exit* Weſt. Now *Falſtaff,* where have you been all this while? When every thing is ended, then you come. Theſe tardy tricks of yours will, on my life, One time or other break ſome gallow's back.

Fal. I would be ſorry, my lord, but it ſhould be thus: I never knew yet, but rebuke and check was the reward of valour. Do you think me a ſwallow, an arrow, or a bullet? have I, in my poor and old motion, the expedition of thought? I ſpeeded hither with the very extremeſt inch of poſſibility. I have founder'd nineſcore and odd poſts: and here, travel-tainted as I am, have in my pure and immaculate valour taken Sir *John Colevile* of the dale, a moſt furious Knight, and valorous enemy: but what of that? he ſaw me and yielded: that I may juſtly ſay with the hook-nos'd fellow of *Rome,* I came, ſaw, and overcame.

Lan. It was more of his courteſy than your deſerving.

Fal. I know not, here he is, and here I yield him; and I beſeech your grace, let it be book'd with the reſt of this day's deeds; or by the lord I will have it in a particular ballad by it ſelf, with mine own picture on the top of it, *Colevile* kiſſing my foot: to the which courſe if I be enforc'd, if you do not all ſhew like gilt two pences to me; and I in the clear sky of fame, o'erſhine you as much as the full moon doth the cinders of the element, which ſhew like pins heads to her; believe not the word of the noble. Therefore let me have right, and let deſert mount.

Lan. Thine's too heavy to mount.

Fal. Let it ſhine then?

Lan. Thine's too thick to ſhine.

Fal. Let it do ſomething, my good lord, that may do me good, and call it what you will.

Lan. me. *Colevile?*

Col. y lord.

Lan. ous rebel art thou, *Colevile.*

Fal.

Fal. And a famous true fubject took him.

Cole. I am, my lord, but as my betters are,
That led me hither; had they been rul'd by me,
You fhould have won them dearer than you have.

Fal. I know not how they fold themfelves; but thou
like a kind fellow, gav'ft thy felf away *gratis*; and I
thank thee for thee.

S C E N E VII.

Enter Weftmorland.

Lan. Now have you left purfuit?

Weft. Retreat is made, and execution ftay'd.

Lan. Send *Colevile* then with his confederates
To *York*, to prefent execution.
Blunt, lead him hence, and fee you guard him fure.
                              [*Exit with* Colevile.

And now difpatch we t'ward the court, my lords;
I hear the King, my father, is fore fick:
Our news fhall go before us to his Majefty,
Which, coufin, you fhall bear to comfort him:
And we with fober fpeed will follow you.

Fal. My lord, I befeech you, give me leave to go
through *Glo'fterfhire*; and when you come to court, pray,
ftand in your good report, my lord.

Lan. Fare you well, *Falftaff*, I, in my condition,
Shall better fpeak of you than you deferve.   [*Exit.*

Fal. I would you had but the wit; 'twere better than
your dukedom. Good faith, this fame young fober
blooded boy doth not love me; a man cannot make
him laugh; but that's no marvel, he drinks no wine.
There's never any of thefe demure boys come to any
proof; for thin drink doth fo over-cool their blood,
and making many fifh-meals, that they fall into a kind
of male green-ficknefs; and then when they marry,
they get wenches. They are generally fools and cowards; which fome of us fhould be too, but for in-
flammation. A good Sherris-Sack hath a twofold ope-
ration in it; it afcends me into the brain, and there
all the foolifh, dull and crudy vapours which environ it;
makes it apprehenfive, quick, forgetive, full of nimble,
                                                    fiery

fiery and delectable shapes; which deliver'd o'er to the
voice, the tongue, which is the birth, becomes excellent
wit. The second property of your excellent Sherris, is
the warming of the blood which before cold and set-
tled, left the liver white and pale; which is the badge
of pusillanimity and cowardise; but the Sherris warms
it, and makes it course from the inwards, to the parts
extreme; it illuminateth the face, which as a beacon,
gives warning to all the rest of this little kingdom, Man,
to arm; and then the vital commoners and inland petty
spirits muster me all to their captain, the heart; who
great, and puft up with this retinue, doth any deed of
courage; and this valour comes of Sherris. So that
skill in the weapon is nothing without Sack, for that sets
it a work; and learning a meer hoard of gold kept by a
devil, till sack commences it, and sets it in act and use.
Hereof comes it, that Prince *Harry* is valiant; for the
cold blood he did naturally inherit of his father, he hath,
like lean, steril and bare land, manured, husbanded, and
till'd with excellent endeavour of drinking good and
good store of fertil Sherris, that he is become very hot
and valiant. If I had a thousand sons, the first humane
principle I would teach them should be to forswear thin
potations, and to addict themselves to Sack.

Enter Bardolph.

How now, *Bardolph* ?

Bard. The army is discharged all, and gone.

Fal. Let them go; I'll thro' *Glocestershire*, and there
will I visit master *Robert Shallow*, Esquire: I have him
already tempering between my finger and my thumb,
and shortly will I seal with him. Come away. [*Exe.*

S C E N E VIII.

Enter King Henry, Warwick, Clarence, *and* Gloucester.

K. *Henry.* Now, lords, if heav'n do give successful end
To this debate that bleedeth at our doors,
We will our youth lead on to higher fields,
And draw no swords but what are sanctify'd.
Our navy is address'd, our power collected,

Our

Our fubftitutes in abfence well invefted,
And every thing lies level to our wifh :
Only we want a little perfonal ftrength :
And paufe us, till thefe rebels, now a-foot,
Come underneath the yoke of Government.

  War. Both which we doubt not, but your Majefty
Shall foon enjoy

  K. Henry. Humphry, my fon of *Glocefter,*
Where is the Prince your brother ?

  Glou. I think he is gone to hunt, my lord, at *Windfo*

  K. Henry. And how accompanied ?

  Glou. I do not know, my lord.

  K. Henry. Is not his brother *Thomas* of *Clarenc*
    with him ?

  Glou. No, my good lord, he is in prefence here.

  Cla. What would my lord and Father ?

  K. Hen. Nothing but well to thee, *Thomas* of *Clarenc*
How chance thou art not with the Prince thy brother
He loves thee, and thou doft neglect him, *Thomas* ;
Thou haft a better place in his affection
Than all thy brothers : cherifh it, my boy,
And noble offices thou may'ft effect
Of mediation, after I am dead,
Between his greatnefs and thy other brethren.
Therefore omit him not ; blunt not his love,
Nor lofe the good advantage of his grace,
By feeming cold, or carelefs of his will.
For he is gracious if he be obferv'd :
He hath a tear for pity, and a hand
Open as day, for melting charity :
Yet notwithftanding, being incens'd, he's flint,
As humorous as winter, and as fudden
As flaws congealed in the fpring of day.
His temper therefore muft be well obferv'd :
Chide him for faults, and do it reverently,
When you perceive his blood inclin'd to mirth :
But being moody, give him line and fcope,
Till that his paffions, like a whale on ground,
Confound themfelves with working. Lear   , *Thoma*
And thou fhalt prove a fhelter to thy fri
A hoop of gold to bind thy brothers in,

                           Tha

That the united veſſel of their blood,
(Mingled with venom of ſuggeſtion,
As force, perforce, the age will pour it in)
Shall never leak, though it do work as ſtrong
As *Aconitum*, or raſh gun-powder.

   Cla. I ſhall obſerve him with all care and love.

   K. Henry. Why art thou not at *Windſor* with him,
    Thomas ?

   Cla. He is not there to-day; he dines in *London.*

   K. Henry. And how accompanied ? canſt thou tell that ?

   Cla. With *Poins*, and other his continual followers.

   K. Henry. Moſt ſubject is the fatteſt ſoil to weeds:
And he the nob'e image of my youth,
Is over-ſpread with them; therefore my grief
Stretches it ſelf beyond the hour of death.
The blood weeps from my heart, when I do ſhape
In forms imaginary, th' unguided days
And rotten times that you ſhall look upon,
When I am ſleeping with my anceſtors.
For when his head-ſtrong riot hath no curb,
When rage and hot blood are his counſellors,
When means and laviſh manners meet together,
Oh with what wings ſhall his affection fly,
Tow'rds fronting peril and oppos'd decay ?

   War. My gracious lord, you look beyond him quite:
The Prince but ſtudies his companions,
Like a ſtrange tongue; wherein, to gain the language,
'Tis needful that the moſt immodeſt word
Be look'd upon, and learn'd; which once attain'd,
Your highneſs knows, comes to no farther uſe,
But to be known and hated. So, like groſs terms,
The Prince will in the perfectneſs of time
Caſt off his followers; and their memory
Shall as a pattern or a meaſure live,
By which his grace muſt mete the lives of others;
Turning paſt evils to advantages.

   K. Henry. 'Tis ſeldom, when the Bee doth leave her
    comb
In the dead carrion. — Who's here ? *Weſtmorland ?*

                 SCENE

S C E N E IX.

Enter Weſtmorland.

Weſt. Health to my ſoveraign, and new happineſs,
Added to that, which I am to deliver:
Prince *John*, your ſon, doth kiſs your grace's hand:
Mowbray, the Biſhop, *Scroop*, *Haſtings*, and all,
Are brought to the correction of your law;
There is not now a rebel's ſword unſheath'd,
But Peace puts forth her Olive ev'ry where.
The manner how this action hath been born,
Here at more leiſure may your Highneſs read,
With every courſe, in his particular.

   K. Henry. O *Weſtmorland*, thou art a ſummer bird,
Which ever in the haunch of winter ſings
The lifting up of day.

             Enter Harcourt.
Look, here's more news.

   Har. From enemies heav'n keep your Majeſty:
And when they ſtand againſt you, may they fall
As thoſe that I am come to tell you of.
The Earl *Northumberland*, and the lord *Bardolf*
With a great pow'r of *Engliſh* and of *Scots*,
Are by the Sh'riff of *Yorkſhire* overthrown:
The manner and true order of the fight,
This packet, pleaſe it you, contains at large.

   K. Henry. And wherefore ſhould theſe good new
     make me ſick?
Will fortune never come with both hands full,
But write her fair words ſtill in fouleſt letters?
She either gives a ſtomach, and no food;
(Such are the poor in health) or elſe a feaſt,
And takes away the ſtomach; ſuch the rich,
That have abundance and enjoy it not.
I ſhould rejoice now at this happy news,
And now my ſight fails, and my brain is giddy.
O me, come near me, now I am much il!

   Glou. Comfort your Majeſty!
   Cla. Oh, my royal father!
   Weſt. My ſoveraign lord, chear up your ſelf, look up
                              War.

War. Be patient, Princes; you do know thefe fits
Are with his Highnefs very ordinary.
Stand from him, give him air: he'll ſtrait be well.

Cla. No, no, he cannot long hold out thefe pangs;
Th' inceſſant care and labour of his mind
Hath wrought the † mure that fhould confine it in,
So thin, that life looks through, and will break out.

Glou. The people fear me; for they do obferve
Unfather'd heirs and loathly births of nature:
The feafons change their manners, as the year
Had found fome months afleep, and leap'd them over.

Cla. The river hath thrice flow'd, no ebb between;
And the old folk (time's doting chronicles)
Say it did fo a little time before
That our great Grandfire *Edward* fick'd and dy'd.

War. Speak lower, Princes, for the King recovers.

Glou. This apoplex will, certain, be his end.

K. Henry. I pray you take me up, and bear me hence
Into fome other chamber: foftly, 'pray
Let there be no noife made, my gentle friends,
Unlefs fome flow and favourable hand
Will whifper mufick to my weary fpirit.

War. Call for the mufick in the other room.

K. Henry. Set me the crown upon my pillow here.

Cla. His eye is hollow, and he changes much.

War. Lefs noife, lefs noife.

S C E N E X.

Enter Prince Henry.

P. Henry. Who faw the Duke of *Clarence* ?

Cla. I am here, brother, full of heavinefs.

P. Henry. How now! rain within doors, and none
　　abroad ?
How doth the King?

Glou. Exceeding ill.

P. Henry. Heard he the good news yet ?
Tell it him.

Glou. He alter'd much upon the hearing it.

P. Henry. If he be fick with joy,
He'l recover without phyfick.

　　　† *r* wall.　　　　　　　　　　*War.*

War. Not fo much noife, my lords ; fweet Prince,
    fpeak low ;
The King, your father, is difpos'd to fleep.
   Cla. Let us withdraw into the other room.
   War. Will't pleafe your grace to go along with us ?
   P. Henry. No ; I will fit, and watch here by the King.
                      [Exeunt all but P. Henry.
Why doth the crown lie there upon his pillow,
Being fo troublefome a bed-fellow ?
O polifh'd perturbation ! golden care !
That keep'ft the ports of flumber open wide
To many a watchful night : fleep with it now !
Yet not fo found, and half fo deeply fweet,
As he whofe brow with homely biggen bound
Snores out the watch of night.   O Majefty !
When thou doft pinch thy bearer, thou doft fit
Like a rich armour worn in heat of day,
That fcald'ft with fafety.   By his gates of breath
There lies a downy feather which ftirs not :
Did he fufpire, that light and weightlefs down
Perforce muft move. My gracious lord ! my father !
This fleep is found indeed ; this is a fleep,
That from this golden * rigol hath divorc'd
So many *Englifh* Kings. Thy due from me
Is tears, and heavy forrows of the blood,
Which nature, love and filial tendernefs
Shall, O dear father, pay thee plenteoufly.
My due from thee is this imperial crown,
Which, as immediate from thy place and blood
Derives it felf to me.   Lo, here it fits,
Which heav'n fhall guard : and put the world's whole
    ftrength
Into one giant arm, it fhall not force
This lineal honour from me.   This from thee
Will I to mine leave, as 'tis left to me.   *[Exit*

S C E N E XI.

Enter Warwick, Gloucefter, *and* Clarence.

K. Henry. Warwick ! Gloucefter ! Clarence !
Cla. Doth the King call ?

                              War.

    * rigol, *or* circle ; *meaning the* crown.

War. What would your Majesty? how fares your Grace?

K. Henry. Why did you leave me here alone, my lords?

Cla. We left the Prince my brother here, my Liege;
Who undertook to fit and watch by you.

K. Henry. The Prince of *Wales!* where is he? let me
fee him.

War. The door is open, he is gone this way.

Glou. He came not through the chamber where we
stay'd.

K. Henry. Where is the Crown? who took it from
my pillow?

War. When we withdrew, my Liege, we left it here.

K. Henry. The Prince hath ta'en it hence; go feek
him out.
Is he so hasty, that he doth suppose
My sleep my death? find him, my lord of *Warwick,*
And chide him hither strait; this part of his
Conjoins with my disease, and helps to end me.
See, sons, what things you are; how quickly nature
Falls to revolt, when gold becomes her object?
For this, the foolish over-careful fathers
Have broke their sleeps with thought, their brains
    with care,
Their bones with industry: for this engroffed
The canker'd heaps of strange-atchieved gold:
For this, they have been thoughtful to invest
Their sons with arts and martial exercises:
When, like the Bee, culling from ev'ry Flow'r,
Our thighs are packt with wax, our mouths with honey,
We bring it to the hive, and like the Bees
Are murder'd for our pains; this bitter taste,
Yield his engrofsments to the * dying father.
                Enter Warwick.
Now where is he? that will not stay so long,
Till his friend, Sickness, hath determin'd me.

War. My lord, I found the Prince in the next room,
Washing with kindly tears his gentle cheeks,
With such a deep demeanour in great sorrow,
That Tyranny, which never quaft but blood,
                                        Would

  † *ending.*

Would by beholding him have wash'd his knife
With gentle eye-drops. He is coming hither.
  K. *Henry*. But wherefore did he take away the Crown?
          Enter Prince Henry.
Lo, where he comes. Come hither to me, *Harry*.
Depart the chamber, leave us here alone.   [*Ex*.
  P. *Hen*. I never thought to hear you speak again.
  K.*Henry*. Thy wish was father, *Harry*, to that thought:
I stay too long by thee, I weary thee.
Dost thou so hunger for my empty chair,
That thou wilt needs invest thee with my honours,
Before thy hour be ripe? O foolish youth!
Thou seek'st the greatness that will overwhelm thee,
Stay but a little; for my cloud of dignity
Is held from falling with so weak a wind,
That it will quickly drop; my day *is* dim.
Thou hast stoln that, which after some few hours
Were thine without offence: and at my death
Thou hast seal'd up my expectation:
Thy life did manifest thou lov'dst me not,
And thou wilt have me die assur'd of it.
Thou hid'st a thousand daggers in thy thoughts,
Which thou hast whetted on thy stony heart,
To stab at half an hour of my frail life.
What! canst thou not forbear me half an hour?
Then get thee gone and dig my grave thy self,
And bid the merry bells ring to thy ear
That thou art crowned, not that I am dead.
Let all the tears that should bedew my herse
Be drops of balm to sanctifie thy head;
Only compound me with forgotten dust,
Give that which gave thee life unto the worms.
Pluck down my officers, break my decrees;
For now a time is come to mock at form.
Henry the Fifth is crown'd: up vanity,
Down royal state. All you sage counsellors hence,
And to the *English* court assemble now
From ev'ry region, apes of idleness:
Now neighbour-confines, purge you of your scum;
Have you a ruffian that will swear? drink? dance?
                     Revel

Revel the night? rob? murder? and commit
The oldeſt ſins the neweſt kind of ways?
Be happy, he will trouble you no more:
England ſhall give him office, honour, might:
For the Fifth *Harry* from curb'd licence plucks
The muzzle of reſtraint, and the wild dog
Shall fleſh his tooth on every innocent.
O my poor kingdom! ſick with civil blows:
When that my care could not with-hold thy riots,
What wilt thou do when riot is thy care?
O, thou wilt be a wilderneſs again
Peopled with Wolves, thy old inhabitants.

   P. *Henry*. O pardon me, my Liege! but for my tears,
                            [*Kneeling*
(The * moiſt impediments unto my ſpeech,)
I had foreſtali'd this dear and deep rebuke,
Ere you with grief had ſpoke, and I had heard
The courſe of it ſo far. There is your Crown,
And he that wears the crown immortally
Long guard it yours; if I affect it more,
Than as your honour and as your renown,
Let me no more from this obedience riſe,
Which my moſt true and inward-duteous ſpirit
Teacheth this proſtrate and exterior bending.
Heav'n witneſs with me, when I here came in
And found no courſe of breath within your Majeſty,
How cold it ſtruck my heart! If I do feign,
O let me in my preſent wildneſs die,
And never live to ſhew th' incredulous world
The noble change that I have purpoſed.
Coming to look on you, thinking you dead,
(And dead almoſt, my Liege, to think you were)
I ſpake unto the Crown, as having ſenſe,
And thus upbraided it. The care on thee depending
Hath fed upon the body of my father,
Therefore thou beſt of gold art worſt of gold;
Other, leſs fine in carrat, is more precious
Preſerving life in med'cine potable:
But thou, moſt fine, moſt honour'd, moſt renown'd,

                     D 2   Haſt

   * *moſt*.

Haft eat thy bearer up. Thus, Royal Liege,
Accufing it, I put it on my head.
To try with it (as with an enemy,
That had before my face murder'd my father)
The quarrel of a true inheritor.
But if it did infect my blood with joy,
Or fwell my thoughts to any ftrain of pride,
If any rebel or vain fpirit of mine
Did with the leaft affection of a welcome
Give entertainment to the might of it;
Let heav'n for ever keep it from my head,
And make me as the pooreft vaffal is,
That doth with awe and terror kneel to it.
   K. *Henry.* O my fon!
Heav'n put it in thy mind to take it hence,
That thou might'ft † win the more thy father's love,
Pleading fo wifely in excufe of it.
Come hither *Harry,* fit thou by my bed,
And hear, I think, the very lateft counfel
That ever I fhall breathe. Heav'n knows, my fon,
By what by-paths and indirect crook'd ways
I met this Crown; and I my felf know well,
How troublefome it fate upon my head.
To thee it fhall defcend with better quiet,
Better opinion, better confirmation:
For all the foil of the atchievement goes
With me into the earth. It feem'd in me
But as an honour fnatch'd with boift'rous hand,
And I had many living to upbraid
My gain of it by their affiftances,
Which daily grew to quarrel and to blood-fhed,
Wounding fuppofed peace. All thefe bold fears
Thou feeft with peril I have anfwered.
For all my reign hath been but as a fcene,
Acting that argument: And now my death
Changes the mode; for what in me was purchas'd,
Falls upon thee in a much fairer fort.
So thou the garland wear'ft fuccefivly;
Yet though thou ftand'ft more fure than I could do.
                      Thou

* *join.*

Thou art not firm enough, fince griefs are green;
And all thy friends, which thou muft make thy friends,.
Have but their ftings and teeth newly ta'en out;
By whofe fell working I was firft advanc'd,
And by whofe pow'r I well might lodge a fear
To be again difplac'd: which to avoid
I cut them off, and had a purpofe now
To lead out many to the Holy land;
Left reft and lying ftill might make them look
Too near into my ftate. Therefore, my *Harry*,
Be it thy courfe to bufy giddy minds
With foreign * wars; that action, hence born out,
May wafte the memory of former days.
More would I; but my lungs are wafted fo
That ftrength of fpeech is utterly deny'd me.
How I came by the Crown, O God forgive!
And grant it may with thee in true peace live.

  P. Henry. My gracious Liege,
You won it, wore it, kept it, gave it me;
Then plain and right muft my poffeffion be;
Which I with more than with a common pain
'Gainft all the world will rightfully maintain.

    Enter Lord John *of* Lancafter *and* Warwick.

  K. Henry. Look, look, here comes my *John* of Lancafter.

  Lan. Health, peace and happinefs to my royal father!

  K. Henry. † Thou bring'ft me happinefs and peace,
fon *John*;
But health, alack, with youthful wings is flown
From this bare, wither'd trunk. Upon thy fight
My wordly bufinefs makes a period.
Where is my lord of *Warwick*?

  P. Henry. My lord of *Warwick*.

  K. Henry. Doth any name particular belong
Unto the lodging where I firft did fwoon?

  War. 'Tis call'd *Jerufalem*, my noble lord.

  K. Henry. Laud be to God! ev'n there my life muft end.
It hath been prophefy'd to me many years.

              D 3

   * *quarrels.*
   † *Thou bring'ft me happinefs, Son* John.

I fhould not die but in *Jerufalem*:
Which vainly I fuppos'd the Holy land.
But bear me to that chamber, there I'll lye:
In that *Jerufalem* fhall *Harry* die,   [*Exeunt.*

ACT V. SCENE I.

GLOSTERSHIRE.

Enter Shallow, Silence, Falftaff, Bardolph, Page, *and* Davy.

Shal. BY cock and pye Sir, you fhall not away to-night.
        What, *Davy*, I fay.

Fal. You muft excufe me, mafter *Robert Shallow*.

Shal. I will not excufe you: you fhall not be excufed:
Excufes fhall not be admitted: there is no excufe fhall
ferve: you fhall not be excus'd. Why *Davy*.

Davy. Here, Sir.

Shal. *Davy*, *Davy*, *Davy*, let me fee, *Davy*, let me fee;
William Cook, bid him come hither. —— Sir *John*, you
fhall not be excus'd.

Davy. Marry, Sir, thus: thofe precepts cannot be ferv'd;
and again, Sir, fhall we fow the head-land with wheat?

Shal. With red wheat, *Davy*. But for *William* Cook;
are there no young Pidgeons?

Davy. Yea, Sir —— Here is now the Smith's note
for fhooing, and plow-irons.

Shal. Let it be caft and paid —— Sir *John*, you
fhall not be excus'd.

Davy. Sir, a new link to the bucket muft needs be had.
And Sir, do you mean to ftop any of *William*'s wages
about the fack he loft the other day at *Hinckly* fair?

Shal. He fhall anfwer it. Some Pidgeons, *Davy*, a
couple of fhort-legg'd Hens, a joint of mutton, and any
pretty little tiny kickfhaws: tell *William* Cook.

Davy. Doth the man of war ftay all night, Sir?

Shal. Yes, *Davy*, I will ufe him well. A friend i'th'
court is better than a penny in purfe. Ufe his men
                                                    well,

well, *Davy*, for they are arrant knaves, and will back-bite.

Davy. No worse than they are bitten, Sir; for they have marvellous foul linnen.

Shal. Well conceited, *Davy.* About thy Business, *Davy.*

Davy. I beseech you, Sir, to countenance *William Visor* of *Woncot*, against *Clement Perkes* of the hill.

Shal. There are many complaints, *Davy*, against that *Visor*; that *Visor* is an arrant knave on my knowledge.

Davy. I grant your worship that he is a knave, Sir; but yet God forbid, Sir, but a knave should have some countenance at his friend's request. An honest man, Sir, is able to speak for himself, when a knave is not. I have serv'd your worship truly, Sir, these eight years; and if I cannot once or twice in a quarter bear out a knave against an honest man, I have but very little credit with your worship. The knave is mine honest friend, Sir, therefore I beseech your worship let him be countenanc'd.

Shal. Go to, I say he shall have no wrong: look about, *Davy.* Where are you, Sir *John?* come, off with your boots. Give me your hand, master *Bardolph.*

Bard. I am glad to see your worship.

Shal. I thank thee with all my heart, kind master *Bardolph*; and welcome, my tall fellow; [*To the Page*]Come, Sir *John.*

Fal. I'll follow you, good master *Robert Shallow.* *Bardolph*, look to our horses. —— If I were saw'd into quantities, I should make four dozen of such bearded-hermites-staves as master *Shallow.* It is a wonderful thing to see the semblable coherence of his mens spirits and his: they by observing of him do bear themselves like foolish justices; he by conversing with them is turn'd into a justice-like servingman. Their spirits are so married in conjunction, with the participation of society, that they flock together in consent like so many wild Geese. If I had a suit to master *Shallow*, I would

D 4　　　　humour

humour his men with the imputation of being near their
master: If to his men, I would curry with master *Shallow*, that no man could better command his servants.
It is certain that either wise bearing or ignorant carriage
is caught, as men take diseases, one of another: therefore let men take heed of their company. I will devise matter enough out of this *Shallow* to keep Prince
Henry in continual laughter the wearing out of six fashions, which is four terms or two actions, and he shall
laugh * without *Intervallums*. O, it is much, that a lye
with a slight oath, and a jest with a sad brow, will do
with a fellow that never had the ache in his shoulders.
O you shall see him laugh, till his face be like a wet
cloak ill laid up.

Shal. Sir *John.*

Fal. I come, master *Shallow*; I come, master *Shallow*.

SCENE II.

LONDON.

Enter the Earl of Warwick, *and the Lord Chief Justice.*

War. How now, my lord Chief Justice, whether away?

Ch. Just. How doth the King?

War. Exceeding well: his cares are now all ended.

Ch. Just. I hope not dead.

War. He's walk'd the way of nature,
And to our purposes he lives no more.

Ch. Just. I would his Majesty had call'd me with him,
The service that I truly did his life
Hath left me open to all injuries.

War. Indeed I think the young King loves you not.

Ch. Just. I know he doth not, and do arm my self
To welcome the condition of the time,
Which

* *with.*

Which cannot look more hideously on me,
Than I have drawn it in my fantasy.

Enter Lord John *of* Lancaster, Gloucester *and* Clarence.

War. Here comes the heavy issue of dead *Harry* :
O, that the living *Harry* had the temper
Of him, the worst of these three gentlemen :
How many nobles then should hold their places,
That must strike sail to spirits of vile sort!
　Ch. Just. Alas, I fear all will be overturn'd.
　Lan. Good morrow, cousin *Warwick.*
　Glou. Clar. Good morrow, cousin.
　Lan. We meet like men that had forgot to speak.
　War. We do remember, but our argument
Is all too heavy to admit much talk.
　Lan. Well, peace be with him that hath made us heavy.
　Ch. Just. Peace be with us, left we be heavier.
　Glou. O, good my lord, you've lost a friend indeed,
And I dare swear you borrow not that face
Of seeming sorrow, it is sure your own.
　Lan. Tho' no man be assur'd what grace to find,
You stand in coldest expectation.
I am the sorrier : would 'twere otherwise.
　Cla. Well you must now speak Sir *John Falstaff* fair,
Which swims against your stream of quality.
　Ch. Just. Sweet Princes, what I did, I did in honour,
Led by th' * impartial conduct of my soul ;
And never shall you see that I will beg
A ragged and forestall'd remission.
If truth and upright innocency fail me,
I'll to the King my master that is dead,
And tell him who hath sent me after him.
　War. Here comes the Prince.

　　* *imperial.*

D 5　　　　　　SCENE

S C E N E III.

Enter Prince Henry.

Ch. Juſt. Heav'n ſave your Majeſty.

P. Henry. This new and gorgeous garment, Majeſty,
Sits not ſo eaſy on me as you think.
Brothers, you mix your ſadneſs with ſome fear:
This is the *Engliſh*, not the *Turkiſh* court;
Not *Amurath* an *Amurath* ſucceeds,
But *Harry, Harry.* Yet be ſad, good Brothers,
For to ſpeak truth, it very well becomes you:
Sorrow ſo royally in you appears,
That I will deeply put the faſhion on;
And wear it in my heart: Why then be ſad,
But entertain no more of it, good brothers,
Than a joint-burthen laid upon us all.
For me, by heav'n, I bid you be aſſur'd
I'll be your father and your brother too:
Let me but bear your love, I'll bear your cares:
Yet weep that *Harry's* dead, and ſo will I.
But *Harry* lives that ſhall convert thoſe tears
By number into hours of happineſs.

Lan. &c. We hope no other from your Majeſty.

P. Henry. You all look ſtrangely on me; and you moſt,
You are, I think, aſſur'd I love you not.
                                    [*To the Ch. Juſt.*

Ch. Juſt. I am aſſur'd, if I be meaſur'd rightly,
Your Majeſty hath no juſt cauſe to hate me.

P. Henry. No! might a Prince of my great hopes forget
So great indignities you laid upon me?
What! rate, rebuke, and roughly ſend to priſon
Th' immediate heir of *England!* was this eaſy?
May this be waſh'd in *Lethe*, and forgotten?

Ch. Juſt. I then did uſe the perſon of your father;
The image of his power lay then in me:
And in th' adminiſtration of his law
While I was buſy for the common-wealth,

                                    Your

Your Highnefs pleafed to forget my place.
The majefty and pow'r of law and juftice,
The image of the King whom I prefented;
And ftruck me in the very feat of judgment::
Whereon as an offender to your father
I gave bold way to my authority,
And did comm't you. If the deed were ill,
Be you contented, wearing now the garland,
To have a fon fet your decrees at naught?
To pluck down juft'ce from your awful bench?
To trip the courfe of law, and blunt the fword
That guards the peace and fafety of your pefon?
Nay more, to fpurn at your moft royal image,
And mock your working in a fecond body?
Queftion your royal thoughts, make the cafe yours;
Be now the father, and propofe a fon;
Hear your own dignity fo much profan'd;
See your moft dreadful laws fo loofely flighted;
Behold your felf fo by a fon difdain'd:
And then imagine me taking your part,
And in your pow'r foft filencing your fon.
After this cold confid'rance, fentence me;
And as you are a King, fpeak in your ftate,
What I have done that misbecame my place,
My perfon, or my Liege's foveraignty.
   P. Henry. You are right, Juftice, and you weigh this
       well,
Therefore ftill bear the balance and the fword:
And I do wifh your honours may increafe,
Till you do live to fee a fon of mine
Offend you, and obey you, as I did:
So fhall I live to fpeak my father's words,
Happy am I that have a man fo bold
That dares do juftice on my proper fon;
And no lefs happy having fuch a fon,
That would deliver up his greatnefs fo
Into the hand of juftice. You committed me;
For which I do commit into your hand
Th' unftained fword that you have us'd to bear,
With this remembrance that you ufe the fame

                                      With

With the like bold, juſt and impartial ſpirit
As you have done 'gainſt me. There is my hand
You ſhall be as a father to my youth :
My voice ſhall ſound as you do prompt mine ear;
And I will ſtoop and humble my intents,
To your well-practis'd wiſe directions.
And Princes all, believe me I beſeech you :
My father is gone † wail'd into his grave,
(For in his tomb lie my affections)
And with his ſpirit ſadly I ſurvive,
To mock the expectations of the world,
To fruſtrate Prophecies, and to raſe out
Rotten opinion, which hath writ me down
After my ſeeming. Tho' my tide of blood
Hath proudly flow'd in vanity till now;
Now, doth it turn and ebb back to the ſea,
Where it ſhall mingle with the ſtate of floods,
And flow henceforth in formal Majeſty.
Now call we our high court of Parliament,
And let us chooſe ſuch limbs of noble counſel,
That the great body of our ſtate may go,
In equal rank with the beſt govern'd nation ;
That war or peace, or both at once, may be
As things acquainted and familiar to us,
In which you, father, ſhall have foremoſt hand.
                              [*To Lord, Chief Juſtice*
Our coronation done, we will accite
(As I before remember'd) all our ſtate,
And (Heav'n conſigning to my good intents)
No Prince nor Peer ſhall have juſt cauſe to ſay,
Heav'n ſhorten *Harry's* happy life one day.   [*Exeunt*

—† *wild.*

SCENE IV.

Gloucestershire.

Enter Falstaff, Shallow, Silence, Bardolph. *the Page and*
Davy.

Shal. Nay, you shall see mine orchard, where 'in an
arbour we will eat a last years pippin of my owngraffing,
with a dish of carraways, and so forth : come cousin
Silence ; and then to bed.

Fal. You have here a goodly dwelling, and a rich.

Shal. Barren, barren, barren : beggars all, beggars all,
Sir *John*, marry, good air,. Spread *Davy*, spread
Davy, well said *Davy*.

Fal. This *Davy* serves you for good uses ; he is your
servingman and your husbandman.

Shal. A good varlet, a good varlet, a very good varlet,
Sir *John*. By th' Mass I have drank too much Sack at
supper. A good varlet. Now sit down, now sit down :
come, cousin.

Sil. Ah, sirrah, quoth-a,

We shall do nothing but eat and make good cheer, [Singing.
And praise heav'n for the merry year ;
When flesh is cheap, and females dear,
And lusty lads roam here and there ;
So merrily, and ever among, so merrily, &c.

Fal. There's a merry heart, good master *Silence*. I'll
give you a health for that anon.

Shal. † Give Mr. *Bardolph* some wine, *Davy*,

Davy. Sweet Sir, sit ; I'll be with you anon. most sweet
Sir, sit. Master Page, sit : good master Page, sit : pro-
face. What you want in meat we'll have in drink ; but
you must bear ; the heart's all.

Shal.

† *Good Mr.* Bardolph, *some wine,* Davy.

Shal. Be merry, Mr. *Bardolph*, and my little foldier there be merry.

Sil. [Singing.] *Be merry, be merry, my wife has all,*
For women are Shrews, both short and tall ;
'Tis merry in hall, when beards wag all,
And welcome merry Shrovetide.
Be merry, be merry.

Fal. I did not think master *Silence* had been a man of this mettle.

Sil. Who I ? I have been merry twice and once ere now.

Dav. There is a dish of leather-coats for you.

Shal. Davy.

Dav. Your worship—— I'll be with you ftreight. A cup of wine, Sir ?

Sil. [Singing.] *A cup of wine,*
That's brisk and fine.
And drink unto the leman mine ;
And a merry heart lives long-a.

Fal. Well faid, master *Silence.*

Sil. If we shall be merry, now comes in the fweet of the night.

Fal. Health and long life to you, master *Silence:*

Sil. Fill the cup and let it come. I'll pledge you wer't a mile to the bottom.

Shal. Honeft *Bardolph*, welcome ; if thou want'ft any thing and wilt not call, beshrew thy heart. Welcome my little tiny thief and welcome indeed too: I'll drink to master *Bardolph*, and to all the cavileroes about *London.*

Dav. I hope to fee *London*, ere I die.

Bard. If I might fee you there, *Davy.*

Shal. You'll crack a quart together ? ha, will you master *Bardolph* ?

Bard. Yes, Sir ; in a pottle pot.

Shal. By God's liggens I thank thee ; the knave will ftick by thee, I can affure thee that. He will not out ; he is true bred.

Bard. And I'il ſtick by him, Sir.

                        [*One knocks at the door.*

Shal..Why , there ſpoke a King : lack nothing, be merry, Look, who's at door there, ho : who knocks ?

Fal. Why now you have done me right.

Sil. [Singing.] *Dò me right, and dub me Knight, Sa-mingo.* Is't not ſo ?

Fal. 'Tis ſo.

Sil. Is't fo ? why then ſay an old man can do ſome-what.

Dav. If it pleaſe your worſhp there's one *Piſtol* come from the court with news.

Fal. From the court ? let him come in.

S C E N E V.

Enter Piſtol.

How now, *Piſtol* ?

  Piſt. Sir *John*, ſave you, Sir.

  Fal. What wind blew you hither, *Piſtol* ?

  Piſt. Not the ill wind which blows no man good; ſweet Knight : thou art now one of the greateſt men in the realm.

  Sil. Indeed I think he be but goodman *Puff* of Bar-ſon.

  Piſt. *Puff* ?

Puff in thy teeth, moſt recreant coward baſe !

Sir *John*, I am thy *Piſtol* and thy friend ;

And helter skelter have I rode to thee ;

And tidings do I bring, and lucky joys,

And golden times, and happy news of price.

  Fal. I pr'ythee now deliver them like a man of this world.

  Piſt. A footra for the world and worldlings baſe,

I ſpeak of *Africa*, and golden joys.

  Fal. O baſe *Aſſyrian* Knight, what is thy news ?

Let King *Cophetua* know the truth thereof.

  Sil. And *Robin Hood*, *Scarlet* and *John*.

                                    Piſt.

Pift. Shall dunghil curs confront the *Helicons*?
And fhall good news be baffled?
Then *Piftol* lay thy head in fury's lap.

Shal. Honeft gentleman, I know not your breeding.

Pift. Why then lament therefore.

Shal. Give me pardon, Sir. If you come with news
from the court, I take it there is but two ways, either
to utter them, or to conceal them. I am, Sir, under
the King, in fome authority.

Pift. Under which King? *Bezonian*, fpeak or die.

Shal. Under King *Harry*.

Pift. Harry the Fourth? or Fifth?

Shal. Harry the Fourth.

Pift. A footra for thine office.
Sir *John*, thy tender Lamb-kin now is King,
Harry the Fifth's the man. I fpeak the truth.
When *Piftol* lyes, do this, and fig me like
The bragging *Spaniard*.

Fal. What, is the old King dead?

Pift. As nail in door: the things I fpeak are juft.

Fal. Away *Bardolph*, faddle my horfe. Mafter
Robert Shallow, choofe what office thou wilt in the
land, 'tis thine. *Piftol*, I will double charge thee with
dignities.

Bard. O joyful day! I would not take a knighthood
for my fortune.

Pift. What? I do bring good news?

Fal. Carry mafter *Silence* to bed: mafter *Shallow*, my
lord *Shallow*, be what thou wilt, I am Fortune's fteward.
Get on thy boots, we'll ride all night. Oh, fweet *Piftol!*
away *Bardolph*: come, *Piftol*, utter more to me; and
withal devife fomething to do thy felf good. Boot,
boot, mafter *Shallow*. I know the young King is fick
for me. Let us take any man's horfes: the laws of *England* are at my commandment. Happy are they which
have been my friends; and wo to my Lord Chief Juftice.

Pift. Let vultures vile feize on his lungs alfo:
Where is the life that late I led, fay they?
Why here it is, welcome this pleafant day. [*Fxeunt.*

SCENE

SCENE VI.

LONDON.

Enter Hoftefs Quickly, Doll Tear-fheet, *and Beadles.*

Hoft. No, thou arrant knave, I would I might die that I might have thee hang'd; thou haft drawn my fhoulder out of joint.

Bead. The conftables have deliver'd her over to me and fhe fhall have whipping cheer enough, I warrant her. There hath been a man or two kill'd about her.

Dol. Nut-hook, nut-hook, you lye: come on; I'll tell thee what, thou damn'd tripe-vifag'd Rafcal, if the child I go with do mifcarry, thou hadft better thou hadft ftruck thy mother, thou paper-fac'd villain.

Hoft. O that Sir *John* were come, he would make this a bloody day to fomebody. But I pray God the fruit of her womb mifcarry.

Bead. If it do, you fhall have a dozen of cuhions again, you have but eleven now. Come, I charge you both go with me, for the man is dead that you and *Piftol* beat among you.

Dol. I'll tell thee what, thou thin man in a cenfor's, I will have you as foundly fwindg'd for this, you blue-bottle rogue; you filthy famifh'd correctioner, if you be not fwindg'd I'll forfwear half kirtles.

Bead. Come, come, you fhe-Knight-arrant, come.

Hoft. O, that right fhould thus o'ercome might! Well, of fufferance comes eafe.

Dol. Come, you rogue, come; bring me to a juftice.

Hoft. Yes, come, you ftarv'd blood-hound.

Dol. Goodman death, goodman bones.

Hoft. Thou † Atomy, thou.

Dol. Come, you thin thing: come, you rafcal.

Bead. Very well.   [*Exeunt.*

† *Anatomy.*

                                                SCENE

SCENE VII.

Enter two Grooms strewing rushes.

1 *Groom.* More rushes, more rushes.

2 *Groom.* The trumpets have sounded twice.

1 *Groom.* It will be two of the clock ere they come from the coronation: dispatch, dispatch.

[*Exeunt Grooms.*

Enter Falstaff, Shallow, Pistol, Bardolph, *and the Boy.*

Fal. Stand here by me, master *Robert Shallow,* I will make the King do you grace: I will leer upon him as he comes by, and do but mark the countenance that he will give me.

Pist. Bless thy lungs, good Knight.

Fal. Come here, *Pistol,* stand behind me. O, if I had had time to have made new liveries, I would have bestow'd the thousand pound I borrow'd of you. But it is no matter, this poor shew doth better; this doth infer the zeal I had to see him.

Shal. It doth so.

Fal. It shews my earnestness of affection.

Pist. It doth so.

Fal. My devotion.

Pist. It doth, it doth, it doth.

Fal. As it were to ride day and night, and not to deliberate, not to remember, not to have patience to shift me.

Shal. It is most certain.

Fal. But to stand stained with travel, and sweating with desire to see him, thinking of nothing else, putting all affairs in oblivion, as if there were nothing else to be done but to see him.

Pist. 'Tis *semper idem;* for *absque hoc nihil est.* 'Tis all in every part.

Shal.

Shal. 'Tis fo indeed.

Pift. My Knight, I will enflame thy noble liver, and make thee rage.

Thy *Dol* and *Helen* of thy noble thoughts

Is in bafe durance and contagious prifon ;

Hauld thither by mechanick dirty hands.

Rowze up Revenge from Ebon den, with fell *Al. flo's* fnake,

For *Dol* is in. *Piftol* fpeaks nought but truth.

Fal. I will deliver her.

Piftol. There roar'd the fea ; and trumpet clangour founds.

S C E N E VIII.

The Trumpets found. Enter the Kirg and his train.

Fal. God fave thy grace, King *Hal*, my royal *Hal*.

Pift. The heav'ns thee guard and keep, moft royal imp of fame.

Fal. God fave thee, my fweet boy.

King. My Lord Chief Juftice, fpeak to that vain man.

Ch. Juft. Have you your wits ? know you what 'tis you fpeak ?

Fal. My King, my *Jove*, I fpeak to thee, my heart.

King. I know thee not, old man : fall to thy Prayers :

How ill white hairs become a fool and jefter !

I have long dream'd of fuch a kind of man,

So furfeit-fwell'd, fo old, and fo profane ;

But being awake, I do defpife my dream.

Make lefs thy body hence, and more thy grace,

Leave germandizing. Know, the grave doth gape

For thee, thrice wider than for other men.

Reply not to me with a fool-born jeft,

Prefume not that I am the thing I was :

For heav'n doth know, fo fhall the world perceive,

That I have turn'd away my former felf,

So will I thofe that kept me company.

When thou doft hear I am as I have been,

Approach me, and thou fhalt be as thou waft ;

The

The tutor and the feeder of my riots;
Till then I banifh thee, on pain of death,
As I have done the reft of my mif-leaders,
Not to come near our perfon by ten miles.
For competence of life, I will allow you,
That lack of means enforce you not to evil:
And as we hear you do ‡ reform your felves,
We will according to your ftrength and qualities
Give you advancement. Be't your charge, my lord,
To fee perform'd the tenour of our word.
Set on.   [*Ex. King, &c.*

S C E N E IX.

Fal. Mafter *Shallow*, I owe you a thoufand pound.

Shal. Ah marry, Sir *John*, which I befeech you to let me have home with me.

Fal. That can hardly be, Mr. *Shallow*. Do not you grieve at this; I fhall be fent for in private to him: look you, he muft feem thus to the world. Fear not your advancement, I will be the man yet that fhall make you great.

Shal. I cannot perceive how, unlefs you give me your doublet and ftuff me out with ftraw. I befeech you, good Sir *John*, let me have five hundred of my thoufand.

Fal. Sir, I will be as good as my word. This that you heard was but a colour.

Shal. A colour I fear that you will die in, Sir *John*.

Fal. Fear no colours: go with me to dinner: come lieureant *Piftol*, come *Bardolph*. I fhall be fent for foon at night.

Enter Chief Juftice and Prince John.

Ch. Juft. Go carry Sir *John* Falftaff to the *Fleet*,
Take all his company along with him.

Fal. My lord, my lord.

                                 Ch. Juft.

‡ *redeem.*

Ch. Juſt. I cannot now ſpeak, I will hear you ſoon,
Take them away.
   Piſt. Si ſortuna me tormento, ſpera me contento. [*Exes*

      Manent Lancaſter *and Chief Juſtice.*
   Lan. I like this fair proceeding of the King's.
He hath intent his wonted followers
Shall all be very well provided for;
But they are baniſh'd, till their converſations
Appear more wiſe and modeſt to the world.
   Ch. Juſt. And ſo they are.
   Lan. The King hath call'd his parliament, my lord.
   Ch. Juſt. He hath.
   Lan. I will lay odds, that ere this year expire,
We bear our civil ſwords and native fire
As far as *France.* I heard a bird ſo ſing,
Whoſe muſick, to my thinking, pleas'd the King.
Come, will you hence?   [*Exeunt.*

E P I-